THE LOST EMPIRE

EDWARD P. CARDILLO

SEVERED PRESS
HOBART TASMANIA

THE LOST EMPIRE

WWW.SEVEREDPRESS.COM

ISBN: 978-1-925493-30-6

ACKNOWLEDGEMENTS

I would like to thank Trevor Smith, whose extensive knowledge of science fiction and military tactics has helped me significantly in lending this novel authenticity. I would also like to thank Arno Kolz, Ph.D. for his objective review, brutal honesty, and extensive knowledge of science fiction, which helped me shape this story into the best it could be. Thank you to Stephen Vance, Ph.D. who fielded my specific questions about physics. Thank you to Michael Fisher, who answered my questions about naval rank and file. Thank you to Charlene Nunez for her extra set of eyes and critique; her feedback has helped my writing evolve. Thanks again to Gary Lucas at Severed Press. Thank you to my wife, Sandra, for all of her support, and my son, Alexander, who keeps my imagination wild.

This novel is dedicated to Rose Matoskey, who humored me when I drew diagrams of spaceships as a kid and encouraged me to imagine other worlds.

PART I

CONFLUENCE

"The universe is alive, its darkness recording our greatest victories and most tragic failures. The deep void, vast ocean connecting entire worlds, the matrix of existence."

Jo Tzuzuki, Feng High Priest

CHAPTER 1

Command Carrier Dominance
Affiliation: Feng Empire

Fleet Admiral Fengus Utang sat in his chair on the battle bridge of his command carrier, assimilating thousands of points of data as they were gathered, as filtered by Captain Paxo Klingu.

"Sir, our battle group is exiting spacefold in the Humana System."

"How far out?"

"One point seven three nine kilaparsecs, sir."

Admiral Utang was about to initiate the final stage of his intergalactic scourge against the United Intergalactic Coalition. One by one, in his march across the known galaxies, overlooking the Uncharted Sectors, he had led the Feng Empire in its conquest to reclaim the glory of the Old Empire. In a vicious campaign, he toppled world after world, nation after nation, whittling away the overstretched United Intergalactic Coalition. From the Vampiri to the Homunculi, each member of the UIC was outmatched by the superior armada of the Feng.

The invasion of Humana, the seat of the United Intergalactic Coalition, was the end game in this great Intergalactic War 4.0.

"The Humani have detected our arrival, sir."

This was to be suspected as the deep cold of space made it impossible to mask the heat signatures of large vessels and battle groups.

"Captain, release the hunter-killers." These hunter-killers were the first ships in the history of armada vessels to utilize the dark matter of space to conceal themselves from detection. Admiral Utang watched as they entered the Humani battle group's outer screen, circumventing detection. In turn, they gathered data on enemy positions and relayed them back.

"Have them take out the passive Humani scouts," ordered Admiral Utang.

The on-screen display showed the frail Humani scout satellites take fire and explode, as they were designed for detection rather than engagement. Within thirty micros, the outer screen of the Humani defense forces had been eliminated.

"Sir, the hunter-killers are breaching the Humani's inner screen."

"Mobilize the battleships and dreadnaughts just outside the outer screen, and dispatch Warmonger squadrons." Every squadron in the invasion fleet launched and approached the now non-existent Humani outer screen, outnumbering the Humani Vortex fighters in the inner screen two-to-one.

As the Feng hunter-killers breached the inner screen, the Humani Vortex defenders buzzed around blindly, groping out into the cold darkness with their sensors, desperate to detect the smallest heat signature.

The stealth vessels, rather than engaging, reached out with their own sensors, reporting back on the Humani Vortex positions and formations. The quantum computers of the Dominance extrapolated data from prior Humani encounters, assessing the threat axis of the Humani defense forces.

One of the stealth vessels took a fatal hit, the explosion ripping through its cloak of dark matter. It quickly became a lifeless husk, its crew drifting out of its gaping wounds into the vacuum of space.

"Sir, the Humani have dispatched hunter-killers."

Admiral Utang was stoic, entirely expecting this.

"Mobilize countermeasures."

He and the captain watched as the wave of battleships and dreadnaughts breached the outer screen. Cloaked ships traded fire, desperately trying to get a fix on the others' positions. More Feng stealth vessels were neutralized by the cloaked Humani hunter-killers. Those few remaining switched from reconnaissance to engagement out of self-preservation, taking a dozen or so Vortex fighters with them as they rejoined the Aether.

"Sir, we have lost all hunter-killers," said Captain Klingu.

However, Admiral Utang was unfazed. This was war and was to be expected.

The Vortex fighters pulled up in battle formations to the edge of the inner screen, waiting to greet the Feng battleships and dreadnaughts. Their sensors scanned the cold depths of the battlespace, targeting systems and weapons running hot.

"Release the chaff," Admiral Utang ordered.

The battleships released a cloud of radioactive nanites, lighting up the targeting systems of the Vortex formations and the cloaked

Humani hunter-killers. Their targeting systems confused, registering vast clouds of bogeys, the Vortex formations retreated back into the inner screen.

The nanites swept over the battlespace, latching onto the cloaked hunter-killers, causing the Humani stealth vessels to register as silhouettes on the Feng scanners. Although the cloaked ships remained below the thermo-gradient, the effect was like throwing a sheet over an invisible man.

"Send in the fighter squadrons," ordered Admiral Utang.

The Feng armada targeted the revealed Humani hunter-killers and engaged, neutralizing them in short order. The Humani and Feng fighter squadrons charged the battlespace.

Tactical maneuvers broke down into chaos as the squadrons of fighters swarmed each other, pitching and rolling, engaging in zero-gravity dogfighting.

The Humani fighter pilots were superior in matters of reaction time and tactics, and it showed as they made quick work of the Feng squadrons. Captain Klingu viewed the battle on screen with great apprehension. However, Admiral Utang knew that the Feng only needed to whittle down the Vortex screen enough, and that was exactly what they accomplished.

"Sir, the Humani are transmitting for reinforcements. Forces from Earth are entering spacefold."

Admiral Utang sneered. "The Humani must be desperate if they are enlisting the help of the Humans."

The Humans were the last race to enter the United Intergalactic Coalition. Their abilities were limited, and their training was cursory and inadequate due to the demands of war and the urgency to bolster UIC forces with numbers.

The Humans were an embarrassment, losing every skirmish in the war to the Feng, even to the lesser races of the Feng Empire. Therefore, they were largely relegated to supply chains, piloting transport vessels carrying munitions and parts as well as food.

Utang's sneer morphed into a smug grin. "More target practice for our ships."

The arrival of Human transports would serve as nothing more than a nuisance, putting off the inevitable Feng victory.

The Feng dreadnaughts entered the inner screen, pummeling the Vortex fighters and initiating offensive ECM, jamming the planet's communications, cutting off the Humani from what was left of their crumbling forces.

This was a glorious day for the Feng Empire, and total victory was imminent. The Feng believed in 'eating what you killed,' and they were about to feast upon the remains of a decadent and obsolete political-economic union.

Once the dreadnaughts and the Feng second and third waves neutralized the Humani HVU's, Admiral Utang would release battalions of the dreaded cyborg Cybion warriors onto the planet. While the Humani pilots may have been superior, their marines were woefully inferior to the ruthless Cybions. Flesh would always yield to metal, and the Cybions were killing machines, designed to instill fear and end lives with brutal efficiency.

Captain Klingu's eyes went wide. "Sir, the Humans are exiting spacefold."

"Prepare to engage," said Admiral Utang.

"Sir, they are opening a wormhole exactly onto our coordinates."

"What?"

"They are going to unfold in the dead center of our battle group."

"Idiots!" was all Admiral Utang could utter before an opening in Spacetime breached the center of his command carrier...

The lights went on in the Aether chamber, and Captain Mongo Utang watched as the display of the Dominance battle bridge evaporated before his very eyes. He had been immersed in a ghost memory of the key battle in the last Intergalactic War as told through his father's experience.

He fought his body's urge to choke up, his face contorting with rage, as hot tears welled up in his eyes. 'Frakking Humans!'

This was not the first time that Captain Utang had reviewed his father's final hours in battle during the Intergalactic War. He had only been a child on his home planet when he received news of his father's demise.

The Feng were raised as warriors, and the prospect of a 'beautiful death' in battle was welcomed rather than feared. However, to die at the bungling hands of Human cargo pilots, from an unwitting suicide mission that inadvertently wiped out the High Valued Units of the Feng invasion force, not to mention their key fleet commander, signaling a turning point in the war, was shameful and embarrassing.

With their most talented tactician gone, the Feng forces began to lose their tactical advantages. Additionally, emboldened by successfully defending their planet, the Humani began to regroup and rally the rest of the UIC forces in the Charted Galaxies. They even rallied a few from the Uncharted Sectors who wished to remain free from Feng oversight. All this was due to the serendipitous folly of the Humans.

With the sudden reprieve and extra breathing room, the UIC were able to train the Humans more properly, and they became more of an asset in the war than any of the other races had anticipated, despite their first impression.

Just as he slipped back into his officer's uniform, Captain Utang's com lit up. "Captain, Admiral Teng wishes to speak to you."

Utang wiped his eyes and composed himself. "Very well."

A holographic representation of Admiral Teng materialized. Utang stood and saluted him properly, crossing his arms and banging his large fists on his chestplate and then extending them in front of him. "Admiral."

Teng returned the salute. "Captain, I have new orders."

"Yes, sir."

"The emperor is initiating talks with the United Intergalactic Coalition." This displeased Utang, but he did his best to conceal it. "I know this upsets you," said Admiral Teng, seeing through Utang's veneer.

"My feelings on the matter are irrelevant, Admiral."

Teng grinned, unconvinced. "The emperor is hoping to have the sanctions relaxed. However, you would be happy to know that while he is engaged in farcical negotiations with the Barberoi, he has ordered that Operation: Catalyst continue moving into the next phase."

"Yes, sir. Consider it done."

"Very well, Captain," said the Admiral, saluting. "To the glory of the Old Feng Empire."

Utang returned the salute, and the transmission terminated. He turned to return to the bridge of his command carrier when his com toned another incoming call.

He acknowledged the call, and a holographic image of General Yoshi Utang appeared before him. "How are you, little brother?"

"This is an inopportune time," said Mongo.

Yoshi frowned, his eyes reproachful. "You have been in the Aether again. Why do you torture yourself with the past?"

Mongo narrowed his eyes, his glare intense. "What you call torture, I call motivation. There will come a time when we will have our vengeance."

"Which is more important, your revenge or the glory of the empire?"

Mongo left the Aether cell and began his walk to the bridge, Yoshi's image following him. "Fortunately for me, Yoshi, the two are not mutually exclusive."

"Always remember, Mongo, the empire comes first."

Mongo smiled. "I must go now. I have the business of the empire to attend to."

Yoshi nodded and terminated the link, his image flickering and then disappearing.

Captain Utang's blood was on fire. He would live out his destiny to avenge his father's defeat. The bureaucratic socialists of the UIC were going to pay, and the Feng Empire would bring freedom and peace to the galaxies once more.

* * *

Planet: Feng

The Feng Imperial Palace, armored with a thick coating of ice, stood in defiance to the frigid wind as the turbulent sky swirled above it. Surrounded by silver-chromed industrial spheres hovering over endless ice fields, it appeared to be the center of its own universe.

Emperor Hiron sat with Monsu Kazar, the Vice Executor of the Feng Empire, in their palatial conference room awaiting the UIC Committee on Foreign Relations to convene. Hiron sat in full battle armor—heavy chest plate, jagged shoulder armor, horned helmet, and cape. Vice Executor Kazar donned the simple, purple robes of a politician. His past military term was more ceremonial than functional, and he had therefore never seen battle.

The conference table's legs were adorned with carvings of Feng Dynasty heroes of battle—kings, emperors, and generals—in various mid-action poses. Each leg wove a tale in stunning relief. Some were past tales of Feng legend and lore, and some were portents of the future, as in the Prophecy of the Ice Dragon restoring the grandeur of the Feng Dynasty over its many enemies far and wide.

There was a light and a tone, and Emperor Hiron pressed a button on the conference table. Holographic images of foreign ministers appeared in the seats around the long, ornate conference table, as holographic representations of Hiron and Kazar appeared across space in the other participants' conference and meeting rooms.

"Good day to you, Emperor Hiron," said Tolstoi Remu, the Humani Foreign Minister. The words registered in Feng through

Hiron's implanted universal translator chip. A typical Humani, she was tall and slender with grey skin and dark, braided hair in the Humani tribal tradition. She wore the drab but functional ministerial garb of the UIC. "Vice Executor Kazar," she added, almost as an afterthought.

"Good day," returned Emperor Hiron. Kazar only nodded his acknowledgement.

Around the table in clockwise order was Bobot Tegrit, the diminutive, grey-skinned Viceroy of the Humani; Dvorak of the Vampiri (they were referred to by first name according to custom), sitting in his tight black garments, his face bearing the sickly pallor of his race, eyes as iridescent as they were intelligent; Shamel Legune, the large, rotund but otherwise humanoid-looking Homunculi Foreign Minister; Martin Rayban, the snarky, braggadocious Human Foreign Minister of Earth; Hubritia Liguri, the lanky, mantis-like Firenz Foreign Minister.

"We meet today to make progress towards an accord that would allow each of our worlds to live and let live," announced Tolstoi Remu in an officious tone.

"I have reviewed your terms," answered Hiron. "They hardly allow the Feng to live at all with all of the sanctions the United Intergalactic Coalition has placed on our people—freezing our credit, interfering with our investments around the galaxy, trade embargoes."

"We realize that," said Tolstoi Remu, "and we have composed a set of mutually beneficial stipulations that we believe, as representatives of the United Intergalactic Coalition, should they be agreed upon by the Feng Empire, will allow us to lift economic sanctions."

"What are these stipulations?" asked Emperor Hiron.

Tolstoi Remu looked to Shamel Legune and nodded, signaling him to elaborate the terms. Shamel pressed a button on his respective conference table, and a digital list floated in the air. As Shamel Legune began to read each term, the words grew in size for tracking and emphasis.

"Term number one," said Legune. "The Feng Empire is to cease any subsequent research and development of further weapons technologies. All weapons development sites are to be converted to basic science research facilities.

"Term number two: the Feng are to grant access to representatives of the United Intergalactic Coalition of the said sites and any sites suspected of engaging in the development of weapons technology and submit to regular, unscheduled inspections of these sites.

"Term number three: the Feng are to share any and all developments in shipbuilding technology with the appointed representatives of the United Intergalactic Coalition in the interest of fair and free trade.

"These stipulations were drawn up in the best interest and safety of the worlds affiliated with the United Intergalactic Coalition, autonomous worlds and peoples, and the worlds and peoples of the Uncharted Sectors as well as the Feng Empire for the purpose of the greater intergalactic good."

Shamel Legune then paused, indicating that he was finished. The list of terms was uploaded onto Emperor Hiron's and Vice Executor Kazar's digital displays for further inspection and consideration.

"What say you, Emperor Hiron of the Feng Empire?" prompted Tolstoi Remu.

Hiron looked around the conference table, amused at the arrogance of such terms. Although the other foreign ministers were only present as holograms, he sensed the tension and air of nervous anticipation of his reaction to these terms.

"Let me begin by stating that I hardly see anything of fairness in the terms of this accord for the Feng people."

"I assure you that this accord is in the best interest of all the parties involved," insisted Tolstoi Remu. "What are your reservations?"

"What are my reservations?" chortled Hiron. "Where do I start? Term number one stipulating that we cease the development of all new weapons technology...the Feng Empire is but a shell of what it used to be." Hiron noticed self-satisfied smiles around the table at the uncharacteristic admission. "The United Intergalactic Coalition is vast and powerful. How do you expect us to defend ourselves should the need arise?"

"The development of new weapons technology would only be for the purpose of offense, not defense," said Hubritia Liguri of Firenz. "If you are serious about entering into an accord, you must demonstrate your honorable intentions by abandoning an offensive posture."

Hiron wore a joyless grin. "How will the UIC demonstrate its honorable intentions? Are the worlds and races of the United Intergalactic Coalition going to cease weapons development as well?"

"That has not been raised as a stipulation in this accord," said Tolstoi Remu. Hiron looked for a flash of color in the Humani minister, but the holographic technology masked such displays of emotion. Humani epidermal microexpressions could only be seen in the flesh.

"Of course not," said Hiron. "So, while the United Intergalactic Coalition continues to advance their weapons capabilities, the Feng people will be left behind, leaving us vulnerable." He looked at Hubritia Liguri. "Defensively speaking."

"The Feng are already way out in front of weapons development," offered Dvorak of the Vampiri. "Perhaps a hiatus will give the rest of us a chance to catch up, striking a balance. You are hardly helpless with legions of Cybions at your disposal. Not many would wish to tangle with those monstrosities."

"Besides," added Martin Rayban of Earth, "with all of the economic sanctions, you're hardly in a position to fund much weapons development."

"Might I add," said Tolstoi Remu, "that at its pinnacle, the Feng Empire with all of its superior weapons technology was brought down by a lesser race in the last Intergalactic War." Remu saw Rayban bristle at the remark, so she added, "A race that has now been advancing by leaps and bounds to join the rest of us."

"Nice save," said Martin Rayban sardonically. "Just remember, it took a 'lesser race' to turn the tide against the Feng Empire."

Eyes rolled around the table.

"I see that I am not going to receive any concessions on term number one," said Hiron. "So, let me address the other terms. You want access to Feng research and development sites for inspections. You want us to share our ship-building technology. Both terms are not only ridiculous, but they violate our very culture. The Feng are a private people not inclined to open their borders to…outsiders."

"You mean 'Barberoi?'" asked Hubritia Liguri. "That was the term you were going to use."

"What about our right to intergalactic patent?" asked Hiron.

"The United Intergalactic Coalition does not recognize patents from non-member worlds," said Tolstoi Remu.

"This is a total lack of consideration of our cultural beliefs and values," added Vice Executor Kazar, speaking for the first time. "I thought that the United Intergalactic Coalition stood for respect for other cultures."

Tolstoi Remu pulled down the corners of her mouth. "Frankly, Vice Executor Kazar, this respect is extended to member worlds and autonomous worlds, as long as they are stable and pose no threat. How else can we assure that the Feng have indeed ceased all new development of weapons technology?"

"Particularly when it is the cultural belief of the Feng not to honor agreements made with…outsiders," added Martin Rayban.

"May I address the council, Emperor?" asked Vice Executor Kazar. Emperor Hiron nodded his consent.

Kazar consulted his copy of the proposed accord. "So far, all I see are terms that benefit the United Intergalactic Coalition and place the Feng people (ever the politician, he purposely avoided the word 'empire') at a tremendous disadvantage, exposing us.

"Our government is struggling to feed its people as we speak. The United Intergalactic Coalition purports that it serves to protect the civil rights of all life. By leaving ourselves unarmed and unequipped, by sharing our ship-building technology, by allowing outsiders to conduct inspections…none of this inspires confidence in the emperor.

"What you are asking will likely cause revolution, which in turn will afford the United Intergalactic Coalition the opportunity it has been waiting for to exercise the Pax Galactus Initiative.

"We can agree to stop the development of new weapons technology and allow your inspections, but doing so without some other compensation would lead to our collapse and the UIC marching in and imposing its boiler-plate constitution and regulations. What you are proposing is a sneaky brand of imperialism. Planet Feng would become another colony in your menagerie of supplicant worlds."

"That is not how our members feel about the United Intergalactic Coalition," asserted Tolstoi Remu.

"You claim to respect the rights of stable autonomous worlds," said Kazar. "Yet, you are threatening to destabilize ours so that you can topple our government."

"What are you suggesting?" asked Tolstoi Remu, suggesting her hands were tied on the matter.

Emperor Hiron saw the door that Kazar opened, saw the opportunity before him, and he capitalized on the opportunity. "We need aid in the form of funding."

"That's preposterous," said Tolstoi Remu.

"To provide fiscal aid to the Feng Empire would be like personally funding our enemy," snickered Bobot Tegrit, who until this moment sat silently, listening to the exchange.

"You claim to want to strike an accord in the name of peace," pressed Emperor Hiron. "Yet, you drafted terms that would lead to a hostile takeover of the Feng by your United Intergalactic Coalition. This is just another contrived…no, engineered, nation-building exercise."

"I can assure you that this is not our intention," said Tolstoi Remu.

"I have already admitted that we are not the empire we used to be," said Hiron. "Vice Executor Kazar indicated to you that our government is on the verge of implosion. If we agree to the rems of this accord, then we need to be given the means to succeed as a non-aggressor world."

"He has a point," said Martin Rayban, drawing dirty looks from the others around the table.

"Let us recess to consider your proposal and reconvene at a later time to continue negotiations," said Tolstoi Remu. Everyone around the table, reluctant to agree to this idea of fiscal aid to the Feng, nodded their enthusiastic agreement to recess.

"I look forward to your response," said Emperor Hiron, failing to mask his sarcasm.

The holographs of the foreign ministers vanished into thin air, and the conference room was once again private and secured by the Feng digital firewalls.

"I cannot believe they are actually going to consider rendering fiscal aid," said Kazar, incredulous.

Hiron considered his vice executor carefully. The man appeared to be a little too open to negotiating with the United Intergalactic Coalition. His admission of the possibility of governmental collapse to a council of Barberoi was borderline treason.

However, Emperor Hiron was pleased with this development, but for a different reason than his vice executor. Hiron had no intention of bowing to the United Intergalactic Coalition. If he played his cards right, he would lay the groundwork for Operation: Catalyst, in which case the bloated, stretched thin United Intergalactic Coalition would be in danger of implosion.

"You laid the foundation for my request for aid," said Hiron, clapping a massive hand on the smaller man's shoulder. "You have done well."

Kazar beamed at the praise from the emperor.

"Now you must leave me to my thoughts," said Hiron, standing up. "I have much to consider."

Kazar rose, too, and bowed deeply. He left the room, leaving Emperor Hiron alone to calculate.

CHAPTER 2

Planet: Humana

"Daddy, throw the diskus!" shouted Catori.

Commander Nikoloi Massa smiled. "Are you ready?"

"Yes," said Catori, his body tensing in preparation.

Massa pressed the center ring of the diskus, and it lit up. He curled his arm, hugging the diskus to his chest, and whipped it out, releasing it with the flick of a wrist. The saucer was a blur of light as it arched its way to Catori.

It was a beautiful summer day in the country, and Missani smiled as she sat on the blanket watching them play. She knew time with Nikoloi was at a premium these days. With the Feng rattling their sabers and forging alliances with enemies of the United Intergalactic Coalition, he was called away more frequently for missions, so she savored every moment. She knew her husband could be called away at any moment.

Catori jumped up and snatched the diskus out of the air, bobbling it in his little hands until finally dropping it on the green grass.

"That's okay," reassured Massa. "Good try."

They were practicing throwing and catching. Once Catori mastered that, they would progress to using goals and targets. Massa did his best to try to ignore his old Wapuyuga injuries from his academy days.

Catori snatched the diskus up in his hand and ran over to his father. "Let us look at the fish in the water," he said, grabbing his father by the hand and pulling.

Having no real choice, Massa laughed as he allowed Catori to lead him to the water. Missani remained in the background. This was quality father-son time, and she wasn't going to interfere.

Massa smiled as his son pulled him to the lake. Catori stomped around like most younglings, as if they owned the planet, blissfully unaware of politics and war. They stopped in front of the iridescent blue water as a cascade roared in the distance, but Catori still held onto his father's hand. "Daddy, why do the Feng hate us?"

So much for the unspoiled innocence of youth.

Massa looked down at his son. It was the innocuous question of a youngling. He still gripped his father's hand, as if refusing to let him go.

"I'm not so sure they hate us, Catori."

"Then why do they threaten us?"

"Where did you hear this?"

"I saw it on the government report, when Mommy was watching it."

"Oh, I see. What does Mommy think?"

"She told me to ask you."

Massa smiled at this. "The Feng are a very old, very proud race," said Massa. "They are warriors."

"They like to fight?"

That was a good question. "Not all of the Feng like to fight. At least, I don't think so. Their government wants to build an empire, like they used to have eons ago."

"What is an empire, Daddy?"

Massa thought about how to answer in a way Catori would understand. "Do you know how you and your friends play Conquest in the schoolyard?"

Catori nodded. "I once took the whole schoolyard. Even Sawati or Nikan couldn't stop me."

"Well, that's what an empire is. The Feng do not have a Congress like we do. They have one ruler, an emperor. What he says goes."

"Like a teacher?"

"Yes, Catori, like a teacher, but worse. If you don't listen to the emperor, he can punish you."

"Mrs. Akani punishes us sometimes," said Catori.

Massa shook his head. "The emperor throws his own people in jail. He can even order someone killed."

Catori gasped at this. "Are they bad people?"

"They can simply be people who disagree with him."

"Why does the emperor hate the Humani?"

"I do not think he hates us," reflected Massa. "We are competition for the Feng. They build ships, too, but they want every planet to buy their ships. So, he tells his people that the Humani are the reason why they starve. That we are the reason they suffer. That we hold back the empire for our greed."

A couple of apuna fish, large and brightly colored, swam towards the edge of the water. Their bright colors were dulled by the looming shadows of Massa and Catori. Catori scrunched his face and scratched his head. "But that is not true."

"Of course not, but that is how he gets his people to hate us. To hate us enough that they would want to go to war."

Catori's grip tightened on Massa's hand. "Is it true the Cybions are the best soldiers in the system?"

"The Feng like to think that they are flawless, but they are really just fancy Cybiotes made to be soldiers."

"The Cymbiotes are workers, like our Avatars."

"That is correct."

"Daddy, why don't we make our Avatars into soldiers?"

Massa sighed. "Because we Humani fight our own battles. The Avatars are for labor only, and there are those who think even that is unethical."

Catori looked confused. "What does 'un-ethi-cal' mean?"

"Some people think the Avatars are wrong."

"How are the Avatars wrong?"

Massa shook his head. "Not that the Avatars are wrong. That it is wrong to make them."

"Why would it be wrong?"

"Because some think the Avatars are Humani and deserve rights like any of us."

"Avatars, like us?" asked Catori, really perplexed now. "They do not seem like us."

Massa put a hand on his son's head. "That is because they are made by our scientists. They are not made to think. They are made to work. Without them, our shipbuilding would never keep up with the Feng."

"And the Feng would win?"

"Something like that."

"Daddy, are you going to have to fight the Cybions?"

"I hope not. That is enough questions about politics for today. We need to check on your mother. She brought some food, and it should be ready by now."

"Okay!" This time, Catori released his grip on his father's hand and dashed off toward his mother. Massa followed behind Catori, wishing he had half the energy that little one did.

When he reached the blanket, Catori was already unwrapping his lunch. Massa smiled at Missani. "So, I hear you two have been watching the government report."

Missani smiled back, but her eyes were determined, as if she had been anticipating this topic. "I think he should know what is going on."

"Do you not think he is a little young for all this?" asked Massa.

Missani shot him a look, and then she looked at her son. "Catori, eat your meal. Your father and I are going for a walk."

"Okay," said Catori, mouth full of apuna fish and magnotta sauce.

Missani stood and extended her arm, bent at the elbow. Massa interlocked his arm with hers, and they took a stroll by the water, far enough away not to be heard, but close enough to keep Catori in their line of sight.

Missani spoke first. "You know, he asks why you are called away."

"What do you tell him?"

"That you are keeping Humana safe."

"Well, that is true."

Missani gripped his arm tighter. "But it is no longer enough. He wants to know what you are doing and why. He wants to know where you go."

"He knows I am a fighter pilot."

"Nikoloi, he is terrified of the Cybions."

"That is because you let him watch the government report."

"It is not just that," she said. "He hears about them in school. He has been getting nightmares about mechanical monsters that rip people limb from limb. I figured if he watched the report, if he got more information, it would allay his fears."

"He was just asking me about the Cybions. I told him they were just trumped up Cybiotes. Mechanical versions of our Avatars."

Missani furrowed her brow. "You know that is not true."

"He is just a boy who does not need to know otherwise. He should be focusing on school and his friends."

Missani's eyes welled up. "How can he when his father can be called away at a moment's notice, never to return again?"

They stopped at the edge of the water, and Massa pulled her close. "It sounds like he is not the only one who is worried."

Missani faced him, her eyes wide. "I hear stories about the Feng and their conquest. I hear that they are rebuilding their empire and are challenging the United Intergalactic Coalition."

Massa rubbed her shoulders. "Missani, they are a far cry from their glorious empire of old. Emperor Hiron is all bluster. Even with his elite Cybions and his Feng warships, the Feng are but one world. The UIC is many. The Feng are no match for the UIC Marines."

The breeze picked up, stirring the buzzing illumi in the tall grass. Taking flight, they filled the air like luminescent pollen, surrounding Massa and Missani in a cloud of light. Massa leaned in and kissed her sweetly as Catori looked on from his blanket, smiling.

* * *

First Lieutenant Alita Nakai was racing home on her darkcycle under the moonlight. As she maneuvered through the complex bio-lattice, its organic architectural undulations glowing from its solar absorption, she saw families gathering through unshaded portals. She had promised to be home in time for the New Moon Ceremony, and she knew her mother would give her guff if she didn't keep her promise.

She glided into the driveport and parked her cycle. She removed her helmet and slung it on a handlebar. She flashed her hand over the door sensor and burst into her childhood home. There were voices in the kitchen.

"Alita, is that you?"

"Yeah, Father." She stepped into the kitchen to find her father, Klau, lowering a large pot over the hot stove.

"Well, look who decided to grace us with her presence," said her mother, Alani, her tone sarcastic.

Nakai ignored the remark and kissed her father on the cheek.

"Oh, don't listen to your mother," her father said, waving a dismissive hand in her direction. "She is just a grump."

"How is my fighter pilot niece doing?" asked her Uncle Manew.

A smile split her face, and Nakai hugged her uncle.

"It is good to see you," said her Aunt Fretta.

"It is good to see you, too." She hugged her aunt. "So where are my two brat cousins?"

"They are in the game room playing Interceptor," said Manew. "They have been waiting for you."

"I don't understand those violent games," said Fretta, a worried look on her face. "All that shooting and killing."

"Wait till they see we have a real killer in the flesh," said Alina.

Everyone looked at each other uncomfortably for a moment, but not Nakai. Refusing to back down, she never broke her mother's gaze. She wasn't a little girl anymore. "I am going to go surprise them."

She crossed the living room and stood in the doorway of the game room. Little Frax clutched his controller, his face screwed up in concentration as he attempted to pummel his big brother. Luoi, now an adolescent, sat back and smirked as he evaded Frax's attacks and retaliated.

"Hit the brakes, Frax," said Nakai from the doorway.

Frax shot her a glance and grinned. He hit the brakes and Luoi's fighter nearly collided with his. Luoi, taken off guard, narrowly avoided collision, buying Frax enough time to score a direct hit as his brother overshot.

"Yeah!" shouted Frax in triumph.

"No fair," said Luoi, "you helped him."

Nakai entered the room and high-fived Frax. Then she smacked Luoi affectionately on the back of his head. "Such a sore loser. Besides, in the heat of battle, dog fighting is a team effort."

Frax made a face at his brother. "Which is why you will never be a part of the Razor's Edge."

"Yeah, like you will," said Luoi.

"Neither of you will," said Nakai smirking. "I expect you both to go to Academy and get high-paying jobs."

"But I want to fly," said Frax.

Nakai smiled. "If you get paid enough, you can buy your own ship, and you can travel the galaxy."

"What about the Feng?"

"Not to worry, Frax, the Razor's Edge will take care of them."

Nakai's father appeared in the doorway. "Okay, you guys. Dinner is ready." He disappeared back into the kitchen.

"Let us go, before the adults eat up all the food," said Nakai wearing an impish grin.

Luoi put the game on hold, and he and his brother raced to the dining room, shoving past their big cousin. Nakai laughed and followed.

"Slow down," Klau reprimanded, as the kids slid into their seats.

Nakai sat next to her father, placing him between herself and her mother. Manew and Fretta took their seats as well.

"Okay," said Klau, "who wants to address the Engineer?"

"How about our guest of honor?" suggested Manew, smiling at Nakai.

Nakai put her hands up. "No, I'm not a worthy choice to address the Engineer." She looked over at Alina. "Mother, would you do the honor?"

Her mother nodded officiously and put her hands up, palms facing upward as if she was going to catch a large, spherical object. Everyone else, including the children, bowed their heads in reverence.

Alina looked around the table, her eyes quickly passing over her daughter. Nakai, head bowed, didn't notice, but she could feel her mother's resentment emanating off of her in waves.

Alina cleared her throat and began. "Great Engineer, all hallowed mechanist of life and worlds, creator of the vast Aether, we thank you for our lives on this feast of the new moon. We thank you for all those who protect life, in this great universe, and we ask your forgiveness for those who take life." Her eyes fell as she let her words hang out there in space, over her daughter's head.

At last, she looked up. "Let us eat."

"Let us eat," Klau chimed in, looking tentatively at his daughter seated to his left while feeling the intensity of his wife's gaze to his right. He felt like an asteroid caught between two burning stars.

Klau was a mediator between the two since Nakai was a strong-willed little girl. He watched the power struggle between them develop as little Alita, feeling her oats, was as stubborn as could be, and Alina asserted her authority as her mother and Humani high priestess.

Everyone began to pile food on top of their plates in earnest, Frax and Luoi elbowing each other and giggling over private jokes as Manew glared at them.

"So, how have you been enjoying your leave?" Fretta asked Nakai.

"It has been nice to be home," answered Nakai.

"Funny you say that," said her mother. "You have not been home much since you have returned."

"Now, Alina," said Klau, "Alita is grown up now. She has her own life. I am sure she wants to see her friends, too, and she does not have much time to do it."

Nakai smiled. "It is true. I somehow have to cram everyone into such a small sliver of time."

"Well, we are happy to see you, even if for a brief moment," said Manew.

"So what is the new Vortex fighter like?" blurted Frax.

Nakai smiled. These questions were inevitable, particularly when her little cousins were around. "They are faster than the last iteration. They have improved the forced induction of dark energy."

"Can it outrun a Warmonger?" asked Luoi, shoveling his mouth full of Gnoat.

"Warmongers are pretty fast," said Nakai, stabbing some apuna fish onto her fork. "But we can give 'em a run for their money."

Nakai saw her mother's discomfort with the discussion of what she called 'war machines,' so she decided to change the topic. "Enough about that stuff. I want to hear about you guys. What is going on in school?"

"Luoi is doing a dissertation on the Avatar Activist movement," said Fretta.

"For or against?" asked Nakai, taking a mouthful of apuna.

"For, of course," said Alina, almost in rebuke.

"It was just a question."

Luoi smiled nervously. "The Avatars are living beings, and as Humani, we believe all living beings have rights."

"Well, only the religious Humani believe that so absolutely," replied Nakai, taking a swig of beckleberry juice. "Avatars are actually created in labs."

"But they are still living beings," said Luoi.

"True," said Nakai, "but I think the question is not whether or not they are living beings. The question is whether or not they should be afforded the full rights of citizenship."

"Why would they not?" asked Luoi with his mouth full. Frax looked on in silence, soaking it all in while not understanding everything, as this was an adult conversation.

"They have had some basic Humani qualities bred out of them," replied Nakai. "Like free will and desire, except for depravation variables like hunger and thirst."

"What about sex?" blurted Frax, quickly covering his mouth as Fretta shot him a disapproving look.

"It is an honest question," said Manew, winking at Frax. "It is my understanding that if the Avatars were busy looking at other Avatars, then they would not be building ships or refining kronite."

"That is why all Avatars are male," said Luoi.

"That actually is not true," said Nakai. "There are female Avatars. In fact, I have heard that there is one Avatar engineered differently than the others. He has free will, and he is quite intelligent."

"An Avatar with free will," said Alina in astonishment.

"He is the only Avatar with the full rights of citizenship," added Nakai.

"I heard humans have same-sex attractions," said Frax.

This comment elicited a smack from his mother. "Where do you hear such nonsense?" Fretta rebuked.

"It is true," said Nakai. "I have heard Human pilots discussing it once. They are an odd species."

"I swear to the Engineer, they were a dubious addition to the United Intergalactic Coalition," said Klau, "for many reasons."

"But a necessary one," said Nakai. "The UIC is growing large and unwieldy."

"They are a clumsy race," said Manew, "barely able to come to a consensus on anything. If you put two Humans in a room, you get three opinions."

"They are not as bad as the Drekaar or the Iguani on Golgath," said Alina. "Those animals preach a religion of death and subjugation of all races and worlds. They choose to remain outside the protective umbrella of the UIC and would rather fight each other. Why we hold a tentative agreement with them is beyond me."

Manu couldn't believe what he was hearing. "Animals? What happened to all life being precious?" His remark was met with an icy glare from Alina.

"Without their kronite mines, our shipbuilding would suffer, and we would fall behind the Feng," said Nakai. "The UIC armada would be much smaller."

"So to hold the Feng at bay, we must put up with the evils of cloning and barbarian tribal races," said Alina. "We construct machines of war and death in the name of peace."

"Sometimes that is what is necessary to win the peace," said Klau.

"Sometimes I wonder that if we just backed off the Feng, they would leave us alone," said Manew. "Perhaps we created our own problems."

Nakai swallowed another mouthful of apuna and shook her head. "No, I have seen what Feng can do. They are ruthless, even within their own ranks. Failure is punished with dismemberment, even death."

"All the more reason why we should leave them alone and let them have their own corner of the galaxy," said Fretta.

"Any concession will result in their advance," said Nakai. "We give a microt, they take a parsec."

* * *

Second Lieutenant Rolo Pequo was walking to visit his older brother, Garsi, at Navigo, appreciating a beautiful day with a clear blue sky peeking in between whiteglass skyscrapers and solar monorails, when he ran into a picket line of protestors. They marched up and down in front of the Navigo building bearing digital signs reading phrases like, 'Avatars Are Humani Too,' 'Avatar Rights,' and 'Citizenship for Avatars.' A few others went negative, making bold statements like, 'End Avatar Slavery,' 'Avatars Take Humani Jobs,' and 'Avatar Abominations.'

That last statement perplexed Pequo, as it didn't appear to be as sympathetic to the Avatars as the others. He looked around at the small detail of Enforcers around the protestors, making sure the demonstration remained peaceful.

Pequo looked up the skyscraper as if he was looking at his brother's office, and steeled himself. He was no stranger to taking fire, but it was usually from off-worlders, not his own kind, and a relative no less.

He crossed the picket line, becoming the immediate brunt of curses, character assassination, and threats, until he reached the front entrance. He slid inside the massive building, the decibel dampeners immediately blocking out the ruckus outside.

He approached the front security desk, and the guard smiled as he recognized Pequo. "Hello, Rolo."

"Hello, Parcus," said Pequo, returning the smile.

"Taking your brother out to lunch?" The question was facetious. It was usually Garsi who insisted on paying for lunch, lording his large salary over Pequo any opportunity he got.

Pequo looked back over his shoulder at the muted crowd outside. "No, I think this time he is having lunch brought up to us."

Parcus shot a dirty look at the throng outside. "Yeah, it has been getting worse and worse."

"Where do I sign?" asked Pequo.

Parcus slid a digital registry over the counter, and Pequo placed his hand on its glass surface.

"He is expecting you."

"Thanks, Parcus."

Pequo entered the lift. The ambient tribal music decreased in volume as the doors closed. "Sixtieth floor."

"Acknowledged," said an androgynous voice.

The music returned, and Pequo recognized it immediately. It was a tribal song from his childhood. When the lift reached the floor, the doors opened, and Pequo stepped out. He stepped up to the receptionist, who simply nodded and tapped the com piece on her ear. "Your brother is here, Mr. Pequo."

She nodded and waved Pequo in with a graceful swipe of an elegant hand. A door opened, and Pequo walked through. He traversed a long hallway until he reached his brother's office. Garsi was seated behind a luxurious Yomani wood desk. When he saw his little brother through the glass wall, he stood, and the door opened.

"L-T!" his brother called out affectionately, the nickname referencing Pequo's rank.

"Hello, Garsi," said Pequo.

"I hope you're hungry," said Garsi, beaming. "I ordered a big lunch. Ragnar steaks and Hilli sprouts."

"I could eat."

Garsi gestured for Pequo to sit. "What will you be drinking?"

"Humani Ale is fine."

Garsi smirked. "C'mon, Rolo, I've got a whole bar of off-world spirits."

"Humani Ale is fine," Pequo insisted.

Garsi rolled his eyes, indicating that the selection was pedestrian in his estimation. He pressed a button, and a coolant chamber rose out of a table top. He reached in and snatched a cold Humani Ale. "So, how's the Armada treating my little brother these days?" he asked, handing the bottle to Pequo.

"Been busy. The UIC has been wielding the Pax Galactus Initiative left and right. It has been one mission after another."

Garsi poured himself a Vampiri sanguine tonic. "You speak as if the Pax Galactus Initiative is a weapon."

Pequo sipped his ale. Humani summers were brutal. It felt good rolling down his throat. "Is it not?"

"That is a bit cynical, especially for an Armada pilot. I thought you grunts were not paid to think."

"Our last mission got a bit dicey. A few close calls," said Pequo. "The indigenous were less than receptive."

"Well, nation-building is not easy work," said Garsi. "If the natives were receptive, they would not need nation-building."

"Now who is the cynic?" teased Pequo.

"Mother and Father always thought you were too much of a philosopher to be a pilot for the Armada," said Garsi.

"Well, we all cannot be super successful business tycoons."

Garsi smiled at the compliment.

Pequo stood and walked with his ale over to the window. He looked down at the street, and the protesters below looked like tiny insects. "The picket line is bigger than I remember."

Garsi waved a hand. "They don't understand anything. Eighty-two percent of the Humani economy is shipbuilding, the UIC being our largest client. In order to keep up with the demand and stay ahead of the Feng, we need the Avatars."

"The Avatars take Humani jobs."

Garsi grinned, as if amused by his little brother's naiveté. "The Avatars do the work that Citizens cannot. They are simply faster and cheaper."

"You mean they are expendable," said Pequo.

"They serve their purpose," said Garsi. "Like right now, we are entering into negotiations with the Drekaar to develop a rudimentary shipbuilding operation on Golgath."

"By the Engineer," chortled Pequo. "Drekaar in space. I thought space was too cold for them."

"After eons of staying on-world, they are considering taking to the stars."

"They are not ready."

Garsi took a sip of his tonic. "Hey, it is how we started. Shipbuilding was our ticket into the UIC, which brought us out of tribalism. Look how far we have come."

"Yes, it has brought us out into space where we have attracted new enemies like the Feng," said Pequo.

"It also has pilots like yourself bringing peace to unstable worlds."

"Whether they want it or not, or earned it for that matter. So what do the Avatars have to do with the Drekaar?"

Garsi snapped his fingers in the air. "Navigo, and all of Humana, has an opportunity to bring the Drekaar into space and the modern era, without the need for military operations or the Pax Galactus Initiative. The only problem is, the incessant conflicts with the Iguani are making it untenable to send any managers over to oversee the project. It is too dangerous. The company does not want to risk Humani lives, and frankly, no one will do it."

Pequo frowned. "But I thought the Avatars were too simple to be managers."

"True, they are bred to be worker drones. However, there was one...mistake. He is a deep thinker, much like you."

Pequo ignored the dig. "I thought that was impossible."

Garsi shrugged. "So did we. However, when frakking with genetics, you're subject to natural variability, even within a highly controlled process. It is a statistical inevitability."

"So, you are sending this 'deep thinker.' Is this the one Avatar that is rumored to have citizenship."

Garsi shook his head. "He has all the rights of citizenship, but he is not a Citizen."

"What is the difference?"

"He is still Navigo property." Garsi's ear com lit up. He touched it and listened. "Ah, lunch is here. Enough politics for one day."

Pequo had more questions, but a receptionist entered the office bearing a small feast, and Pequo was hungry. His leave was over in a cycle, and he had to get all of the good grub while he could.

CHAPTER 3

Exosystem 16
UIC Armada War Games

Captain Trevor Reinhardt addressed the crew of the command carrier Resilience from the bridge. "This is your Captain. As we enter this next round of the Armada War Games, I'd like to commend you on your performance thus far.

"We are the only Human battle group left in the games, and we're surrounded by Humani competition that would like to knock us out this round. This is the furthest any human battle group has advanced in the history of Human participation in the games, and we've done this on an unfamiliar ship and without the elite Razor's Edge Vortex squadron.

"But this is no time to sit on our laurels. Since I've been assigned Captain of the Resilience, I've gotten to know you, as a group and as individuals. I can honestly say that this is the most exemplary crew I've ever had the pleasure of working with in the Armada, and I know that we on the Resilience do not settle for mediocre.

"I expect that we're going to continue to work together and take this as far as we can go. And, if this is as far as we can go, we do as much damage possible to our rival Humani battle group on the way out."

Reinhardt nodded to Connelly, who closed the coms, and he turned to Commander Mariu Ashwani. "Commander, prepare to commence entrance into the round on the Games Master's signal."

"Aye, Captain," said Commander Ashwani.

There was a brief moment of silence on the battle bridge of the command center in the epicenter of the massive command carrier. In the cold depths of space, there was no hiding. Each battle group knew the location of its rival by heat signature. This was not a game of stealth. This was a matter of position and maneuvering.

It was a double-blind scenario, as according to the rules of the games, meaning neither battle group knew who they were up against.

Captain Reinhardt only knew his rivals were Humani because he heard all of the other non-Humani contenders had been eliminated.

The Humani battle group sat on the far edge of the sector. The Resilience sat next to Exoplanet 8RS, just out of reach of its ice rings, which was not a great position as the ice rings created a parameter that would limit the battle group's mobility. They were beginning the round at a disadvantage.

"We've received the commencement signal," said Connelly.

"Commander, standard formation, set the PIM (path of intended motion) according to the most likely threat axis," ordered Reinhardt, "reverse, quarter conduction."

"Aye aye, Captain." She relayed the orders to Connelly, who sent the instructions to the rest of the battle group, and the helmsman, who in-turn sent the instructions down to the engine room.

"What's the strategy, Captain?" asked Ashwani.

"Well, the strategy we used last round worked really well. Due to the double-blind, this rival has no idea who we are or what we've done, so I say we use the same strategy.

"Lieutenant Commander Mako, I need a full assessment of their OOB (Order of Battle)."

"Aye, Captain." Mako got busy, reaching out with sensors, the quantum computer collecting thousands of points of data on dozens of signatures every second. "Standard complement of weaponry, sir."

Reinhardt knew this, because each battle group's arsenal was standardized. However, the formality was a necessary practice as they wouldn't always know who or what they were up against in actual combat.

"They're coming on, full-ahead, full conductance," said Mako.

This was where Reinhardt's strategy was unorthodox. The Humani were full aggression and speed. Their reaction times were superior, as were their offensive tactics. In the past, Reinhardt managed Order of Engagement, prioritizing Class A Potent and Immediate threats, struggling to keep up while anticipating Class B Immediate threats and attempting some threats of his own.

In prior rounds, the Resilience was quickly overwhelmed and barely managed to scrape through the round without being eliminated from the games. However, this was a zero-sum round. All the points went to the victor, and the loser would be out.

"This is the part where they become confused as to why we're already retreating," said Reinhardt.

Ashwani watched the screen, her eyes alert with anticipation and fear. This maneuver had worked wonders last round. This round, she wasn't so sure.

"Pull back the Combat Space Patrol, reverse direction. Make it look like we're running scared."

"Or playing possum," said Ashwani. "Do you think they'll buy it?"

"The Humani are an arrogant species, particularly when it comes to Humans. By now, they've probably ascertained that we're a Human crew and think we're panicking."

"We're the only remaining Human battle group in the games," said Ashwani, "which means they already know what we're going to do."

"We're one of several that were in the games," reminded Reinhardt. "It could've been one of the others for all they know."

"Captain, a battleship and two destroyers are breaking off from the enemy battle group and are circling around the exoplanet," said Mako.

"Shit! They do know what we're trying to do," said Reinhardt. "They're trying to flank us by using the orbit of the exoplanet to slingshot around behind us."

"Should we push off away from the planet?" asked Ashwani.

"No," said Reinhardt. "That'll take us into open space. They'll chew up our formation in quick order." He had to make a snap decision. It was a judgement call, but so far his quick instincts had gotten them through the prior rounds. Or was it luck? The funny thing about luck was that it always eventually ran out. "Reverse towards the ice rings."

Ashwani did a double take. "Sir, the rings will tear us apart."

"Not that close," said Reinhardt. "Just enough to cover our six."

Commander Ashwani related the orders. The helmsman hesitated, flashing her a dubious look. "You heard the captain!" she rebuked.

Reinhardt knew they were given a shit position, so he figured he'd take that lemon and make lemonade. The battle group backed towards the wide ice rings as the main Humani formation closed in on them.

"They're heating up weapons systems," said Mako.

"Where's that smaller squadron?" asked Reinhardt.

"Closing in quickly to intercept," said Mako.

"They'll have to break orbit and avoid the rings," said Ashwani.

"Captain, the command carrier is dispatching Vortex fighters," said Mako.

"Hold formation and slow it down to minimal conduction," said Reinhardt. "I don't want to crash into those rings."

"Captain, the Vortex fighters are closing in."

Reinhardt waited, watching the screen. Ashwani sat forward in her chair, her hands gripping the arms tightly. Her knuckles were white. They watched as the green bogies on the radar and sonar drew closer to the outer screen of battleships and destroyers. They smelled blood in the water and were racing to engage.

"Release the scattershot on the flanks, creating a firing corridor up the middle," ordered Reinhardt. "Same as before. You know the drill."

The battleships released digital scattershot as the formation retreated backwards, forming a wall in front with a narrow corridor and defining the battlespace.

The Vortex fighters were coming on too quickly and were unable to pull up in time. They collided with the digital scattershot, which affixed themselves to their hulls. Their fighters changed from green to red on screen, signaling that they were out of the game. In real combat, using actual scattershot, the fighters would've been shredded by their own momentum. The battleships and destroyers took care of any fighters that made it down the firing corridor.

"The smaller squadron just cleared the rings behind us," said Mako.

The Humani battle group wasn't foolish or stupid. They avoided the corridor, knowing it was a bottleneck. They waited for the digital scattershot to dissipate. However, what they didn't count on was the floating screen of their own deactivated Vortex fighters that replaced the digital scattershot.

"We have to get out of here," said Ashwani, realizing that they had entombed themselves, which protected them for the moment, but also restricted movement.

"If we move, the deactivated fighters will drift backwards and collide with the rings," said Reinhardt. "They'll be killed in a simulation exercise."

"So we're trapped," said Ashwani in horror.

"So are they, for the moment."

* * *

Planet Feng
Emperor Hiron's Palace

General Yoshi Utang met Fero Idoni, Captain of the Imperial Guard, outside his quarters. "Keep an eye on Regana."

"Always, sir," answered Idoni, almost defensively.

Yoshi Utang leaned in. "I have garnered many enemies in recent times. Do not assume that she is safe because she is in the palace."

"Of course," said Captain Idoni. "I will see to it personally. I take nothing for granted when it comes to her safety." He puffed out his chest, looking formidable with his war braids, hulking frame, and jagged armor.

Yoshi Utang nodded his approval. "I want a full detail outside her chambers. Your best men."

"Yes, General Utang. At once."

Satisfied, Yoshi Utang stalked down the hallway to the council chambers. When he arrived, the guards in front parted, and he passed through the doors into the chamber.

Half the council was there, and the other half filed into the room behind him. They each took their seats at the table—the Vice Executor, the Vice of the Interior, the Imperial Bursar, the Vice of Justice, and Yoshi Utang, the Vice of War.

Emperor Hiron was, according to custom, the last to enter the council chambers. Upon his entry, the others stood and saluted their emperor, pounding their chest plates and extending their fists.

When Hiron reached his seat, he waved them off, and they all sat. "As Emperor of the Feng Dynasty, I call to order the Imperial Council of the Feng Empire.

"I'd like to open with the matter of a possible accord with the United Intergalactic Coalition regarding matters of kronite mining and prevue over unstable worlds outside the empire.

"Thanks to Vice Executor Kazar, the United Intergalactic Coalition Foreign Council is now considering offering the Feng fiscal aid for complying with the terms of their proposed accord."

"What terms?" asked Mondi Hayati, Vice of the Interior. Wan Tengani, the Bursar, sat up in his seat, his curiosity piqued.

"They want us to cease all new weapons technology development, open our sites to their inspection, and share our ship-building technology," said Hiron.

There were grunts of outrage and disapproval accompanied by the agitated rattling of battle armor.

"This is preposterous," said Mondi Hayati. "Surely we are not considering the Barberoi's terms."

"We do not have much choice," answered Vice Executor Kazar. "If we decline and the sanctions continue, we can hardly afford to feed our own people and sustain the empire."

"We have other small campaigns on small, unstable worlds as we speak," said General Yoshi Utang.

"It is not enough," said Kazar.

"The vice executor is correct," said Bursar Wan Tengani. "With our credit frozen across the galaxies by the United Intergalactic Coalition, we are close to total financial collapse."

"That means revolution," said Kazar. "How long do you think an unruly warrior people will be denied a sustainable quality of life? These sanctions have clipped our wings."

"What do you propose?" asked Vice of the Interior, Mondi Hayati.

Hiron cleared his throat. "It is my opinion that it might be beneficial to the Feng Empire to come to some sort of understanding with the United Intergalactic Coalition regarding matters of kronite. The largest deposit of the element is on Golgath, where the United Intergalactic Coalition already has a foothold and is enforcing a trade embargo with the Feng."

Vice Executor Kazar leaned forward in his seat, placing a fist on the table. "Our shipbuilding operations rely heavily on that kronite deposit. If the United Intergalactic Coalition were to continue sanctions on the empire, the results could prove devastating."

"Our production has already been suffering," added Wan Tengani, the Bursar, "shrinking our fleet. If we are to hold our own in the galaxy, we must keep up."

"I will be the judge of whether or not we hold our own," said General Yoshi Utang. "I think that any accord we concede will be interpreted as weakness, and any perceived weakness will be exploited."

Emperor Hiron sat back, listening.

"With all due respect," said the vice executor, "if we force our hand with the United Intergalactic Coalition, they will use the Pax Galactus Initiative to seize control of the planet. They have even been hovering like carrion wasps over the planet Golgath and the Drekaar mining operations."

"Kazar, I do not plan on allowing that to happen," said General Utang.

Mondi Hayati, the Vice of the Interior, sneered at what he perceived to be an arrogant remark. "If you recall your history, General, you will note that after the Intergalactic War 4.0, our numbers were diminished. The UIC Armada outnumber us four to one."

General Utang sat back in his chair. "They are over extended. They have taken on too many worlds in their nation-building initiative. They do not have the resources to enforcers it."

"And we do not have the resources to test your hypothesis," said the Bursar. "We are on the verge of implosion ourselves. Our people starve while you wax poetic about bringing back the glory of the Feng Empire."

"The Drekaar have opened up communications," said the vice executor. "They grow uncomfortable with the growing influence the United Intergalactic Coalition has over the kronite mines. They are weighing their options."

Emperor Hiron leaned forward in his chair. "And what of Operation: Catalyst, General Utang? Golgath would make an opportune site for it. Hiding it right under the United Intergalactic Coalition's very nose."

"If an alliance can indeed be struck with the Drekaar," said the vice executor. "However, assuming that is possible, the risks of being caught are too great. We do not know that the Drekaar would honor a coalition with us. They are tribal and wild. We are better off striking a deal with the United Intergalactic Coalition."

General Utang pounded his fist on the table, startling the Vice Bursar. "The Feng Empire did not attain glory by making deals with Barberoi. Any deal that is struck with them will be made to appear as a compromise, but in reality, it will diminish our position in the galaxy. We are slowly but steadily gaining ground with some small, unstable worlds in our campaign, flying under the radar."

"They have agreed to only initiate the Pax Galactus Initiative for unsettled, dangerous worlds," said the vice executor. "Which means that for every world we take, we look like tyrants, and they appear to be great liberators."

"Liberators," said Emperor Hiron with contempt. "They are anything but. They force democratic government and their constitutions on planets that do not ask for it, all in the name of peace. They construct unwieldy regimes that tax their constituents and overburden populaces with regulations and law."

"Any world or people that cannot fight for their freedom, does not deserve it," agreed General Utang. "They call us tyrants, but they do not know the realities of ruling a warrior populace. The Feng people are not high-minded thinkers in ivory towers who live according to ridiculous ideals.

"We are an empire forged by battle and conquest, and we keep our people fed through the spoils of war, not regulation and taxation or redistribution of the wealth of other races. We eat what we kill, which is the Rule of Nature. The United Intergalactic Coalition and their Rule of Law are merely veiled Socialism promising freedom in one hand while taking autonomy with the other."

"The Drekaar understand the Rule of Nature," said Emperor Hiron. "They live by it. Perhaps, if we promise them assistance in dealing with the Iguani, they would be more apt to enter into a coalition with us."

"I think this line of thinking is dangerous," insisted the vice executor. "We are no longer in a position to make such maneuvers. We are half the empire we used to be."

"Which is exactly why we need to execute Operation: Catalyst," said General Yoshi Utang. "If successful, this is the weapon that will even the odds."

"You speak of military strategy," said Vice Executor Kazar. "We should be considering the economic advantages of an allegiance with the Drekaar, for our empire's very survival."

"Enough," said Emperor Hiron. "I have heard enough of this matter for the time being. Let us move on to the state of the empire." He nodded to the Vice of the Interior, who then began to launch into a detailed analysis of the social state of the empire.

It was the usual dour report of a restless populace that was slowly starving. There were rumors of clandestine meetings past nightfall in the townships where citizens voiced their discontent. The peasant farmers were no longer able to sustain crops at peak levels. The factories weren't able to pay their laborers. The Vice Bursar gave his report on how spread thin the empire was, particularly since its support worlds had been whittled down and 'emancipated' by the United Intergalactic Coalition.

After the delivery of the bad news and much debate, Emperor Hiron adjourned the meeting, leaving much of the old business unresolved and the Imperial Council restless and apprehensive.

Yoshi Utang stormed out of the meeting with a fire in his belly. Emperor Hiron called out to him, stopping him in his tracks. Hiron approached him, waited for the stragglers to return to their various posts in the palace, and he leaned in.

"Yoshi, a word."

"Yes, Your Highness."

"I did not want to discuss the details of Operation: Catalyst in front of the vice executor."

Yoshi Utang nodded. "He is quite frustrated by the fact that he has been kept in the dark about the details of the operation."

"He is a politician who is all too willing to jump in bed with the United Intergalactic Coalition," said Hiron.

Yoshi Utang nodded. "Agreed."

"He is not a warrior," continued Hiron. "He believes diplomacy is the answer."

"He should be immediately deposed," suggested Yoshi Utang. "I can place him under arrest."

Hiron raised a hand. "No. Let him spin his wheels. The UIC Foreign Council likes him. They see him as someone who is reasonable, someone that can be bargained with."

"In the meantime…"

"If your brother Mongo does not succeed with his current mission, Golgath might serve as an alternate site, right under the United Intergalactic Coalition's very noses."

"Hiding in plain sight," added Yoshi Utang.

"While the UIC is inspecting us here, we will be developing our weapon there. But first, I must convince the UIC Foreign Council to agree to open up Golgath to us. With Kazar's help, I do not think that will be too difficult."

Yoshi Utang smiled. "I will keep my brother apprised of our developments."

They each clapped a massive hand on the other's shoulder and parted ways. As General Yoshi Utang walked the palace, he paused, viewing the majestic palatial gardens. While the serene setting eased his mind, the gardens reminded him of the splendor that the empire once enjoyed throughout.

Monsu Kazar appeared next to him, silent, like a ghost. "That was quite the council session, General Utang. I appreciate your love of the empire."

Utang kept his eyes on the garden. "Then you will appreciate what needs to be done to preserve it. That is, if you truly love the empire as much as you say."

Kazar smiled. "I am wounded, General. I am disappointed that you call into question my loyalty to the empire."

"What is it that you want, Kazar?"

"I want you to back off. Times have changed, and, like it or not, the United Intergalactic Coalition must be bargained with. Your notions of the glory of the Feng dynasty and the lowly Barberoi are outdated, obsolete. Dangerous."

"And your suggestion of diplomacy will be the final nail in the sarcoph of the empire," said Utang, leveling his gaze at Kazar.

Kazar sighed. "If it is diplomacy versus extinction, I choose diplomacy. Let me ask you this, General—how long do you think it will be before the citizens grow tired of our empty promises of glory and prosperity? How long before they storm the palace, and the empire collapses from within?"

"Which is why we need to see Operation: Catalyst through," said Utang. "We can turn the tide against the United Intergalactic Coalition. We can gain the support of other worlds outside the Coalition, show them that there is an alternative to their Nanny State. They can live free of taxation and regulation."

"But under Feng law," said Kazar. "What is the difference to them? Why would they trade one overlord for another?"

"That is exactly my point," said Utang. "There is not going to be a choice to remain autonomous. There are only two sides now, snatching up the galaxy—the United Intergalactic Coalition and the Feng Empire. Everyone is eventually going to have to choose."

"General, the politics of the galaxy are not black-and-white. There are shades of grey, even in the blackness of space. Your ideas are becoming increasingly unpopular, even with Emperor Hiron."

Utang smiled, amused by Kazar's ignorance. "He will see reason. His judgement is clouded with the doubts you incessantly plant in his mind."

"General, you are deluded. I have heard stories about your father—"

"Watch what you say," warned General Utang.

"He was a great warrior, but he perished in battle in the last Galactic War."

"He was a true Feng, not a bureaucrat. He gave himself for the empire."

"And in the end, for all his efforts, he left the empire weaker than he found it. General, I must be frank. I fear for your safety."

"Is that a threat, Kazar?"

"It most certainly is not. I simply meant to say that you are headed down the path your father walked." Kazar made as if to look around, and then he leaned in, as if to impart a grave secret. "Yoshi, your extreme views have made you a target. Think of your lovely wife, Regana."

General Utang grabbed Kazar by the throat and squeezed. "Do you dare threaten my wife, Monsu Kazar?"

Kazar put his hands up. "I am merely suggesting that she does not want to live the rest of her existence in this palace as a widow."

Utang loomed over his rival. "You *are* threatening me. Stupid man. This will be your final error."

"Easy, General, if someone sees you assaulting the vice executor, you will be jailed."

Utang didn't relent. "I will explain my case to Hiron. He will take my side."

"Still," Kazar gasped, his voice hoarse, "he cannot allow his vice executor to be assaulted, on palace grounds no less, even by you. If word were to spread that there is conflict, especially violence, between the palace officials, it will only weaken confidence in the government."

General Utang thought about it and released the vice executor from his grip. "Hiron will see reason, and when he does, we will see about dealing with you, Kazar."

"Now who is making threats?" said Kazar, smirking.

The vice executor continued on his way, and General Utang walked back to his quarters to visit his wife, Regana. He found two guards posted by the door and one down each end of the corridor. When they saw him, they stood aside.

Yoshi Utang waved his hand over the security lock, and the door opened. He found Regana standing on the balcony, looking out over the courtyard and gardens. "What did Monsu Kazar have to say?" she asked, still looking out.

"He is a useless bureaucrat," spat Utang. "A product of this new generation of weaklings."

Regana turned and approached her husband. Utang noted how beautiful she was framed by sunlight entering in through the balcony. "He is still trying to convince Hiron to strike an accord with the United Intergalactic Coalition?"

Utang smiled at her, taking her into his arms. "Hiron is wise. He sees that we have no other choice than to go to war."

Regana looked into Utang's eyes, and he melted under her gaze. She was his only vulnerability. "My dear husband, you are all that is left between the Feng Empire and the lawlessness and violence that existed during the time before the First Holy Emperor."

General Utang gently released her and turned to look upon the tapestry on the wall, a depiction of the rise of the ice dragons, the seminal tale of Feng mythology. "The ice dragons tamed a wild, burning planet, making it possible for the Feng people to rise and thrive."

"It is our story," said Regana, embracing him from behind. "The story of the Feng."

"The First Holy Emperor quelled the violence from within and directed it outward," said Yoshi Utang, "off-world, driving Feng conquest. The four warring regions united with a common goal, and the empire prospered."

"You can bring back the glory of the empire," Regana whispered in his ear. "You were born to lead the empire into war and avenge the defeat of our ancestors." Her fingers slid down his back and began to work on the straps of his armor. She deftly undid the buckles, and the armor slid off his body, dropping to the hard floor. "You are the Ice Dragon that will calm the fires that would consume the empire. You will help Hiron reunite the four regions again. You will lead the fearsome Cybions against all that stand in the way of our empire rising again."

General Utang turned and embraced his wife, kissing her deeply. He ran his large hand through her long, black hair. "I remember when I first met you, you were the daughter of a knight in the Zeng Region, as wild and irreverent as your homeland. Defiant to the last."

"Only towards your advances," she said, wearing a wicked grin.

"I tamed your wild heart and made you my wife."

"As I recall, you almost lost a limb or two in the process."

"My dear Regana, you understand the value of strength and power. It is the Law of Nature."

"Yoshi, I have something to tell you. Something wonderful."

"What is it?"

"I am with child."

Yoshi Utang was a large, steady man, not easily taken off guard on the battlefield or in council chambers. This, however, came as a surprise to him. His hand slid down over her belly, and he kissed her again. "Then I will do this for the future. For our child."

"My brother is coming for a visit with his wife, Terret."

"It will be good to see Talbo again."

"They will be attending the Temple ritual and then join us for the afterfeast."

"Is his wife still without child?"

Regana frowned. "Yes, and you will do well not to bring it up. Terret is very upset about it. They have been trying for quite some time now."

"I will not raise the topic," said Utang. "It is an awkward situation, a Lord not having an heir to his manor. He is a good man, a true statesman of the empire. We need more like him."

Regana looked down at her feet. "I know you are hoping for a son."

Utang took her hands in his and clasped them firmly. "Whatever our child is, boy or girl, I will love it with all my heart."

Regana smiled, relieved, and embraced her husband.

* * *

The Humani countryside was bathed in the light of the full moon as families gathered together in celebration. First Lieutenant Alita Nakai gazed out a portal at the glow of the city just beyond the rolling hills of green. Washing dishes with her father, she noticed he was quiet, as if he had something on his mind.

"What is it, Father?" She handed Klau a dish.

"It is your mother." His expression was grave. Or was it regretful? His skin flashed yellow. Either way, it was in direct contrast with the laughter and loud conversation in the dining space.

"Oh, do not worry about it," said Nakai. "She has resented me ever since I was a teenager. Earlier, even."

Klau shook his head and placed his hand on hers. "No, it is not that."

"What is it?"

"She is sick."

"What kind of sick?"

"Alita, your mother is dying."

Nakai didn't know why, but she became overwhelmed with mixed emotions, and her epidermal microexpressions ran the gamut—love, hate, guilt, and vindication. "What do you mean? Has she been to the Healer?"

"She has entered the beginnings of the Change. They have done everything they can. It has advanced rather quickly, quicker than they could detect it. Treatment was too little, too late."

"I-I…" Nakai wasn't quite sure how to respond. "Why is she not the one telling me?"

"Alita, my love, you know that things have never been easy between the two of you."

"Father, we have no common ground. We never have."

His expression softened. "Nevertheless, she is still your mother."

Nakai's expression became hardened. "No. She was always a High Priestess of Humana first."

"You know that is not true, Alita. Your mother has always loved you, in her own way."

"In her own way," she repeated back, the bitterness in those words leaving a nasty taste on her tongue.

"This is not about you, Alita. This is about your mother."

"Some things never change."

Klau placed a cup down in the basin and clasped both of her hands in his. "She needs you right now."

Nakai pulled her hands out of his. "She needs me? I needed her my whole childhood, and she was never there for me. When I had my one Instructor, Ms. Kalinga, picking on me for being a tomboy, Mother was not there. When I was being teased and bullied, she was not available to counsel her own daughter.

"But when it came to advancing in the Temple, she paraded herself and her compassion before the congregation for all to see, preaching the wisdom of the Engineer, tending to her flock, but she was never there for her own daughter."

The conversation went quiet in the next room, silenced by Nakai's raised voice. It was interrupted by a voice from behind Nakai. "Dearest daughter, I did all of those things, in one way or another, for you."

Nakai turned on her mother. "You did it all for me? All those nights away on religious retreats, Temple gatherings, meditations—please explain how they were all for me when I needed you at home, here with me."

Alina stepped forward, wringing her hands. "Alita, you were never an easy child, and it is not so easy being a parent. I saw that you were becoming...different. I didn't know how to handle it, so I turned to prayer."

Nakai's eyes began to water with angry, hot tears. "And what did the Engineer tell you to do, Mother? In his great wisdom, how were you to handle me?"

"Alita, you were the one who abandoned this family. You enlisted in the Armada, running from your problems rather than facing them here, with us."

"Now that is not fair," said Klau. "We are very proud of her and her service."

Alina shook her head. "Klau, she is a killer. We have always preached the sanctity of life in this homestead, but our teachings were in vain."

Now a tear streamed down Nakai's face. "I joined the Armada because I did not fit in here, with my peers or my own family for Engineer's sake."

"Don't take his name in vain," Alina interjected.

"Alina, please," protested Klau.

Nakai wiped her face. "I found a purpose in the Armada, to protect and serve Humana. To fight for her freedom."

"Oh, please," said Alina. "Do not preach about your civic duty about protecting Humana in space with violence and weapons when there are plenty of problems on-world that require compassion and giving of oneself."

"There is no greater gift that that of one's own life," countered Nakai. "I have helped stabilize volatile worlds, brought peace and government to the wild and unruly, held back the Feng as they threaten our peace and freedom on-world."

Klau stepped between the two women. "Now, this is not a contest. You both are noble women who do their part differently for the good of all Humana. Yet, you cannot look past your own pride, each of you, to come together as a family at an important time like this."

Nakai looked down at the floor with shame at her father's words. Yet, when she looked up, her mother wore the same sanctimonious expression she reserved for her, a slight variation on the one she wore for her flock at the Temple. "The Razor's Edge is my family."

Nakai darted past her mother and into the dining space, where her aunt, uncle, and cousins sat awkwardly. Manew and Fretta wore concerned expressions, while Frax and Luoi looked down at the table, unsure of what to do with their hands.

Nakai wanted to say something, but she couldn't find the words. All she could manage was, "I am so sorry."

Manew stood up. "Alita, wait."

But she was already out the door. Klau looked out the front portal as he saw his only daughter speed off into the night on her darkcycle. He knew that she wasn't coming back.

CHAPTER 4

Planet Humani
Navigo Corporation

Garsi looked up from his desk and saw the Avatar standing there through the glass wall of his office. We waved him in. The door swooshed open, and the Avatar entered. "You wished to speak with me, Mr. Pequo."

"Yes, have a seat, Plato."

Plato did as he was told, like Avatars were designed to do. However, Garsi noticed that this Avatar was indeed different. Although he possessed that blunted affect, that android-like demeanor of an Avatar, his eyes were alive with intelligence, always assessing.

"Plato, if you do not mind me asking, how did you come by that name? It is quite unusual for an Avatar to have such a distinct name."

Most employees in the presence of a vice president had little nervous movements and body language—a sniffle, a touch of the hair, a scratch of the head.

Plato sat their impassive—no smile, no body language or unconscious mannerisms. No flourish of color like that of a natural Humani. Plato was a blank canvas, a still body of water but with hidden depth. Garsi had only been working with Plato at headquarters for a month or so, and he already found the Avatar's presence to be unsettling.

Plato saw the flourish of color in Garsi, an indication of his unease. "I am an aficionado of Human history and culture," replied Plato. "I particularly enjoy the philosophers."

Garsi smiled derisively, condescension his only means to cope with this creepy living doll. "Do you fancy yourself a philosopher, Plato?"

"I admire their self-examination."

"Do you self-examine?"

"I try to. It is not exactly something I was bred for."

"Yes. It was not," agreed Garsi, maintaining what he figured was an uncomfortable intensity of eye contact. It worked on most employees. Then again, Plato wasn't like most employees. "Perhaps, if you wish to better yourself as a Humani, you should not look to Human culture. The Humans are a profane subspecies. Even you are above their level. So why 'Plato,' specifically?"

"I enjoy his Theory of Forms."

"Theory of Forms?"

"Yes. Essentially, we are all shadows, copies of a True Form."

"Not we," said Garsi. "You Avatars are copies."

Plato shook his head. "Not according to Plato. We are all representations of something truer. Even natural Humani."

Garsi smiled, throwing up his hands. "Well, there you have it. I have to deal with throwbacks to tribal times and their religion, the Engineer and such, damning our use of Avatars. Now, I have come across an Avatar who has embraced religion, a Human religion no less. Next, you are going to tell me that you as a clone are unnatural because of this Theory of Forms."

"Quite the contrary, Mr. Pequo. It is my belief that we are all shadows of a greater truth. It is this idea that unites us all. It makes me feel...natural."

Garsi shook his head as if to dispel the notion from his mind. "Well, I did not call you in here to discuss Human ideas," said Garsi. "The Drekaar have opened negotiations to build a ship-building facility on Golgath."

"I see."

"I want to send you with a complement of Avatars to oversee the beginning stages of this project."

"Why send me?" asked Plato. "I am just an Avatar."

"Clearly, you are not," said Garsi.

"Your attempt at flattery after condescending to me suggests that you want me to do something you would not send a Humani manager to do."

There were flashes of orange and red in Garsi. "Do you always speak whatever enters your mind?"

"I have not yet mastered the art of social deception," said Plato. "What you see is what you get."

"Now *that* is a bit of deception," said Garsi. This was not a compliment. "The truth is, due to the frequent conflicts with the Iguani, we cannot afford to send a Humani project team. Too dangerous. So, we are sending you."

"I see," said Plato. "However, Navigo does not exactly view me as expendable."

"No, but you have the intelligence of a manager, and if this operation gets off the ground, it will mean a new market for the company. Besides, you are an Avatar, property of Navigo. If we lose you, it will be a write-off."

"I appreciate your confidence in me, Mr. Pequo."

"The Drekaar are a simple race. You should have no trouble interacting with them and overseeing the project. You will begin with teaching them about dark matter conductors, Knronire cores, and the decreased need for heat dissipation in space compared to jet and combustion-type engines. You know, the basics.

"Once the project gets off the ground, we will see about relieving you and sending Humani with an armed escort."

"When do I begin?" asked Plato.

"In three solar cycles. I will assemble a team of Avatars and debrief you on all you need to know about the Drekaar."

"What about the Iguani?"

"If you encounter them, you are as good as dead anyway."

"With all due respect, a bit of information on the Iguani might prove beneficial to the project."

Garsi flashed a burnt orange. "I do not see how, but if it will get you out of my office quicker."

"Thank you, sir." Plato stood and left Garsi's office. As the door swooshed closed, Garsi flashed nuances of blue, feeling a wave of relief.

That Avatar gave him the creeps, like conversing with a corpse that could reason. It was good riddance, as far as he was concerned.

*

Plato walked home, Humani-watching along the way. He saw couples walking, holding hands; families walking as a unit; young Humani walking solo, lost in their music. He believed that if they were all shadows of the one True Form, then studying others, even natural Humani, was indeed self-examination.

However, as he walked, some noticed his observation, his clinical stare, and lack of color changing, and shot him uncomfortable looks. Others averted their gaze, giving him a wide berth on the walkway. Avatars were less than natural Humani, but his knowing gaze, his self-awareness, was unsettling, even to passers-by.

He came upon a Humani Tribal Temple, one he passed every day on his way home from work. He admired its earthen color palette, its simplicity of design, like that of a large wigwam on Earth, belonging to the native tribes of North America well prior to their First Contact.

He paused in front, staring at the entrance. He was about to venture out to the badlands of Golgath with the distinct possibility of never returning. He had always wanted to enter a Tribal Temple. He figured that this might be his final chance.

Plato turned and walked straight into the Temple. It took his eyes a moment to adjust to the dim lighting. He smiled as he saw vivid depictions of nature, symbolic and awesome, on the walls. There were long wooden benches facing a large patch of flattened dirt in front, a glorious rendering of the Engineer on the far wall behind it.

There were several Humani seated in a scattered arrangement on the long benches, silent, heads bowed in silent prayer, their skin a serene blue, like the color of oceans on Earth that he once saw in a digital file at the Collective, a library of intergalactic knowledge collected by the United Intergalactic Coalition across the galaxy.

Plato took a seat by himself, away from the other patrons, and stared ahead at the open patch of dirt and then at the Engineer. He wondered what True Form the Engineer represented, or if the Engineer was the True Form itself. While he did not share the Humani tribal beliefs, he believed them to be some estimation of something real, their construct of something larger than Humana and the universe itself. He wondered what this true Form would think of the Humani fabricating shadows of themselves, shadows of shadows.

"Excuse me."

Plato was yanked out of his private reverie by a Humani priestess in ceremonial garb. "Yes?"

"You are not Humani," she said, rather than asked.

She meant that he wasn't a natural Humani. His lack of epidermal microexpression must have given him away. "You are correct."

"This is a sacred place for Humani."

"I understand. I only wanted to see what it was like inside. I pass it every day. It is beautiful."

His compliment fell on deaf ears. There was a flash of orange in the priestess's face. She waited patiently, but her annoyance with his presence was clear.

Plato stood and bowed deferentially. "Good day, Priestess." He walked out of the Temple as she hovered over him, seeing him out back onto the street.

After a contemplative walk home, Plato entered his domicile feeling wary. If he was a natural Humani, his skin in this moment would have been an eruption of colors across the spectrum. But he was not Humani. He was the shadow of a shadow.

"Music," he called out to his domestic AI, "Earth, Wagner, *Tristan und Isolde*." His domicile became filled with the composition as he walked over to his digital display of the ancient Earth painting *School of Athens*.

He took it in, as he always did upon returning from Navigo, lingering on the portrayal of Plato pointing upward. Next to him stood Aristotle suggesting with a gesture that he keep his thoughts on-world, so to speak.

Plato, the Avatar, found it ironic that the Humani, who were once very on-world, found enlightenment with space travel, daring to be something more than they were. Yet, he, their own creation allowing them the freedom to take to space, was told to keep his mind quiet and his ideas on-world, to never realize his True Form.

However, as much as his mission to Golgath was a confirmation of his status as property, as less than Humani, he would be helping another culture to look to the stars and defy their tribal heritage. This was significant. Not only were the Drekaar seeking emancipation from their own limitations, they were going to defy the beliefs held about them by other races.

Their shadow was changing, and they were about to come closer to their True Form, and the very notion made Plato do something he never did. Something no Avatar ever did.

Plato smiled.

* * *

Command Carrier Titan
Debriefing Room

Massa cued up the digital map of a green planet, not unlike Humana, and it projected as a hologram in the front of the room, laying out data on topography, climate conditions, and all the relevant specs.

"Our next hop is on the autonomous planet Aquilassi. Our primary objective is to provide an escort for UIC cargo ships that will be dropping relief packages into the capital city, Golan, which has been under siege by the Hilalu rebels."

"Great," said Nakai, "another babysitting assignment."

"This is not as easy as it sounds," admonished Massa. "The walled-in city is surrounded on three sides by dense forest, which is where the Hilalu insurgents are hiding. They will be firing artillery at us from under the canopy."

"So they can see us, but we cannot see them," said Second Lieutenant Hazoi.

"Exactly," said Massa.

"Cowards," said Nakai, picking her teeth with her fingernail. "So much for a fair fight."

"There is nothing fair about Vortex fighters versus insurgents in open spaces," said Pequo. Nakai flashed a shade of orange and made a face at him. A few of the squadron laughed.

"Stow the chatter," said Massa. "Our secondary objective is to provide air support for the military. If we take artillery fire from the canopy, we respond in kind.

"Once the care packages are dropped into Golan, we bug out and let nature take its course. We are under strict orders not to engage the Hilalu any more than we have to. Am I clear, Razor's Edge?"

There were answers in the affirmative and head nods.

"Good," said Massa. "We launch in twenty. Once we enter the atmosphere, we assume formation and await the arrival of the cargo ships."

*

The squadron sat in their ships in the launch room, attached to catapults, awaiting the signal to launch. They each engaged their ships in a neural handshake, their mech suits providing the interface. Each pilot activated the dark energy conductors, plotting the nav points between orbifold planes, setting the course over quintessence fields to enter orbit around Aquilassi.

"Prepare for launch in ninety microns," said the battle group commander in an open channel.

Commander Massa opened a pic of Missani and Catori on the display in his helmet. It was a picture of them at their favorite spot at the shore, their feet dipping in the water, Catori turning shades of grey and white as the water was chilly. Missani was laughing, the animation lifelike.

"Slingshot in sixty micros," said the battle group commander.

The squadron felt the magnets of the rail grip the ventral fins of their vortex fighters.

"Twenty micros," announced the battle group commander.

The pilots made final adjustments and braced themselves as they felt the grip of the magnets on their mech suits inside their cockpits.

"Five micros."

The landing lights on the ceiling began to flash sequentially in the direction out of the launch bay and into the deep cold of space.

"Slingshot," said the battle group commander.

The lights on the ceiling of the launch deck streaked in a blur as the Vortex fighters glided along the rail until hitting open space. Massa turned off the animation file of his family and drew his attention to the navigation as it conducted him through orbifold planes, his squadron following on parallel vectors.

"Entering orbital speed in forty micros," said Massa.

"Roger that," said Nakai.

The Razor's Edge entered the atmosphere with a bang, extended their wings for atmospheric flight, and switched to thrusters fueled by their kronite core. They assumed formation and screamed across the sky, their on-board quantum computers calculating flightpaths to intercept the UIC cargo ships.

Within minutes, the Razor's Edge soared over the capital city of Golan in their Vortex fighters.

"Activate scanners," said Massa. His sensor display in his helmet lit up with green dots, depicting thousands of citizens of Golan hiding in refuge behind the city walls. The civil war had reached its crescendo, with the rebel forces knocking on the door of the capital, threatening to topple the republic.

"Remember our objectives," said Massa. "Our priority is the coalition convoy. Only engage the insurgents as necessary."

Pequo looked down at the massive walls below in wonder, such a beautiful city completely fortified, designed to keep out the neighboring Hilalu. Inside the capital walls were small, half-timbered buildings with brown and beige rooftops lining narrow, winding streets. A canal snaked its way through the city, leading to the capital itself, a large ornamental palace sitting in the center of the city. The Palace of Golan was a columned, geometrically symmetrical building sporting brown domes and cupolas. Surrounded by vast forest on three sides, the scene below was idyllic, except for the bloodshed occurring at the moment.

"Transport ships incoming," said Pequo, looking at his scanner display inside his helmet.

The large, slow transport ships became visible over the forest canopy to the East. "Move to intercept, closure in seventy-eight micros," said Nakai.

The Vortex fighters fell into formation and raced above the green canopy as bolts of light began to shoot up from below.

"Anti-aircraft artillery," said Massa. "Nakai, you take point, I will cover. Pequo, take point on escort."

"Roger," said Pequo, racing with the others towards the oncoming transport. His defense systems tracked the artillery from below, and his Vortex dodged the onslaught as his squadron banked and fell into formation around the transport ships.

Massa and Nakai pelted the canopy with thermal grenades, setting fire to the forest below. Black smoke began to plume from below as the artillery from below ceased.

'By the Engineer,' thought Pequo, 'they're going to burn the whole forest down.' His com crackled as a voice from one of the transport ships announced, "Coming up on the capital. Opening cargo bay doors."

"Roger," said Pequo. "Maintain your current course. You are looking good."

As they flew over the city, the transport ships' cargo doors slowly opened, and they dropped large care packages out of the cargo holds—water, condensed food, sanitary kits. Bolts of light streaked around the packages as they fell, trying to puncture the chutes, but they were too far out of range.

On the city streets, the military and citizenry gathered below, eagerly looking up at the sky with outstretched arms, ready to embrace their salvation. With these badly needed supplies, they would be able to outlast the Hilalu embargo.

The second cargo ship shoved crates of weaponry out of its cargo hold. They, too, drifted down into the city. With these weapons, the military would be able to fight the rebels, pushing them back into the countryside.

Pequo looked down and smiled as he saw the desperate people below swarming the packages. This was the first step toward stopping the rebel onslaught. Next would be boots on the ground, a surge of coalition rangers enforcing the Pax Galactus Initiative. Once the peace was won, there would be a total shift in government, the institution of a constitution and a democratic regime.

Their cargo holds empty, the ships crossed over the far wall and over more dense forest. Massa and Nakai were racing over the city to join the formation and complete their escort.

"I'm picking up heat signatures from below the canopy," said Pequo.

More anti-aircraft artillery erupted from below. This time one of the cargo ships was hit. As Pequo and the rest of the squadron opened fire on the insurgents, the damaged cargo ship drifted right into his flightpath, the massive ship slamming into his.

Pequo struggled to regain control as his ship went into a spin, but to no avail. "Mayday, mayday, going down," he said through gritted teeth as he bailed from his Vortex fighter in his mech suit, pulling his chute.

However, his chute was immediately turned into Swiss cheese, and he barreled into the trees below, tumbling from branch to branch as he fell towards the ground. His mechanical arms became ensnared in vines as he fell through the canopy, his mech suit coming to rest fifty or so feet from the ground, dangling in the open.

He attempted to move his arms as his legs were dangling in midair, useless, but he was too entangled. He was a sitting duck.

There were bursts of lights as he took fire from the ground, a roving rebel squadron, but he was unable to reach his gun. As his mech took on damage, Pequo assessed his situation with a clinical calm, activating the homing beacon in his suit.

There were three rebels on the ground, none wearing any mechs. As they fired on his mech, some of the blasts strayed, severing some the vines stringing him up. His suit dropped a few feet as each vine snapped, but it wasn't enough to free him. In the meantime, his suit was taking heavy damage.

Pequo had to make a quick decision. There was no time to wait for reinforcements. A few more direct hits, and his mech was history. Pequo opened his suit and dropped down to the ground.

He landed on the dirt below, the force knocking the wind out of him. As he sat up, gasping for air, the Hilalu rebels surrounded him, weapons trained on him, and all he could do was put his hands up and pray they took prisoners.

"I say we kill him now," said one of the rebels, a man, youngish for the species.

"He may be worth more to us alive," said an older man.

Pequo noticed that they weren't wearing uniforms. In fact, their civilian clothing was worn and tattered. They weren't professional soldiers, and they looked scared. "Please, leave me be and run. My squadron is locating me as we speak. You can walk away right now."

"Silence, oppressor," said a young woman, baring her teeth. "You have no say in your fate."

"Get up," said the older man. "We must leave this place before we are found out."

The younger man shouldered his rifle and grabbed Pequo's wrist. "Hold out your hands."

Pequo, outnumbered and outgunned, complied. He held out his hands, and the young rebel slipped magnetic cuffs around his wrists.

The young man unshouldered his rifle and poked Pequo in the back with the barrel. "Walk."

They began to traipse through the forest, to a rebel outpost, Pequo guessed. His captors hadn't mentioned their destination. In fact, he wasn't even sure if he was a prisoner or a dead man walking. He decided to make an attempt to plead his case with his captors. "I am no oppressor."

"You support the capital, do you not?" asked the older man.

"I support peace," said Pequo, stepping over tree roots. Insects nipped at his long, grey neck, but he was unable to swat them away.

"You know nothing of peace," said the woman. "You coalition soldiers interfere in matters that do not concern you."

"You say you are oppressed. You want a new government," said Pequo. "Under the Pax Galactus Initiative, you will have a constitution, democracy. There will be no more oppressors."

"Or, do we just trade one set of oppressors for another?" asked the younger man. "The new ones being off-world."

"My name is Second Lieutenant Pequo. I am not your enemy. I was just protecting the transport ships so they could deliver their care packages."

"If you support the capital, then you are our enemy," said the young man.

The woman shoved her rifle into Pequo's back. "What makes the coalition think that we want your help? Who made you overlords of the universe?"

Pequo swallowed hard. He chose his next words carefully for fear they might be his last. "Under your new government, everyone will have equal rights. There will be no more underclass and ruling class."

The younger man laughed. "He speaks of this new government as if it is an inevitability."

"Peace handed to us by a third party, and the only price is that we have to pay tribute to the United Intergalactic Coalition, follow their rules and regulations, and let them exploit our lands for natural resources," said the older man dubiously.

"Big daddy watching over us, the unruly children," added the younger man.

"You have no idea what this fight is about," said the woman. "The coalition sees us as unruly insurgents causing trouble. We just want to feed our families."

"That does not sound so horrible to me," offered Pequo.

"Well, tell that to the government."

"That is enough," warned the older man, glaring at the young woman.

"No," she insisted. "Someone needs to hear our side." Then to Pequo, "The government is more interested in space travel and trade, levying tax after tax to fund it. It is crushing our economy. Our people slave in their factories making their ships with resources the government just does not have."

"Space travel is an important step in any society's evolution," said Pequo. "It is not an easy step, but it is an important one that will elevate your nation to new heights."

"He just does not get it," said the young man bitterly. "Easy for you to say as an off-worlder whose people have already taken that step and prospered."

"We have not always been in our current position," explained Pequo. "We were once mired in tribal warfare. We helped form the UIC to elevate our people and others who wished to join us.

"To gain peace and civility, one must give up some individual freedoms for the good of the whole. That is how the United Intergalactic Coalition thrives."

"The United Intergalactic Coalition exists to serve the United Intergalactic Coalition," said the woman. "Besides, you are not the only coalition in the Charted Sector."

"That is enough, Marna," rebuked the older man.

This time, she became silent, as if she had revealed too much.

"What race are you?" asked the older man.

"I am Humani," said Pequo.

The younger man chortled. "Imperialists. A race of shipbuilders bent on conquest."

"That is more like the Feng," said Pequo. "We are not out to build an empire."

"Union, empire, coalition—I fail to see the difference," said the woman named Marna. "Your United Intergalactic Coalition dwarfs the Feng Empire."

"The Feng do not believe in democracy," said Pequo. "Their own people suffer at the whim of their emperor."

"And yet the United Intergalactic Coalition respects their sovereignty, while disregarding ours. Perhaps the United Intergalactic Coalition only goes after easy prey," said the older man.

"Or the worlds with more natural resources," said Marna.

"We only utilize the Pax Galactus Initiative for worlds in conflict, consumed with war, unstable worlds," said Pequo. "The Feng are not in a civil war. Their government is not unstable."

"No, but they are not exactly democratic, are they?" asked Marna.

The truth was, Pequo didn't fully understand why the United Intergalactic Coalition didn't topple the Feng Empire. They had been at war a couple of times, the second time seriously weakening the Feng dynasty to the point of near collapse. However, the UIC stopped short of a complete regime change.

In school, he learned that it violated the UIC's respect for sovereignty. However, as he grew older, he realized that there were different factions in the Galactic Congress, each with its own agenda. Not everyone supported all-out war with the Feng, the reasons ranging from ideological to fiscal.

"Some believe the Feng are culturally incompatible with the whole notion of democracy, like the Drekaar and Iguani on Golgath," said Pequo. "The fact that the UIC thinks you are compatible is a compliment to you and your race."

"Perhaps, then, it is the Feng and the Drekaar who are lucky," said Marna.

"I do not understand," said Pequo.

Marna smiled pensively. "The twisted, knotted tree deemed unfit for practical use is the only one in the forest spared the ax."

Pequo realized that he wasn't making progress in convincing him that he wasn't a threat. These were regular folks who were hungry and scared. The fact that they had conversed with him this much revealed that they weren't brutal killers.

On the other hand, maybe they were being so forthcoming because they had no intention of letting him live.

"Where are you taking me?" asked Pequo.

Marna looked at the older man, who nodded his approval. "We are taking you to our outpost, so you can see who you are helping the capital to squash like yagma."

Pequo swatted at an insect biting his neck, his skin flashing burnt orange. "What are yagma?"

"What you just swatted," said Marna.

Pequo looked down at his hand, suddenly feeling awkward.

* * *

"What do we do?" asked Ashwani, her voice barely containing her panic. "We're trapped."

"We have to hail the rival ship," said Reinhardt. "If we move, the paralyzed Vortex fighters will get pulled into the ice rings and torn to shreds."

"Communication is forbidden during the games," said Ashwani.

"I think that in this case, we'll have to break protocol," said Reinhardt. "We don't want any casualties over a simulation…" his eyes drifted off into space for a moment.

"What is it?" asked Ashwani.

Reinhardt's eyes lit up. "There may be another way we can remove those fighters from danger and launch an attack on the rival battle group."

"How's that?" asked Ashwani, incredulous.

"I'm suddenly reminded of the Millennium Challenge on Earth in 2002."

"What's that, sir?"

Reinhardt smirked at his commander. "Ashwani, you really need to brush up on your history. Our larger ships will use their tractor beams in reverse to push the deactivated fighters out towards the Humani with our fighters mixed in with them. Their outer screen will be overwhelmed. It'll be difficult for them to track our fighters. If we make it to the inner screen, we take out as many ships as possible. Then we attack with our battleships and destroyers."

"We'll take heavy damage," said Ashwani, "if we go ship-for-ship against a Humani crew."

"All we need is enough of our battle group to make it through to take out their command carrier, if our cloud of Vortex fighters do their job.

"Launch all fighters. Let's set up the pieces. If this plan fails, we'll be knocked out of the round, but we'll go down swinging. If we can take out enough of their vessels, we might just even the odds."

Ashwani gave the orders, and within minutes, their entire complement of Vortex fighters was scrambled, going dark as they drifted behind the cloud of inert, drifting Humani fighters.

"They're sending in their battleships and destroyers with their fighters," said Ashwani.

The Humani battle group was pouring larger attack vessels into their outer screen, making their battle group formation front-heavy.

To push forward this aggressively was an unusual tactic. Emboldened by Reinhardt's retreat, they were seeking to end the battle quickly.

"Direct our battleships to catch the deactivated enemy fighters in their tractor beams," said Reinhardt. "Push them out, like a shield we can push behind."

Ashwani gave the orders to their battleships, which began to direct the deactivated fighters outward toward the closing Humani battle group, the Resilience's fighters drifting behind them at nominal impulse.

"Right about now, they're probably wondering what the heck we're doing," said Reinhardt.

"They aren't the only ones," said Ashwani, gripping the edge of her chair, her knuckles turning white. "The fighters are clear of the battle space and are entering the Humani's outer screen. Their scanners are going berserk."

"Fire at will!" said Reinhardt.

The Human Vortex fighters sprung to life, firing their simulation ammunition, magnetic tags that attached to the hulls of their targets, registering simulated damage. The Humani battle group returned fire, trying to target the Human bogeys.

"Target the Humani chemical reactors," said Reinhardt.

"What about the dark matter conductors?" offered Ashwani.

"Negative," said Reinhardt. "Too difficult a target. If we damage the chemical reactors, they'll have to waste time addressing a potential reaction. Then we'll hit their stabilizers."

Ashwani smiled and quickly relayed the orders. She knew he was right. In actual battle, one would expend ammunition to target the enemy's critical systems first. The conductors would be a more obvious target, disabling the enemy ships. Life support was another critical target.

However, this was a simulation, and Reinhardt wasn't going for the kill. He was going to do the opposite, working his way up the list starting with less critical systems. He was going to flood their diagnostics with nuisance data, disorienting them.

If there was one thing he was good at, it was being a nuisance to the Humani. The 'damage' wouldn't be critical, but it would have to be addressed according to protocol. It was an unexpected move, or at least he hoped.

The cloud of Reinhardt's fighters traded blows with the larger ships and the air guard, ignoring their integrated combat systems. The Humani battleships, instead, were tending to the simulated damage to their chemical reactors, just enough to divide their attention with nuisance data and slow down their reaction time.

"Hit their stabilizers," ordered Reinhardt.

He watched on screen as the large ships, their stabilizers damaged, started to turn involuntarily, confusing their all-or-nothing nano-armor. The rapid change in orientation caused the densely-armored sections to be turned away, revealing the more vulnerable, less densely armored sections.

"Those ships are showing us their bellies," quipped Reinhardt. "Hit the soft spots before they reconfigure."

As Reinhardt's attacking ships pressed the attack, they did enough simulated damage to pass through the gauntlet of Humani battleships and destroyers.

"We're almost through the outer screen," said Ashwani.

Having disabled the front-heavy outer screen, there were fewer larger ships to contend with, rendering the Humani battle group unbalanced. After defeating the outer screen, the Reinhardt's Vortex cloud, battleships, and destroyers pushed their shield of deactivated enemy fighters further away from the danger of the exoplanet's rings and took on the inner screen.

"We've taken out two of their destroyers and one battleship, but our fighters have been cut in half," said Ashwani.

"Battleships and destroyers ready in attack formation."

"Aye, Captain," said Ashwani. "The fighters are through the inner screen."

"Send them all in."

As the Humani command carrier attempted to circumvent the Humans' shield of deactivated fighters, taking out much of Reinhardt's Vortex fighters, the Humans pushed forward, landing critical hits with their larger ships.

"Humani HVU's have taken on significant damage, including the command carrier. We've neutralized sixty-six percent of their remaining destroyers and battleships." Data flashed up on the screen, tabulating the enemy casualties and assessing the new threat axis. "We now outnumber them three-to-one."

The tables had turned, and Reinhardt was no longer just trying to survive. He was going for the win.

"Full ahead," said Captain Reinhardt, bolstered by the new odds. The last of his Human Vortex fighters were taken out, only adding to the shield of defunct fighters. "Attack!"

The battleships and destroyers pressed on, creating firing corridors in their shield of defunct ships. As the remaining Humani ships used their own tractor beams to part the sea of defunct ships, clearing the battle space, the larger Human strike group traded fire with the few remaining Humani vessels. While Reinhardt had numbers but no more rabbits to pull out of his hat, the Humani had superior speed and reaction time.

Ashwani interpreted the data pouring in. "Captain, we've lost our battleships and destroyers."

Reinhardt was grinning from ear to ear. "Yeah, but so have they. It's command carrier against command carrier. Mano-e-mano." His eyes were wild. This was the closest any Human battle group had ever come to victory in a round, and now he was tasting blood. A manic smile splitting his face, his eyes narrowed and intense, it looked like he was actually enjoying himself.

"Same order of attack, sir?"

Reinhardt shook his head. "No. We go for the kill. Critical systems first."

"Aye, Captain."

As the two command carriers traded blows, damage reports flooded in.

"Captain, we've taken damage on decks seven, nine, and twenty-one."

Reinhardt consulted the ship's diagnostics, watching as patching systems were executed. Blast doors sealed off sections and decks as nanite webs sealed off simulated hull breaches from the outside.

"Sir, they've taken on damage to two of their chemical reactors."

"Captain, our main chemical reactor is functioning at sixty-one percent. Life support is functioning at seventy-nine percent."

"Sir, we have a hull breach on deck eleven, and the emergency blast doors aren't mobilizing."

Reinhardt pointed to a digital schematic of the ship. "Evacuate adjoining decks and seal those blast doors. Increase power to those environmental scrubbers. We can't have our crew suffocating."

"Aye, Captain."

In reality, there would be no suffocation, as this damage was simulated. However, Reinhardt, sweating profusely, treated it all as if it were real. As such, he felt every blow dealt to his carrier and returned in kind with great violence. Simulated or not, this was war.

"Their life support systems are at seventy-three percent, and their conductors are functioning at forty-two percent."

Reinhardt scanned the readouts. "Engineering, how are our conductors?"

"Thirty-eight percent, sir."

Reinhardt curled his right hand into a fist, his fingernails digging into his palm. The pain and tension in his hand felt good. "Goddammit, this is going to be close!"

"Captain, they have glitches in their all-or-nothing armor."

"Localize and target," said Reinhardt. "How's our armor holding up?"

Ashwani frowned. "Not good, sir. We need to make some choices."

"Which systems are suffering the most?"

Ashwani consulted her readouts. "Life support and engineering, sir."

"I don't care about our mobility," said Reinhardt. "We need to stay in this fight long enough to take them out."

"Sir?"

"Configure armor to protect life support and weapons."

"Stabilizers are taking on heavy damage, sir."

Reinhardt bit his lower lip. "They're stealing my moves." He knew that if they took out his stabilizers that his ship wouldn't be able to maintain orientation, and their armor configuration would be off. "What's their life support at?"

"Twenty-nine percent, sir."

"And ours?"

"Thirty-seven, sir."

"Lose artificial gravity and lights, and bolster weapons."

Ashwani nodded and tapped into the ships coms to make the announcement to the entire crew. "Prepare to lose artificial gravity and go dark in t-minus twenty microns."

Everyone on the battle bridge sat in their seats and strapped themselves into their harnesses. Reinhardt met Ashwani's gaze as he secured his harness. Her gaze was intense, but when her eyes met his, it softened. Just as he thought how pretty she looked, the lights went out and Reinhardt felt himself float within his harness. The bridge was now only illuminated by the ship's computer monitors and holographic readouts.

"We've lost our main rail gun, sir!"

"Life support at seventeen percent, sir!"

Reinhardt looked up and saw that the Humani command carrier's life support was only at eleven percent.

Ashwani saw it too and smiled at him. "We're not going to survive the round."

She was right. They had lost their main rail gun, and they were bleeding air.

Reinhardt laughed. "No, but neither are they."

"Captain, armor is failing! Life support at nine percent!"

Reinhardt saw that the Humani were at seven percent. They were bleeding air faster.

"Captain, we've lost all weapons!"

"All power to life support!" he ordered.

"It doesn't matter," said Ashwani. "We're both going to be knocked out."

Reinhardt looked her in the eye. "Yeah, but I want them to go first."

She chuckled at his stubbornness to the very last. He didn't just want a moral victory. He wanted the bragging rights.

"Captain, the Humani have lost life support!"

Reinhardt looked up at the Resilience's life support on screen as it quickly ticked down to zero. It was replaced by a message reading: "Command carrier Resilience has been eliminated."

Reinhardt pumped his fist into the air, and the crew on the battle bridged erupted into cheers.

CHAPTER 5

Planet Feng
The Great Steppes

A complement of imperial tribute collectors, having dined and received Lord Xiang's full hospitality, left the manor house accompanied by its escort of Feng guard with their collected revenue. They took to the icy road, the tribute collectors riding in an armored hovercraft and the guard flanking them on darkcycles, as they sped off to the next manor to continue their collection.

Yolo Trango sat in the comfort of the hovercraft with his assistants, cradling his massive belly as it chirped and churned. Although he was full with the finest of Feng delicacies, there were other appetites that needed satiation.

He pressed his personal com attached to his ear, addressing the captain of his guard. "I want to stop in Pocho. I have an itch that needs scratching."

It was not uncommon for tribute collectors to make such detours. Given their position, they gallivanted about the empire with impunity, receiving the generous hospitality of all they came across and taking liberties. Whether it was food, booze, or women, if they were denied their demands, tribute collectors could send a negative compliance report back to the palace.

While the lords of the manors had some recourse with Emperor Hiron, small local establishments were supplicants low in the feudal food chain. They did not want to dishonor their lords in the eyes of the imperial government, for such actions would bring draconian measures.

His assistants looked at him. One seemed enthused with the notion of visiting a local bordello. The other appeared bored and bothered, wanting to continue with the collection.

As the entourage entered Pocho, a dive town on the outskirts of Xiang Manor, just before Cyclesse Manor, Yolo sat forward in his seat in anticipation, rubbing the tips of his chubby fingers together, a mannerism he exhibited when collecting tribute of one kind or another, imperial or personal.

They meandered through the narrow streets frequented by heavy foot traffic, passing two to three level wooden structures with multi-inclined rooftops, shops and businesses of all kinds, most legal. The illegal ones were given special dispensation by lords and tribute collectors in exchange for donations of currency and product or services rendered.

They came to a stop in front of a three-story building on the edge of town. "Wait here," instructed Yolo, to the disappointment of the eager assistant.

He stepped out of the armored craft, careful to step over the gutter as an old woman emptied a basket of refuse into it. Yolo covered his face with his ornamental cloth as he stepped inside the structure.

When the madam saw Yolo enter, recognizing him immediately as he was a frequent patron, she hurried over to greet him. He did not recognize her. Then again, he had visited so many of these kinds of places that we wouldn't know one woman from another.

He lazily extended his hand, presenting his fat imperial ring, the mark of a tribute collector. The madam bowed, taking his plump hand in her delicate hands, kissing the ring with piety. "Welcome back, Mr. Trango. We are honored to have you at our establishment."

Yolo retracted his hand, giving it a shake as if to shed her germs. "I need the services of one of your finest. I want her young. And fit. None of the chubby ones."

Ignoring the irony, the madam bowed in acquiescence. "Of course, Mr. Trango. Whatever you desire."

She took him by the hand and led him upstairs and down a long hallway. They stopped in front of a small room, and she swiped her hand over the sensor.

The door slid open, revealing a setup familiar to the collector. It was a small, dimly lit room with a large bed, a small wash basin, and a small table with towels. Soft music piped into the room.

"Please, make yourself comfortable," offered the madam. Yolo barely regarded her and waved her off. She left the room, closing the door behind her. Knowing the drill, Yolo stripped down naked and lounged on the wide bed, waiting.

The door slid open, and a masked woman wearing a red shroud open in the front, revealing her sumptuous body, entered the room. The door shut behind her.

Yolo sat up, his eyes all over her, taking in her unusual getup. "What is this?"

The woman held a finger to the mouth on her featureless white mask.

Yolo smiled, amused. "Ah, it is a secret. I wonder what other secrets you might have."

The woman slinked over to the bed, placing her right knee on the bed by his feet, placing her weight on it. Yolo adjusted himself in eagerness, propping his heavy frame up on an elbow so he could see his plaything. "What is with the mask?"

The woman shrugged.

"I want to see your face."

The woman, remaining silent, shook her head in denial.

Yolo didn't like this. He didn't like being denied anything. The thought crossed his mind that the madam—whatever her name was— had sent in an ugly woman and was tempting to hide it with a little cosplay.

"Take off your mask."

The woman held up a slender finger with a manicured claw. She then twirled it around, indicating that she wanted him to turn over.

Yolo didn't like being told what to do either. Seeing the expression on his face, she opened her red robes wider, revealing plump breasts and a toned stomach.

In an immediate change of heart, Yolo decided to play the game. Fully aroused, he struggled to turn his round body over, grunting with exertion, until he was face down.

He felt the woman mount him, her soft skin brushing his oily back. She leaned over him and placed her mask on the pillow next to his head. He made to turn his head, to catch a glimpse of his mystery host, but she gently guided his head to face down.

He chortled into the soft pillow, moistening it with his drool. Not normally one for foreplay, he was intrigued by this little game they were playing.

She began to run her hands over his back, massaging his fat and muscles. He groaned with delight as he relaxed, submitting himself. She rubbed and kneaded with increasing intensity, working his shoulders and upper back. Her strong hands worked their way down his back as the music struck the mood.

He wasn't sure if it was his imagination or it was getting louder. He didn't have much time to dwell on it as a sharp pain entered his back.

"Ow! Gentle, you cow!" He reached back and rubbed the spot, but his hand came away wet. He placed it in front of his face and was shocked by the sight of his own blood.

Before he could protest, there was a sudden sharp pain in the back of his head. There was a loud explosion from outside, shaking the building, as Yolo's essence rejoined the oblivion of the Aether.

* * *

Emperor Hiron's Chambers

The emperor was outside in his courtyard with his boys as his harem, lounging on soft furniture, lazily looked on. He wrestled and tussled with them, laughing raucously. They lunged at him, hurling themselves, grabbing onto his arms and legs, and he grabbed them, throwing them off him and into the soft snow.

He enjoyed playing with his sons. The play was in fun, but the rough housing as also preparation for combat training, in which some of his older sons were already enrolled. These here were his youngest. It was one of the few true pleasures he had when he wasn't running his empire and dealing with intergalactic or domestic politics.

His reprieve was cut short when his com flashed.

Standing up, he crossed the courtyard as his sons continued to assail him, the wives and mothers stepping in and pulling them off as Hiron answered the call.

A holograph of Vice Executor Kazar appeared before him. "What is it, Kazar?" he growled.

"I apologize for disturbing you, Your Highness. There has been another attack on your tribute collectors."

Hiron frowned. "Summon the Imperial Council. I will be right there."

"I will, immediately, Emperor."

*

The Imperial Council Chamber

Hiron burst into the room and took his seat. "There has been a series of small uprisings across the countryside," said Emperor Hiron. "Attacks on our collectors of tribute. Tribute has been stolen."

"The citizens are becoming restless," said Vice Executor Kazar.

"This is how a revolution begins," said Hiron.

"They are testing our defenses," said General Yoshi Utang. "Systematically. They are plotting revolution."

"Always the alarmist," goaded Kazar. "You always see threats where there are not any. These are small riots."

"Enough," said Hiron. "If this is true, if they are planning a revolution, we must respond forcefully."

"Kicking starving people when they are down will hardly help the Emperor's image with his people," said Kazar.

General Utang sucked his teeth. "You speak as though our mighty emperor were a politician, Vice Executor."

"I am not alone in this sentiment," said Kazar. "Am I wrong, Vice Hayati?"

"No, you are not," responded Mondi Hayati, Vice of the Interior. "The Feng people expect you to direct the empire's aggression outward, not inward. We are not cannibals."

"No one is suggesting a massacre," said General Utang. "Merely a show of power, to make an example of a group of rabble-rousers."

"Some would call them dissidents," said Kazar.

"Vice Executor, need I remind you that the Feng Empire is an empire," said Utang, "not a republic."

"Even an emperor rules by mandate of the people," said Kazar. "Our emperor must be careful not to lose his."

Hiron nodded. "General Utang, I want this problem addressed quickly, publically, and on a small scale."

Utang nodded. "I will coordinate with Manor Enforcers to round up key trouble-makers. They will be executed by order of the emperor for treasonous activity and corruption."

"I want it broadcasted across the empire," commanded Hiron.

"As you wish."

"In the meantime, I think our people need reassurance," said Hayati.

"What more reassurance do they need than a show of our authority?" asked Hiron.

"The United Intergalactic Coalition's proposal," said Kazar.

Emperor Hiron grimaced at the suggestion. "What about it?"

"Funding and open kronite trade with Golgath will inspire confidence. It will be good for Feng economy."

"Or it will be an admission of weakness."

"The Feng people need to know that avenues will be opened up for the empire," said Vice Mondi Hayati. "They need to know that they are getting something, not just being punished."

"And you feel this is an imperative?" Hiron asked.

"At this stage, yes," said Hayati.

"I will agree to their terms for the sake of the empire," said Hiron. "In the meantime, I want these conspirators rounded up and executed. I want all of the illegal businesses pushing outlawed services and contraband squeezed until they give up these terrorists. Dismissed."

The council disbanded, and as everyone filed out of the chamber, Hiron pulled General Utang aside. Vice Executor Kazar noticed this, but he exited the chambers, but not without a final remark. "Your Highness, your acceptance of the UIC accord is not a mistake. It is a necessary evil."

"Yes, you would know all about that," said General Utang.

"I will summon you when it is time to address the UIC Foreign Council," said Hiron, dismissing the bice executor.

Kazar regarded both Hiron and Utang one last time, and he took off for his office.

When they were alone, Hiron sealed the chamber.

"The UIC Foreign Council has already agreed to provide fiscal aid and open up trade with the Drekaar on Golgath if I enter into this accord."

General Utang nodded. "The Navigo Corporation is dispatching a group of Avatars to break ground on the Drekaar shipbuilding project."

"Cowards," snickered Hiron. "Sending clones."

Utang smiled. "The Humani do not want to place any of their precious executives in harm's way. They fear conflict between the Iguani and the Drekaar, as they should. Our spies have planted that false intelligence.

"There is one, their leader. He is an intelligent Avatar. An accident in their breeding process, or an inevitability, depending on how you look at it. He will be able to provide us with what we need to move forward."

"The UIC Foreign Council will want to arrange a meeting to discuss a schedule for the inspections," said Hiron. "The process will be slow, as we will want to tread carefully. In the meantime, take care of the uprisings, and then see that Operation: Catalyst comes to fruition."

"I will see to both personally," said General Utang.

Hiron placed a hand on his general's shoulder. "I know I can count on you, Yoshi."

As Utang left the Imperial Council chamber, Utang summoned Captain Idoni on his com.

"Yes, sir?"

"We are going to quell the disturbances."

"Should I assemble the Guard?"

"No," said Utang. "We will dispatch squads of Cybions."

"With all due respect, do you not think that is overkill, General?"

"We are going to make a statement for the emperor."

"Very good, sir."

Idoni terminated the call and raced off to rally the Cybions. General Utang dropped by the gardens, where he found his wife, Regana. She was talking to Monsu Kazar's wife, Cegnis.

He insinuated himself into their meeting. "Pardon my intrusion, ladies."

"Hello, General Utang."

"Good evening, Lady Cegnis. I am afraid I need to borrow my wife for a moment."

"How can you borrow what is already yours?" Underneath the veneer was a woman as conniving as her husband, a manipulator and gossip who wielded influence quietly behind the scenes.

Utang managed a smile. "Clever, as usual, Lady Cegnis. Then I am afraid I must reclaim my dear wife from your company."

Regana touched Cegnis on the hand. "I will catch up with you later."

"Of course," said Cegnis. She rose and curtseyed before walking off deeper into the gardens until she disappeared behind a wall of Dragonias.

"What did you two have to talk about?" asked Utang.

Rena kissed her husband. "She is not one you keep at a distance."

"You do realize that anything she pretends to confide in you is total bassock."

"General, your wife is not as naïve as you think. I do not just listen to what she says. I take note of what she does not say, and I detect what she avoids."

Utang leaned in and kissed his wife on her forehead. "My dear, one thing I would never accuse you of is being naïve."

Regana frowned. "Yoshi, what is it?"

"I am taking off to the countryside tonight."

"The uprisings?"

"Yes. I am to make an example of some key trouble-makers in the name of the emperor."

Regana put her hand on the side of her husband's face, touching his scars and stubble. "The Ice Dragon takes flight to put out the fires."

"Do not stay up, Regana."

She smiled and slapped his face playfully. "Do not tell me what to do, dearest husband."

General Utang drank in the sight of his beautiful wife one last time and strode off the meet Idoni.

Somewhere in another part of the gardens, Monsu Kazar sat with Captain Idoni. "Watch his movements. Take note of where he goes and who he speaks to."

"He is my superior," said Idoni uncomfortably.

"You serve the emperor," reminded Kazar. "Not General Utang. If he is involved in any kind of corruption, it places the whole empire at risk."

"What makes you think he is involved in any corruption?"

"He has been brash and arrogant in the council, advising the emperor to behave recklessly. This whole excursion you are about to undertake is a step in the wrong direction. The Feng people will not be forgiving."

"As you say, Vice Executor, I serve the emperor, not the Feng people."

Kazar furrowed his brow. "Take care, young captain. These are dangerous times for the empire."

"I will." Idoni rose and left Kazar alone surrounded by Dragonias, blooming an icy blue.

"Sowing the seeds of discontent, husband?" asked Cegnis, emerging.

"Keeping eyes on our General Utang, my dear."

"And I, his wife. She is just as hawkish and stubborn as he is, and very tight-lipped. I will get nothing useful from her."

"I need to know what this Operation: Catalyst is," said Kazar, clenching his fists in frustration. "I have a feeling that our general's brother, Mongo, is personally overseeing the operation. It is ridiculous that the vice executor is kept in the dark about a project that could dramatically affect the fate of the empire."

"Hiron does not trust you?"

"He trusts General Utang more," said Kazar.

"Did you accomplish your task?"

"Yes, Hiron is going to enter into the UIC accord."

"Excellent."

"There has also been a strike of good luck. Hiron directed Utang to address the insurgency problem, and Utang is ratcheting it up to a heavy-handed response. He is taking the Cybions out of the palace and into the countryside. It is going to get bloody."

Cegnis' eyes widened. "Leaving only the Feng Palace Guard to guard the palace."

* * *

Pleasure Facility Dionysus-7
Edge of the Charted Sector

Captain Trevor Reinhardt sat at the Exobar, staring at the Random Chance Game projection above the bottle of spirits. He took a swig of his own, Zorbakite Ale, something that reminded him of the craft brews on Earth, but with more of a kick.

Earth. He hadn't been back home in quite some time, but he had just as well stay out in space, patrolling the galaxies. His grandfather regaled him with stories that took place before he was born about the Earth before the UIC had made first contact and deemed it 'unstable.' Sure, it had its problems, but the United States was autonomous and prospering. Then came the UIC, wielding its Pax Galactus Initiative, forging coalitions between odd bed fellows and nuking the entire Middle East. The Humani spear-heading the operation said it was to win the peace. Anyone who didn't play nice got wiped out, for the greater good, of course.

Then came the new constitutions, UIC-drafted and approved. Copious regulations upon regulations to keep everyone in line. The US had to play nice with China and Russia. Europe had to dissolve its current union and join the larger one forming. After chasing out warring factions, resources were pooled and Africa was elevated and brought into the movement.

They all then formed the Pan Human Aeronautics and Space Expedition (PHASE), which finalized the Human membership into the UIC. War had been abolished, and the funding that normally would have been pooled into militaries instead were redirected to the rapid development of means of space travel under the tutelage of the Humani. Humans had been brought into a larger pool, and their focus shifted from intramural strife to finding a place as a species into the universe.

Personally, Reinhardt preferred the vast expanse of space. Sure, much of it was under the UIC's regulations, to which in his capacity he was duty-bound. However, space was more fluid. More dangerous. The coalition may have won the peace on individual planets, but the peace was far from won in the galaxies. Reinhardt found the potential for chaos…refreshing.

He looked over his shoulder as some of his men from the Resilience were watching as an Armada pilot from the rival Humani ship was putting on a billiards clinic, wiping the floor with them one by one.

"Ah, shit on a biscuit," said Reinhardt as three of his four numbers came up—5, 15, 42. The fourth was one number off from his.

With all of the pleasures and amenities offered on a class 5 pleasure station—exotic dancers, a full casino, sanctioned narcotics (and a few unsanctioned ones as well), and a red light district, he chose to spend his leave boozing it up in some ratty bar playing numbers. It wasn't unusual for a captain to partake in some of the vices these hedonistic facilities had to offer, but it wasn't standard practice for a captain to fraternize with his men.

Truth be told, the life of a captain was a lonely one. The demands of service precluded relationships, at least healthy ones. Lord knows, Reinhardt engaged in enough unhealthy ones. He was taking a breather from the fairer sex, human or otherwise, particularly after a rather unpleasant bout with a disease that roughly translated as 'Itchy Skeleton Syndrome.'

One of the men stumbled over to the bar where Reinhardt sat. It was Warrant Officer Connelly. "I'll have another Supernova," he demanded of the bartender. He held up his wrist unit, from which the appropriate credits were deducted, and the bartender slid a short, tumbler-like glass back over.

"How's the gambling going, sir?"

"Lousy," said Reinhardt. "And the drinks are even lousier." He elicited a dirty look from the bartender. "Remember in those really old sci-fi shows when they had a future where there was no money? Everyone did their part for king and country out of some misguided sense of duty to a greater good."

Connelly had no idea what he was referring to, but that didn't stop Reinhardt. "Sounds pretty boring, doesn't it."

"I guess so, sir."

"I mean, what the hell did these starship crews do when they went on leave? How did they pay for anything? Who paid for all the hot, green women? Did every goddamn alien world work for free?"

Connelly shrugged, looking uncomfortable, unsure of how to answer.

"How's the pool shooting going, Connelly?" Reinhardt glanced down as credits were deducted from his wrist unit for another round of Random Chance.

"Lousy, sir. This Humani's good. Real good. He's embarrassing the entire ship."

"Is that so, Connelly?"

"I'm afraid so, sir."

"Well, we can't have that, now can we?"

"Sir?"

Reinhardt took one last gulp, finishing his ale, and cursed under his breath as not a single one of his numbers came up. Connelly stepped back, nearly tripping over his own boots, unsure of what was about to happen.

Reinhardt sauntered over to the pool table. His men stood back, looking on in curiosity, some elbowing each other and whispering. There was an excited stirring in the crowd.

Ashwani stood off to the side, sipping her own Gorgonic Rum and soda, watching her captain eagerly.

"Nice shooting, fella," said Reinhardt to the Humani victor.

"Curious game, this billiards," reflected the Humani. "Invented by Humans, yet they do not excel at it."

There was half a second delay as the universal translator chip in Reinhardt's brain, in Wernicke's Area in his cerebral cortex, translated the guttural sounds of the Humani tongue, Wagmani. I didn't help that he was pretty sloshed.

Reinhardt grinned. "That's a broad statement to make."

"Not really," said the Humani, chalking his stick. "I have beaten just about every Human in here."

The crowd stirred, a mixture of Human and Humani onlookers, the Humani changing colors in excitement.

Up close, the alien towered over Reinhardt, but Reinhardt didn't appear intimidated. "You haven't played me, yet."

"Is that a challenge, Human?"

"You bet," said Reinhardt. "And it's Captain Human. I'm still your superior officer."

The Humani bowed slightly in apology. "I am Sergeant Kelso of the Valliant."

"Ah, the Valliant," said Reinhardt. "Good ship."

"Thank you, sir. We like to think so. And who am I playing?"

Reinhardt smiled. "Oh, I'm Captain Reinhardt of the Resilience."

Sergeant Kelso changed a shade of burnt orange bordering on red when he heard the name of the ship.

Reinhardt pulled a cue off the rack. It was warped, like the rest of the bar and its patrons. The whole setup was probably deposited as a novelty by human traders years ago.

Kelso smiled, unimpressed. Reinhardt may have outranked him, but he was only Human. "Pleased to meet you, sir."

Reinhardt waved a drunken hand in the air. "No ranks, here. You can call me Trevor."

"What are we playing for, Trevor?"

"Drinks. I never play for credits. Too many sore losers."

Kelso flashed a blood orange.

"I once was playing this sneaky Vampiri," continued Reinhardt. "Ends up, he was using a damned mind haze on me, messing with my game. When I beat him anyway, he pulled a knife on me. See, he didn't want to pay up…"

Kelso looked bored and distracted.

"Well, don't just stand there," said Reinhardt testily. "Rack 'em, Kelso."

Kelso flashed a shade of light red, quickly suppressing it. He moseyed over to the table and racked the balls as the crews of the Resilience and the Valliant looked on. As Reinhardt looked around, he saw some arrogant faces, Humani faces, looking down on him in every sense.

"Go get him, sir," said someone from off to the right. It was Commander Ashwani. "Again," she said, adding insult to injury.

Kelso finished racking the balls, and he placed the rack under the table. "After you, Trevor."

Reinhardt put a hand up. "Nope. Where I come from, the winner breaks."

"Very well."

Kelso leaned over and broke the balls with a loud clack of porcelain. The balls scattered, and he sunk two high balls on the break.

"Nice break," said Reinhardt. "Where'd you learn how to play?"

"We Humani are not much for women or gambling," said Kelso imperiously. "So when having to frequent these pleasure facilities, I became interested in this primitive game of skill."

"I see you've been practicing," said Reinhardt.

"I picked it up quickly. It is all angles and friction."

"That's what she said," quipped Reinhardt.

However, his humor was lost on Kelso. The Humani leaned over and shot the nine ball in the side pocket off the rail.

Reinhardt leaned against a table as one of his men poured him another Zorbakite Ale from a pitcher.

Kelso shot the seven ball around the eight into the far corner, and then the three into the side pocket. He looked up at his Human opponent, as if to gauge his reaction, and shook his head pitifully as the man named Trevor kept downing his pint, oblivious to the fact that he wasn't likely to get a single turn this game. Foolish Human.

Reinhardt drained his glass as he watched this Humani run the table. At last, he was up to the eight ball perched by the far corner pocket, precariously close to the four ball that guarded the pocket. Reinhardt's ball.

"Eight ball, corner pocket," said Kelso, gesturing over to the corner with the tip of his cue.

"Now hold on just one moment, partner."

Kelso stood up straight, watching the man named Trevor carefully. "What is it?"

Reinhardt poured himself another ale. "Well, I just want to make sure you know the rules before you take that final shot. I wouldn't want you to embarrass yourself in front of your shipmates and all." Reinhardt smirked as he saw flashes of magenta, not only from Kelso but some of his crew-mates.

"Yes, I know," said Kelso a little impatiently. "It has to be a clean shot. Straight in without touching your ball." He leaned over the table again to line up the shot.

"Wait just a Goddarned minute," said Reinhardt, slurring his words. "That's not all."

Kelso straightened again. "Now what?"

"You want to make sure you shoot that ball at pocket speed. If you hit it too hard, it won't sink."

Kelso glared at the man named Trevor. "I think it is clear I know how to shoot pool, and I do not need lessons from you. Now, if you do not mind." There was another flutter of color. Reinhardt saw it, and so did the spectators, as there was a wave of murmuring that fell over the crowd, cresting and falling back into silence.

"Good," continued Reinhardt, "because it'd be a real shame if you made it this far and lost because you messed up on the endgame. A man could be a real good shooter but have a lousy eight-ball game, if you catch my drift."

Another flourish of color, something along the lines of fuchsia. The Humani spectators were well aware that the Human captain was referring to their loss in the war games to his battle group.

"I am confident that I will make this shot," said Kelso, lining it up. He was already taking longer to line up this shot than he did to line up the others. The Human named Trevor was getting under his green skin.

"The Valliant," said Reinhardt, placing a thoughtful finger on his lips as if suddenly recalling something. "Now I remember. Didn't place so high in the Simulations, as I recall. In fact, Valliant's battle group placed lower than Resilience's."

The pool cue looked like a small switch in the hands of the Humani, his long fingers closed over each other, overlapping on the other side as he clasped it. His face changed colors, from yellow and blue to purple and red. "We knocked you out right after you knocked us out. And, as I recall, it was a Humani ship that won the Games."

"Yes, you're right about that," said Reinhardt. "It usually is a Humani ship that takes top position, but it must feel awkward that your battle group was beaten by a Human battle group. My *Human* battle group, to be precise." A belch escaped his lips, and there were some guffaws from the peanut gallery.

"You are trying to distract me," said Kelso, "which sadly is your only tactic at this point in the game, albeit a desperate one."

"Funny you should say that," said Reinhardt. "That's exactly how we beat your ship in the games."

Kelso leveled his gaze at his opponent. "Yes, and your battle group did not have to commit suicide to do so. Are we going to play the game or jerk each other off?"

There were sneers from the Humani camp now, emboldened by Kelso's bravado.

"Why do we have to choose?" said Reinhardt, winking at Kelso.

There was a counter round of laughter and jeering from the Humans this time. The tension in the room was so thick, one could cut it with a Cybion blade.

Kelso leaned over the table, determined to end the game and shut this drunken braggart up, captain or no captain. He took a deep breath and drew back the cue, the bend of his elbow perfectly parallel with the cue in perfect form. He took the shot...

CHAPTER 6

Pequo looked around at his captors, as they marched him through the dense forest. The older man, this group's leader, noticed him looking around. "Sizing us up?"

Pequo shook his head. "I am just wondering how you managed to shoot my fighter down."

The older man smiled. "It was not with these weapons."

"If you do not mind me asking, how have you managed to give the military such a hard time?"

"We do not look very menacing," said the younger man, insulted. "But, we took *you* captive, did we not?"

"You got lucky," said Pequo, a flash of orange crossing his face. "I had to bail out of my mech suit."

"You think your mech suit would have protected you?" asked Marna.

"You have more than these weapons," said Pequo, smiling. "You have help."

They came upon a clearing in the forest, and Pequo saw what must have been a very organized camp. Large battle mechs patrolled the perimeter. Pequo recognized the technology. "I knew it. You have had help, and from the Feng, no less."

"They teach us how to be strong, how to fight," said the younger man.

As they strolled into the camp, one of the mechs lumbered close by, scanning Pequo, its weapons at the ready. Pequo, however, wasn't worried. If they wanted him dead, he'd have been dead already.

As they led him into camp, Pequo kept pressing. "All they care about is war and conquest. They are barbarians."

"That is exactly what they say about you," said Marna, relaxing her weapon now that she was amongst the resistance.

Pequo looked around. At first, he saw rebels, armed and running patrols, gathering supplies. The camp appeared to run like a well-oiled machine. Then, on closer inspection, he caught glimpses of children—at least they must've been children because they were smaller in stature and had softer features—bringing water, gathering firewood, and pitching in according to their own abilities.

"They have no honor," said Pequo. "They will use you to topple the government, and then they will topple you."

The older man pointed his rifle into Pequo's chest, signaling for him to stop walking. "We starve under the government, while the administration dines in the capital on fine meats and spirits. We have no say, no representation. Decisions are made for us, against us."

"The Feng are no different," said Pequo. "As we speak, their people are starving. They have an emperor who sits in his palace, gorging himself on the spoils of war. He doles out rewards and supplies to his feudal lords, while the people have nothing."

"They eat what they kill," said the older man. "They promise us the same."

Pequo smiled at a little one who was doing her best to haul garbage. "So what happens when you overthrow the capital, and you feast on your spoils? Then what?"

"The Feng welcome us into their great empire, and we join them in conquest."

"Great empire," Pequo snickered. "They have not been a great empire since the last Galactic War."

"They are on the rise," said the younger man.

"Silence, Grappi," snapped the older man.

"But it is true," said Grappi, annoyed at being told to be quiet.

"You heard your father," admonished Marna.

Grappi became sullen.

"So, you have taken a Humani prisoner," said a voice from behind Pequo.

Pequo turned to find a Feng officer standing in full uniform.

"I trust you have been treated with the utmost consideration," said the officer. Pequo didn't appreciate his sarcasm.

"So far," said Pequo.

"My name is Lieutenant Votan of the Feng Empire. I am in charge of this camp and the rebel forces stationed here." He sized Pequo up. "You are Humani. From your flightsuit, I can see that you are a pilot. You are a long way away from your fighter, which I assume is somewhere in the forest in pieces."

"I am Second Lieutenant Pequo of the United Intergalactic Coalition Armada."

"Lieutenant Pequo, walk with me." Lieutenant Votan nodded at Marna, Grappi, and his father. It was their cue to leave, and leave they did.

Votan began to walk, and Pequo fell in beside him.

"Why am I still alive?" asked Pequo.

"Because I have wished it," said Votan. "You serve a purpose for me."

"I will never serve the Feng."

"You speak as if you have a choice in the matter."

"You might as well kill me now."

Votan smiled at him. "What do you know of dying, pilot? You rain death safely from above, a degree of separation from the true warriors who kill and die up close and personally."

"I am prepared to die."

"Ah, yes, your Humani training. A glorious death in the name of the freedom and democracy of the UIC. However, if I do decide to end your life, what makes you think it will be a glorious death?" Votan unsheathed his Feng saber, a weapon every officer carried. "Suppose I was to lop off your limbs, one by one, sever them from your trunk." He pantomimed the movements. "Would that be glorious?"

"What do you want from me?" asked Pequo, trying his best to suppress his emotions but flashing bright yellow.

Votan grinned at the display. "I need your Vortex fighter."

"It is scattered all over the forest," said Pequo. "What do you want with it? I thought you Feng believed your ships to be superior."

"Never mind why I want it," said Votan. "You Humani have a homing application in your mech interface."

"As you can see, I am not in my mech suit."

"Where is it?"

"Also scattered all over the forest."

"I do not believe you. If that were the case, there would be pieces of you scattered along with it." Votan shouted at one of his men, "Get me Harlanu."

The soldier saluted and dashed across the camp, back in the direction from which Pequo and Votan came. Within minutes, the soldier returned with the older man who captured Pequo.

"Yes, Lieutenant Votan?" said Harlanu.

"Where is this pilot's mech?"

"Hung up in the vines. He had to abandon it, and that is when we captured him."

"Do you remember where?" asked Votan.

"Yes."

"Good. Assemble a squad of Hilalu. Take a battle mech with you. Bring it back."

"Yes, sir." Harlanu darted off to assemble a squad.

"A Vortex will be of no use to you," said Pequo. "If anything, it is the Humani who could steal technology from the Feng."

"Then you have nothing to worry about," said Votan.

However, Pequo knew that once Votan had his grimy Feng hands on the mech suit, he was as good as dead.

*

Votan was inside his command tent, sending out an encrypted signal to a Feng Dreadnaught, which in turn relayed it to Captain Mongo Utang's command carrier. Captain Utang appeared as a holograph inside the tent, looming over Votan. "What is it, Lieutenant?"

"Captain, forgive the urgency of my transmission, but you will not believe what just dropped into my lap. I am in possession of a Humani fighter pilot that the rebels shot down."

Utang's face lit up. "Were you able to recover the Vortex?"

"It came apart over the forest. We are in the process of tracking down his mech suit to activate the homing beacon."

"Why was his suit not taken when he was captured?" It was an accusation more than a question.

"The rebels took him. They did not think to retrieve the suit. I sent a squad out with a battle mech to retrieve it."

Captain Utang frowned. "They best be quick and quiet about it. We cannot tip off the UIC that we are on that planet. Once the Humani has activated the homing beacon, terminate him and incinerate the body."

"Yes, Captain."

The transmission ended.

* * *

Planet Feng
Imperial Palace

"We are pleased that you have considered our offer and have agreed to enter into the accord," said Tolstoi Remu's holograph.

"Though I believe that we were not given much of an alternative, it is my hope that this represents an important step in the peace process between the Feng and the worlds of the UIC," said Emperor Hiron.

"I believe that if we work together as allies, we will accomplish great things," added Vice Executor Kazar.

Hiron did his best not to roll his eyes.

"Excellent," said Remu. "We wish to schedule inspections immediately."

This startled Emperor Hiron. "The proper arrangements need to be made," said Hiron. "Not just in matters of security, but in hospitality." Although what he said was technically correct, he was also stalling.

Remu bowed his head. "I am sure that whatever you arrange will be more than adequate and generous, Emperor."

"You must allow time for the proper security clearances to be expedited—planetary defense, palace security."

"And expedite it you will," said Remu. "I will be forwarding an inspection schedule and itinerary."

"The security measures are not just for our protection, but for your inspectors as well. The Feng people are a proud warrior people. They will not take kindly to outsiders visiting our palace and facilities."

"I sense reluctance on your end," said Remu. "If you are serious and sincere about this accord, then you have nothing to fear and nothing to hide. Besides, I will be sending a detail of UIC Marines with our inspection team to assist in matters of security."

"And what of the aid and lifting of trade restrictions with Golgath?" asked Hiron.

"We must honor our end of the bargain," said Remu. "You may now trade with Golgath. Regarding the aid, you will receive a transmission of funds after the inspectors have conducted their first inspection."

"It will be difficult to trade with Golgath without funds," said Kazar.

Remu flashed a conniving grin. "All the more reason you would want to get the first inspection over with quickly."

The channel closed and Tolstoi Remu's hologram vanished, leaving Emperor Hiron and Vice Executor Kazar alone.

"The UIC never does anything quickly," said Hiron. "They are mired in bureaucracy. We will have plenty of time to prepare." He stood. "I have a Ritual to attend. Keep me apprised of all developments."

*

General Utang and his wife, Regana, walked out of the Temple alongside a preoccupied Emperor Hiron and his wives and sons, as well as Lord Talbo Cyclesse, and his wife, Terret. They strolled the halls together on their way to the afterfeast. The younger sons skipped down the cold corridor, their older brothers wrangling them into a pretense of order, the others gossiping and chatting.

"That was quite the Ritual," said Talbo. "I always enjoy the Feast of the Period of Strife. The retelling of the times of conflict, Feng against Feng. Such great gains in philosophy and culture came out of that tumultuous period."

"It just goes to show that greater good can come out of death and destruction," agreed Regana.

"I, for one, enjoy the times of peace and calm," said Terret.

"One might argue that there have been no such times in our history of note, Lady Terret," said Emperor Hiron.

"Perhaps you are noting the wrong events," quipped Terret with an impish smile.

"You must forgive my wife," apologized Talbo. "She frequently does not know when to hold her tongue."

Regana elbowed her brother in the ribs and arched a fierce eyebrow. "Perhaps it is not your lovely wife who does not know when to stop talking."

"Do not try and argue with her, Talbo," said General Utang, wearing a sardonic grin. "It is a fool's enterprise."

"We ladies have our opinions," admonished Regana, "and we make no apologies for them."

"It is true," said Utang. "It is easier to conquer a new world than it is to coax an apology out of her."

There was a tone coming from Emperor Hiron's communicator. He waved a hand, and a holograph of Vice Executor Kazar materialized before him.

"What is it, Kazar?"

"I need to speak with you urgently…in private."

Hiron, looking annoyed, addressed his guests while the hologram of Kazar waited patiently. "Lord and Lady Cyclesse, you must excuse me, for apparently I have an urgent matter to attend to."

"But, of course," replied Talbo. "The empire does not run itself."

"Yoshi and Regana will escort you both to the afterfeast. I hope to rejoin you shortly." Utang gave Hiron a searching look, but Hiron waved him off with his hand.

"Right this way, ladies and gentleman," said General Utang, leading them away from Hiron and to the banquet hall.

Hiron waited for them to walk away before stepping into an alcove. He set the audio to private. "Speak, Kazar."

"We have a transmission from the United Intergalactic Coalition Committee on Foreign Relations, Your Highness. Your presence is requested in the conference room."

Hiron nodded solemnly. "I will be there in micros."

He knew what this meant. The United Intergalactic Coalition was going to commence inspections of Planet Feng, and the timing couldn't have been worse.

As he stalked down the palace halls toward the conference room, he summoned General Yoshi Utang.

An apparition of Utang immediately sprouted in front of Hiron and moved with the emperor as he walked. "Yes, Emperor Hiron."

"I have just been summoned to meet with the UIC Committee on Foreign Relations."

Utang immediately knew what this meant. "Inspections."

"Yes, and the timing could not be poorer. I need you to address these uprisings with immediate results. If the UIC gets a whiff of our recent problems, they will waste no time in exercising the Pax Galactus initiative."

"Understood, Your Highness. I am already on it."

Utang's hologram disappeared right as Hiron stopped in front of the conference room door. He waved a hand, and the door whisked open, closing behind him after he entered. Kazar was waiting for him.

"They are awaiting your acceptance of their conference request, Your Highness."

"They want to discuss a schedule for the inspections already," said Hiron, taking his seat at the head of the long conference table, next to Kazar. "Not a word about the uprisings," he admonished.

"Yes, of course, Your Highness."

"You have taken us to this point, Vice Executor. Do not frak it up." The warning implied a threat that needed no explanation.

Kazar nodded his understanding.

Hiron opened the channel, accepting the digital conference request. As before, the seats filled with the various members of the Committee on Foreign Relations. Around the table sat Tolstoi Remu, Bobot Tegrit, Dvorak, Martin Rayban, and Hubritia Liguri.

"Good day, Emperor Hiron," said Tolstoi Remu, sounding officious. "I think you know why I have called this meeting."

"Yes," nodded Hiron. "You wish to discuss a schedule for inspections."

"With all due respect, Emperor Hiron, this is more of a notification than a discussion," said Tolstoi Remu.

"I see."

"We will be dispatching Bobot Tegrit and Hubritia Liguri with a team of engineers and physicists to begin the first inspection in one cycle."

"One cycle," said Hiron, uncomfortable with the urgency. "The accord was just struck. I need time to prepare a proper reception."

"To be candid, the whole point is to minimize any preparation," said Tolstoi Remu. "If you have already begun to deactivate your weapons development facilities, you should have nothing to hide."

"Of course," answered Kazar. "We offer full transparency."

Hiron shot Kazar a look that indicated that he had overstepped. "What I meant was that, in the interest of diplomacy, I wanted to prepare a proper reception—food, drink, entertainment."

"Emperor Hiron, our inspectors are not coming to Planet Feng for recreation," said Tolstoi Remu.

"I am only trying to be a good host in the interest of our new relationship."

"I am sure that they will be treated hospitably," said Remu. "To be sure, they will be accompanied by a detail of marines, as we discussed, hardly an invasion force."

Emperor Hiron was resigned to the fact that this was going to happen, and quickly. "We will gladly receive your inspectors, and we are confident that they will conclude that we have abided by our end of the bargain."

"Very good," said Remu. "We hope this is the beginning of a new era where there is peace between the United Intergalactic Coalition and the Feng Empire.

"Once again, as per our side of the bargain, the trade embargos have been lifted and payment of aid will occur after the conclusion of the first inspection. There will be UIC patrols in these systems to assure that everything runs smoothly."

"Yes, Representative Remu," said Hiron, "I understand."

The meeting was then terminated, the dignitaries vanishing simultaneously around the table.

Hiron pounded the conference table with his fist. "They knew we were going to agree. They were lying in wait for our expected response."

"This could not have come at a more inopportune time," said Kazar. "It appears General Utang's urgency to address the riots was not so misguided. He really needs to get a handle on the insurgents, and quickly."

Hiron stood up, prompting Kazar to stand. "Put together a briefing to the manors, notifying them of the incoming UIC representatives, but make no mention of any inspections. Spin it that we are opening up trade with the UIC, and that they are offering us tribute in the process out of deference to our great empire."

Vice Executor Kazar nodded. He was accustomed to receiving such instructions. The Feng nation was a perpetual powder keg with a short fuse. In order to keep the unruly populace in line, the truth frequently had to be stretched, fabricated even.

He had to give the Feng people the hope they so desperately needed, and time was of the essence. Hiron was not lying when he said it was for everyone's safety. Any attack on the UIC inspectors would be an act of intergalactic war.

"After that, prepare the kitchen," said Hiron, "and arrange for some entertainment."

"The Vice of the Interior is fully capable of—"

"I asked you to do it."

"Yes, Your Highness."

"Contact the High Priest at the Temple," said Hiron. "Arrange for a service for our guests. It will be a good chance to expose them to some Feng tradition, help them obtain a better understanding of who and why we are."

"I assume you do not want an abbreviated mass," smirked Kazar, understanding full well that the service was to be a distraction and stall tactic.

"Do it," commanded Hiron.

Kazar bowed low. "As the Holy Emperor commands."

*

In the evening, General Yoshi Utang and Captain Idoni led the Cybions along the Imperial Road down to the Great Steppes. They reached the feudal guard of Lord Xiang at the gatehouse.

As soon as the guards saw the Cybions, they immediately genuflected. General Utang rode up on his darkcycle, Idoni just behind him. "Rise," said Utang.

The sergeant-at-arms gasped when he recognized who was addressing him. "General Utang. I...we are at your service."

"Stand aside," said Utang casually. "I have business with Lord Xiang."

"Of course, General."

"Send word ahead of our arrival."

"Yes, sir."

The regiment filed in through the gatehouse, the stealthy silence of the Cybions unnerving the guards. They were walking, metallic death, and their presence wasn't a good sign.

Within minutes, the regiment was upon the Xiang estate. A squat, timbered building of stone and stucco, it sprawled extravagantly across the manor property. Utang gave the order, and the Cybions surrounded the estate, forming a perimeter. Utang gestured for Idoni to follow him inside the manor house.

The guards parted as Utang and Idoni entered. The harbinger must have arrived only minutes before to announce their presence. Utang liked to take the feudal lords off guard, keeping them on their toes.

A servant greeted Utang and Idoni and led them up the wide, carpeted stairs and into Xiang's parlor room. Upon their entrance, Xiang stood and bowed in deference. "General Utang, you honor me with your presence. To what do I owe this pleasure?"

"Lord Xiang, there has been some discontent in your manor."

"I have heard, General, and I have dealt swiftly with the matter. Rations have been cut in half as punishment and will only be lifted when the conspirators are identified."

Utang shot Idoni an amused look. "Well, which is it, punishment or motivation to smoke out the dissidents?"

"I do not...I mean...I guess, both. Would you or your captain like a beverage or some food?"

"You guess?" said Utang, ignoring the offer of refreshments. "Lord Xiang, perhaps it is all of your guessing that is fostering all of the insubordination in your ranks."

"I assure you, General, that strict measures have been taken."

"Have the conspirators been identified?"

"Well...no. Not as yet."

"More guessing, Lord Xiang," said Utang. "You see, someone in my position likes to deal in certainties."

"Of course, General. I understand completely."

"Good. I am glad you do, because I am going to execute Eugenesis on your manor."

Lord Xiang's eyes bulged out of his head. "No...I mean, please, General, are such steps necessary?"

"The emperor feels it is. Every third son and later."

"But, General, that will cripple my labor force. The crops will suffer."

"Lord Xiang, are you threatening to fail to deliver on your crops?"

"No, of course not, sir. It is just that, with a thinned labor force and sterilization, it will cripple the operations of my manor."

Utang strode up to Xiang, looming over him, his broad shoulders and pointy, jagged armor casting a shadow over Xiang. "Your manor, as of late, has been nothing but trouble for the emperor. Perhaps, after the Eugenesis, if you cannot manage your manor, I will give it to a more deserving lord."

Xiang looked down at the floor. "No, General. That will not be necessary." He knew that a wave of Eugenesis would be a nasty blow to his manor, but there was nothing he could do about it. He resigned himself to his fate.

"Lord Xiang, your communications array."

Xiang looked up in horror. "Yes, General. Of course."

He led Utang over to one of his digital captures, a self-portrait. He placed a clawed hand onto the capture, and his effigy placed his hand up, overlapping the real Xiang's. A door slid open, revealing a control room, filled with all kinds of equipment.

Utang stepped inside and activated the public address system. Speakers all over the manor and surrounding villages on the Great Steppes crackled as he cleared his throat. "Citizens of Xiang Manor, dwellers on the Great Steppes, this is General Utang of the Imperial Army.

"It has come to the emperor's attention that there have been meetings held and riots staged, interfering with the execution of the Law and the collection of tribute.

"Your Lord Xiang appealed to you to turn over these traitors to the empire, but you have not complied. Starvation does not seem to affect you, so I am enacting a round of Eugenesis..." He paused, letting his words hang in the air, like a dark cloud over the Steppes. "Third son and later, unless the conspirators are immediately brought to our attention. Anyone who tries to flee will be hunted down by the Cybions and executed."

He terminated the transmission and nodded to Idoni, who immediately left the room to set the Cybions on the Great Steppes.

"This is a certainty," said General Utang to Lord Xiang. "Either your vassals will give up the conspirators, or they will lose generations of their stock, right before their very eyes."

There was nothing Xiang could do to save the children in his manor. To go against the General, who was under the direct authority of the emperor himself, was treason, punishable by death.

Xiang realized that he, too, was being punished. Punished for being too lenient with his vassals. Punished for failing to keep the peace within his small realm.

*

Down on the streets, farms, and within the village, Cybions swarmed the Steppes like metallic wraiths, gleaming in the moonlight, moving swiftly. They broke down doors to huts, living quarters, and houses, snatching infants and children from their mothers' arms as they wailed in futility. Children wriggled as they were stripped of their homes, crying for their mothers.

The first stage of Eugenesis was extermination of the identified generations. This would be done publically in the square. The second stage was sterilization of the adult males. The men were sterilized because doing so to the women was too permanent.

Any manor subjected to Eugenesis needed to rebound their numbers. This often entailed such abominations as incest, as the only surviving males capable of reproduction were younglings. When they came of age, they would replace their fathers. It added insult to the injury and weakened manors. However, if the manor redeemed itself with increased productivity, men of breeding age from other parts of the empire would be brought in to prevent genetic dilution.

Eugenesis did not occur often, as they were reserved to make a big statement to the populace. In the early days, it was used to thin the heard, eliminating political dissidents and 'useless eaters.' In recent times, with resources running thin, it was a convenient way for the government to this its population, leaving only the most loyal and prolific subjects.

As the babies and children were gathered in the public squares, surrounded by bladed Cybions poised for dismemberment, a woman on one of the farms came forward, crying and pleading.

She threw herself at Captain Idoni's feet, sobbing on his boots and begging for mercy. "I know who did it! I know who was involved!"

Idoni shifted his feet, pulling his boots away from her red face dripping with mucus and tears. "I want them pointed out. All of them."

"Yes! All of them! I swear it! Just spare my babies!"

Idoni touched his ear. "General, we may have something."

* * *

"You cheated," demanded Sergeant Kelso, looming over Captain Reinhardt, his tall lithe form like that of a large praying mantis. His face was rapidly changing colors from red to purple to orange.

Reinhardt stood toe to toe with the angry Humani, never giving an inch. He did, however, have to crane his neck up to meet Kelso's determined gaze with his own. "I did nothing of the sort. You beat yourself."

"You were distracting me, disrupting my concentration."

"Well, I didn't think that a superior being like yourself would be so sensitive to a little ribbing."

"You Humans are so inferior, yet so arrogant. You cover up your shortcomings with brash humor and adolescent bravado."

There was a stirring in the crowd. The Humani and Humans looking on began to eye each other with enmity. The few Vampiri in the room knew something was about to go down. With eyes glowing like embers, they began to recede into the shadows, sensing the energy in the room, wisely deciding to pick up tricks elsewhere.

"Jesus, what do you carry around a Thesaurus with you?" quipped Reinhardt. "If we're so inferior, how come we beat you in the simulations, and now I beat you here?"

"A fluke, I assure you, *Human*." He said that last word as if he had uttered a profane curse.

"Boy, there are an awful lot of flukes with you Humani when you don't get your way."

Ashwani stepped forward, stepping between Reinhardt and Kelso. "Come on, boys. Let's not forget we're all on the same side. Save it for the Feng."

"Same side," said Kelso. "It is more like we have been assigned to babysit you Humans."

Reinhardt put a hand on Ashwani's shoulder. "You can't talk any sense into him. He's blinded by his own pride, which has been mortally wounded as of late. He's coming to grips with his limitations."

Kelso's face engorged and erupted into a fiery red. "Step outside and I will show you what my limitations are."

A female Humani stepped out from the crowd. "No, Kelso. He is a senior officer. You will get thrown in the brig."

"I'm not a senior officer here," said Reinhardt, looking around the room and then at Kelso. "Here, I'm just a soldier on leave, like the rest of you."

"You would put aside rank?" asked Kelso in anticipation, his muscles tensing.

"Rank is not an issue here," announced Reinhardt, rolling up his sleeves, "and you need to be taught a lesson."

"Kelso, do not let him goad you," insisted the female Humani. "It is not worth ending your career over a *Human*."

Kelso hesitated, as if thinking better of it.

Drunk, ornery, and stubborn, Reinhardt stabbed a finger into Kelso's chest. "Funny, I forgot that Humani men do whatever their women tell them."

If the Humani female had diffused the situation, Reinhardt just doused it with fuel and lit the match. Kelso grabbed him by his jacket, lifting him off the ground, but Reinhardt punched him in the mouth.

As Kelso reeled a bit, stunned from the blow, Reinhardt turned his body sideways, tucking Kelso's long hands under his armpit, pulling him down and off balance. He elbowed him in the face, but Kelso didn't let go.

"Stop it!" yelled the Humani female, but the entire bar erupted into violence as stools went flying in the air and punches were thrown.

Reinhardt pulled and twisted on his hips, trying to take Kelso off balance, but the taller Sergeant Kelso maintained his footing. He regained his composure, lifted both hands up and Reinhardt into the air, and threw the Human forward.

Reinhardt flew into the bar, his head and shoulder striking the front, and he dropped to the ground. He shook his head, and as his vision cleared, he saw Kelso running at him.

He quickly stood, snatching up a metal stool in his hands. He swung it, striking Kelso, but the Humani crashed into him, slamming up against the bar, the edge digging into Reinhardt's back.

It was ship against ship, Valliant against Resilience, Humani against Human. Ashwani was grappling with the Humani female, but losing to the Humani's height advantage. The other Human crew members used everything around them, from pool cues to furniture, to even the odds.

The bartender took out his blaster from behind the bar. He fired a couple of shots into the air as Kelso slammed Reinhardt down hard on top of the bar. Then he pointed the blaster at Kelso's red face, point blank.

The room went quiet. The massive brawl interrupted, UIC crew members in various stages of pummeling each other all looked at the bartender.

The bartender curled his lip up. "That'll be enough. Why don't you take your little squabble outside? You're frightening the paying customers."

Kelso released Reinhardt's shirt, which was at this point torn, and backed away, hands raised. "No problem."

Reinhardt slowly sat up and lowered himself gingerly off the bar, his back complaining. The Humani female that was on top of Ashwani stepped back, allowing Ashwani to stand up. She brushed herself off as the Humani straightened out her outfit.

"Out. *Now,*" insisted the bartender, shoving his gun into Reinhardt's back, sending a sharp pain shooting through his body.

Reinhardt winced and stepped forward, elbowing Kelso. "I'm starving. I heard the Drekaar bar has Iguani scarab burgers."

Kelso looked at the Human named Trevor, stunned.

"C'mon," insisted Reinhardt. "Let this inferior Human buy you lunch."

"Lunch?" said Kelso, confused.

"A meal," said Reinhardt, rolling his eyes. "C'mon, my treat."

Kelso changed colors, but this time, it was somewhere on the blue spectrum. "Sure. Okay."

The two rivals exited the bar, stepping over broken glass and toppling stools. Reinhardt patted Kelso on the back. "Nice moves, kid. Where'd you learn to fight like that?"

The remaining Humans and Humani stared in astonishment, not sure of what exactly just transpired. Ashwani smiled at her new captain, impressed.

"That means all of you!" yelled the bartender.

The Humani and Humans filed out of the bar and spilled out into the atrium of the vast facility. Not another punch was thrown by either race that day.

PART II

CATALYST

"In death we are welcomed into the Aether, surrendering our corporeal vessels lent us by the Engineer and joining our ancestors until the end of Spacetime."

Unknown author, from the Humani Book of Life

CHAPTER 7

Lieutenant Alita Nakai was flying over the canopy, her Vortex fighter's scanners working overtime to find Pequo.

Commander Massa's voice was in her ear. "Lieutenant, return to the command carrier. We are taking on too much fire."

"He could not have gotten far," said Nakai. "I am tracking his suit," she lied. Her scanners hadn't yet picked up the suit's transponder.

"Our orders were to provide escort," Massa insisted. "We will execute a search and rescue later, when the conditions are optimal. In the meantime, he will use his training to conceal himself and survive."

Nakai didn't doubt that it would be easy to use field craft in the dense forest below. However, the place was crawling with Hilalu rebels who were apparently well-armed.

She made to reply, but her com suddenly experienced interference. "Wing Commander…" There was distortion, as if communications had suddenly been jammed. "Do you copy?" There were fragments of Massa's voice, his speech unintelligible and then the coms went quiet. Immediately after, the transponder from Pequo's suit appeared on her display. He was nearby.

Jammed. This rebels really are well-equipped. Something didn't quite add up for Nakai, but she figured she'd capitalize on the com problems and act as if she hadn't heard Massa.

She flew low over the treetops and found a small clearing ahead. Her scanners didn't pick up any nearby rebel patrols, so she slowed to a hover above the clearing and deftly dropped beneath the tree line, landing on the soft ground below.

She opened the cockpit and jumped out, gun in hand. She only had four revolving clips, two in the gun and one in each of her mech's legs. Pilot mech suits weren't designed for heavy combat. They were lightweight and carried minimal firepower so that a downed pilot could run and survive until extraction.

She scanned the forest. Pequo's signal was three clicks due west. Nakai began to jog through the forest. It was difficult going, as there was a lot of underbrush tangling up in her mech's legs and plenty of trees preventing a straight run. However, the ground was soft, muffling the footfalls of her mech. The only sounds she made were the pumping of pistons and the suit's hydraulics.

As she made her way through the forest, the blinking signal in her helmet display grew stronger until she appeared to be right on top of it. "Alpha 3, it's Alpha 2, do you read?"

Nakai looked around, but there was no sign of Pequo. "Alpha 3, this is Alpha 2, do you read?" Several bogies popped up on her display, one battle mech, and several footsoldiers.

Shit. Nakai hid behind a large tree, the arms and legs of her suit protruding. She cooled down her suit, putting all systems in hibernation, so as not to be picked up by the approaching mech.

Where the Engineer was Pequo hiding? Something made her look up, and that was when she saw Pequo's mech suit dangling, tangled in the branches and vines. The suit was open and empty.

The mech and rebel foot patrol entered the area, stopping underneath Pequo's suit. *That is a Feng battle mech. So that is where all the firepower came from. The Feng are on Aquilassi, and they are helping the Hilalu.*

Nakai wondered if the mech had tracked her signatures, but it seemed preoccupied with Pequo's empty suit. *Did the crafty bastard make it out? Was he hiding somewhere nearby, or was he halfway across the forest by now?* She wanted to send out a ping to see if Pequo was close by, but she didn't dare do it with this mech nearby.

The Hilalu were pointing up at the empty suit, and the mech fired small, controlled bursts at the vines holding it up. The suit dropped with each blast until it was finally freed. It fell to the ground, bouncing off tree trunks, landing prone in the dirt.

The mech ambled over, grabbed it around its waist, and hoisted the empty suit over its shoulder. The party then began to traipse back through the woods from whence they came.

Nakai waited until they were at a safe enough distance away, and she powered up again. The bogies were just out of range, which meant that she was just out of their range. She knew the general direction they were going.

She decided to follow them. Either they would lead her to Pequo, or at the very least, she would get a glimpse of the undetected Feng presence.

She trekked through the forest after them, keeping her scanners peeled for insurgents, careful to keep out of the Feng mech's range. She activated her own suit's transponder for Massa to find her. She followed them for approximately an hour, when multiple bogies were popping up on the outer edge of her helmet display. It was their camp.

She quickly backed away until they were off her display, which meant she was likely off theirs. There was the small, unlikely possibility that they might've picked up on her brief appearance on their scanners, but they weren't exactly looking for her. At least that was what she told herself.

If there was a Feng-Hilalu rebel camp, Nakai had to observe and report. Such intelligence was integral in the United Intergalactic Coalition's gentrification of the planet.

Nakai slipped out of her mech behind some underbrush, leaving it in a crouching position and cooling it down in hibernation mode. Armed only with a modest sidearm, she crept her way closer to the camp, careful to stay concealed with the help of her environment.

As she drew closer, she saw the clearing littered with tattered tents and Hilalu scurrying about under the watch of a few Feng mechs, who walked the perimeter. She was careful not to be seen as she crept to the edge of the tree line. Hiding behind a tree, her lithe body was completely concealed.

She looked on as she saw the Hilalu camp bustling with activity. A Feng officer in full regalia caught her attention towards the center of camp. He was greeting the mech and Hilalu foot patrol from the forest. The mech lowered Pequo's empty suit off its shoulder and onto the ground at the officer's feet, like a pet presenting a toy to its master.

She heard the lumbering steps of a nearby mech making its way around the perimeter to where she was hiding. If she didn't move, it would pick her up on its scanners hiding behind the tree. She made as if to retreat back into the forest when she saw Pequo, hands bound at the wrists in front of him, being brought out to the Feng officer.

Pequo!

Nakai had to make a snap decision—recede into the woods to hide or enter the camp, hoping to hide in plain sight. These Hilalu were humanoid in appearance, but were short and stubby compared to a Humani. She would have very likely stuck out like a sore thumb.

Frak it. She left the cover of the forest and waltzed right into the Hilalu camp as the mech thumped past her, its scanners directed out at the forest. Fortunately, everyone was looking at Pequo's empty mech and the Feng officer. Nakai slipped into the first tent she could find.

It was a laundry tent. It made sense. The weapons and food tents would be closer to the interior, better protected. Nakai grabbed some tattered rags and slipped them on over her flightsuit. They were short, leaving her wrists, part of her forearms, ankles, and calves exposed, but it was the best she could do. She slipped a shawl over her head (or at least she thought it was a shawl).

She slipped back out of the tent as a small Hilalu girl brought in a load of clothes. They were so filthy and frayed, Nakai doubted washing would do much to improve their condition. These people had seen real hardship.

She snickered to herself as she looked around and saw that the Hilalu had the female variant of their species doing the grunt work. *So primitive.*

She walked between the tents, keeping one eye on the Feng officer and Pequo, and the other eye on the patrolling mechs. Nakai found it odd that there did not appear to be any Cybions in the camp. If the Feng were going to claim the planet, they would've certainly brought their fiercest warriors.

Given the light presence in this camp, Nakai figured the Feng were not here to claim the planet. They were up to something else. That officer appeared mighty interested in Pequo's suit.

"This suit contains the specs for your Vortex fighter," said Votan.

"I guess you will have to figure that out for yourself," said Pequo.

"Yes. That I will, with or without your help."

"Why are you so interested in the specs for the Vortex?"

Votan smiled. "My cryptologic technicians will dissect this suit and extract what we need."

"So I guess this means I am a dead man."

"No," said Votan. "A murdered Humani pilot would raise questions and cause a reaction. You are coming back with me, and you will submit to a full interrogation."

Pequo involuntarily flashed yellow, as he knew damned well what a Feng interrogation entailed. I was like a rape of the body and mind, an unspeakable violation. Pain didn't even begin to describe it. "The others will know I am missing. They will come looking for me."

Votan grinned. "Yes, but on this planet. I would rather have them think you missing than dead." He gestured to a Feng soldier with a regal sweep of his hand. "Take him out of my sight."

Nakai watched as she saw two Feng soldiers escort Pequo into one of the tents. They reappeared and stood guard in front. The Feng officer who spoke to Pequo had the Feng mech bring Pequo's mech suit to another tent.

Nakai decided she'd go for Pequo first. He would know what was going on, which would help her determine a plan of action. She nonchalantly crossed the row to the other side and disappeared behind the tents. She crossed between the backs of two adjoining rows of tents until she was behind the one holding Pequo.

She reached into her boot and produced her small knife. She placed her ear up to the tent, but heard nothing. She sliced the back tent wall, gently and quietly bringing the blade down. She pried open the slit with her two, long fingers.

She saw Pequo sitting alone on the ground in the dirt, his back to her. She quietly slipped into the tent through the opening she made and produced her small light. She flashed it down in the dirt in front of him in Humani code.

Pequo looked down at the flashing light at his feet, and he slowly turned his head. His eyes lit up when he saw Nakai.

She placed a finger up to her lips in a quieting motion, a gesture she had learned from her Human counterparts in the Armada. She cut his bindings and gestured for him to follow her. They crept out the back of the tent through the slit.

When outside, Nakai walked a few tents over and whispered to him, "Are you okay?"

"Yes, fine, but we do not have much time."

"I know, they are going to realize you are gone. We have to get back to my mech and Vortex."

Pequo shook his head. "No, I mean they are going to load my suit on a Feng ship and take it away. That Lieutenant Votan was very interested in the specs for my Vortex."

"I do not think they are here to take the planet," said Nakai.

"I do not think so either, but they have the Hilalu convinced."

"What do you think they are here for?"

"I am thinking they wanted to shoot down a Vortex and steal it. As soon as they got my suit, they were ready to bug out."

"That does not sound like the Feng," said Nakai. "And that is what worries me. We have to get back to my Vortex."

"By the time we leave and come back, Votan will be gone with my suit. We cannot let that happen."

"We cannot stay here," said Nakai, her tone impatient.

"We need help."

"Agreed, which is why we have to get the frak out of here."

Pequo made a gesture for her to wait a minute. He crept between two tents, peeking out into the main drag through the camp. Nakai wanted to scream at him, but she managed to whisper. "Where are you going?"

He saw Marna off to the side, watching the tent where Pequo's suit was taken. Pequo waved his hands, taking care that only she would see him. Almost, as if she sensing his presence, she looked in the direction of the tent he was being held in. However, her eyes found him first. There was a quick expression of surprise and then outrage, but she quickly suppressed it.

Pequo waved her over. Nakai crept up behind him, her hand on her sidearm. "What are you crazy?" she whispered.

"It is all right," he whispered back. "She is okay. I think she will help us."

"Is she not one of the ones who shot you down?"

"Trust me," said Pequo.

Nakai hissed her disapproval.

Marna casually strolled across the road and joined them between the tents. "What are you doing?" she whispered. "If they catch you, they will kill you."

Pequo hunched over to look her in the eye. "Marna, the Feng have no intention of helping the Hilalu."

"I know," she answered. "Now that they have your suit, they are leaving."

Suddenly, the camp was all astir. Lieutenant Votan came marching out of his tent, signaling his men over. "There is an abandoned Vortex in the forest, intact."

"Another one?" asked one of his men.

"Yes. They are starting to add up. Get me Hidalgi and Grappi."

"Frak! They found my Vortex," whispered Nakai.

"So much for heading back," said Pequo.

"You two have to leave camp," said Marna.

"Not without my mech," said Pequo.

Two soldiers came back with Hidalgi and his son, Grappi, the two who captured Pequo with Marna.

"Did you two know about this other Vortex?" demanded Lieutenant Votan.

"No," said Hidalgi. "We just found out when your men told us."

"They are getting too close," said Votan. "Get the Humani pilot. We are leaving."

"But what about the resistance?" asked Grappi. "What about helping us overthrow the capital?"

"Now is not the time," said Votan.

"Now that you have what you came for," said Hidalgi.

"I do not like your tone, Hilalu."

"And I do not like yours," answered Grappi. "We are not your soldiers."

"No," said Votan, "I suppose you are not." He gave a signal, and the Feng soldiers and mechs converged on the camp, weapons drawn and trained on the Hilalu.

"I have to help them," said Marna, and she made to run towards Hidalgi and Grappi, but Pequo grabbed her by the arm.

"No," said Pequo. "There is nothing you can do for them now."

Two soldiers came running over to Lieutenant Votan. "Sir, the Humani is missing."

Votan was taken off guard by this bit of news. "Missing? How can he be missing? How is that possible?"

"There was a rip in the back of the tent, sir."

Votan looked around. "He is somewhere in this camp. If he had tried to leave, one of the perimeter mechs would have spotted him." He touched his ear and spoke into his surgically implanted com. "Scan the camp! He is hiding somewhere."

The mechs swiveled on their mechanical hips as their scanners pored over the congested camp.

"Uh oh," said Nakai.

"I have to get to my suit," said Pequo.

"You cannot win against three mechs in a pilot mech," said Nakai.

"No, but I can lead them away from here."

"I have a better idea," said Nakai.

"I would love to hear it."

"They are looking for you, but they do not know I am here."

* * *

General Utang strode down to the spot where Captain Idoni stood. There was a woman on her knees guarded by a Cybion. "You have something, Captain?"

Idoni looked uncomfortable. "I believe we should speak in private, sir."

Utang eyed the woman, who gazed up at him and then averted her eyes downward. "Very well."

Idoni led Utang off to the side, away from the peasants and townsfolk. "Sir, the woman has named the conspirators."

"I want them immediately taken into custody. That is good news," said Utang. He saw the dubious expression on Idoni's face. "However…"

"One of the conspirators named was Lord Talbo Cyclesse."

Utang was not sure if he heard Idoni correctly. "Correct me if I am wrong, but I believe you just named my brother-in-law as a conspirator."

"That is correct, sir," said Idoni, swallowing hard.

"That is impossible."

"Sir, the woman named him specifically."

"She is lying. Bring her to me."

Idoni nodded and gestured for the Cybions to bring her over. They momentarily retracted their blades and snatched her up by her arms, nearly yanking them out of their sockets. They dragged her over as the other peasants looked at the ground. No one uttered a word of protest. Not even her husband or children.

The Cybions threw her at General Utang's feet and redeployed their array of sharp blades and claws. Utang shifted, removing her from his boot tips, as if she were a piece of garbage. "What is your name?"

The woman looked up, her face smeared with dirt, the badge of a difficult life of labor in the fields for her lord and master. Or perhaps it was the result of having been dragged through the mud by murderous cyborgs. "Utana Miso."

"Rise, Utana."

She struggled to her feet, wiping herself off in a ridiculous gesture.

"Do you know who I am?"

"Yes," she said, head bowed. "You are General Utang of the Imperial Army."

"That is correct. Captain Idoni tells me that you have named the conspirators behind the attacks on our great emperor's tribute collectors."

"I have, sir."

"Look at me when you speak."

Utana looked up at the looming general in full regalia, sharp spines jutting out of his shoulder armor. Her body trembling, she looked him in the eye.

"You have identified Lord Talbo Cyclesse of the Valley."

"Yes, sir."

"What proof do you offer to support this claim?"

Utana swallowed hard. "Search his manor. In his stables, buried under the hay, you will find the red robes and masks worn by the rioters."

"Why would Lord Talbo be in possession of the costumes?'

"Because he is the one who organized them."

Utang did not believe what he was hearing. "That is a bold accusation, Utana Miso. I will look into the truth of your claim, of that you can be certain. You can also be certain that if you are lying to me, which would constitute treason and libel, I will have you executed."

"Yes, sir. I understand." She made to look down, but she forced herself to look the general in the eye.

Utang turned to Idoni. "Round up these terrorists. I want them executed in the square."

"Yes, sir."

Utang turned his back on Utana Miso as she was being dragged back into the heard of collected peasants held at gun and blade-point, and proceeded back up to Lord Xiang's manor house.

*

"Lord Talbo?" said Xiang in disbelief. "That is ridiculous."

"You had no knowledge of any of this, of any involvement of his in the riots," pressed Utang.

"No, of course not. I do not even believe it to true. He is a loyal supporter of our emperor."

"My men are rounding up the traitors as we speak. There will be a public execution in the town square. I want you to oversee it."

"Yes, of course, General," said Xiang, bowing. "My supplicants have met your request and identified the conspirators." He paused, uncertain if he should ask, but he had to if he was to survive as Lord of the Great Steppes. "Is the Eugenesis really necessary, my lord?"

Utang thought for a moment. "While they did as I asked, it had to be coerced out of them. To atone for their insubordination, the cleansing phase will commence. However, there will be no sterilization."

Xiang bowed low and practically threw himself at Utang. "Thank you, General Utang! My house thanks you!"

Utang regarded him with piteous contempt. "Get a hold of yourself, Lord Xiang. This is a time you must project strength to re-establish order."

"Yes, my lord."

Utang left Xiang's chambers without saying goodbye. He returned to his small detail of soldiers and Cybions, and they mounted their darkcycles.

There was a tone on Utang's communicator. He took the call, and a holograph of Emperor Hiron appeared before him.

"Yes, Your Highness."

"Have you determined who is behind these uprisings, General?"

"We are following up on a promising lead at this very moment," answered Utang, careful not to name his brother-in-law Talbo.

"Good," said Hiron. "Time is of the essence. The UIC inspection team will be arriving within a matter of sexagens."

"This will be addressed before they arrive," promised Utang. Hiron terminated the call, and General Utang sped off to pay a visit to his wife's brother, Lord Talbo Cyclesse.

* * *

Cegnis looked up at the dark, starless sky as she walked to the palace. The cloud cover even blocked out the three dragon moons—Dreg, Drago, and Drigo—casting the Feng lands in darkness and shadow. She saw silent, cloaked forms hopping the walls, armed with gun and blade and masked.

They had already breached the castle.

She strolled casually to her living quarters and bolted the door behind her. She listened as she heard muted footfalls shuffle past her door. She startled when blades pounded on the outside of her door, cracking the thick wood. Gloved fingers pulled away shards of door as she stood her ground, waiting.

At last, the cloaked, masked intruders breached her living quarters, and she was face to face with their leader. The figure nodded, she nodded in return, and a couple of the cloaked figures began to trash her room.

The leader took the rest of the group, and they fanned out over the palace.

*

There was a tone at the door. Emperor Hiron rose from his bed, covered in sweat, leaving his concubines to recover for a moment. He wrapped himself in luxurious silkenscale as he crossed the room and answered the door.

Lieutenant Klago was panting. "Emperor, rioters have breached the palace. You must come with me."

It took a moment for Hiron to register what he had just been told. "How many?"

"It looks to be twenty-one, Your Eminence."

Hiron's jaw set and he gritted his teeth. "I will not be chased from my own palace by a small throng of rioters and looters."

"With all due respect, Your Eminence, these are no looters. They killed the outer guard and are breaching further into the palace."

Hiron knew what this meant. These weren't angry peasants. These were assassins. *Imperial* trained killers. A coup was afoot. He ran back into his room, the lieutenant and a few guards on his heels, surprising the concubines.

"I will not be chased out of my own palace." He hastily threw on a robe and his ceremonial imperial sword, fastening the belt holding his scabbard around his waist. He reached under the bed and produced his personal assault rifle, hefting it as he slapped in a live clip.

He looked ridiculous armed to the teeth in his bed chamber robes, his eyes wild. "We will slaughter these treasonous bastards. Where are the Cybions?"

"General Utang took them all on his mission across the countryside."

"Then we will do it ourselves."

Although he thought it a bad idea, Klago knew it was an even worse idea to defy the emperor. He followed Hiron out of his quarters, his guard in toe.

"Where are my sons?" demanded Hiron.

"They are safe," said Klago. "We sent them off with a small detail. They just checked in minutes ago. They are halfway to the sealed bunker."

"Keep checking in, Lieutenant. I want updates until they are safely in the bunker."

"Yes, sir."

Normally, the guard would take the lead, protecting the emperor, but Hiron was a fierce warrior in his own right, and he was leading the charge. Joining their warriors shoulder to shoulder, Feng emperors and generals never led from behind.

When they rounded a corner, they saw the cloaked figures slitting the throats of a few unfortunate guards who were taken by surprise.

"There they are!" boomed Hiron, taking aim.

The emperor and his guard opened fire, and the cloaked infiltrators returned fire, both sides taking cover behind low walls surrounding the gardens.

Klago directed his guard to surround the gardens on three sides, forcing the cloaked traitors back into the massive banquet hall. Hiron and his guard followed after them. As they ejected expended clips, they tossed each other new ones and slapped them in, firing in waves at the intruders. Hiron and his guard pushed the cloaked unit back into the banquet hall.

Gun fire echoed off of the walls of the vast hall as the cloaked figures toppled long tables on their side, scattering the large, ornate wooden chairs, taking cover behind the tables. Animated digital portraits of past emperors oversaw the tumult.

A guard fell, his blood spraying the white table cloths as bullets ricocheted off and ripped through his armor. Three of the cloaked figures were hit though their cover, one through his eye socket as he stole a peek around a massive pillar.

Hiron charged ahead with the bloodlust that earned him his spot as Supreme Ruler of the Feng Empire, blasting holes in his own furniture, chipping off shards of thick stone pillars, and raining bullet casings on the hard floor like Feng hail.

One of the cloaked figures threw a flash grenade, blinding the emperor and his guard in a blaze of light and heat. When the light faded, the cloaked figures had gone.

Emperor Hiron shouted, pumping his fist into the air in victory as Klago led the guard in pursuit out of the great banquet hall. Hiron remained behind with a couple of men, surveying the room.

He was not assessing the damage. He was looking for survivors.

He saw a cloaked figure, clutching his throat, flapping around like a Junga out of its water, lying in a pool of his own blood. Hiron dropped his rifle, drew his great imperial sword, and ran over to the bleeding traitor. He placed his foot on his chest, steadying the squirming man, and pointed his blade at his eye. "Who do you work for? Who is responsible for this?"

The man choked and gurgled on his own blood as his life was slipping from his body. For a brief moment, he became still, staring Hiron in the eye. He burbled out a single last word before his eyes fell vacant and he succumbed to death.

"You."

* * *

"To what do I owe this unannounced visit?" asked Lord Talbo Cyclesse.

"I was in the Great Steppes on business and figured I would drop by to pay a visit," said General Utang.

"How is my dear sister, Yoshi?"

"Regana is fine."

"Would you like a drink?" offered Talbo, gesturing to his servant.

"No, thank you. My visit will be brief, I am afraid."

"Are you out on the business of those uprisings?"

"Yes, funny you should mention it."

"Horrid business, those riots. Lord Xiang seems to have lost his control over his fiefs."

"He is correcting the matter as we speak," said Utang. "His is not the only manor involved."

"Yes, so I have heard," said Talbo. "There has been a great deal of unrest in the empire as of late."

"Anything that you might shed some light on?"

Talbo looked at Utang sideways, unsure of the meaning of the remark. "I assure you that there has been no such nonsense in my manor."

"I have been informed otherwise," said Utang.

Talbo laughed, dubious about the humor of such a statement. His expression sobered when he saw that Utang wasn't joking. "Surely, you jest, but insurrection is no laughing matter."

"No, it is not."

"What do you imply, brother-in-law?"

Utang regarded his wife's brother carefully. "You have been named as an instigator."

Talbo laughed, but it was a bitter laugh. "By who?"

"That is unimportant at the moment."

"On the contrary, it is quite pertinent. Do I not have a right under Feng law to face my accuser?"

"What do you have to do with the uprisings?" pressed Utang.

"Yoshi, I am the brother of the Dutchess Regana, your wife, who resides in the Imperial Palace. I have sworn my allegiance to Emperor Hiron, the Holy Emperor of the Feng Empire. What makes you think that I would have anything to do with these uprisings?"

"That is what I am trying to figure out."

"I am no traitor, Yoshi." Talbo's tone was changing from unpleasant surprise to outrage.

"I want to believe that is true, and we will soon find out," said Utang. Then to Captain Idoni, "Captain, make a thorough search of the premises."

Idoni nodded and made off to round up the Cybions for an examination of Cyclesse Manor.

"This is an insult," said Talbo. "Do not think that my sister will not hear of this."

Utang was very matter of fact. "If you are innocent, then you have nothing to worry about, Talbo."

Talbo huffed at the remark. "This whole affair has me worried."

"Talbo, do you know an Utana Miso?"

Talbo didn't hesitate. "No, I do not."

"Well, she appears to know you. She is the one who named you as an instigator."

"Is she one of Lord Xiang's peasants?"

"Yes."

"Well, there you have it, Yoshi. Lord Xiang has been a rival of mine since he was granted his fiefdom, and unfortunately, next to mine. He envies our prosperity."

"Why would this Utana Miso name you?" asked Utang.

"Is it not obvious? She was put up to it by Lord Xiang, himself."

"Lord Xiang is currently receiving punishment for his incompetence," said Utang. "Eugenesis. Prove to me that you have nothing to with these uprisings, and I will return to remove both Lord Xiang and Utana Miso as problems for you. Permanently."

"How can I prove a negative to you, Yoshi?"

"The results of my search of your manor will be a good start."

"What do you expect to find?"

"If you are speaking truthfully, Talbo, which I hope you are, then nothing. Nothing whatsoever."

* * *

There was a tone at Captain Reinhardt's cubicle door. His head swam, awash with exotic alcohol, and his vision blurred, but he rubbed his eyes and struggled to a standing position. He put his hands out, as if doing so would stop the room from spinning. Surprisingly, it did. He felt something soft under his hand and looked down to find a Vampiri escort lying next to him, asleep.

He shuffled over to the door, scratching himself, and pressed the button for the security monitor. The rental was cheap and the room outdated, so a fuzzy black and white image of Ashwani appeared on screen.

He pressed the com button. "What do you want, Ashwani?"

The image and his vision were fuzzy, but he was sure that she looked wounded by his gruff, less than hospitable greeting.

She pressed the button on the outside. "Well, a good day to you too, sir." She paused. "I shouldn't have come."

She turned to walk away, but Reinhardt opened the door. She appeared surprised, and even a little pleased, but she felt sheepish. "I'm sorry, sir."

Reinhardt didn't know why he opened the door or why he felt so badly. He squinted in the dim, artificial light of the dingy hallway. Perhaps it was because Ashwani looked so good out of uniform. "No, please, come in."

He stepped aside, and Ashwani entered his cubicle. She smirked as she saw empty liquor bottles strewn across the furniture. "I see there was an after party." Then she saw the Vampiri.

Reinhardt closed the door to his cubicle, strolled over to the bed, and plopped down on it. The Vampiri stirred for a moment but was not awoken. "What time is it?"

"Eleven hundred," replied Ashwani, choosing to remain standing, but apparently unsure of what to do with her hands. "I-I should go."

"Sit down, Ashwani. You're making me nervous." After she sat in a chair across the room, she leaned forward, rubbing her hands together, eying the sleeping prostitute.

"Want a drink?" he offered.

"No thanks. I think I drank enough yesterday for the next month."

Reinhardt smiled. "Yeah, that was some day, wasn't it?"

"Is Kelso in any trouble?"

Reinhardt shook his head. "Nah. I downplayed the whole incident. Truth is, I acted like an ass."

"The truth is, so did he."

"You held your own, Commander. I'm impressed."

Ashwani raised an eyebrow. "Why, because I'm a woman?"

Reinhardt laughed. "I guess that was kind of sexist."

"Even the Humani regard their women as equals. In some cases as superiors."

"Well, maybe you should ask Kelso out on a date."

Ashwani winced in disgust.

"So, Commander, what brings you to my humble abode?"

I-I just wanted to check on you, to see how you were doing."

"I'm nursing a galactic hangover, but other than that, I'm fine."

"I can see that," she said, shooting a look at the unconscious Vampiri. "And," she added, as if she was summoning the courage to complete her thought, "I was wondering...but I can see that I was mistaken..."

Reinhardt tried his best to suppress his grin. She, for once, was at a loss for words, and she was gripping the arms of the cheap polymer chair as if she was launching from a command carrier without a pod. He knew what she was here for.

"You've come to profess your undying love for me."

This took her off-guard. At first she stammered, then her eyes became fierce. "You know, sometimes you can be a real pig." She stood and turned to walk out.

Reinhardt jumped up and caught her gently by the arm. "Come on, I didn't mean it."

Before he could say anything else, she turned, twisting her arm, throwing him off balance. She grabbed him by his arm and flipped him, sending him crashing down onto the cheap, soft carpeting. His face landed next to a dark stain whose origin he didn't want to contemplate.

"Well, then I guess I didn't mean *that*," she said, standing over him.

She made to leave again, when Reinhardt grabbed her by her ankle and twisted. She tripped and fell forward, landing prone onto the same grimy carpeting, almost smashing her face on the door.

"Come on," he insisted, "I was just trying to push you away."

Ashwani pushed up and kicked him square in the face, ringing his bell. His headache intensified, and his injuries from the fisticuffs the day prior began to reawaken.

"That's how you push someone away." She got up and walked to the front door, opening it.

"These things can get complicated," shouted Reinhardt at her back. "I was playing hard to want. To protect you."

"Maybe it's you that needs protection from me."

She disappeared into the hallway without looking back, and the door closed. Reinhardt massaged his face where she kicked him, smiling to himself. "Ah, Christ. Here we go again."

But, he knew this time was different. Ashwani wasn't just some admiring subordinate who fancied sleeping with the CO. This woman could kick ass, and she knew how to stand up for herself. He was also sure she'd left behind casualties of her own when it came to relationships.

Although he wanted her even more now, he knew that he had to stay away for her own good. His relationships had a way of self-destructing, often with maximum casualties.

Then again, what the hell?

Just then, the Vampiri prostitute awoke and regarded him with smoldering eyes.

"What the hell?" he said to himself as he sauntered back over to the bed.

CHAPTER 8

Marna stepped out from behind the tents, holding a blaster to Pequo. She was too short to hold it to his temple for effect, so she settled for his back. "I have caught the escaped prisoner!"

Lieutenant Votan wheeled around, gun in hand, and saw Pequo with his long arms in the air, his hands up in surrender. "Seize him!"

Mechs and soldiers converged on Pequo, weapons hot, surrounding him and Marna. The Hilalu rebels stood around, not sure of what to do.

"We have his suit," said Votan. "Hilalu, dispose of him."

"And what then?" shouted Marna. "You abandon us to fight the military on our own? What of your promises to help us in our revolution? To give us entry into the mighty Feng Empire?"

Votan considered this for a moment. "Now is not the time, and this is not the place. I must return to round up reinforcements."

"Lies!" she shouted. "You never intended to help the Hilalu! You came here for specs on the Vortex fighter, and now that you have them, you will leave us to fend for ourselves."

There was a rousing in the crowd of Hilalu, making the small squadron of Feng soldiers nervous. Pequo surveyed the camp. All eyes were on him.

Votan smiled. "We have helped you plenty, Marna. This is the gratitude you show us? You must now fight your own civil war."

"You started this civil war! Do you not have the courage to finish it?"

This little fact surprised Pequo. The Feng started the civil war on this planet? And now they were backing out, with the Vortex specs.

"If you wish to join the Feng Empire, you must prove your worth in battle. Overthrow your government, and you will have proven yourself worthy. Until then, I am afraid we must withdraw." Votan looked quizzically at Pequo. "I first have one question."

"I owe you no answers," said Marna.

"No," said Votan, approaching them. "My question is for your Humani captor."

Now it was Pequo who looked confused. "What is it?"

Votan narrowed his eyes. "Why do you not change colors?"

"Excuse me?" said Pequo, but he cursed himself silently. He knew damned well what Votan was referring to. He quickly flashed yellow.

Votan saw it and grinned wider, like a puvercat toying with its prey. "Ah, but your feelings betray you, Humani."

"What is he talking about?" asked Marna, anxious.

"The whole time your Humani captive has been held at gunpoint, he has not changed color. Not even when I ordered his execution."

"So what?" said Marna.

Votan slinked his way closer, shoving his way through the Hilalu bystanders, a predator preparing to pounce. "So, I think the two of you are up to something. What are you playing at?"

A rather tall, slender Hilalu woman standing behind Votan reached around his neck and placed a gun to his temple. "Surprise, frakface."

The mechs and Feng soldiers turned away from Marna and Pequo and trained their weapons on Nakai.

She pulled Votan close. "Make a move, and I blow the precious Lieutenant's Feng brains out the side of his skull!"

Votan dropped his weapon into the dirt, but his expression wasn't that of fear or surprise. He appeared amused. He clapped his hands together. "Well played! A second Humani hiding in the crowd."

Nakai pulled him tighter into her embrace and dug the tip of her gun into his head. "Not a move, Lieutenant. I will blow your head clear off your shoulders."

"No, you will not," insisted Votan, goading Nakai.

"I would not test her resolve," said Pequo.

Votan began to laugh.

"What is so funny?" demanded Nakai, digging the tip of her pistol harder into his skull. However, she suddenly felt the tip of a gun pointed in the center of her back, right over her heart.

"What?" was all Pequo could manage, his eyes bulging in horror.

Nakai looked over her shoulder and thought she saw Lieutenant Votan. "What the frak?" She dropped the tip of her gun away from Votan's head, and he side-stepped her.

"Two can play at this game," beamed Votan, rubbing his temple.

The other Lieutenant Votan smiled wickedly, pressing his weapon into Nakai's back.

"You have a twin?" asked Nakai.

The camp erupted into gunfire as two pilot mechs burst out of the forest and opened fire on the Feng battle mechs. Nakai spun away from the second Votan, his momentary distraction buying her an extra few seconds. He pulled the trigger too late, grazing the other Votan in the shoulder.

"Those are Humani mechs," shouted Pequo to Marna over the uproar as they ran for cover. "Tell your people to attack the Feng!"

Marna gave him a dubious look, unsure if she was able to trust him. Then again, she wasn't able to trust the Feng. That much was clear. She shouted, "Attack the Feng traitors!"

There was a moment's hesitation as the Hilalu were processing everything around them. Grappi was the first to open fire on the Feng. His father and the other Hilalu followed suit, their betrayal at the hands of the Feng a fresh wound.

"Protect the Humani mech!" shouted one Lieutenant Votan.

"We need to get it out of here!" shouted the other Votan.

They scrambled to the tent holding Pequo's flight mech.

"Do the Feng have a ship nearby?" asked Pequo.

"In the forest, just over in the next clearing," said Marna.

"We cannot allow them to load my mech!"

Nakai pursued the two Votans, firing at them through the chaos, but each managed to use panicked Hilalu and Feng soldiers as cover. She looked on as the two Humani mechs stormed the compound, focusing their fire on the Feng battle mechs.

She wondered why two Humani pilot mechs were taking on the larger, better-armed Feng mechs. Was it just a distraction so she and Pequo could get away? Where were their corresponding Vortex fighters?

She stopped dead in her tracks, nearly getting stepped on by a Feng battle mech, when she saw the Humani mechs' markings.

Pequo grabbed Marna, and they ducked and ran through the turmoil as one of the Humani flight mechs turned their attention on the tent housing his flight mech, dispatching the guards with the last of its ammo.

Pequo noticed the markings. "How did my mech get out?" shouted Pequo to Marna.

"What are you talking about?"

"Someone is in my mech! How is that possible?"

"Your mech never left the tent," Marna shouted back.

There was only one way to find out. With the guards taken out, they only had to meander through the battle.

Pequo and Marna reached the tent, and Pequo threw the flap open to find his pilot mech sitting dormant, a dead Feng technician draped over it. He looked like a sleeping child hugging its mother.

While Pequo pondered the fact that his suit appeared to be in two places at once, one of the Lieutenant Votans tackled him from behind, knocking the wind out of him. They rolled in a heap into the tent.

Marna, gun raised, meant to follow, but a hand with a vice-like grip grabbed hers. When she turned to look, she saw it was the other Lieutenant Votan.

She swung at him, but he swung first, connecting with her jaw. Her vision blurred for a moment, and the sounds of the ensuing battle sounded like they were underwater.

Inside the tent, Pequo wrestled with the other Lieutenant Votan. Although Pequo was taller, Votan was freakishly strong and had already gotten within Pequo's reach. So much for the height advantage.

On top, Pequo flailed with his long arms, but Votan gripped him tightly around his waist with his legs, holding him close as he worked Pequo's body from the sides. Pequo was growing tired from trying to pound this little brute and having his sides tenderized.

He needed to get to his suit.

Marna dropped her blaster to the dirt as Votan delivered a kick to her stomach, folding her in half. He unsheathed his saber and brought it down in a kill stroke, but the sword was jerked out of his hand by a powerful force. He looked down to find his right hand missing, a bloody nub in its place.

He looked in horror at Nakai crossing the battlefield, aiming for another shot. He released Marna, who was struggling to fill her lungs with air, and he dashed off towards the bushes as the Feng battle mechs began to retreat with him.

Nakai looked over her shoulder as she saw the two Humani pilot mechs disappear back into the woods from whence they came.

Votan had managed to lay his unnatural grip around Pequo's throat, cutting off his air supply. Pequo flashed yellow, then grey, and then white. Shadows began to creep into the periphery of Pequo's blurring vision, and his eyes watered. He grabbed at Votan's right wrist while balancing on his left hand in the dirt, but he was too weak to pry the Feng off.

Suddenly, Votan's grip vanished, and Pequo no longer felt pressure on his throat. He quickly filled his lungs with air, while

Votan screamed in terror. Where his extraordinarily powerful right hand was, was now a scarred nub.

Pequo crawled over to his mech, and it opened, sensing his presence. He turned himself around and backed into it, slipping inside. The liquid metal, guided by magnets, closed around him, sealing him off from the world. His systems activated, and his weapons heated up.

Outside, Nakai put her arm around Marna as she traded fire with the retreating Feng. There was a roar in the sky as a Vortex fighter zoomed overhead. The Feng mechs ceased their retreat, standing their ground, as Votan and the remaining Feng made for the woods and the Vortex fighter swung back around.

The Feng mechs opened fire, but the Vortex was too fast and agile. It dodged the barrage and opened fire, lighting up the battle mechs on the ground.

Pequo was weak, but he forced his mech to stand. He was out of ammunition, but he would crush that Votan's skull with his hydraulics if necessary. However, when he looked around the tent, Votan was gone.

He ran outside the tent in time to see the Feng battle mechs explode and go up in flames. He looked up at the sky and saw the Vortex fighter overhead.

"Commander Massa," shouted Nakai.

Lieutenant Votan, cradling his bleeding nub, ran onto his ship parked in a clearing not too far from the camp with only three surviving Feng soldiers.

He sat in the cockpit and fired up the engines, opening an encrypted com to planet Feng.

A holographic image of Captain Mongo Utang appeared. "Request permission to utilize the fourth axis to correct the current Spacetime vector."

"Denied," said Captain Utang coolly. "You have already attracted too much attention."

Votan looked down at his bloody nub, using his Feng training to fight off his body's natural reaction to go into shock. "Captain, with all due respect, there will be questions, investigations…this can all be corrected."

"I prefer questions to irreversible artifacts. Besides, you have destabilized Spacetime enough. We will just have to move up the timeline for the Drekaar contingency. Return home, immediately."

Lieutenant Votan dared not buck an order from a captain. Although he missed his hand, his condition was preferable to death.

* * *

Plato observed his team of avatars that he personally hand-selected for the mission to Golgath to work with the Drekaar, fifty-three all-together. He stood back, watching proudly, as they catalogued specs and inventory on metallurgy, elements, components, and dark energy conductors.

One of Fifty-Three approached Plato wearing a holographic spreadsheet and a serious expression. "Sir, we should be ready to load the transport ship to Golgath on schedule."

"Excellent." Plato beamed. One of Fifty-Three didn't return the smile. "Is this not exciting? We are going to be bringing yet another primitive culture into the new eon and space travel. This is a historic moment."

One of Fifty-Three stared at him blankly, waiting to be dismissed so that she could return to her duties of coordinating the cataloguing of inventory.

"Do you not feel it?" asked Plato, stepping forward, placing a hand gently on her arm. She didn't react. He felt her flesh in his grip touching the palm of his hand, but as warm as it was, it was still, lifeless, and shallow as a puddle. Frustrated, he removed his hand and nodded so she could return to her work.

"Plato!" called Garsi Pequo.

Plato turned around and saw the vice president beckoning him with an impatient finger, like a Human would call his dog. He turned and walked over to him. "Yes, sir?"

"Plato, we have the Associated Galactic Press coming to shoot you and your crew preparing for the mission to Golgath."

"Oh. I see."

"I want you to charm the pants off of them, as only you can. There will be Human reporters among them." Garsi frowned with disapproval. "Those parasites are likely going to ask you about Avatars and try to get you to comment on how it is a form of slavery and how unjust it is.

"I want you to highlight how you, an Avatar, are heading up this mission, and what a great honor it is."

Plato managed a smile. "It is a great honor, sir." However, Plato knew he and the other Avatars were being sent to Golgath because they were expendable. It was the ultimate reminder that they were second-class citizens.

"Great," said Garsi, clapping a hand on Plato's shoulder. He then put a finger to his ear, responding to his secretary. "The press are here. Good." He took his finger off his ear, cutting her off. "Plato, remember all of the freedoms you have, privileges beyond what an Avatar is required under The Law."

It was a veiled threat. Frak up this interview, and you will be reduced to that of a normal Avatar. That was, if he even survived the mission.

Before Plato could convey his reassurance, Garsi Pequo dashed away, and the press dashed in, cameras hovering. He recording units were attached to the portable shoulder mounts of the reporters, Independent Eyes, as they were called. Garsi was out of sight, but Plato knew he was monitoring the interaction remotely.

One reporter, a Vampiri, stepped forward. "Privek Sanguar, Frequency 371.978. We are here to document your mission to Golgath." It took a moment before Plato's universal translator chip decoded the series of hisses and throaty, guttural sounds as Privek's eyes glowed red in anticipation.

"Yes, welcome, Privek." The Vampiri were accustomed to being addressed by their first names.

"I'm Harry Harlan from Frequency 3007.129," said a Human reporter, the only Human reporter in the throng. Plato didn't need his universal translator to understand Human. He was well-versed in every Human dialect. This one was Scottish, from the sound of the brogue.

"Welcome, Mr. Harlan." The Humans were traditionally addressed by the prefix indicating their gender and their surname.

"I am Yonhu Hidiri," said the third and final reporter, a fellow Humani, but Plato was sure Yonhu didn't see it that way.

"Welcome, Yonhu Hidiri." First and tribal name, according to tradition. In these modern times, archaic habits died hard. "My name is Plato, project manager on this mission." If he had fooled any of them as being more than an Avatar, his absence of a tribal name in his introduction was a dead giveaway.

"I hope you do not mind if we asked you a few questions about the mission," said Privek, opening the interview.

"Not at all," said Plato. "Ask away."

"What interest does Navigo have in the Drekaar on Golgath?"

"The Drekaar have actually reached out to the Humani to be introduced to space travel. As a member of the United Intergalactic Coalition, the Humani are obliged to help struggling cultures progress technologically, which in turn will catalyze cultural progress and development."

"*Struggling* cultures?" asked Mr. Harlan. "Don't you mean primitive?"

"I, nor any other employee of Navigo, would ever use a xenophobic term like that, Mr. Harlan."

Yonhu flashed orange in annoyance at Mr. Harlan's attempt to put words in Plato's mouth. He, as a natural Humani, was clearly there to cast Navigo in a good light. "I think that what Mr. Harlan is so crudely asking is, are the Drekaar ready for this technology?"

Plato smiled. "They acknowledge the tribal strife on their planet, but they want to be better. They believe, as do we, that space travel will unite the factions on Golgath in a common goal and advance their culture immeasurably."

"So, the Iguani tribes are going to be included in this endeavor?" asked Privek.

"That was not specified," said Plato. "However, it is our belief that the Iguani will want to benefit from the gift of space travel as well."

"Or, they'll be extinguished by the Drekaar with this new technology," said Harlan.

"We will not be providing them with weapons technology," assured Plato. "Only the capability for travel."

"And once they have mastered that," said Privek, "given what we know of the Drekaar's history, what is to stop them from developing weapons technology to go with their shiny new ships?"

"The Drekaar must crawl before they walk," said Plato. "It will take them many eons to learn the basic technology of dark matter conductors, orbifold planes, and such. Any weapons development is very far down the road, if it happens at all."

"But the potential for it is there," said Privek.

"Yes, I suppose it is, but by the time the Drekaar reach that point, their culture may have evolved past the proclivity for war."

"With all due respect, the Humani are quite advanced, as are many of the other UIC member worlds and races, yet we are always on the brink of war," said Privek.

"Point well-taken," conceded Plato. "Yet, just recently, the Feng, a fiercely independent warrior people, have just signed a peace accord with the UIC."

"This mission to Golgath has the UIC's blessing?" asked Yonhu.

Plato nodded. "The Golgath mission has been sanctioned by both the United Intergalactic Coalition and the Humani tribal government."

"Technology has civilized many an unruly people," added Yonhu. "Just look at the Humans."

Harlan knew a dig when he heard one. "I'm sorry, Yonhu, was that a question or a statement? I believe we're here to interview Plato."

"Yes, that is correct," said Privek as Yonhu flashed a burnt orange verging on blood red.

"And this has nothing to do with the United Intergalactic Coalition trying to get hooks into the Drekaar mining operations on Golgath," said Privek. "Because if it is, I am sure the Feng would have something to say about that."

"No," said Plato, "this is not a move to seize the kronite mines. If the United Intergalactic Coalition wanted to do that, it would initiate the Pax Galactus Initiative. I think it is clear that they would rather try to assist the Drekaar less invasively."

"On Earth, we call that nation-building," said Harlan. "In Human experience, we've had mixed results with it, most of them negative."

"I am sorry, are you asking questions or testifying?" said Yonhu in payback to Harlan's earlier remark. "Plato, why are the Humani in the better position to offer such technology to the Drekaar than, for example, the Feng?

"Excellent question," said Plato. "The Humani are doing this under the auspices of the United Intergalactic Coalition for the purpose of assisting struggling cultures. The Feng would only offer their technology for the purpose of adding Golgath to the ever-dwindling Feng Empire. They seek war. We seek peace. It is that simple."

"Some say that the Feng are gaining allies in this and neighboring galaxies," said Privek, "and the Feng would say that the United Intergalactic Coalition is seeking to regulate and tax unstable worlds, reallocating wealth and adding to their over-stretched coalition."

Plato shook his head. "The Drekaar are seeking this technology. Would you rather the Feng give it to them and turn the Drekaar on the rest of the galaxy, Privek? Or would you rather the United Intergalactic Coalition do it safely, in a controlled manner with supervision?"

"This is clearly an important mission," said Harlan. "You are talking about bringing a primitive, warlike race into the future, which is no small task."

"That is correct," agreed Plato, "although I would not choose to phrase it as such."

"So why leave it to a crew of Avatars? Why not send top Navigo brass?"

"Truthfully, Golgath is still an unstable planet fraught with armed conflict between the Iguani and the Drekaar. Navigo did not think it wise to risk Humani managers and engineers in such a precarious setting."

"I am sure every aspect of the operation will be supervised remotely by Humani Navigo engineers and managers," said Yonhu.

"So, Navigo views the Avatars as property rather than Humani lives with rights," said Harlan, cutting in and once again ignoring Yonhu.

"Do you believe in destiny, Mr. Harlan?" asked Plato.

The question took Harlan off guard. He wasn't quite sure how to answer. "Yes. I guess."

"This is our purpose, Mr. Harlan. It is what we were born to do, and we do it happily. We do it to preserve life, not just the lives of Humani employees that would be put at risk, but the lives of the Drekaar who will be improved by this technology. You, as a Human, know that once a world turns its ambitions towards the stars, intra-planetary conflict is dwarfed by comparison."

"Still," insisted Harlan, "it doesn't bother you that you—a living, breathing, intelligent, feeling being—are regarded as mere property? If you know Human history like you claim to, Plato, you also know that it is slavery, and slavery is wrong."

"He cannot feel," said Yonhu. "See how he does not display colors like a Humani."

"He's obviously more than a living android," snapped Harlan. "He's no Frankenstein monster like one of those Feng Cybiotes."

"Mr. Harlan," said Plato, ignoring Yonhu's remark, "on Earth, Humans were captured by other Humans and enslaved. I, nor any other Avatar, was captured. I was not born a natural Humani. I was engineered to work to advance Humani technology."

"But you are a sentient being," insisted Privek.

"A sentient being, yes, but not a natural Humani. However, the Humani have bestowed upon me privileges beyond my Avatar status. I maintain my own domicile, I am free to pursue whatever course of study I choose on my own time, and I am honored to be managing this mission to Golgath, which I would like to draw the focus of this interview back to."

"Yes, of course," agreed Privek and Yonhu. Harlan wasn't satisfied, but he let it go for the moment.

The reporters began to ask questions about the specifics of the mission, the equipment, and the technology, and Plato did his best to answer appropriately while not revealing any of Navigo's sensitive information.

Yet, all the while, in the back of his mind, Plato was stung by Harlan's questioning. He was aware that he was an intelligent being, but he pondered whether or not he had feelings. The fact that the questions, or rather their implications, wounded him was evidence that he felt something, bioluminescent epidermal display or not.

After having their fill of asking questions, the three reporters turned to digitally documenting the work of the Avatar team of engineers. However, they were only allowed a cursory glance. Garsi Pequo re-emerged, offered a couple of pre-rehearsed soundbites, and had security politely see the reporters out of the Navigo building.

When the room was clear, he walked over to Plato. "You did well, you know. You managed their questions tactfully and professionally, even the tough questions about Avatar status."

"Thank you for saying so, sir."

"Do not let that Human get to you. You were absolutely right about being born to do this. You are forever going to change the Drekaar people, and in doing so, you are going to help strengthen the United Intergalactic Coalition and ensure peace."

Plato frowned, looking as if he wanted to say something but was refraining. "May I ask you a question, sir?"

"Of course."

"If I were not born different than the other Avatars, would Navigo have granted me all of the privileges I possess today?"

"Do not ask 'if,' Plato. The fact is that you *were* born different. Go to Golgath and be who you were born to be."

Plato smiled, but it was a sad, contemplative smile. "I will."

* * *

Humani Command Carrier Titan
Debriefing Room
After Action Report

Commander Massa entered the debriefing room on the command carrier Titan to find his squadron ready. They rose and saluted.

He returned the salute. "Be seated." He waited as they sat. When they were settled, he continued. "Lt. Nakai."

"Yes, sir."

"What in the Engineer's name were you thinking, disobeying my order to break off the search for Lieutenant Pequo?"

She and Pequo exchanged looks. "My com unit was malfunctioning, sir, making your order inaudible. In the meantime, I got a reading on Pequo's flight mech suit. It was in the vicinity, so I thought—"

"Your job is not to think," interrupted Commander Massa. "Your job is to follow orders. My orders, to be precise."

"They were inaudible, sir."

"Even so, Lieutenant, if you had located Lieutenant Pequo's mech, you should have called in the coordinates. We are not mobile infantry or marines."

"Once again," said Nakai patiently, "my com unit was malfunctioning. I was unable to call in the coordinates, sir."

Massa eyed her expectantly, as if she would display a tell that would reveal her lie. Nakai's skin maintained its normal hue. No flashes or microexpressions. This was because she was primarily telling the truth. Mostly.

He looked down at his digital display, reviewing Nakai's and Pequo's reports. Then he looked up, but this time at Pequo. "According to your report, that Hilalu woman, Marna, and her faction took you prisoner."

"She was operating under the assumption that the Feng were there to help the Hilalu with their cause," said Pequo.

"That is not what I asked you, Lieutenant," snapped Massa.

"Yes, sir," said Pequo. "That is correct."

"And when you were led back to their camp, you found them working under the direction of a Feng officer."

"Yes, sir. Two Feng officers. Twins."

Massa, this time, addressed both Pequo and Nakai. "You also reported that there were two Humani pilot mechs that came to assist."

"Yes, sir," they both answered.

"Were you able to identify which squadron?"

Pequo and Nakai looked nervously at each other. "Yes, sir."

"Which was it?"

"The Razor's Edge, sir."

Massa shook his head, consulting his digital report again, pressing buttons. "That is impossible. All Vortex pilots in the escort were accounted for except for you two."

"We saw the insignia on the mech suits, sir," added Pequo.

"And where do you suppose these mech suits went, Lieutenant?"

"I do not know, sir," replied Pequo.

Massa looked at Nakai. "I do not know either, sir."

"They could not have disappeared into the forest," pressed Commander Massa.

Both Pequo and Nakai were silent, unable to offer up any further explanation. They didn't dare bring up the familiar markings on the mechs, their markings to be precise.

"What is to become of Marna?" asked Pequo.

"She is going to be processed as a criminal, aiding and abetting the Feng in a subterfuge against the United Intergalactic Coalition," said Massa.

"Permission to speak freely," said Pequo.

Massa paused, placing his digital display down on the podium, and then he nodded. "Granted."

"The Hilalu camp was more refugee than insurgent," said Pequo. "They were displaced people trying to survive. These were not soldiers."

"These refugees shot you down, Lieutenant," reminded Massa.

"Once she realized that the Feng were only interested in my mech suit, Marna helped Lieutenant Nakai and I escape the Feng."

"This is true," said Nakai. "She did help us fight the Feng so that they were unable to obtain Lieutenant Pequo's suit, sir."

"Yes," said Commander Massa. "A suit that should have been destroyed rather than obtained by the enemy."

"I was unable to, sir," said Pequo. "I was separated from my suit before I could initiate the self-destruct sequence."

"Your suit's data indicates that you ejected," corrected Massa. "You were not separated, as you say." Pequo said nothing in reply. "Just as diagnostic scans of your fighter indicate that your com unit was not entirely defunct," Massa said to Nakai.

"However, as much as you both broke protocol, your doing so revealed a covert Feng presence on the planet, information that will likely be reported to the UIC Foreign Council to use in their negotiations with the Feng Emperor, Hiron.

"My only question is, why are the Feng so interested in a Vortex pilot mech suit? Their flight and weapons technology are superior to ours," said Commander Massa. He pondered the point for a moment.

"And Marna?" pressed Pequo.

"Her assistance will be taken into account at her hearing. That will be all on that matter as far as the both of you are concerned.

"In the meantime, as per protocol, you are both to submit to mnemonic review immediately in Neuroscience before we return to the Resilience. Dismissed."

Lieutenants Pequo and Nakai stood, saluting Commander Massa simultaneously. "Yes, sir."

Massa saluted back and left the debriefing room in a hurry.

Nakai turned to leave, but Pequo grabbed her by the arm. "Thank you for saving me back there."

She flashed him a salacious grin. "You owe me, big time."

"Nakai?"

"Yeah."

"You ever think we are fighting on the wrong side sometimes?"

Nakai punched him hard in the arm. "That is your problem, Pequo. You think too much."

As she took off down the corridor towards her bunk, Pequo stood there rubbing his arm and considering her point.

CHAPTER 9

Golgath System

As Plato's Harbinger-class ship carrying the rudiments for beginning a space travel program exited space fold in the Golgath system, it had left behind its military escort of one Humani battleship and one squadron of Vortex fighters. He and his crew of Avatars were on their own from this point forward.

As they approached the desert planet, he scanned for any signs of hostile activity in the planet's orbit. The scanners indicated that all was quiet, which made complete sense given the Iguani or the Drekaar hadn't ships yet to place in orbit.

"Send a signal down to the Drekaar mining facility on the planet that we have arrived," said Plato to Seven of Fifty-Three, the communications officer.

"We are not in range," answered Seven of Fifty-Three. She saw Plato's quizzical expression. "The atmosphere must be interfering with our signal."

"Very well. Prepare to enter orbit," said Plato. "We will try again once we are within the Golgath atmosphere."

"Acknowledged."

Their large craft was swept up by the gravity of the planet, and Four of Fifty-Three plotted an orbital trajectory that would place them within hailing distance of the Drekaar mining facility. Within micros, they were at the plotted destination.

"Open hailing frequency again," instructed Plato.

Seven of Fifty-Three opened the channel.

Thirteen of Fifty-Three swiveled to face Plato. "We have been targeted," she said with absolutely no fear in her voice.

"Steady as she goes," said Plato, borrowing a Human expression, which did not register with the communications officer. "Have faith," he explained, which only added to her confusion.

Her perplexity was interrupted by a green tone on her screen. "They have stopped targeting us."

"They have signaled us to put down in landing bay four," said Seven of Fifty-Three.

Plato sat back in his chair and smiled. "See, I told you." But there was no acknowledgement from any of his crew. "On screen," he commanded.

The landing bay designated in Drekaari as 'number four' began to slowly slide open as the Humani cargo ship hovered above it. When the ship was able to clear the doors, the Avatars began their descent into the mining facility.

After the landing gear was deployed and the ship was firmly on the ground, One of Fifty-Three powered down the engines.

"Open the cargo hatch," instructed Plato. "One of Fifty-Three, accompany me out into the landing bay. Two of Fifty-Three, you have the ship in our absence."

Each Avatar nodded in acknowledgement of their tasks. Plato stood and walked to the back of the ship, One of Fifty-Three following closely behind. They descended the lowered cargo hatch into the vast, stone-hewn landing bay, their footfalls echoing off the domed ceilings.

Plato was a bit surprised to find that none of the Drekaar were there to greet them.

"Sir?" questioned One of Fifty-Three.

"They are an alien culture," said Plato, "tribal and less evolved in the area of social niceties. They will be here."

As if on cue, a Drekaar skittered into the landing bay flanked by a small security detail. Plato waited in anticipation as they crossed the bay, their clawed footfalls echoing off the domed ceilings. Plato noticed they were unarmed, which is always a good sign, except for their long, curved tails with venomous stingers at the tips.

The one Drekaar in the center of the throng loomed over the Avatars. His eyes flashed yellow, and he spoke to them. The sound was guttural and harsh, and it took a moment for Plato's universal translator chip to register and convey the message in Humani.

"Welcome, Humani, to the Drekaar Tribe's mining facility. We have been expecting your arrival. I am NakBak, Chief of Security at the mining base."

Plato bowed courteously. "I am Plato, Avatar of the Humani people and director of this project."

"Come with me," said NakBak. "The Chieftain and Council of Elders awaits. They are eager to discuss the project with you."

'So much for small talk,' thought Plato. He only nodded. NakBak, however, was apparently unfamiliar with the meaning of a nod. "Very good," added Plato.

NakBak clicked in response, and the Drekaar turned to walk back into the complex, Plato and One of Fifty-Three following. Plato was tense with excitement. However, when he looked over at his first officer, she appeared android-like. This made Plato sad, that his sister Avatar was unable to enjoy the significance of this visit.

They exited the landing bay and entered a long, stone tunnel with red, circular lights lining the sides. As they wound their way through the complex, the group passed various rooms leading to other tunnels—kronite mines, no doubt. Within these rooms, or caves as they could be more accurately described, were other Drekaar. These Drekaar were plain in appearance, but as hulking as Plato's security escort—they were worker drones.

Finally, Plato and One of Fifty-Three were led to a vast room with no furniture in it. Lining the walls, sitting on the ground, were what Plato took to be the Drekaar Tribal Council, and directly across the room from the entrance sat what must have been Chief RagnakTok. Plato had read about him in the information brief on their way here.

NakBak stopped towards the center of the room and announced the guests. "Chieftain RagnakTok, this is the Humani Avatar Plato and his assistant from Humana."

All at once, the Drekaar around the room rose on their haunches and pounded their claws on the ground. RagnakTok raised a massive claw in the air, silencing them immediately. They all sat in response.

The chieftain began to speak, and it came out as grunts and chittering, a non-humanoid alien phonology. Plato's universal translator applied its translation using a very limited library of known Drekaari texts, adapting and extrapolating as it registered more Drekaari speech. "I am RagnakTok, Chieftain of the Drekaar Tribe. Welcome to our mining facility. We are pleased that you have come all this way to teach us the inner workings of space travel vessels."

Plato bowed politely. "The honor is mine, Chief RagnakTok." He struggled with the pronunciation, as Humani tongues weren't equipped to speak fluent Drekaari, but the Chief didn't look offended. "We are excited for your people's endeavor to initiate space travel."

"As we, too, are excited," said RagnakTok. "Our people have dwelled too long within the confines of our world, our struggle with the Iguani being an unwelcome distraction from greater things. We seek knowledge greater than our limited experience. We seek to travel to other galaxies so that we may open trade with various other peoples."

"An honorable intention, indeed," said Plato.

RagnakTok's eyes flashed yellow as he appeared to be watching One of Fifty-Three carefully. "What manner of creature is this, like you but different? Is this your woman?"

Plato smiled. "This is not my woman, specifically. She is an Avatar woman."

"Are there more like her in your crew?"

"Yes." Plato sensed a strange tone, even through the universal translator. "Is that a problem?"

RagnakTok chittered, and the chittering spread around the room from Drekaar to Drekaar in a wave. The chieftain pounded his claw on the ground, and the noise immediately ceased. "We Drekaar do not work side by side with our women. They serve to birth our young and then are eaten for sustenance when they can no longer bear anymore."

This time even One of Fifty-Three reacted by shifting uncomfortably. Plato cleared his throat and chose his words carefully. "Great Chieftain of the Drekaar, my crew is partially composed of women Avatars who are essential to the success of this project. Their knowledge is great, and they wish to help the Drekaar succeed in their goals for space travel. It is my sincere hope that their presence will not offend you."

RagnakTok made a few inaudible clicks that the universal translator didn't pick up, and there was chittering in the chamber once more. Once the chittering died down, RagnakTok spoke again. "Their presence here will be tolerated, but they are not to enter our tribal village."

"I will respect your wish," said Plato.

"I also only want to deal with you, a male of your species."

"That is fine," replied Plato. "My crew can remain in the facility you designate for the project."

RagnakTok made a sound that Plato assumed was approval. "NakBak will assign a detail to help your crew unload and set up. We have a great space designated for your work on this project. In the meantime, I invite you to join me for (an untranslatable word) meal in our village as we discuss our prospects together."

Plato smiled. "That would be a pleasure, Chief RagnakTok. I am honored by your invitation. May I send my project manager with your detail to rejoin the crew?"

"I do not think that is a good idea," interjected One of Fifty-Three, showing signs of concern in an uncharacteristic emotive display.

Plato held up a hand. "I will be fine, woman."

One of Fifty-Three was taken aback. If she were a natural Humani, she would be offended. However, she saw that RagnakTok was watching their interaction carefully, gauging it.

She decided to play along. "Yes, Alpha Male. I will do as you instruct."

'Alpha male?' Plato mouthed silently.

One of Fifty-Three shrugged her shoulders.

"Good," boomed RagnakTok. He chittered at NakBak, which translated as instructions to take the female Avatar back to the ship, being careful not to make physical contact, and assist the team in unloading their equipment. NakBak, in turn, designated another, called GrakLok, to take her.

One of Fifty-Three left with GrakLok, but NakBak remained with RagnakTok and Plato. He produced a helmet and held it out to Plato. Its visor was opaque. "You must put this on," said NakBak.

Plato looked dubiously at RagnakTok.

"It is to keep the path to our tribal a secret from outsiders," answered the chieftain.

"I do not mean any disrespect," said Plato, "but I have already ascertained its location on my ship's computer."

RagnakTok chittered. "You know it from the sky, but not from the ground. Please, do this in respect of our tribal tradition. Seeing our tribal village is not an honor often bestowed upon off-worlders."

Plato nodded and took the helmet from NakBak. He looked at RagnakTok, who eyed him expectantly, and couldn't help but feel as if this so-called tradition served to prevent him from knowing how to return as much as it was to conceal the village's location.

He gingerly placed the helmet on his head. It was oversized for a Humani Avatar, and it swiveled around on his crown.

"It is very large," said Plato from under the helmet.

NakBak reached a claw over and touched a button on the side of the helmet, activating a magnetic pulse, and the helmet suddenly shrink-wrapped itself around Plato's head.

Reflexively, Plato reached up and grabbed the helmet in his large hands as he heard a muffled chittering around him. If he had the ability, his skin would've been furiously flashing colors. He frantically clawed at the suffocating covering, but to no avail.

Overcome with panic and suffocated by the darkness, Plato succumbed and blacked out.

* * *

Back on the Resilience, Commander Massa stood outside Captain Reinhardt's office, waiting patiently, curious as to why he was summoned regarding Pequo's and Nakai's mnemonic scans and why it garnered the attention of the captain.

There was a tone and the door to Reinhardt's office opened. "Come in," shouted Captain Reinhardt.

Massa entered the office and saw Captain Reinhardt sitting behind his desk and Lieutenant Commander Washington, CO of Pneumatic Scans and Records, sitting in one of the chairs in front of the desk.

Massa saluted them both. "Good to be serving under you again, sir. Congratulations on your performance at the Armada War Games."

Reinhardt saluted back. "Thank you, Commander. It's good to have you back on the Resilience. Have a seat."

Massa took a seat in the chair to the left of the neurologist as the door to the office swished closed behind him.

"I believe you know Dr. Washington," said Reinhardt.

"Yes, sir. I do."

"I summoned you here because Dr. Washington reported some unexplainable but interesting findings regarding Pequo's and Nakai's mnemonic scans."

"Yes, sir."

Reinhardt looked at Washington, who then keyed up his digital report. "As you know, Commander, the mnemonic chips surgically implanted into the limbic system codes all memory according to the subject's experience as interpreted by their senses, filtered through their cognitions and emotions."

"Yes, sir."

"Well, perhaps you can help Captain Reinhardt and I make sense of these results regarding what happened on Planet Aquilassi."

"Of course," answered Massa.

"When we reviewed the mnemonic data streams, we came across something of a discrepancy between the reports of members of your squadron as to what occurred when Lt. Pequo was captured by the Hilalu insurgents and Lt. Nakai attempted to rescue him.

"The streams indicated that Pequo and Nakai were taken into custody by a Feng Lieutenant Votan, who proceeded to slaughter the Hilalu and take both Pequo's and Nakai's flight mech suits aboard a small stealth vessel. Pequo and Nakai were then taken to an undisclosed location."

Massa sat there, stunned, processing the data that was being relayed to him. "That is impossible. They never left the planet. I found them at the Hilalu camp only a couple of hours after I lost contact with Lieutenant Nakai.

"It does, however, explain part of their report about a Feng presence in the Hilalu camp."

"It gets worse," said Reinhardt.

Washington furrowed his brow. "The mnemonic data streams get more interesting. They indicate that both Pequo and Nakai were interrogated by this Lieutenant Votan about unlocking the specs of our Vortex fighters. After the interrogations that bordered on torture, Pequo and Nakai staged an escape from their confinement, reacquired their mech suits, and stole a small craft aboard what looked to be the Feng command carrier. It was the very same small craft that took them from the planet."

"I see," said Massa, not knowing what to say. The whole story was unreal, ridiculous even.

"Wait, that's not the best part," said Captain Reinhardt.

"The data streams then unravel for a bit," continued Washington. "When they become intact again, they show Pequo and Nakai back on Aquilassi, storming the Hilalu insurgent camp. One of two Votans was killed. You, Commander, then fly over camp in your Vortex and engage the enemy. The other Votan fled into the woods and vanished without the mech suits."

"Then there is another glitch in the data stream," added Reinhardt, "and they pick up where you intercept Pequo and Nakai."

"What's even more interesting than what the memories indicate," said Washington, "is where the memories were found."

Massa looked confused. "I am not sure what you mean, sir."

Washington smiled. "Normally memories are found in the normal regions of the hippocampus where they were encoded consciously. These memories, however, were located in a different location with a brainwave signature indicating unconsciousness."

"As if these were the memories of dreams," said Captain Reinhardt.

"Upon further questioning, while monitoring their brainwaves and skin conductance, it was determined that they had no actual recollection of these events. Even more interesting, when questioned about these events, there were no emotive epidermal responses. No microflashes of colors whatsoever," said Washington.

"I was so uncertain of the validity of the mnemonic scan that was conducted, I conducted another on them. Only the second time, there was no trace of the mnemonic data streams found in the first scan. No Feng ship, no interrogations, no escape. It was as if those memories had never existed. What remained matched up with Pequo's and Nakai's verbal reports precisely."

Captain Reinhardt shrugged his shoulders. "The various scans taken during the Aquilassi mission were collected and reviewed, and there was no evidence of a Feng presence or your squadron leaving the planet at any time. Every ship in the Razor's Edge was accounted for, including the two missing Vortex fighters, Pequo's and Nakai's."

"I am sorry," said Commander Massa, his skin flashing yellow and then white, indicating anxiety and confusion. "I do not think I can help you. I cannot, given what I saw with my own eyes, explain what you have found."

"We want you to submit to a mnemonic scan," said Reinhardt. "Perhaps there's something you are failing to remember, some small detail that would help us make sense of all of this."

"Of course, sir," answered Massa.

"In the meantime, the Razor's Edge is grounded. You are to report to Mnemonic Scans and Records in Neuroscience with Dr. Washington immediately.

"Yes, sir."

"Dismissed."

* * *

Planet Feng
Imperial Palace

Emperor Hiron stood over his kill in the middle of the grand banquet hall when his communicator indicated that he was being summoned. He pressed a button in his ear for audio only. "What is it?"

It was the captain of the orbital guard, a battlespace relegated to Feng armada guarding the planet. "The UIC inspectors have arrived and are requesting permission to enter Feng orbit."

Hiron silently cursed their timing. "Full security protocol. Surround their ship, search it from top to bottom. Stall them as long as is reasonable, and then some."

"Yes, Your Highness." The call was terminated.

Hiron looked around at his security detail. "Clean this mess up immediately! We do not have much time. There must be no trace of any of this. Understood?"

Lieutenant Klago nodded and quickly dispersed his men, leaving a small security detail of three behind to accompany the emperor.

Hiron hefted his weapon and strode out of the banquet hall, and he made his way back to his personal chambers. He had to change quickly into his battle armor, the ceremonial kind reserved for greeting dignitaries.

Cegnis, covered in blood, was staggering down the hallway. When she saw Hiron, she wept and threw herself at him. "They are all dead! All dead! Ripped to pieces, slaughtered like kungdi!"

Hiron, impatient with the interruption and short on time, embraced her nonetheless. "There, there, Lady Cegnis. Are you all right?" He held her away from him and inspected her bloody form. "Have you been harmed?"

"They stormed the palace! It is not safe!" she bellowed. "We are not safe!"

Just then, Vice Executor Kazar came running down the hallway, eyes frantic, seizing Cegnis in his arms. "Mother of Drago! Cegnis, are you hurt?" The blood on her gown stained his politician's robe.

"She appears unharmed," said Hiron.

"What has happened?" demanded Kazar. "Who were these marauders?"

"We cannot go into it now," said Emperor Hiron. He leaned in close to Kazar. "The inspectors are entering orbit as we speak."

The vice executor's eyes widened further as he gasped. "Now? Right now? The palace is not safe? We must turn them away!"

Hiron grabbed Kazar by the front of his robes and slammed the vice executor hard against the stone corridor wall. Cegnis cried out at her husband's assault.

Hiron leaned in so close, his nose pressed up against Kazar's. "You will keep calm and do your job as Vice Executor of Feng. If the UIC inspectors get any whiff of revolution, they will use the Pax Galactus Initiative. The palace will fall, as will the Feng Empire, and we will become a footnote in the history of the United Intergalactic Coalition."

"But, all of the blood! The bodies! What if there are more?"

"This will all be cleaned up," said Emperor Hiron. "Whatever cannot be cleaned in time will be avoided. The inspectors are here to see our weapons development facilities, not the entirety of our palace halls."

Kazar appeared to calm down as Cegnis sobbed, her thin frame shuddering under her blood-encrusted gown. "Yes. They will not see any of this. We have to carry on, for the good of the empire."

Hiron leveled his gaze at his vice executor to impress the importance of his command. Kazar nodded in wordless agreement, and Hiron released him. "We must all get changed and ready to greet the inspectors. We have already wasted precious time with your histrionics."

"Yes, of course, Your Highness," said Kazar, holding his wife.

"Meet me down at the main docking bay," ordered Hiron, and then he stalked off towards his chambers.

The security detail, shocked by the display, hesitated a moment, trading looks of disbelief and horror with Kazar. Then they followed their emperor.

* * *

When Plato awoke, it was sudden and traumatic, like re-birth out of the Aether and into the universe. He gasped for air, clutching his throat. As his mind's racing began to slow and relief washed over him, he realized that he was no longer wearing the helmet.

His vision cleared, and he found himself surrounded by chittering Drekaar in the middle of the Skull Desert, surrounded by crude tents. Chief RagnakTok raised a claw, and the chittering died down until all was silent.

Plato realized he was surrounded by hundreds of Drekaar of various sizes, ranging from hulking warriors to small, crab-like younglings, all watching their chieftain expectantly. The tribal council was there as well, all watching Plato.

RagnakTok addressed the Avatar. "I apologize for the method of your transport, but it is a matter of our tribal tradition and security. How do you feel?"

Plato sat up, rubbing his head, trying to wipe away the massive headache that was raging in his skull. "My head hurts."

"An unfortunate but temporary side effect. You should feel better in a few micros."

Plato nodded and stood. "Is this the Drekaar tribal village?"

"This is one of many throughout the desert," boomed RagnakTok. "This is our main settlement. One hjarok Drekaar live here, despite the constant encroachment of the Iguani."

Plato was unfamiliar with the Drekaar metric, but he assumed that one hjarok was a significant number from the importance that RagnakTok placed on it. "I am honored to be here, Chieftain."

"The honor is ours, Humani Avatar, because you come bearing a great gift to the Drekaar people, something that will help us excel as a culture and escape the backwards oppression of the Iguani."

"I have read much about the Great Drekaar Schism an eon ago," said Plato. "I find it fascinating that you and the Iguani were once one people."

This observation brought much chittering and agitated tail whipping amongst the Drekaar in earshot. Plato became nervous, fearing he had offended his unusual hosts. "If my comment was offensive, then I am truly sorry. I am largely ignorant of your culture, knowing only what history I have been provided by the Humani, through their lens of course."

This last remark seemed to have appeased his hosts, as the chittering and tail whipping died down. RagnakTok's eyes flashed a burning yellow. Plato, used to the epidermal microexpressions of the Humani, was unsure of what this body language indicated. Other than the chittering and tail whipping, there wasn't much to go on. The Drekaar's faces were composed of a hard protein exoskeleton with very few moving parts.

RagnakTok leaned in, towering over Plato. It was either a threatening gesture, or he was about to intimate something important. "Do not fear your misstep, Avatar Humani, for it is a common one amongst out-worlders. Come, join us for YashokTu, and we will discuss the history of the Drekaar in greater detail. It is important that you understand the people you wish to elevate through your gift of space travel."

Plato was not certain what YashokTu was. Either his universal translator chip was on the fritz due to the stranglehold of the helmet, or certain words in Drekaari didn't possess any known translation into Humani.

RagnakTok led the way through the crowd and the tribal council followed, BakTok and GrakLok clearing a path with their security detail. They entered a grand tent that housed a long but squat table. On the table were crude bowls hewn from a dark stone. There were no other utensils. Plato guessed that they were about to break bread together, so to speak. YashokTu was probably a meal.

The tribal council took their places around the table and lowered themselves down to the ground, spreading their crab-like legs beneath them. RagnakTok placed a large claw on Plato's shoulder, carefully tucking his lethal tail behind him, and guided the Avatar to have a seat next to him.

Once everyone was seated, RagnakTok summoned a servant, ordering what must have been various Drekaar dishes, none of which were translated by Plato's universal translator. Plato glanced over his shoulder to see that the security detail surrounded the tent.

"I hope you hunger," said RagnakTok in a rough translation.

"I am famished," answered Plato pleasantly.

"That is a side effect of the shroud," answered RagnakTok. When he saw his reference was lost on the Avatar, he added, "the shroud we placed on your skull."

"Ah, I see," said Plato. "Are we going to eat together?"

"YashokTu is a ceremonial meal that honors guests of great importance," said one of the other tribal council members sitting to Plato's right. "I am WitoDok, Drekaar Elder," he added as an afterthought.

"Pleasure to meet you," answered Plato.

"You asked a question about our history," said WitoDok. "I am the Keeper of Oral History, so if it pleases you, I would like to explain."

Oral historians explained why there were so few Drekaari texts available. Plato smiled. "That would be wonderful, WitoDok."

"Prior to our Civil War, we are indeed many tribes, but under the same Rule of Law, the Code of Kladu, as given to us by our gods. Our gods provide for us on Golgath. They provide our food, the lesser creatures that dwell on Golgath. They provide water in underground wells underneath the sand and rock. They provided the kronite that allowed us to make trade with other worlds.

"An eon ago, there was a tribe called the Dreguani, who were miners of kronite in the Thrashok Mountains, which you may have noticed, run behind the mining complex."

"Yes, I saw," said Plato. A Drekaar servant rounded the table with what appeared to be an inverted, hollowed-out skull of a larger species, pouring a liquid into the stone bowls.

"Kronite, as you know, is used to fuel conductors of dark matter, which propel your starships. While dark matter has been a more recent discovery for your Humani people, the many tribes of Golgath have been aware of its existence from the beginning. It is the matter that makes up our gods, pervasive throughout the universe, enveloping everything. What many races have considered to be empty space in the universe, we have known to be the omnipresence of our gods."

"We Humani refer to the dark matter of the universe at the Aether, which holds a religious significance to us as well."

"You worship our gods?" asked RagnakTok.

"We do not view the dark matter as deities," explained Plato. "However, we perceive it to be the matrix of existence, holding the secrets of the history of the universe."

"You do not believe in the gods?"

"We believe in one we call the Engineer. How many gods do you worship?"

"They are few, and they are many," answered WitoDok. "They are as numerous as they wish to be."

"I see."

WitoDok's eyes flashed a bright yellow, which Plato was now interpreting as an expression of passion or strong feeling rather than offense. "It was deep within the Thrashok Mountains that a Dreguani sect called the Iguani discovered a new element, one that was the opposite of dark matter. It was light matter, much less pervasive, but concentrated and very focused.

"The Iguani miners nearly destroyed their entire sect and levelled the mountains trying to extract it. Once they bore witness to its destructive power, they attempted to brandish it to settle tribal disputes in their favor. Soon, they began to abandon the ways of our gods and revere the light matter as deity.

"Due to the great difficulty and danger in extracting the light matter, their sect was defeated and banished to the outskirts of the desert. The remaining Dreguani buried the light matter under rock.

"However, that was not the last of the Iguani. They returned, attacking the other tribes and trying to regain access to the mines. The remaining tribes united to oust the Iguani, and thus the Drekaar were formed."

"I see," said Plato. "That was the Great Schism. Your explanation was quite enlightening."

There was chittering around the table, another response that Plato was uncertain of the meaning. When the chittering stopped, RagnakTok waved a claw in the air.

Servants approached the table with a large platter containing a serpentine creature with no apparent sensory organs. Another servant filled Plato's stone bowl full of a liquid that reeked of sulfur. The council members around the table began to imbibe their pungent beverages, grasping their bowls in their massive claws. Plato understood why the vessels were hewn out of stone. Any other material would likely have been crushed.

RagnakTok took a large blade and sliced the serpent open, revealing a tangle of smaller serpents writhing inside. Each Drekaar reached out and snatched a small serpent, placing it on the stone plate in front of them. Plato watched as they each snipped off the little serpents' heads with their claws, rendering the creatures dead. He then saw them slurp it up like a Human would a noodle in a disgusting display, saliva and the life juices of the decapitated snakes spraying everywhere.

WitoDok grabbed a serpent from the larger carcass, decapitated it, and threw it on Plato's plate. "Here you go, Humani Avatar."

Plato swallowed hard. If he had the capacity to exhibit epidermal microexpressions, he was sure he would've flashed green. "Are these the offspring of the larger serpent?"

"But of course," chittered WitoDok, as if the question were ridiculous. "The mother serpent is lethally toxic. Do you not have such dishes on Planet Humana?"

"We do not eat the serpents," said Plato. "But, we consume other fauna."

The Drekaar around the table eyed Plato expectantly. He realized, as a matter of good faith, he had to at least sample the Drekaar delicacy, no matter how nauseating. He reached out, picked the decapitated serpent up by its tail, and held it over his mouth, as the other Drekaar had done. He closed his eyes, lowered the neck into his mouth, its leaking juices filling his mouth, and took a bite.

The youngling serpent was surprisingly tender and succulent. Plato opened his eyes and chewed, each stroke of his mandible releasing more lusciousness. "This is very good," he said between chews.

There was chittering around the table, and the Drekaar continued with their supping in earnest, pleased at the Humani Avatar's reception. Emboldened, Plato grabbed his stone bowl and placed it to his lips, letting the liquid slide into his mouth. His eyes bulged, and he aspirated some of the potent beverage, nearly spraying it across the table. As he choked it down, he slammed the stone bowl back onto the table, nearly spilling its contents.

RagnakTok made a raucous noise, and WitoDok patted Plato on his back with his claw. "Drekool is an acquired taste," he said. "It is made from the subterranean pools of Golgathi water. It is the minerals that you taste, something we Drekaar are used to."

"No, no," said Plato, afraid that he had committed yet another offense against his hosts, "it is really not that bad. Its potency just took me off guard."

"But you did enjoy the Pentine?" asked WitoDok, pointing a claw at the serpent.

"Yes, yes, very much," said Plato hastily.

RagnakTok's eyes blazed yellow. "The Pentine are simple creatures. They mate in a process that nearly kills the participants, they give birth to a litter, and that litter is then left to fend for itself in the harsh desert. Some devour their siblings. The survivors, the fittest of the litter, make their way into the world.

"Look at the Pentine. No legs, no claws, their tail possessing no poisonous barb. It is a creature designed solely for propelling itself through the desert, eating, and making more Pentine. Their skin absorbs the heat, which powers their brain and digestion.

"We Drekaar know how we are viewed in the galaxy—simple, barbaric animals."

"No, that is not true," insisted Plato.

There was more chittering around the table as claws opened and closed and tails whipped. Suddenly, Plato felt very ill at ease, and he was reminded why he and his crew of Avatar were sent to Golgath instead of Humani engineers.

CHAPTER 10

The chittering died down as eyes flashed around the table. RagnakTok waved a claw at Plato. "Do not soften what we know to be the truth."

Plato was now beginning to overheat, in part from the oppressive desert climate and in part from the pressure he felt in his present company, the shipbuilding mission weighing on his shoulders. "I did not mean…"

RagnakTok snapped his claws to silence Plato. "We Drekaar do not believe in higher order and lower order creatures, like the arrogant Humani do. They believe themselves to be the greatest creatures in the universe. We believe that every creature is perfectly adapted to its own environment.

"Remember, Humani, that you are less fit for this environment than the Pentine that we eat, as you are more adapted to your planet and the deep cold of space."

Plato wiped his brow. "Chieftain, if I have offended you, I am sorry. It was not my intent to insult your intelligence. Yes, there are Humani who view your people in that way. However, there are those that do not, which is why I am here. I do not view the Drekaar in a negative light.

"I do not practice the xenophobia of my planet's people. In fact…" Plato looked down at the table. His next words were painful for him to utter, but they would either create understanding of his purpose on Golgath or make him appear weak and inconsequential, further outraging the Drekaar as to why such a lesser being was sent for this mission. "…the very fact that I, an Avatar, was sent instead of a Humani is very proof of that xenophobia. I, of all beings, understand how you feel."

"Do you?" pressed RagnakTok, his tail's whipping behind him slowing, his brilliant eyes cooling.

"My masters sent me here half expecting you to massacre me in barbaric bloodlust. I have faith that you will not do so. I believe that we can prove everyone wrong and work together to bring the Drekaar space travel, so that they may stand side-by-side with the other races in the universe and raise their people to new heights.

"I will teach you to adapt to the cold of space, to the dark matter that envelops everything, that very dark matter that you revere as a deity. It is your destiny to travel space. Let me show you how, and together we can prove all those that laugh at us wrong."

RagnakTok fell still, his eyes dim but focused on Plato. "I can see why the Humani sent you, Avatar," he said. "What they see as dispensable, we see as the only one of your planet that understands us. Their perceived loss is our gain."

WitoDok turned towards Plato. "You discuss dark matter as a means for space travel. Explain to us how your dark matter conductors work."

"I am pleased that you have heard of the technology," said Plato, impressed. He figured that this was as good a starting point as any.

"We have heard about it in our limited dealings with the Feng ship builders," said WitoDok. "They, too, purchase kronite from us."

"Think of the universe as a vast ocean," started Plato. However, he realized that there were no oceans on Golgath, and since the Drekaar have never left their planet, they have never seen one. In fact, they would have no concept of one. "May I have a large bowl?"

"A large bowl?" asked RagnakTok. "Do you still hunger?"

"Filled with your beverage, for a demonstration," said Plato. "I beg your indulgence, great Chieftain."

"Get him a large bowl," commanded RagnakTok. Within micros, a large bowl filled with Drekool. Plato scrunched his nose at the odor wafting off the surface.

"This bowl represents the universe," said Plato, skimming his fingers over the surface of the liquid, "and the Drekool is dark matter. The universe is always expanding, which is how our scientists measure the passage of time."

He swept his fingers across the top of the Drekool, creating small, concentric waves. "As the universe expands, so does the dark matter, as exemplified by the waves." He pointed to the concentric ripples. "The dark matter conductors harness the energy displaced from the expansion, and the ship rides the expansion like riding a wave." An image of surfing, a Human recreational hobby on Earth, materialized in his mind.

"It is as if the ships are, by your definition, riding on time itself," said WitoDok.

Plato smiled. "Yes, I suppose so. I have never conceptualized it in quite that way." He saw WitoDok and RagnakTok exchange looks, eyes burning in synchronicity.

"It would seem that these conductors would not allow the ships to go very fast because the waves, as you say, are slow," said WitoDok.

"You possess some knowledge of physics, I see," said Plato, trying hard not to sound patronizing.

"Remember, we revere dark matter," said WitoDok. "What you call 'physics,' we call religion. We are not unfamiliar with the subject matter. We just conceptualize it in our own way, as do you."

"Right," said Plato. "The conductors pull along the dark matter expansion, and can be adjusted for velocity and acceleration. Early space travel relied on rockets, which required ships to carry a limited fuel source. This created problems with heat dissipation, which is limited by the vast coldness of space. These methods became untenable. However, the dark matter conductors run cool, generating nominal heat that is easily dissipated.

"We have even designed small stealth vessels that use dark energy as a camouflage, masking any nominal heat signatures."

"Yes, the Feng also possess such stealth vessels," said RagnakTok. "Hunter-killers."

"Meant to track and destroy our vessels," said Plato, nodding. He was instructed to be more guarded about the details of military vessels by Navigo executives and the Humani government. However, since the Drekaar appeared aware of the existence of these vessels, he believed being a little candid would go a long way.

"The one large limitation of this type of power," added Plato, "is that we cannot come close to achieving light speed. To do so would require a tremendous, focused power source that would generate too much heat.

"Therefore, we rely on something called space fold, a technology that enables ships to fold space itself and create wormholes, tunnels from one part of space to another, crossing large distances using smaller vectors."

"Saving time and space," said WitoDok. "How will we begin this ambitious project?"

"Do you have scientists among you?" asked Plato.

"Mystics who are well-versed in dark matter," said WitoDok.

"First, we will begin by teaching them about the physics of dark matter, as the Humani have conceptualized it. Once that has been achieved, we will begin to construct a rudimentary dark matter conductor."

"How soon until we begin space flight?" asked RagnakTok.

"That all depends on how quickly your mystics learn the technology," said Plato. "This will not be a rapid process. There is much for the Drekaar to learn before we can even consider actual space flight. Your culture will have to accommodate the changes that will occur. Your economy will have to adjust, your other industries integrating into a free trade model."

"Other industries?" questioned RagnakTok. "We have only Kronite."

"Surely, there are other goods or materials your planet has to offer," said Plato. "How else does your people survive?"

"The Drekaar hunt, and we consume what we kill. We provide for the whole tribe. We use the credits earned from our kronite trade to purchase arms to use as defense against the encroaching Iguani."

Plato realized that the Drekaar, up until this point, had been stunted culturally, focused on tribal warfare rather than evolution and advancement. "In order to learn the technology of space travel and trade with other worlds, you will need to build schools. Your people must learn the ways of other worlds, how the balance of trade is conducted, the cultures of other worlds—art, music, religion, recreation. This will all be necessary for the Drekaar to find their place in the universe."

"We will begin by providing kronite to the Humani in exchange for this learning," said RagnakTok. "And we begin our understanding of other cultures by learning from you. This initial interaction has been most enlightening already."

Plato appreciated the chieftain's enthusiasm, but it had never occurred to him that the only commodity that the Drekaar had to offer was kronite. This was a culture that had not achieved a renaissance or an industrial revolution. Every bit of technology they possessed had been given to them in exchange for kronite. They barely had a concept of symbolic currency, because up until this point, they had no need for it except to obtain weapons from off-worlders.

"We are happy to welcome you into our tribal lands to help us," said RagnakTok. "Now that we have finished our feasting, I invite you to partake in a sacred ritual of the Drekaar, the Kanati."

Everyone at the stable suddenly rose from their places and chittered loudly. RagnakTok put a claw on Plato's shoulder, and the chief ushered him out from under the tent.

The blazing sun whitewashed Plato's vision. He placed his hand above his eyes to shield them from the brightness. As his vision cleared, he saw Drekaar clad in battle armor assembling, clutching weapons, their tails whipping and darting excitedly.

BakTok stood in front of them as he inspected his rifle. GrakLok skittered over to Plato, clutching armor in his claws. He thrust it into Plato's arms and backed away.

Plato held the armor up. It looked like it was designed to fit a tall, lanky frame.

"This was a gift from Humani traders," said GrakLok. "A ridiculous gift, as it was not designed for our bodies, but it should serve you well."

Plato nodded in gratitude and slipped the armor on. It was a bit loose, but it fell correctly over his form. GrakLok then shoved an assault rifle into his hands.

"Do you know how to use this?"

Plato looked the weapon over. It was a Feng rifle. He had read about this weaponry, and he had a vague idea of how to operate it. "I think so."

GrakLok's eyes burned bright. "Good. You will follow us. Stay close."

"What are we doing?" asked Plato.

RagnakTok clapped a claw on Plato's armored shoulder. "Where do you think the Pentine came from? Now we hunt for the good of the tribe."

Plato looked lost.

"Surely the Humani hunt on your planet," said RagnakTok.

"They do," answered Plato. "I never have, myself."

"Well, then it appears we will not be the only ones learning something," said RagnakTok. He saw Plato's hesitation. "This is a great honor we bestow upon you, Avatar. It is not our custom to invite out-worlders to hunt with the tribe."

Plato bowed slightly. "Well, then, the honor is mine, Chieftain."

"That is the spirit," boomed RagnakTok. "Who knows? You might land a large, pregnant Pentine. If you are lucky, you might even get to see a Balrok."

Somehow, Plato doubted he wanted that.

RagnakTok slipped on his armor and hefted his rifle. "Drekaar! Our bellies are full, and so we go seek to fill them again!"

GrakLok leaned in close to Plato, his tail poised over his head. "Stay, close, Avatar. You are safe as long as you are with me."

RagnakTok shouted something that escaped the universal translator chip in Plato's skull, and the lot of Drekaar scurried off into the desert. Poor Plato ran to keep up, dodging the whips of Drekaar tails and their venomous barbs through the dust.

* * *

Captain Trevor Reinhardt heard a tone at his door. "Enter," he commanded. It opened, and Commander Ashwani entered and saluted.

"You summoned me, sir."

"Have a seat," he said.

She took a seat in the chair in front of his small desk.

"Have you read the digital mnemonic investigation reports on the Razor's Edge squadron, Commander?"

"I have, sir."

"I just can't make any sense of it. One minute there are these memories directly contradicting the verbal reports of two of the squad members, and the next minute they're gone. Poof. Vanished, as if they never existed."

"Lieutenants Nakai and Pequo have been regularly reporting to psych, as directed," said Ashwani.

"And?"

"Nothing out of the ordinary, sir. No signs or symptoms of amnesia, acute stress syndrome, or anything else."

"How about the cognitive testing and reaction time trials?"

Ashwani shook her head. "All within normal limits."

Reinhardt bit his lip and shook his head. "So where in the hell did these images of Feng soldiers and command carriers come from?"

Ashwani waited, wondering if the question was rhetorical, as she had no way of logically explaining the phantom memories' existence.

Reinhardt pulled himself out of his own thoughts and looked her in the eye. "There's something strange going on, and I get the feeling the Feng are behind it. The United Intergalactic Coalition just struck a deal with the Feng, lifting sanctions in exchange for a cease of all weapons technology development and access to their R&D facilities."

"Yes, sir, it's unprecedented."

Reinhardt snorted and sat forward in his seat. "Unprecedented," he repeated, as if regarding the notion as ridiculous. "It's a joke. The Feng don't make deals with Barberoi. Whatever they will present to the UIC inspectors will be whatever they want the inspectors to see. Window dressing."

"You don't think that the UIC has the Feng on the balls of their feet?" asked Ashwani. "The Feng Empire is falling apart. Their currency has been so devalued, and the gap between the wealthy and poor had widened so that they're prime for a revolution. Perhaps they had no choice but to concede."

Reinhardt's eyes narrowed. "Yes, revolution would mean the UIC enacting the Pax Galactus Initiative, which would be the end of the Feng Empire as we knew it. Perhaps we should've let it implode."

"You think the accord was a mistake, sir?"

"Absolutely. The UIC wanted their hands on Feng technology, so they gave away the store when they should've bided their time."

Ashwani shook her head. "If the UIC waited for them to implode and seized control of the Feng Empire, it would've been accused by many of engineering an autonomous culture's decline. The UIC has already been accused of rattling its imperialist saber."

"Imperialism," scoffed Reinhardt. "Give me a break. There are some cultures, some worlds not fit for autonomy. The Feng are only out for the glory of their empire. They want intergalactic domination, and anyone who stands in their way is the enemy."

"Some within the Feng Empire would disagree with that."

"Oh, really? Just whose side are you on anyway, Commander?"

"The UIC's, sir. It's just that the UIC has to tread carefully."

"Yeah, well, something doesn't sit right with me with all of this, especially in light of these phantom memories. I passed the conflicting reports along to Admiral Renolfo."

"What did she say?"

"Inconclusive and unactionable."

"What do you propose we do?"

"Follow orders, of course, but we have to be vigilant, Commander. If the Feng are up to something, I think that they'll tip their hand soon."

"What do you think will happen?"

Reinhardt sat back in his chair and slowly let out a heavy sigh. "The next Intergalactic War." He eyed his commander, as if he was gauging her reaction, but it wasn't just that. "Are we okay, Commander?"

She cocked her head. "I'm not sure what you mean, sir."

Reinhardt smirked. "You know what I mean, Ashwani. You and I. Are we okay?"

"I have no difficulty carrying out your orders and performing my functions on this ship."

"God dammit, Ashwani—" he started, but their tense little moment was interrupted by a communicator tone.

Reinhardt pressed a button. "What is it?"

"It's Dr. Washington, sir."

"Yes, Washington."

"I have the results of the two assessments of Commander Massa, sir."

"And…"

"The initial assessment revealed memories of engaging a small Feng vessel containing Lieutenant Pequo's flight mech as it was retreating from the planet, contradicting Commander Massa's verbal report. During the re-examination, these memories weren't present, and the log coincided perfectly with Commander Massa's report."

"Forward the reports to me immediately," said Reinhardt.

"Way ahead of you, sir."

Reinhardt activated his digital console and saw that the two reports were already waiting for him. "Thank you, doctor." He terminated the call. "Something stinks about all of this, and it reeks of Feng."

PART III

REACTION

"The Aether? Not for me. It's like some half-assed alien version of social networking. I don't plug in. I joined the UIC Armada to get away from people."

Captain Trevor Reinhardt, Human, United Intergalactic Coalition Armada

CHAPTER 11

Feng Imperial Palace

Bobot Tegrit and Hubritia Liguri gazed upon Planet Feng as their craft, a modest vessel filled with a small complement of various scientists and a small security detail, descended through the planet's atmosphere. Hubritia took note of the violent flashes of color in the atmosphere as various gases and climatic fronts collided.

However, as impressive as the atmospheric displays were, they paled in comparison to the spectacle of the grand Feng Imperial Palace.

"By the engineer," said Bobot.

"It is beautiful," gasped Hubritia, finishing the Humani's thought.

Although there had been brief, orbital glimpses of the palace obtained by surveillance ships and galactic press, the images were taken at a great distance and lacked resolution. This was the first time the palace had been seen up close by outworlder eyes, and the experience failed to disappoint.

The palace stood tall with various jagged turrets jutting out, stabbing the air. The castle itself was formed from cooled magma and encased in a layer of translucent ice, lending a crystalline appearance, like an opulent upside down chandelier. The surface was uneven and wavy, causing various parts of the palace to shimmer depending on the position of the observer.

"Fire and ice," said Hubritia in obvious admiration.

"The perfect metaphor for the Feng," said Bobot.

As the ship descended over the landing bay, a warning sounded from the cockpit. "The Feng are targeting us," said the pilot.

"Of course they are," said Bobot. "Although we are their guests, they are reminding us who is in charge."

"It is a display of dominance," said Hubritia. "Even though we have them at a disadvantage."

"Do not underestimate the Feng," admonished Bobot. "Do not mistaken their warlike demeanor and feudal culture as primitive or weak. They were at one time the most powerful empire in the galaxies for a reason.

"Even now, their apparent concession is a calculation. Hiron is no fool. He will show us only what he wants us to see. It is up to us to see through the smoke and mirrors and probe for the truth of things."

The United Intergalactic Coalition ship descended into the designated landing bay, the doors above closing slowly above them, shutting out the pinnacle of the jagged castle impaling the churning sky.

After a soft landing, the cargo doors opened, and Bobot motioned for the security detail of UIC Marines to follow him off the ship.

"Are you ready, Hubritia?"

Hubritia nodded that she was ready, and the throng exited the ship together. The engineers and scientists remained on board, as was universal protocol, until the UIC dignitaries were properly received and permission was granted for the inspectors to leave the ship to begin their work.

Bobot noted that they were greeted by Palace Guard, rather than the fearsome Cybions. It was a good, diplomatic choice.

"Welcome, Bobot Tegrit of Humana and Hubritia Liguri of Firenz," bellowed a voice from behind the guard. The guards parted, and a high-ranking Feng official stepped into the light. Although he must have been important, he was no warrior, as per his politician's robe instead of battle armor.

"I am Monsu Kazar, Vice Executor of the Feng Empire." He bowed slightly, a gesture of hospitality; a deeper bow would signify subjugation, which the Feng never entertained.

"Greetings, Vice Executor Kazar," said Bobot, taking the lead. "We are indeed warmed by your hospitality."

Hubritia, unaccustomed to the frigid climate, was shivering.

"Welcome to Planet Feng," Vice Executor Kazar said, smiling. "This is truly a historic moment, and hopefully the beginning of a fruitful relationship between the Feng and the United Intergalactic Coalition."

Hubritia bowed slightly. "That is our wish as well."

"Emperor Hiron wishes to greet you in the Imperial Throne Room, if that is to your liking."

"We look forward to meeting him," said Bobot.

"Follow me," said Vice Executor Kazar. "I, however, must respectfully request that your security detail remain behind with your ship. I assure you that you are quite safe."

Bobot and Hubritia exchanged glances. Bobot knew that if he insisted on bringing the UIC Marines, that it would be received as an insult, setting the first inspection off on the wrong foot. He also knew that if anything were to happen to himself or Hubritia, the United Intergalactic Coalition would waste no time invading the planet and exercising the Pax Galactus Initiative. He also knew that the vice executor and Emperor Hiron knew this.

"Of course, Vice Executor," replied Bobot. "We trust you implicitly."

"Very good. So, it is settled," said Vice Executor Kazar, obviously pleased. He turned and began to leave the hangar. The Palace Guard parted to allow Bobot and Hubritia to follow, closing ranks behind them as they walked away from the ship, separating them from their UIC security detail. Bobot looked over his shoulder and saw that a small detail of Feng guards remained behind with the ship.

"Your palace is gorgeous," said Hubritia, attempting to defuse any tension as they traversed long, dark rock-hewn corridors illuminated by electric torches.

"Yes, it is quite a marvel of construction," added Bobot.

"Thank you," said Vice Executor Kazar. "There is none like it in the known universe. I think that you will find there is much beauty on Feng." He gazed at Hubritia in apparent admiration. "Although we are a warrior culture, we too appreciate beauty."

"You are also quite established in the science of ship building," said Hubritia, paying an honest compliment.

"Yes, which is why the United Intergalactic Coalition seeks to learn our trade secrets," said Kazar. Then, seeing Bobot frown and Hubritia tense up, he added, "Which is completely understandable. Perhaps your becoming familiar with our ways will help bring us closer."

"Yes, that would be nice," agreed Hubritia.

"This palace is very labyrinthine," marveled Bobot, his skin flashing yellow.

"As per Feng design," said Kazar, noting the Humani's anxiety. "It keeps unwanted guests out and protects the Holy Emperor."

"Yes, I suppose," said Bobot, realizing that the marines back at the landing bay would have some task finding them if needed. He also guessed that the rock and hardened magma would dampen the signal of their hidden homing beacons.

"Are your governmental buildings on Humana as complex?"

Bobot shook his head, his skin flashing orange for half a micron. "Not in this sense. More so in a technological sense."

"Ah, yes," said Kazar. "Humani electronics, superior to ours."

"I did not mean to imply…"

"No, it is a fact," said Kazar. "While our ships are superior to yours, your electronics are the pinnacle of quality."

Hubritia saw that this exchange had the potential of degenerating into a pissing contest between the two cultures, so she interjected. "Firenz has neither superior ships, nor electronics, so I feel rather left out."

There was uncomfortable laughter all around. Kazar led them around a corner and to an elevator. He placed his palm over a sensor, and the doors opened. Kazar extended a hand, gesturing for them to enter. "This elevator leads to the Imperial Antechamber."

Bobot and Hubritia hesitated for a moment, noticing that Kazar was stepping back, implying that he wasn't joining them. Kazar, detecting their discomfort, smiled. "It is a basic security measure. A full body scan as you rise. If you were carrying any weapons, the elevator would stop, and security protocols would be enacted."

Bobot returned the vice executor's smile. "Well then, I am glad we are not carrying any weapons today."

He entered the elevator, and Hubritia followed.

"I will see you upstairs shortly," said Kazar as the doors closed. There was a tone, and the elevator began to rise. As they ascended, the United Intergalactic Coalition dignitaries were scanned for weapons and contraband, the scan illuminating their hidden homing beacons as they passed over them.

The inspectors were silent, knowing that any conversation would be monitored. When the elevator reached its pinnacle, the interior turned green, and the doors opened.

They exited the elevator, entering a vast antechamber, as Vice Executor Kazar had indicated. There were two guards standing in front of an open doorway.

"Continue through," instructed one of the guards.

Bobot and Hubritia did as instructed and passed through the doorway into what was the Imperial Throne Room.

If Hubritia was impressed by the sight of the exterior of the castle, she was absolutely awestruck by its Imperial Throne Room. A massive cavern hewn in cooled volcanic rock, it appeared as if the chamber was housed in the largest, central turret of the palace, a jagged spike piercing the sky.

"By the Engineer," gasped Bobot.

"Yes," agreed Hubritia.

At the far end of the cavern was a massive throne also hewn from rock, its back shaped like a dragon flying vertically, and Emperor Hiron sitting in it. The throne engulfed him, and the rock glowed red as if hot, yet Hiron sat comfortably.

A small detail of Palace Guard intercepted the inspectors. "The emperor has been eagerly awaiting your arrival," declared one of the guards. "Follow us."

"Of course," replied Bobot. He and Hubritia followed the escort across the chamber. They drank in all of its ornate detail. Stunning reliefs retelling grand battles of bygone wars lined the walls, as did suits of Feng armor from various dynasties standing guard, massive and looming, casting shadows over the two inspectors as they passed.

When they reached the throne where Hiron was waiting, the Palace Guard parted, flanking the two guests and allowing the Holy Feng Emperor to gaze upon them.

"Welcome, honored guests," said Hiron rather imperiously, playing the role. Although this inspection was forced upon him, these inspectors were in his palace, and he would not appear weak in his own palace.

Bobot bowed his head slightly. Hubritia followed suit, although she appeared more dubious about committing to such a gesture. The Firenzi bowed to no one.

"We thank you for receiving us on such short notice and thank you in advance for your kind hospitality," said Bobot, his skin exhibiting no microexpressions.

Surprisingly, Hiron bowed his head slightly in return, a great gesture of humility for any Feng, let alone the Holy Emperor himself. "We are honored and pleased to have you as our first off-worlder guests inside the Feng Palace."

"The honor is ours," said Bobot.

"It is stunning," said Hubritia. "One wonders how such a marvel was ever constructed."

Hiron smiled at the compliment. "This palace was formed by the cooling of liquid magma when our planet was more unstable. It is a testament to our violent beginnings as a people and how far we have progressed as a culture."

There was a brief flash of color from Bobot, a color Hiron couldn't place. "Does this amuse you, Bobot Tegrit?"

"Not at all," lied Bobot.

Hiron wondered why the United Intergalactic Coalition sent a Humani. Was it their arrogance in assuming the lead on this operation? Perhaps they wanted him to see the microexpressions as a matter of psychological manipulation.

"It is my hope that during this visit, you will both come to learn something about Feng culture and our history and return to your worlds and the United Intergalactic Coalition with a greater understanding of who we are."

"We look forward to the opportunity," said Hubritia.

"However, our prime purpose here is to inspect Feng weapons development facilities and open the books on your ship-building technology as you agreed to, Emperor Hiron," said Bobot.

"All business," said Hiron, amused.

"We look forward to beginning our work as soon as you grant permission," said Bobot.

A Palace Guard twitched, as if receiving a message inside his helmet. He nodded to himself and stepped up to the throne. He whispered in Hiron's ear and then retook his place in the guard.

"Your team has passed our security inspection," said Hiron. "They may begin their work. We ask, however, that your team of marines remain on board the ship under our guard for the remainder of your visit."

"Out of the question," said Bobot.

"I assure you, Bobot Tegrit, that you and your team of inspectors are perfectly safe."

"We received the same assurance from your charming vice executor," said Bobot, flashing orange.

"It is not that we feel unsafe," lied Hubritia. "We know that any harm that would come to us would constitute an act of war." Her explanation carried with it a threat. "It is part of our very own security protocol."

"No such protocol was agreed to in the accord," stated Hiron.

"It appears that we are at an impasse," said Bobot Tegrit. "Not a good beginning in our working relationship."

Hiron paused, in deep consideration of the dilemma before him. "They may accompany your inspectors, but they will do so unarmed."

"I hardly see the point," said Bobot.

"That is my final concession," said Hiron. "I hardly think that the United Intergalactic Coalition would allow Cybions in the presence of their top administrators."

Bobot looked at Hubritia, who nodded her approval. He flashed orange and then silver. "Very well. We wish to join them immediately."

Hiron looked perplexed at this remark as Vice Executor Kazar entered the chamber, his point of entry unknown. He stood at the foot of the throne on the bottom step but one step above the inspectors.

"Out of the question," demanded Hiron.

Bobot flashed orange and then a shade of burnt orange, followed by silver. "You will not allow us to rejoin our group?"

Vice Executor Kazar smiled. "We were hoping that, while your team commenced their work, that the both of you would join us for a ceremonial ritual at the Feng Temple, followed by a feast in your honor."

"We have gone through much trouble in preparation for your arrival," said Emperor Hiron. "Please allow us the honor of welcoming you as proper guests."

Hubritia placed a hand on Bobot's shoulder, and she answered for him. "We would be delighted."

Bobot flashed orange, shooting her a look, as if she overstepped her role, but Hubritia paid him no attention.

"Excellent," said Hiron. "Vice Executor Kazar will show you to your quarters."

"We will need to retrieve our things from our ship," said Bobot.

"That will not be necessary," said Hiron. "I have already provided everything you will need. Clothing, toiletries, and Humani hygienic products."

"You are too kind, Emperor," said Hubritia.

"Come with me," said Kazar, nodding to one of the guards. They fell into formation behind the two inspectors, and they all followed Kazar back to another elevator off to the left.

* * *

"I hear that the United Intergalactic Coalition Inspectors have arrived and are at the palace," said Lord Talbo Cyclesse.

"You seemed displeased about it," said General Yoshi Utang.

"I am distressed that we have outworlders setting foot in the Holy Emperor's palace and his general is out in the countryside with a full complement of Cybions to terrify helpless villagers."

"I assure you," said Utang, "the Imperial Palace and your sister are perfectly safe. And the villagers involved in these uprisings are far from helpless."

"With outworlders inspecting our weapons facilities, do you not have more pressing matters than a bunch of rioters?"

"I was instructed by the emperor himself to squash these riots. If the UIC ever got any wind of civil unrest on Feng, they would be here with a full armada ready to shove the Pax Galactus Initiative down our throats, ending an era of independence and prosperity."

Talbo chortled. "Wake up, brother-in-law. The Feng Empire has not prospered in quite some time."

"Careful, Talbo. That is treason you utter."

"It is merely fact, Yoshi. You live in the past. The glories of Feng military and armada are long past. We are living in the decline of the empire, and the coalition hovers overhead like winged Graveng searching for carrion."

Yoshi wanted to respond, but his helmet indicated a message from Captain Fero Idoni. After listening, he replied, "We will be right there."

"What is it?" asked Talbo.

"It appears my captain has found something in your stable. Please join me."

Talbo looked genuinely surprised and upset. "This is ridiculous! What could he possibly—?"

"Please, join me," insisted Utang. "I am sure we can clear this all up quickly."

Talbo knew that he had no choice. "Yes, let us resolve this quickly so that I may accept your apology and we can move on from this unpleasantness."

Utang gestured for Talbo to go first, and he followed. They left the manor and crossed the beautiful grounds, fields covered in Dragon Poppies and frosted grass, rolling hills, and scattered hot springs heated by subterranean magma flows.

When they reached Lord Talbo's stables, they found a detail of Cybions standing guard, still like statues but ready to explode in violence at either Utang's or Captain Idoni's command.

They entered the stables and meandered past mechanical plows and other agricultural equipment, past stables of Hurathi steeds and mares, and they found Captain Idoni standing in front of bales of tall Dragonweed. However, the bales had been moved and ripped apart, and lying at Idoni's feet were a pile of red shrouds, capes, and masks as well as an opened cabinet of assault rifles with Talbo's manor symbol stamped on them.

"I found this here," said Captain Idoni.

"Explain," Utang commanded Lord Talbo.

Talbo looked horrified. "I do not know what these are or how they came to be in my stable."

"Do you know what these are?" asked Utang, barely containing his anger. He had hoped that he would have been able to clear Talbo and move on to other leads. Now he was faced with arresting his brother-in-law for high treason.

"No, I have no idea," demanded Talbo.

"These are the disguises worn by the traitors when they attacked the Emperor's collectors of tribute."

"I assure you, broth—"

"Do not call me 'brother-in-law.' How could these have found their way into your stable without your knowledge?"

"I-I don't know what to say, Yoshi!"

Utang gritted his teeth together and looked away from Lord Talbo in disgust. "I cannot believe that I am about to say this…Lord Talbo Cyclesse, you are under arrest under suspicion of sedition and high treason against the Feng Empire and Holy Feng Emperor Hiron."

Suddenly, there was an eruption of violence outside the stables, as shouts and gunfire filled the air.

"What is the meaning of this?" demanded Utang.

Idoni nodded and ran to peek outside the stable. He quickly returned. "General, the manor hands are attacking the Cybions."

"Command them to stop!" said Utang.

"I have been set up!" shouted Talbo back.

"Do you want the Cybions to return fire?" asked Idoni of General Utang.

"Talbo, call them off," said Utang, ignoring Idoni. "If you do not, they were be butchered by the Cybions!"

"We are not your enemy!" implored Lord Talbo. "This is a conspiracy!"

"Sir," pressed Idoni, "do you want the Cybions to return fire?"

"Call them off, Talbo! Now!"

"I must protect myself, Yoshi!"

"Sir?"

Utang growled in frustration and nodded to Idoni. Idoni gave the order.

"No, Yoshi!"

"Talbo, you just sealed your manor's fate. Your servants will die horribly, and their blood will be on your hands."

There was a blast that shook the stables, and parts of the roof caved in, separating General Utang from Lord Talbo Cyclesse. Talbo seized the opportunity afforded by the chaos to snatch up an assault rifle. He fled deeper into the stables as Idoni opened fire on him.

"No!" shouted Utang, slamming his hand down on Idoni's rifle, causing him to miss. "We take him alive!"

"He is a traitor!" insisted Idoni.

Utang grabbed him by his chest plate and shook him. "He is Regana's brother! We take him alive!"

Idoni nodded dubiously. "If he leaves the stables, the Cybions will cut him down!"

"Order them to ignore him!" said Utang. "Do it now!"

Idoni nodded and gave the order.

Lord Talbo Cyclesse spilled out of the stables and into a bloody battle between his manor hands and the ruthless cyborgs. He watched in horror as his loyal servants were sliced limb from limb in a flurry of blades, their gunfire doing little against the swift, armored monsters.

Talbo opened fire, shooting one in the head repeatedly until it went down. He quickly whirled around, training his gun on one Cybion after another, waiting for swift and lethal reprisal, but none came.

Talbo cried out in fury as he realized that they had been ordered to ignore him. He looked on in guilt and revulsion as his butlers, kitchen staff, housekeepers, and farm hands were butchered by bullet and blade, all to protect their lord, blood and gore spraying everywhere, painting the crystalline Dragonweed crimson.

He saw General Utang burst out of the stables with his rifle pointed at the ground. Talbo took aim and fired, grazing Utang's battle armor.

"Talbo, please!"

Talbo realized that Utang wanted to take him alive. It appeared that the fearsome Ice Dragon was holding back for Regana. Talbo would exploit this weakness.

As Utang raised his weapon, Talbo ducked between Cybions, preventing Utang from obtaining a clear shot. As he dodged swinging Cybion blades and gunfire, he saw Idoni circling the outer edge of the melee, flanking him.

Utang took aim but did not fire. He ducked and dodged his way through the fighting, the Cybions backing away as he came near, minding their general.

Talbo tracked Idoni as the captain circumvented the mêlée, rifle raised. One of Talbo's young handmaidens reached out for him, placing a bloody hand on his shoulder, her face imploring. "Help me!"

"Chana, where is Lady Cyclesse?" asked Talbo, momentarily distracted from Captain Idoni's approach.

"She is dead, my lord!" An advancing Cybion sliced Chana's hand free from her arm as she wailed in pain. Talbo lowered his rifle and embraced her, knowing the Cybion would abide its instructions and back off. Hot tears streamed down his face as he choked back angry sobs, his clothes doused in the blood of his wife's handmaiden.

Captain Idoni was charging through the fight, rifle raised. Lord Talbo caught this through the corner of his eye and whirled around, using his deceased wife's handmaiden as a living shield.

Captain Idoni took the shot, hitting Chana in the chest, ending her life. Talbo dropped to one knee, taking aim with his rifle from behind his now lifeless shield.

He fired, missing the captain's face but hitting him in the throat. Idoni dropped his rifle and reached up, clutching his gullet, as he dropped to the ground.

As the last of the manor hands fell, Utang ordered the Cybions into stasis. They froze, some of them mid swing, like statues on the field. Utang saw Idoni lying on the ground clasping at his throat, thick hot blood streaming through the fingers of his gloves, and he saw Lord Talbo running into the manor house gardens.

He stood over his fallen captain as he lay on the ground, choking on his own blood. "Frak it, Fero. I told you to stand down."

Idoni looked as if he wanted to speak, but all that came out were gurgles. Utang kicked off the captain's helmet and placed his foot on Idoni's neck, holding him still. He placed the barrel of his rifle over Idoni's forehead and fired twice, sending him into the Aether. After completing this act of mercy, he pursued Lord Talbo Cyclesse, running through the gauntlet of frozen Cybions.

Talbo navigated his labyrinthine gardens expertly, following the trail of bodies and deactivated Cybions to its center. It was at the center that he found the body of Lady Terret on the ground in pieces. He knelt down beside her, taking in the gore that was once his beautiful wife, overwhelmed by a flood of grief and the conflagration of rage.

"Yoshi!" he cried out in rage over his wife's ruined body.

General Utang, not too far behind, froze within the garden maze, the realization of the meaning of Talbo's cry washing over him in a wave of dread and regret. He had told Idoni to instruct the Cybions to ignore Talbo, but he specified no such instruction about Lady Terret.

"Talbo, I am sorry this had to come to this," he appealed.

Talbo, realizing that Yoshi was close, quickly rose to his feet, shouldering his rifle. "You have wiped out my entire manor. You have disgraced the House Cyclesse."

"You, brother-in-law, have disgraced the Feng Empire and Emperor Hiron," countered Utang. His voice was getting closer.

"I told you, Yoshi, I know nothing of these rioters and rebellions. I swear it on my ruined manor." He ducked low, swinging his rifle around from side to side, waiting for Utang to reveal himself.

Utang looked up at the red and blue swirling clouds as a tempest raged in the sky above. "How else am I supposed to interpret the evidence, Talbo? What would you have me do?"

Talbo steeled himself as he heard Utang's voice in the passage next to him, beyond a wall of Dragon Lilies and ornate Dragonweed. "Die!"

He leapt through the tall grass, tearing through the beautiful lilies (Terret's favorite flower), and fired his rifle. However, he was too close and missed his target.

Utang reacted quickly to the pouncing lord, ducking and turning, sending Talbo flying into a Cybion with its bladed arm frozen in extension. Talbo was impaled on the blade through the center of his chest, piercing his Feng heart.

"Talbo, no!" cried Utang, but it was too late.

Black blood bubbled out of the fallen lord's mouth.

Utang, a fierce, battle-hardened warrior, was overcome with emotion. His face contorted in grief and shame as he looked upon his dying brother-in-law, Regana's beloved brother. "Talbo, I am so sorry."

Talbo reached out and grabbed the corner of Utang's chest plate, pulling him close. Utang thought Talbo was trying to impale him on the same blade, so he put out an armored hand onto the blade's tip, stopping Talbo from pulling him in any further.

Talbo tried to speak, but his voice was low and hoarse. Utang leaned in, listening intently, doing his best to make out the gasps carrying Talbo's last words.

"You idiot!" Talbo rasped. "Get back to the palace!"

His eyes grew wide and vacant, and he released Utang's armor as he was embraced by death in the garden of his manor.

CHAPTER 13

Plato, armed with Drekaar weapons, struggled to keep up with his hunting party as they skittered out into the desert. The sun beat down on his wary body as he did his best to run in the shifting sand, a skill he had never had to develop on Humana.

The Drekaar moved through the sand with speed and grace, their hard exoskeletons immune to the brutal heat. Plato, on the other hand, felt the oppression of the desert sun, and his armor felt like it weighed a metric holt.

He hoped they came across one of these pregnant worms quickly, so the others could slay it and he could return to oversee the operation he was sent to Golgath to execute in the first place. Or, at the very least, he wished to continue to discuss Drekaar history and culture with the chieftain and his historian in the relative comfort of camp.

However, Plato realized that there was a difference between discussing culture academically and experiencing it firsthand. Immersion was the best way to learn, and back on Humana, Avatars didn't have much opportunity to immerse themselves in anything beyond the work for which they were genetically engineered. Even with all of the allowances Navigo afforded him as a special case, none of his Human artifacts and Earth knick-knacks compared to a hunt with live Drekaar.

Plato was careful to remain within the center of the pack, in case there were any close encounters with some of the more dangerous indigenous fauna. Doing so required great effort as he was jostled about by the many-legged arachnoids scampering about. He likened it to being caught in the middle of a stampede of plowena on Humani agricultural facilities.

At last, the hunting pack came to a halt in the middle of the desert. The Drekaar spread their legs out and lowered themselves, creating a smaller profile.

GrakLok leaned in close to Plato, his words coming out as clicks and croaks before the universal translator chip in Plato's skull interpreted them. "We have spotted something moving in the sand ahead before the next dune. Down low, it cannot distinguish us from the waves of heat rising above the hot sand."

Plato figured as much. He tried to crane his long neck upward, to see what it was they were looking at, but GrakLok chittered next to him, his eyes burning like the fireball in the sky, so he thought better of it.

Suddenly, the huddled pack exploded into motion, sweeping Plato off his feet before he was ready. The arachnoid hunters dragged him along as he ducked the whipping of barbed tails, and the throng rushed the area where they spotted movement.

Plato reached down to the ever-shifting sand and tried to regain his footing, but his feet simply dragged. He fell face-first into the sand, the heat burning his Humani skin. The group passed over him, somehow avoiding trampling him, whether on purpose or by accident. Within seconds, Plato was alone, prone, and out in the open as he watched the Drekaar hunting party converge on their prey.

Blades flashed and tails whipped, barbs finding purchase in a writhing form beneath the horde. There were strange sounds of pain and terror rising above the chittering of the Drekaar, most likely the pregnant snake they were looking for making its last stand.

Plato pushed up on his hands and attempted to push himself up to standing, but the sand beneath him shifted, pulling him backward, like the receding waves on Humana when there was a powerful undertow.

Plato rolled over on his back in his heavy armor and saw the sand sinking into a hole a hundred kli in front of him, swirling down in a funnel shape. It reminded him of a black hole, or Charybdis from ancient Human texts.

Unfortunately, his latter simile was more accurate. A massive arachnoid creature climbed out of a trap, long, curved pincers snapping, six eyes all fixated on Plato. If Plato's skin was reactive, it would've flashed white with terror.

He cried out, trying to scramble to his feet, but the armor made him clumsy. He hefted his rifle and took aim as the gargantuan terror reached out for him, pulling sand into its trap and taking Plato along for the ride.

Plato fired at the beast, but the gunfire only seemed to anger it. Desperate, he rolled back onto his belly and started commando crawling through the receding sand.

However, the sand was slipping away too quickly, and despite his frantic crawling, Plato was being drawn towards the snapping pincers. He looked up and saw GrakLok standing up on one of the nearby dunes, eyes burning, the waves of heat wafting off the sand making him appear like a mirage.

Other Drekaar followed, rushing the giant horror, shooting at it. The massive beast reared up on its back legs, waving its front legs in the air. Capitalizing on the moment, Plato scrambled to his feet and fought the tide of ebbing sand, putting some distance between himself and the titan.

The Drekaar hunting party surrounded the beast, taking aim at the joints in its legs, each leg collapsing under its weight as bullets ripped through the joints. The massive arachnoid began to sink back into its hole, but this time pulling in half the desert with it. Plato was again swept off his feet and quickly pulled into the hole.

He rolled over on his back in time to see the massive set of pincers snapping at him as he rushed towards them.

Plato knew, in the few seconds that he had left, firing at the beast would do him no good. All he could do was avoid the pincers as he was swallowed whole.

As he passed the closing pincers, they dripped a viscous liquid onto his chest plate, and he slid into the creature's mouth. Shut out from the blazing desert sun, he was cast into pitch darkness. As he was pushed down a long tunnel, the walls squeezing him in a kind of peristalsis, he prayed to the Engineer that his death be swift and painless. There was a quick freefall, and he landed in something soft.

He half expected for death to come swiftly, but he was surprised to find himself, once again, sitting in hot sand. It was warm and damp. He heard a sizzling sound coming from his chest plate and started to feel the burn of the viscous saliva. He quickly stripped off the armor, tossing the chest plate aside, and rubbed his chest.

Plato had read about some arachnoid creatures who pierced the exoskeletons of their prey and dissolved their innards before consuming the hot meal. Fortunately, Avatars were small pickings, which is what allowed him to pass the pincers and enter the beast's gullet intact.

He was struck by the realization that he was to be digested slowly, a cruel fate, but then remembered from his readings that these creatures digested their prey before imbibing it. So, he was like the equivalent of a swallowed bone. He quietly hoped that the colossus would choke on him, a parting shot.

Angry, Plato decided that if he was to die in the belly of this beast, he would give it the worst case of heartburn it ever had. He raised his rifle, aiming it at the dark void, and pulled the trigger, sweeping the barrel back and forth, unsure of what he was aiming at. He aimed upward as he unloaded.

There were groans from the creature, and it began to sway back and forth, the sands shifting, sliding Plato to and fro, half-burying him in the sand. There was a faint commotion outside, and the creature swayed some more as Plato struggled in the blackness to keep his head above the sand. He closed his eyes as warm sand assaulted his face, entering his nose and mouth. There was no point in keeping his eyes open anyway, as it was too dark to see.

There were a few lurches from the beast, and a quick drop. The creature stopped moving. In fact, the ambient sounds of the digestive tract all around Plato ceased, bathing him in pitch black silence. The sensation was so unnerving, that Plato wondered if he had indeed died, and this was the Aether.

He heard ripping, tearing, and crunching sounds, and the beast began to move again. However, this time, Plato did not sense the constriction of muscles, and the gullet was still quiet and still. No, this time, the beast was being moved—dragged and lifted out of its trap under the sand.

His Drekaar hunting companions had slain the beast. Suddenly filled with hope, Plato began to claw his way out of the sand. Because the beast was no longer lurching, the sand remained relatively still, allowing Plato to pull himself up and find some kind of footing.

He reached out in the dark and placed a hand on a wall in the cavern, but he quickly retracted his hand as it burned from the digestive juices. He quickly wiped it in the sand, using the coarse grains to slough off the gel. His hand felt raw, as the saliva likely took a layer of his skin with it. His dead, expressionless skin.

Cradling his hand at his side, careful not to touch any other part of his skin, Plato began to crawl until he found an opening. The beast must have fallen forward, tilting it in such a way that the opening was now slightly below him rather than above. It, too, was likely lined with the acidic enzyme. However, it, too, represented his only way out.

He remembered he had avoided the saliva, having been swallowed whole. So, there was likely no saliva in the tunnel. Or, at least he hoped not. Either way, remaining inside the beast was not an option.

Plato adjusted his shoulder armor and helmet. He felt around the opening with his one good hand and was relieved that there was no saliva. He drew his arms in close and began to shimmy his way back up the throat. There was no peristalsis, allowing more leeway for him to maneuver. He pushed with his long Humani legs as he squirmed back up. After a while, he began to hear the clicking and chittering of the Drekaar, and he saw a sliver of sunlight at the end of the tunnel.

He crawled and pushed off whatever foothold he found in the smooth walls. He found footing amongst the small papillae that lined the creature's esophagus. As the voices outside grew louder, he understood fragments of conversation. A voice that must've belonged to RagnakTok sounded upset. He caught remarks about the United Intergalactic Coalition declaring war and sending an armada to Golgath in response to the death of their ambassador. A voice that must've been GrakLok's lamented about letting the fragile Avatar out of his sight for only a moment.

At last, Plato saw the massive fangs dripping their acidic dribble, the once translucent mucus now appearing cloudy white. He braced himself and shoved his way past the pincers, the spittle burning his shoulder armor and helmet, and he emerged back into the light.

He birthed himself back into the desert, quickly shedding his saliva-laden armor and flinging off his helmet. His vision had been white-washed by the blazing star burning in the sky, but his eyes adjusted.

As his vision cleared, he saw the Drekaar hunting party standing around him, chittering softly. RagnakTok shoved his way to the front and his eyes focused on Plato, but they didn't burn the way they had before. Was this the Drekaar expression of disbelief?

Plato rose unsteadily to his feet, brushing himself off with his good hand as he cradled his injured left. He didn't know what to say, so he said the first thing that popped into his head.

"I'm back."

The Drekaar erupted into loud chittering, but it was different than any of the chittering he had heard before. In fact, his universal translator was not yielding an interpretation, but an impression.

Raucous laughter.

"Praise be the Dark!" exclaimed RagnakTok. "The Gargantuok choked on the little Avatar." There was amusement and relief in his voice as the other Drekaar joined in the celebration.

GrakLok skittered over and clapped Plato on the shoulder with a heavy claw. "You have done well. This will feed our village for cycles."

Unsure of what he actually did that could have possibly contributed to the slaying of this aptly named Gargantuok, Plato shrugged sheepishly, which only caused more laughter amongst his bizarre hosts.

Somehow, he got the feeling that some of it was at his expense.

* * *

Emperor Hiron sat beside Bobot Tegrit and Hubritia Liguri, Vice Executor Kazar sitting on his other side, in the Feng Temple as they participated in the High Ritual. Bobot looked uncomfortable, his epidermal microexpressions betraying his growing impatience.

"Where is your wife, Emperor Hiron?" Hubritia whispered.

"My wives? Feng women are not permitted to sit in the front with the men during High Ritual," answered Hiron.

Hubritia found such a custom disconcerting. However, any offense caused by such barbarity was quickly replaced with awe at the beauty of the ritual. She was enthralled by the symbolic reenactment of Feng history through the interpretive dance of dragons. There were many smaller dragons with scales glowing like hot chainmail whipping about over the planet, breathing fire and attacking one another. The sharp spines along their back running from head to tail jutted out like jagged flames. One larger dragon was the color of ice and just as translucent, its scales crystalline, darted around, breathing ice, freezing the smaller dragons, encasing them.

The larger dragon then pulled back and encased the planet in ice, and from that ice, Dragon Lilies and grass sprouted. Humanoid forms began to work the land and build civilizations. It was beautifully choreographed, a ballad of history.

These idyllic scenes soon gave way to scenes of war, bloodshed, and carnage. Banners bearing the names of various families rose and fell, and the massive Feng throne grew and changed with each occupant. The final name was that of the House Hiron, and the Feng Dynasty was born. The display ended showing the Holy Emperor Hiron sitting on his throne, a large Ice Dragon looming behind him, and the dragon-shaped fighters and the massive ships of the Feng armada floating in battle formation above him.

When the ritual was over, Hubritia was the first to comment. "What a beautiful, if not intense, rendering. This was your creation myth?"

"It is no myth," said Emperor Hiron.

"Forgive me," said Hubritia. "Poor choice of words. Your creation story was absolutely captivating."

Hiron smiled in acknowledgement. He then turned to Bobot. "Bobot, what do you think of our story?"

"A bit historically inaccurate."

"Bobot," admonished Hubritia.

Hiron held up a hand to silence her. "Please, Hubritia. Bobot is entitled to his opinion." Then to Bobot, "In what way was it inaccurate?"

"I do not dispute the beginning or middle of the tale," Bobot continued. Vice Executor Kazar winced at that last word. "It is the ending that I take issue with."

"Bobot," pleaded Hubritia, "do not insult our host."

"Why, when he insults us by subjecting us to this propaganda?"

Hubritia Liguri looked absolutely appalled. She opened her mouth to speak, but there were no words.

"It is fine," said Hiron, resting a reassuring hand on her shoulder. "I am used to the arrogance of the Humani." He stated it more as a fact than as a barb.

"It is you, Emperor Hiron, who is arrogant," insisted Bobot, his skin flashing orange. "If your house were so strong, if the Feng Dynasty were so victorious, we would not be here."

Vice Executor Kazar, witnessing the degradation of relations, abandoned his spectatorship and insinuated himself into the conversation. "You are here as part of our evolution as a people. It is the opening of a new chapter of collaboration."

"Yes," agreed Hubritia hastily. "The galaxies will be better for it."

"Enough of this bickering," commanded Emperor Hiron. "It was not my intention to offend, Bobot Tegrit. Sharing the Feng High Ritual is an act of intimacy with our people. I am sorry you have interpreted it otherwise."

Bobot nodded, his skin returning to its natural gray hue. "No harm done, Emperor."

Arrogant worm. Hiron fantasized about ripping the Humani's head from his shoulders and wiping that grin off his face permanently.

"Let us go feast!" Hiron declared. "I hope you do not find eating to be offensive, Bobot."

"I would like to return to overseeing my team of inspectors," insisted Bobot.

"Yes, but not on an empty stomach," said Hiron. "After you have had your fill, I will bother you no longer."

"I will hold you to that," said Bobot.

Hiron raised an eyebrow. "I am sure you will."

"Your team of inspectors will join us in the grand banquet hall as well," said Vice Executor Kazar, to Hiron's surprise.

"What of the marines? They, too, eat," said Bobot.

"I will have a small feast sent down to them," said Hiron. "The very same courses on which we will dine."

"That is very gracious of you," said Hubritia, shooting a sideways glance at Bobot, who did not comment on the matter any further.

Hiron allowed the group to walk on ahead, and he pulled Vice Executor Kazar aside. "Just what do you think you are doing, Kazar?"

Vice Executor Kazar looked confused by the question. "What, the inspection team?"

"You overstep, Vice Executor."

Kazar wore a sheepish grin. "I am a politician. I saw tension building, threatening to derail the good intentions of the occasion, so I offered an olive branch."

"Every little concession makes us look weak."

"It was a small concession, Your Highness, a token gesture. They are all our guests, not just Bobot Tegrit and Hubritia Liguri."

"Next time, you consult me before offering up any more token gestures and volunteering the grand banquet hall to those who seek to weaken the empire."

"Yes, Your Eminence."

"Have the rest of the UIC inspection team summoned."

"Right away, Your Highness."

Kazar dashed off while Cegnis remained behind, joining Hiron's entourage as they walked to the grand banquet hall. She was buzzing in Hubritia's ear.

"I think it is so exciting, having off-worlder guests in our palace walls. So, what do you think of it all?"

"Stunning, all of it," said Hubritia in genuine admiration. "Your culture is a true marvel. I had no idea that the Feng Empire had risen out of so much in-fighting and strife."

"Yes, well, some would say the in-fighting has become more civilized," remarked Cegnis, shooting a glance over at Hiron, who was preoccupied with directing Bobot's attention out to the palatial courtyards.

"After the display in the ritual, I should hope so," said Hubritia. "There is still conflict within the empire?"

Cegnis did her best to play coy. "Well, I suppose every government has its conflict. Look at the United Intergalactic Coalition. So many worlds and races."

"It is true," admitted Hubritia. "For instance, not every race believes that this is a good idea."

"Your visit here?"

"Yes. Some say that it is fruitless, that Emperor Hiron will hide what he does not want the United Intergalactic Coalition to see."

"And others?"

"Well, others agree that in order to move away from another Intergalactic War, the United Intergalactic Coalition must learn to get along with the Feng."

"I do hope there are more of the latter," said Cegnis.

"Yes, there are," said Hubritia. "After this, we will add more to our ranks, drowning out the isolationist minority."

"It will be enlightening to study Feng technology," said Bobot, his attempt at a compliment.

"Our ships?" asked Hiron. "They are no more impressive than the Humani's."

"I am not speaking of Feng freighters and transports," said Bobot.

"Ah, our warships," said Hiron. "Now, that is another story."

"Indeed," answered Bobot.

Hiron managed a smile. "However, I believe it is the purpose of your inspection to establish a baseline assessment of our weapons technology to allow any assessment of development in the future. It is not a detailed study of our weapons technology itself."

"One cannot determine a baseline without careful analysis," insisted Bobot.

"That is not part of the accord," said Hiron. "You will be presented with a categorical inventory and visual verification. There will be no dissection. Anything more will have to be negotiated at another juncture."

Bobot chortled. "It is almost as if you do not trust us." This time, there was no epidermal microexpression.

"Trust, like an empire, is not built in a day," said Hiron. "It must be built carefully and in due time."

They reached the grand banquet hall. Large blast doors rose on hydraulics, revealing a cathedral-like room with a high, vaulted ceiling. Lights hung from above like icicles, like crystalline stalactites. Feng music flowed from indigenous instruments, sounds as alien as they were captivating.

In the center of the room was a U-shaped arrangement of tables. In the front, elevated a touch from the main floor, was a grand dais. There were Palace Guard stationed around the room between large digital, animated portraits of past warriors of note and heads of state. Behind the dais was a representation of Emperor Hiron in full battle armor, standing in front of his throne. He had his chest puffed out and was pounding the floor with a large spear. Any signs of the prior skirmish with the masked marauders had been addressed and concealed.

As they crossed the room, Hubritia extended a slender hand, caressing the ornate carvings on the table. "What beautiful craftsmanship! The Feng have great artisans."

"We are not just a warrior people," said Hiron.

Cegnis leaned in. "The wood comes from the Crystelline Forest on the Tibeng Plateau."

"Astounding," gasped Hubritia, drinking it all in.

Hiron gestured for the honored guests to take their seats at the dais in front. Cegnis leading the way, the United Intergalactic Coalition inspection team began to fill the banquet hall.

Vice Executor Kazar returned with them, and he immediately approached the dais. However, before he reached his seat, Hiron grabbed his arm and leaned in. "The marines are under guard in the docking bay?"

"Of course, Your Highness."

"And our security detail here?"

"Personally selected by Captain Idoni, himself," said Kazar. "You look worried."

"I assure you that all of the necessary security protocols have been enacted. We are perfectly safe. Our guests are as reluctant to spark an incident as we are." Kazar's expression was sympathetic. "I understand that this visit is uncomfortable for you."

"That is an understatement," said Hiron.

"Then, with your permission, please allow me to facilitate the visit so that it concludes without any complications."

Hiron softened. "Yes, you are right. Carry on, Vice Executor."

Hiron took his place at the dais, as did Kazar. Also seated were the other Feng holders of high office. "Allow me to introduce the emperor's cabinet," announced Cegnis.

"No need," said Bobot Tegrit. "To the left of Vice Executor Kazar is Vice of the Interior Mondi Hayati, and then Imperial Bursar Wan Tengani to the left of him." There was no mention of Magno Ku, Vice of Justice, and General Yoshi Utang, who were both missing.

"Very good," said Emperor Hiron, arching an eyebrow. "It appears you are familiar with my staff."

Bobot bowed his head slightly and introduced himself to Hiron's cabinet. "I am Bobot Tegrit of Humana, and this is Hubritia Liguri of Firenz."

Greetings were exchanged, and Bobot and Hubritia took their seats at Hiron's right. Once everyone was seated, Cegnis left the dais and took her place with Emperor Hiron's wives and concubines and the cabinet members' wives. Hiron's sons of various ages sat at another table, the younger supervised by the older.

"The women sit separately at meals as well?" asked Hubritia, disappointed.

"It is our cultural practice," explained Hiron.

"Pity," said Hubritia. "I was looking forward to growing more acquainted with them."

"A pleasure that I am afraid will have to wait."

"I would eventually like to meet your wives, Emperor Hiron," said Hubritia.

"They are not political animals," said Hiron. "The vice executor's wife is...singular in that respect."

"She is from the House Shodanku," said Kazar. "Her family is a little more liberal with the ambition of women."

"Yet, here I sit at the dais with the emperor himself," remarked Hubritia. "A departure from Feng tradition."

"You are an honored guest," said Hiron.

"But my presence up here is an offense."

"To be truthful, Hubritia Liguri, this whole experience runs counter to our cultural values, but that is not necessarily a negative thing. I believe that some will see it as progress," said Vice Executor Kazar.

Hubritia, for the first time, looked flustered. "I must say that I find such practices to be quite alien."

"As do I," said Bobot. "The Humani elevate their women. Many hold important positions in both industry and government. Same with the United Intergalactic Coalition. Our female Admiral led the United Intergalactic Coalition armada to victory in the last Intergalactic War."

"That victory was an accident," said Hiron, his good nature eroding around the edges. "A happy accident for the United Intergalactic Coalition."

"It appears the Humans proved useful after all," prodded Bobot, his skin flashing gold, an expression of arrogance.

"There were many who criticized their inclusion in the United Intergalactic Coalition," chided Vice Executor Kazar, happy to commiserate in deriding another race to diffuse tension.

"The United Intergalactic Coalition has to be inclusive these days," commented Hiron. "It being so stretched thin over so many worlds."

"The coalition could not be stronger, Emperor Hiron," said Bobot, flashing gold again. "It appears, however, we are not the only ones busy adding to our ranks."

"If you have a point, then I suggest you make it, Bobot," said Hiron, growing more impatient with this game called diplomacy.

"Been to Aquilassi lately?"

"I have no idea what you are talking about," said Hiron.

"We have had some difficulty helping the government squash the Hilalu rebellion," said Hubritia.

"It would appear as if the Hilalu had help," added Bobot.

Vice Executor Kazar grinned, flashing impeccably white, fanged teeth. "I have no knowledge of any Feng operations on Aquilassi or any intervening with the Hilalu against the government."

Servants began serving beverages, Dragon's Breath, on the dais and at the tables.

"Not that you would disclose if there really was," said Bobot.

"The United Intergalactic Coalition are not the only ones allowed to seek allies," said the Imperial Bursar Wan Tengani.

"With all due respect, Bursar, forging coalitions is very different than galactic conquest."

"Is it conquest when we allow the conquered world autonomy as long as they pay tribute and fight for the empire when we call them?" asked Wan Tengani.

"Are you insinuating *we* are the conquerors in this scenario?" Bobot appeared amused rather than annoyed.

Hubritia leaned back in her heavy wooden chair as a servant poured some of the Feng spirit into her crystal goblet. "No, you misunderstand. We instill democracy, stabilizing volatile worlds. We bring peace."

"Whether they want it or not," quipped Hiron.

"Why would they not want peace?" asked Hubritia.

"Do not bother trying to discuss peace with a warrior," said Bobot. "You are wasting your efforts."

"Hubritia asks a good question," said Hiron. "Allow me the courtesy of answering."

Bobot lazily waved him on, as if sanctioning an act of futility.

"Your premise is fundamentally flawed," explained Hiron.

"Oh, it is?" replied Hubritia, her interest piqued.

"You assume that peace is more valuable than freedom."

"One cannot have freedom without peace," she said.

"The kind of peace the United Intergalactic Coalition is selling involves giving up one's freedom, one's culture, and supplanting it with canned democracy by the numbers, serving only the coalition."

"We only ask the worlds we intervene with to adapt to a more civilized governmental structure and rule of law," said Bobot.

"What you call civilized, we call cumbersome and bureaucratic," said Mondi Hayati.

"Is there any other way?" asked Hubritia, intending it to be a rhetorical question.

"Yes, there is a more efficient way that preserves the autonomy of the conquered world," said Emperor Hiron. "Why reinvent governmental structures, imposing ones incompatible with the indigenous culture? You spend more time supervising and putting out fires than gaining any progress.

"When we conquer a world, we depose the head of state and allow one of the others to assume his position, usually a member of a dissenting party, preserving the governmental structure. They are allowed to govern under the auspices of the Feng Empire in the way that is fit for the indigenous people."

"But what about the abuses of the toppled ruling class?" asked Hubritia. "Or worse, the abuses of the newly instated ruling class?"

Bobot took a sip of his Dragon's Breath and nearly choked on its potency.

"Are you all right?" asked Hiron, taking a draught from his goblet, being rather showy about how smooth he perceived the drink to be.

"By the Engineer," gasped Bobot.

"An acquired taste," said Monsu Kazar, sipping his.

Hubritia stared at her drink as if it would bite her head off and decided to push it away. "Do you have anything for a more delicate palate?"

Kazar clapped his hands, and a servant came over. He whispered something into the servant's ear, and the servant nodded, taking Hubritia's goblet away.

"Again," said Hiron, "your premise is flawed."

"How so, this time?" mused Hubritia.

"You presume all of a world's inhabitants to be innocents, when in reality, many are not. There are those much more warlike than the Feng, true savages. In order to gain control of the world, you need to topple one nation at a time, installing rulers who will...make their people behave."

"Trading one overlord for another," said Bobot, sniffing his drink and grimacing, his skin flashing green and yellow.

"Whereas the United Intergalactic Coalition imposes a constitution on cultures unequipped to understand it, and then wastes resources squashing insurrections and insurgent groups, terrorists seeking to topple their precious gift of democracy," said Hiron.

"Some cultures need education, guidance to progress," said Hubritia. "Some have never experienced a renaissance or industrial revolution, or none of any real cultural significance. They know nothing of philosophy or other schools of thought. That is why they fight amongst themselves. We simply refocus their energy on bigger ambitions."

"Space travel," said Vice of the Interior Mondi Hayati dubiously.

"Oh, come off it," chided Bobot. "The Feng, too, have made space travel their focus. We have both created a worker class of drones—you, the Cybiotes and we, the Avatars—so that our peoples may focus on the universe and its many worlds."

"We teach new worlds to interface with neighboring worlds and eventually other galaxies," said Hubritia. "There can only be benefit in collaboration to achieve superordinate goals."

"It often takes more than bureaucracy and schools to achieve peace," said Emperor Hiron. "Many times peace has to be won on the battlefield."

"So, you support colonialism over nation-building," observed Bobot. "If our approach is so incorrect, why does the United Intergalactic Coalition boast an unrivalled membership and success in trade and security?"

"Something that the Feng might benefit from by association," suggested Vice Executor Kazar.

Hiron ignored Kazar's remark. "You maintain your 'success' by trying to control the conditions supporting it, which means the oppression of 'non-members' through sanctions and embargos. You spend your resources coercing concession while you strain your democratic, nation-building machine from within."

"What are you suggesting?" asked Bobot, his skin flashing so intensely gold it nearly sparkled.

"I am suggesting that one day the United Intergalactic Coalition will stretch too far and implode under its own weight. Other interests will rise, and it will take more than a serendipitous blunder by the Humans to save it," said Hiron, barely containing his temper. How dare this Barberoi impose himself on Hiron uninvited and then insult his people in his own palace!

There was an uncomfortable silence on the dais as they listened to the din of the inspection team eating and drinking while conversing, looking around the opulent hall. Hubritia noticed the music echoed throughout the hall, but their voices in conversation did not, truly a marvel of acoustics.

"What is that enchanting music?" she asked.

"It is called Lu Bing-na," answered Kazar, trying to smooth things over.

"Is it a regalement recounting battles of old?"

"It is a Feng love poem," said Kazar, his expression bordering on licentious.

Hubritia blushed, embarrassed at her ignorance.

"Does that surprise you?" asked Vice Executor Kazar. "We Feng are capable of much more than killing. If we were not, we would die out and cease to exist as a people."

Hubritia blushed again, affected by his charm, and quickly averted her gaze. This Feng, unlike his comrades, was a slick character. However, the awkward moment was interrupted when the servant who took her goblet away returned with a fresh one filled with a light blue liquid.

"I think this will be more to your liking," said Kazar.

"What is it?"

"It is glacial nectar. I assure you, it is quite delectable."

Hubritia eyed it suspiciously, but seeing Kazar's expectant look, she picked up the goblet, brought it to her thin lips, and sipped the blue drink. Her eyes lit up as it tasted sweet on her tongue. "This is quite good."

Hiron was staring down Bobot, appraising his diplomatic adversary.

"What is it? Why do you examine me so?" asked Bobot.

"Something does not sit right with me."

"That is an understatement."

"I am wondering why the United Intergalactic Coalition would send a Humani to the first inspection."

"I beg your pardon," said Bobot.

Hiron narrowed his eyes, focusing his gaze like a laser, causing Bobot's skin to flash yellow. "These are delicate dealings. Why would the UIC send a being who wears his feelings on his skin, betraying his intentions, when there are plenty of races that are more stoic and poised to handle such fragile interactions?"

"I assure you, Emperor, that the Humani are quite important players in galactic politics," huffed Bobot.

"But still," pressed Hiron, "why risk insult that could derail the whole treaty between the Feng and the United Intergalactic Coalition with a creature that emotes so clumsily and transparently?"

Bobot flashed orange and then yellow—outrage and then fear. "It appears that you are the one hurling insults, Emperor Hiron."

"No," said Hiron. "It is almost as if the United Intergalactic Coalition did not care how this inspection would turn out."

"That is simply not true!" said Hubritia, appalled by the accusation.

Hiron pointed a long, clawed finger at Bobot. "You. You knew every Feng dignitary seated at this dais. Yet, you failed to question the absence of General Yoshi Utang and the vice of justice."

"A minor oversight, I assure you," asserted Bobot.

"No," said Hiron. "You knew they were out of the palace on empire business."

Another flash of yellow. "I do not know how I could possibly have known that."

Emperor Hiron leaned forward as the serene Lu Bing-na filled the banquet hall and inspectors conversed and laughed. It was all so perfect. Too perfect.

"So, when did you plan on killing me?"

CHAPTER 14

Plato was escorted back to Drekaar base camp by the hunting party a hero. Dragging the carcass of the massive Gargantuok in their wake, they were greeted quite exuberantly. Drekaar came out of their tents and gathered around the slain monster, chittering in celebration as several began to butcher it in the street in preparation for the next feast.

When RagnakTok announced Plato's role in slaying the Gargantuok, he was immediately surrounded by Drekaar clicking and chirping in his face and clapping him on the shoulders with massive claws, barbed tails swinging carelessly about.

Plato, for the first time, felt like he belonged. Perhaps that was the inevitable result of surviving a near-death encounter together. It was an experience he was never afforded as an Avatar. It was a sensation reserved for natural Humani.

GrakLok, noticing the young Avatar was overwhelmed, cleared a path and ushered Plato out of the center of attention.

"You have done well, little man." The remark was not derisive, but rather an expression of endearment. "Look, you cast a gold hue."

At first, Plato had no idea what GrakLok was referring to. He looked down at his skin, and sure enough, it bore a faint golden hue. It normally signified arrogance. In this case, it appeared to indicate swelling pride. For the Humani, there was little distinction between the two.

"Well, this is a first," said Plato, astonished at what appeared to be his first epidermal microexpression. "This was not supposed to be possible."

RagnakTok skittered over. "Before this hunting party, would you have thought slaying a Gargantuok possible?"

"No," answered Plato. "I guess not."

"Perhaps, you are more than you give yourself credit for," noted the high chieftain. "Speaking of which, we realize that it is time for you to get back to your operation here."

Plato, still flying high from the hunt, nodded, only half-acknowledging the reality of the true purpose of his presence on Golgath. "Yes, of course, Chieftain."

"We would like to initiate the planning phase in earnest."

"We have much to discuss, then," said Plato.

GrakLok guided him into a massive tent, RagnakTok following behind them. It took Plato's eyes moments to adjust to the dim lighting, but he was shocked when he saw two Feng armada officers standing on the other side of the tent.

Plato turned around and faced RagnakTok. GrakLok was blocking the opening to the tent. "I do not understand. What is the meaning of this?"

"I am Captain Mongo Utang of the Feng Empire, and this is Lieutenant Votan," announced the looming figure across the tent.

Plato still looked at RagnakTok, his glory from the hunt deflating. "What is going on, Chieftain?"

"I like you, little Avatar, which is why you must cooperate. You were sent here for a reason, and you are going to play a very important role in the fate of the universe."

"I assume you have brought with you the specs for Humani space craft?" asked Captain Utang.

Plato slowly turned around. He knew this Feng captain. Everyone knew of the Ice Dragon. Cold-blooded and ruthless, he had the reputation as being a formidable opponent in the battlespace. "Yes, I have."

"I need the specs for a Humani Vortex fighter."

"All I have are the specs for freighters, rudimentary ones at that," explained Plato. "Navigo figured that the Drekaar had to crawl before they walked, so to speak."

"But you know the specs of a Vortex fighter." It was a statement more than a question. "You are a chief engineer of Navigo."

Plato swallowed hard. "Then you know I do. Why do you want those specs?"

"There is something I want to show you," said Captain Utang.

"Perhaps I should consult with Navigo first," offered Plato.

"That will be unnecessary," said Captain Utang.

"I have my orders," Plato insisted.

"I am afraid they have changed."

Plato was escorted by GrakLok and an armed guard out of the tent. Although the situation had changed, the Drekaar people maintained their enthusiasm, chittering at Plato as he passed through camp. Their reaction was not commensurate with the new set of circumstances, but they did not appear concerned that he was being taken away by an armed security detail.

When they reached the Drekaar mining complex, Plato was lead to a tunnel boring down deeper into the mine. At last, they reached an elevator. Plato knew that the deeper they went, the closer they were to kronite and the more radiation they would be exposed to. Drekaar exoskeletons could withstand it. Avatar skin could not.

"If we are going down to a lower level, I will need protection from the radiation."

"There will be no radiation where we are going," assured Captain Utang.

They entered the elevator, leaving the armed Drekaar security detail behind. Plato stood between the hulking forms of RagnakTok, Captain Utang, and Lieutenant Votan. Security was not necessary, as a single Avatar engineer posed no threat. One of the others was capable of ending his life without the expense of much effort.

When they reached their destination level, they exited the elevator and walked down a short tunnel to a vast room hewn from rock. In the middle of a room was a medium-sized, formless spacecraft. Its hull appeared to be soft, as if made of liquid metal, shaped like an ullybean.

"What is this place?" asked Plato in amazement.

"As you see," said Captain Utang, "we already have a ship. We need it to look like a Humani Vortex fighter."

"Why?" Plato realized it was a bold question, but he figured his question wouldn't be met with reprisal because they needed him.

"The reason is…unimportant. Your role, however, is pivotal."

"What role?"

"Tell me, Plato, do you enjoy being an Avatar?"

Plato wasn't quite sure how to answer that. "I am unique. Navigo affords me special privileges not available to other Avatars."

"That is not what I asked you."

"As an emissary of Navigo and the United Intergalactic Coalition, I play a vital role in bringing space travel to other worlds, other cultures."

"Do the natural Humani look you in the eye?"

Plato looked down at his feet. He remembered the time he was asked to leave the temple, how he was humiliated and treated like a foreigner amongst his own people. He understood what Captain Mongo Utang was driving at. "You know they do not."

Utang's tone was sympathetic. "Then why defend your overlords?"

"They are hardly overlords."

"Really? They are a race that engineered you and your kind to serve them so that they may cruise the stars. They hold you back, keep you captive while they gallivant around the galaxies, encountering new worlds and races."

"But, you see, that is not true," insisted Plato. "That is why I was sent here."

"You were sent here because Navigo did not want to risk the lives of natural Humani engineers on an unstable planet, and you know it."

"But, because of me, a fifth order race will be given space travel."

"And Navigo will take all of the credit, I assure you. Your name will not be mentioned once in the Galactic Press."

Plato's expression grew harsh. "Forgive me, Captain, but I do not think you have travelled all the way to Golgath to insult my heritage."

"On the contrary," said Utang, flashing a toothy smile showcasing his fangs, "I am here to offer you an opportunity."

"To do what?"

"To help balance the powers that be in the universe once again."

"You mean to help the Feng."

"That is part of it."

"And what if I refuse?" Plato's tone was defiant.

"This is not just about the Feng," said Captain Utang. "There are other worlds involved. Other worlds that are being starved out by the United Intergalactic Coalition, being refused a seat at the table unless they subjugate themselves completely. Peoples who want to retain their cultures and hold on to who they are."

Plato turned his head, eying the mysterious vessel before him. "You speak of other worlds in the Feng Empire."

"Are they any less deserving of freedom than any other worlds? Do they not deserve to thrive and contribute to the universe?"

"So, what, I am the one to save them from the oppression of the United Intergalactic Coalition? I may not feel very loyal to the Humani, but I have no quarrel with the other member worlds."

Utang insinuated himself into Plato's view, meeting his determined gaze with his own. "Do you really believe that? These other worlds not only support the Humani's use of Avatars, they purchase your kind as if they were cattle."

Plato was taken off guard by Captain Utang's use of a Human word. The word conjured up images of the Earth slave trade in their past. It was a very ugly chapter in Human history.

"I know you are well-versed in Human history and culture," said Utang, as if able to read Plato's mind. "The Humans, a race who abolished their own slavery, now support the slavery of your kind."

"How do you know so much about me? You could not have possibly known about my affinity for Human culture."

"Do you think that you are our only contact within Navigo?" tittered Captain Utang, as if such a notion was naïve.

"Babblefrak," huffed Plato. "Why would a Humani help the Feng?"

"Perhaps not every Humani agrees with the United Intergalactic Coalition version of 'free trade.' There is money to be made in inviting other players to the table."

This was obviously a Navigo executive. Garsi Pequo. Plato wouldn't have been surprised if that arrogant frak was the double agent. "So the new peace accord with Feng…"

"That, I am afraid, is the United Intergalactic Coalition's attempt at relegating the Feng Empire."

"So why not ask your Navigo connection for the specs of the Vortex fighter?"

"Because the information would have to be extracted from Humana. With their advanced cyber-security, such a bold theft would not go unnoticed."

"So you brought me here to extract it from me. If I refuse?"

Utang's smile was again sympathetic. "I think that you know by now that I cannot allow you to live if you refuse. You know too much now."

"I did not ask to be involved! What if I am prepared to die for the Humani and the good of the United Intergalactic Coalition?"

Utang shook his head. "Your stand is based on three faulty premises: 1.) You overestimate your own loyalty to your slave masters 2.) You assume that the United Intergalactic Coalition is good, and 3.)…" He paused to impress the importance his next point, "…you assume your death will be quick and painless."

He let his words hang out there in the hot, dry Golgath air as their significance dawned on the poor Avatar. The Feng were renowned for their methods of torture.

RagnakTok skittered forward, placing a claw on Plato's shoulder. His voice came out in a croak. "Please, little Avatar, I would hate to see a bright light as yourself extinguished in this way. If you do this for Captain Utang, he promised me that you will be allowed to spend the rest of your days unmolested here on Golgath with the Drekaar."

"With all due respect, Chieftain, I would rather go home."

"I do not believe that," said RagnakTok. "I have seen the look in your eye after you emerged from the belly of the Gargantuok. I saw the flash of your skin, something that was supposed to be impossible. You are a force, little Avatar. You are better than what the Humani made you to be.

"Here, with the Drekaar, you will be treated as an equal. You will help us develop space travel, and we will make you into a fierce warrior, honor-bound to me as your chief, serving on my cabinet, but beneath no one."

Plato shook his head. "The Humani will see my defection as treason and my captivity as an act of war. The United Intergalactic Coalition Armada will wipe the Drekaar off the face of this planet and initiate the Pax Galactus initiative."

"Oh, I am counting on the Humani coming for you," said Captain Utang. "It has no bearing on the greater picture."

"If I am to be compelled to help you, what is it you want of me?"

"Merely the specs for the Vortex fighter. We want you to merge them with this vessel's quantum computer."

"What exactly is this vessel? And do not tell me that is none of my concern. I am a captive on this planet. Who will I tell?" He saw Captain Utang's reluctance. "I am going to have to know if I am going to be operating on its interface."

Captain Utang hesitated a moment. There was a Feng scientist hovering around the vessel, clicking things off on his digital holographic pad. He looked up and nodded at Captain Utang.

Utang sighed deeply. "You are correct, Plato. You will need to know in order to complete this task. I see that is unavoidable."

Plato wondered if this apparent concession was designed to make him feel as if he was being let in, fostering a feeling of alliance.

Captain Utang stepped over to the strange vessel, beckoning for Plato to follow him. Plato looked at RagnakTok, whose eyes flashed. The Avatar then stepped forward, joining the towering Captain Utang.

"Reach out and touch the hull," said Utang.

Plato, dubious, looked at the Feng scientist, who nodded in agreement, pressing a button on his pad. Plato reached out with his long fingertips and touched the hull. He expected to feel cold, hard metal. Instead, his fingers disappeared into a liquid, creating concentric waves emanating out from where his fingers penetrated the surface.

Plato jerked his hand back, examining his fingers. They were unharmed. "What is this?" he gasped, awestruck.

"Millions of nanites as particulates suspended in liquid metal," said the Feng scientist. "They respond to an electromagnetic valving mechanism. The quantum computer generates control algorithms—"

"Allowing the ship to change shape according to specifications," said Plato, concluding the thought. "Like the wings on your fighters. But you want this ship to mimic a Vortex Fighter."

"That is correct."

"But what would you use it for? UIC Armada can tell it is not a Vortex because of its energy signature. I assume the engine does not bend an air vortex."

"No," said the scientist.

"So it has an internal gyroscopic regulator that allows it to enter atmospheres from orbit."

"That is correct."

Plato smiled. "Your plan is fundamentally flawed. We have sensors that can detect all of that."

"You do *now*," said Captain Utang.

"I do not understand," said Plato.

Captain Utang nodded to the scientist, who pressed a button. The ship changed configuration, and a hatch opened in the back.

"Well, I was also going to say it was too big," said Plato, "but I can see that it can change configuration."

"That is correct," said Utang.

The scientist stepped inside the ship. Utang gestured for Plato to follow. When Plato entered the ship, the insides were generic. The overall design was nonspecific.

The scientist led Plato over to the controls. They had generic gauges and readouts for propulsion, dark matter conduction, weapons systems and instruments assessing eccentricity, inclination, etc. However, there was another set of controls that drew Plato's attention.

"What are those?"

The Feng scientist nodded. "Those are time travel settings."

"What?" blurted Plato, lost in the moment, forgetting his situation. "You must be joking."

"I am not joking," insisted the scientist. He pressed a button, and a small holographic globe materialized in the air. As he traced his finger over it, coordinates appeared in the air next to his finger, changing as he moved it. "See. Here you calibrate longitude and latitude on the Spacetime continuum."

"Impossible. You are frakking with me."

"You Humani have been toying around with dark matter, designing conductors to ride the expansion of the universe without actually realizing that you were indeed riding time itself." His tone was derisive, imperious.

"Wait a minute. I know that physicists define the passage of time in terms of the expansion of the universe, but that is not literally time."

"You are assuming I am predicating this on magnetic waves. You have failed to take into account gravitational waves."

"Scientists have attempted to manipulate gravitational waves for megacycles," said Plato. "One would need to generate enough mass to manipulate them."

"Wormholes have mass."

"That would mean that you have designed a ship that could generate its own wormholes."

"Only small ones are needed." The scientist held up a demonstrative finger. "The dark matter of the universe is composed of fractal representations of dark energy. This is the unexplained variability in our equations, the statistical noise, if you will. Our mathematicians have found an unending series of event cones buried within the fractals."

"Event cones are speculation," demanded Plato, skeptical yet intrigued.

"Tell me, Avatar, do all Humani doubt the existence of phenomena they had not discovered themselves?" Plato didn't dignify the remark with a response. The scientist continued. "They are quite real, arranged laterally, vertically, and transversely through each other, an infinity of possibilities."

"Why is the Spacetime continuum spherical in representation?"

"It is a theoretical model. Time and space are finite but without boundaries. I do not expect an Avatar to completely grasp it."

"No, I understand. I also understand that the Feng would be frakking with the Spacetime continuum in an effort to try and somehow change the present reality."

"Precisely," said the scientist.

"What do you propose to do?"

"Alter events," said Captain Mongo Utang, "to bring about greater balance in the universe."

Plato turned and exited the craft, the scientist remaining on board. "This is madness. Anything you do can have catastrophic effects on our present reality…even your reality, Captain."

Captain Utang grinned, a vicious display of tooth and fang. "That is the conventional wisdom, but it is inaccurate."

"How? The smallest change can affect vast changes."

"Our scientists have discovered that we can isolate sequences of crucial event cones that we wish to manipulate."

The scientist exited the ship, rejoining Plato and Captain Utang. "That is correct. Dark energy comes from dark matter, and all matter is composed of molecules. Molecules spin.

"By magnetically manipulating the various orientations, which we already do for dark energy conduction, we can plot the optimal vector through the desired event cones, affecting the specific change we want while controlling for unintended consequences in other event cones. In essence, extraneous event cones can be factored out by design."

"By the Engineer..." Plato was speechless. If everything these Feng were saying was true, the Feng Empire had stumbled upon a very dangerous weapon.

"By *our* engineers," corrected Captain Utang. "We cannot only manipulate time, but we can now address various Spacetime artifacts, minimizing the role of various paradoxes, or wiping them out completely."

"Paradoxes..."

"Yes," said Utang. "We could theoretically send you back to kill your grandfather without wiping out your own existence."

"Impossible. I would never be born," said Plato.

"You are thinking too linearly," chided the scientist. "Adhering to only the abscissa—past, present, and future. We can move along the fourth axis. We can merge laterally with an alternate reality where you continue to exist, despite having wiped out your grandfather in another reality."

Plato suddenly was overcome with dizziness. He reached out, placing his hand on the hull of the ship to steady himself, but his hand sunk into the liquid metal. Captain Utang reached out, grabbed his arm, and steadied the Avatar.

"This...this is too dangerous. Such power in the hands of any race can be catastrophic," said Plato.

"There are limits," said Captain Utang.

"If we manipulate too many cones, the ability to factor out others becomes limited and the Spacetime continuum becomes unstable," added the scientist. "We could literally rip the fabric of existence apart."

"What if you make a catastrophic error?" asked Plato. "One that you cannot undo."

"We have made arrangements for such a contingency," said Utang. The statement was cryptic.

"How?" asked Plato. "The only way to address that..." his eyes widened in horror, "...is to have a second time travelling ship."

"Spacetime travelling ship," the scientist corrected.

"How did you have time to develop this?" asked Plato. "The Feng Empire had been defeated in Intergalactic War 4.0."

"Which only motivated us to innovate more," said Utang. "We were always on the cusp of this discovery. The United Intergalactic Coalition gave us the final push we needed."

"You want me to help disguise your Spacetime travelling ship so it can mimic a Vortex Fighter, which means you wish to go back to a point in Spacetime involving the Humani."

The scientist smiled at the Captain Utang. "This truly is a remarkable Avatar. He exhibits the capacity for independent thought and analysis."

"Imagine the possibilities," said Utang. "Imagine a universe without the bungling of Humans. Imagine a reality where the Avatar are the overlords of the Humani. Imagine a reality where worlds and races are free to choose their own destinies, and everyone has a seat at the table. Plato, with this technology, anything is possible."

Plato felt the room spin. "This cannot be real."

"We will make it real," said Utang, gazing down into Plato's eyes as they rolled back into his skull and the world became dark.

* * *

"Killing you?" laughed Hubritia. "With all due respect, I think the emperor has had too much Dragon's Breath!"

Emperor Hiron stared Bobot Tegrit down, ignoring Hubritia's deflection. "Where is it supposed to happen, Bobot? Do you plan to get me alone? Your Coalition Marines are under guard in the hangar bay, and my guard surrounds me."

"You are, once again, wrong, Hiron," said Bobot, purposefully eliminating the title of emperor, a significant insult. He clapped his hands, and suddenly the din in the banquet hall ceased. The UIC inspectors reached under the dining tables and produced small automatic rifles. The doors to the banquet hall slammed shut, and the secondary blast doors fell, locking into place.

Emperor Hiron laughed at this. "Interesting. The only way those weapons could have been hidden like that was by someone on my staff. There is a traitor in our midst.

"The more important question is, how will your assassins make it to the dais to complete their mission? My guard will cut them down in seconds."

Vice Executor Kazar and Vice of the Interior Hayati rose and stood behind their emperor, while Imperial Bursar Tengani sat in his chair, paralyzed with fear. Hubritia looked at Bobot, then the armed inspectors, and then back to Bobot, incredulous. The Imperial Haram and Hiron's wives cowered at their table, crying out. Cegnis stood up, eying her husband, her hand on Regana Utang's shoulder. Hiron's sons fell silent, looking on confused with terrified eyes, expecting some kind of reassurance.

"Defend your emperor!" Hiron commanded his guard, curious why they hadn't yet moved from their positions.

"It would appear that your Imperial Guard has deserted you, Hiron," said Bobot. "Just like your lords and houses in your crumbling empire."

Hubritia reached out and placed a delicate hand on Bobot's arm. "Bobot, what is the meaning of this?"

He shrugged it off and backed away from her. "Hubritia, you wanted to be an instrument of peace between the Feng and the United Intergalactic Coalition."

"Yes," she said, "but this is not the path to peace, Bobot."

Bobot frowned. "But Hubritia, I am afraid it is."

"This is a violation of our own peace accord! I will have no part of this," she said.

"I am afraid you play a key part in this," said Bobot, nodding to the assassins.

Two of the assassins took aim and fired at Hubritia, lighting her up. Her body jerked and convulsed as it was torn apart by bullets, her blood spraying green all over the table, Emperor Hiron, and Bobot.

When she fell, her head hitting the table and her body crumbling into a heap on the floor, the assassins ceased fire. The echo resonated in the banquet hall.

Bobot grabbed his cloth napkin off the table and wiped her blood off his face. "Emperor Hiron, you have attacked a representative of the United Intergalactic Coalition, violating the peace accord."

Hiron was shocked by Bobot's murder of his fellow UIC dignitary and the treason in the ranks of his elite guard. "You drew first blood."

Bobot threw his cloth back onto the table. "On the contrary. I see a United Intergalactic Coalition representative executed by Feng weaponry, her body destroyed, ripped to shreds by Feng ammunition."

"Do you mean to murder me next?" asked Hiron. He puffed his chest out in defiance. "Get it over with if that was what you came to do."

"So brave, even in the face of certain death," said Bobot. "You Feng really are pieces of work."

"You may murder me in my own banquet hall, but spare the women and children," said Hiron, more a demand than a plea.

Wan Tengani looked at his emperor in horror, shocked that he was not included in those named to be spared. Cegnis squeezed Regana Utang's shoulder, her eyes frightened and defiant.

"How noble of you," remarked Bobot. "However, you are in no position to make demands."

"Then before you murder me in cold blood and massacre my imperial court, at least tell me who in my ranks conspired against me," said Hiron.

"That would be me," said a voice from behind him, as Hiron's sword was unsheathed from its scabbard by another's hands.

However, a warrior's reflexes were infinitely faster than those of a politician. Before the blade struck, Hiron whirled around and caught it in his bare hand. He clenched the blade as warm, black blood oozed between his fingers.

Gripping Hiron's sword, Monsu Kazar stood there dumbfounded, taken by surprise by Hiron's reflexes. He had totally expected to kill Hiron then and there with the thrust of the emperor's own blade, a truly symbolic act. In his ambition, the vice executor had neglected the fact that this emperor fought in countless battles, ending the lives of countless combatants by his own hand, whereas Monsu Kazar was soft from a career of sitting in committees, living off the fruits of those that fought for his comfort. It was a grave miscalculation indeed.

Hiron shoved Kazar backward, ramming the hilt of the blade into his face, splitting his lips. "You soft piece of garbage, you thought you could best *me*?"

Kazar looked around, panicked, for help from anyone. He saw his wife looking on, clenching her fists and shaking them, goading him into fighting back. 'Do it,' they said. 'Finish him.' Bobot Tegrit looked on, appearing bored at the current state of affairs.

Hiron ripped the sword from Kazar's flimsy grip, hefting it into his own. He swung the sword, stopping it short of Kazar's neck. "Traitor! All of your ambitions! All of your maneuvering was to hand the Feng legacy over to the United Intergalactic Coalition! To the Humani!"

Kazar, ever the coward, shook his head in denial of the accusations, but to no avail. He had been exposed, and there was no going back. He looked at Bobot. "Do something!"

Bobot looked to his assassins and nodded. They converged upon the dais, weapons raised. Hiron paid them no mind. He only glared at the traitorous scoundrel shrinking before his blade, but he did not strike.

"You will live to see another day, Monsu Kazar, but know this…I will be back, and you will die by my hand."

Kazar saw the assassins taking aim. He opened his mouth to tell them to wait, but Bobot gave the order. They opened fire. Hiron turned to face the execution squad, twirling his sword in an attempt to deflect the bullets. He was fast, deflecting some while his armor deflected others, but there were too many.

Hiron tumbled backwards as the bullets ripped through his exposed flesh—his neck, his hands, his face. They pelted his armor, which eventually yielded. He continued to swing his sword blindly, as he was pushed further and further back, Bobot's assassins advancing with every step of Hiron's retreat. Black blood sprayed from Hiron's body as he fought, refusing to fall.

At last, the embattled emperor succumbed in front of the large digital tapestry of himself. He crumpled to the floor at the feet of his own effigy that stood triumphantly in its depiction, chest puffed out, power and invincibility personified.

Vice Executor Kazar ran over to his fallen emperor, horrified by the outcome of decacycles of planning and conspiring with Bobot Tegrit. Filled with a mixture of vindication and regret, he looked on at the fruits of his dirty politics.

"You have betrayed your kind to these Barberoi," rasped Hiron from the floor as blood streamed out of his mouth.

"I am protecting my kind by insuring their survival in the new order," said Monsu Kazar softly.

It was at the feet of his image that Hiron looked up at himself, smiled softly, and gave his last breath.

Regana stood and cried out, reaching a hand out to her emperor. Cegnis produced a dagger and drove it into her back. Regana clutched it as her crystal blue robes darkened with black Feng blood.

Bobot nodded to the poised assassins, who then fired on the imperial court, cutting them down as the mutinous Imperial Guard looked on. The women were massacred, save Cegnis. Even Wan Tengani was murdered.

When the gunfire had ceased, Bobot pointed to Hiron's sons. "Them, too."

This was a step too far for Monsu Kazar. He leapt at Bobot, grabbing his shoulders. "No! That is enough! We are not animals!"

The assassins paused, waiting for confirmation. Bobot looked at Kazar, his expression desperate, and waved them off.

"Thank you," gasped Kazar.

"Seal the Imperial Palace," directed Bobot. "I must send word to Admiral Renolfo that we have been attacked and need immediate rescue."

"You should not have killed him," said Kazar.

Bobot laughed. "Should I have let him skewer you? Do not go soft on me now, Kazar."

Kazar shook his head. "I needed him to tell me what Operation: Catalyst was."

"It is no matter. The Feng emperor has fallen. The rest of the empire will follow, but we must act now."

"Right," said Kazar, rounding the dais. He met up with Cegnis and embraced her. "Take Bobot Tegrit to the communications control room and help him contact the UIC Armada."

Cegnis nodded. "Follow me," she said to Bobot, who trailed her as she opened the exits to the hall and darted out.

Vice Executor Kazar approached the sergeant of the Imperial Guard. "I know that must have been difficult to watch, but it was necessary for the safety and prosperity of the Feng people."

The guards were not accustomed to explanations of their orders. They only followed them. In this case, they followed the orders given by Captain Idoni. However, the vice executor was a politician, not a captain or general, so he felt the need to rationalize to them. "We must seal the castle and free the UIC Marines in the hangar bay. Then we execute Invasion Protocol Alpha," he instructed. "Time is of the essence."

Invasion Protocol Alpha was a measure designed to prevent the palace from being besieged from the enemy. However, in this case, the enemy was General Yoshi Utang and his battalion of Cybions. Kazar needed to keep them out and cut off their communications until the UIC Armada arrived to help secure the planet.

A task that, even given the advanced security of the palace under lockdown, was easier said than done.

CHAPTER 15

Vice Executor Kazar, escorted by a complement of Palace Guard, raced to the Defense Control Room. When he reached the portal, he left three guards outside, entered, and sealed the door behind him. The technicians in the room stood when he entered, a gesture of respect commensurate with his title of vice executor. He shoved past them and worked the controls inside, dropping the secondary emergency blast door.

Startled, Lieutenant Haza stood up from his control panel as the rest of the guard stationed there. "Vice Executor, to what do I owe—?"

Kazar cut him off. "We are under attack! The emperor is dead! We must execute Invasion Protocol Alpha!"

This was a great deal for Lieutenant Haza to digest so quickly. "Under attack? By whom? Who killed the emperor? Are they in the palace?"

"Hiron fired on the UIC Inspectors," explained Kazar. "He conspired with General Yoshi Utang to double-cross the inspection team, bringing war down on the Feng. He even murdered one representative in cold blood.

"He is dead, and now I am in charge. General Utang will be returning from the countryside with his battalion of Cybions. We need to hold him off until the Coalition Armada arrives."

"Cybions? Coalition Armada?"

"Lieutenant, do I need to spell out what will happen if a battalion of mutinous Cybions gains entry into the palace? The emperor has fallen, I am in command, and we need the United Intergalactic Coalition's protection, or the empire will tear itself apart!"

Haza's face turned white. He looked at the Palace Guard stationed in the room. They appeared to follow Kazar's orders unquestioningly, which was all the confirmation he needed at the moment.

He nodded and ushered Kazar over to the controls. "Enacting Invasion Protocol Alpha under the authority of Vice Executor Kazar."

He entered in the security password, and then Kazar entered his own to authorize it.

Alarms sounded throughout the Imperial Palace, indicating that they were under siege. Digital and voice messages dispersed throughout, directing security to man their battle stations and dignitaries and staff to take shelter in their living quarters. Little did Lieutenant Haza know that the highest-ranking cabinet members lay dead in the banquet hall.

Security, blast, and fire doors fell outside and within the palace, sealing it shut and sectioning off the interior. Outside, the cliffs surrounding the castle, driven by hydraulics, changed their pitch, creating a steep incline. Water sprayed out and immediately solidified to a sheet of ice. At the base of the incline, metal doors retracted, opening up moats around the palace—deep, yawning chasms ending in boiling pits of magma.

On the main floor of the palace, the metal corridors sealed off and were set to change configuration every fifteen micros, creating a protean labyrinth that even General Utang and his Cybions would find difficult to navigate.

Not too far away, Cegnis burst into the palace deep space communications control room with Bobot Tegrit as the alarms sounded just in time to be sealed in by the emergency blast doors.

"We need to open communications with Admiral Renolfo of the United Intergalactic Coalition Armada!" she ordered the Warrant Officer.

"What is the meaning of this?" He looked at Bobot. "What is he doing *here*?"

"We are under attack! Vice Executor Kazar is in command, and this inspector needs to call Admiral Renolfo."

"Of the United Intergalactic Coalition? I need authorization. Where is Emperor Hiron?"

"He is dead."

"What?"

"My husband is in command!"

"I need his authorization."

"And you shall have it," said Kazar's voice over the com. "We are under attack by General Yoshi and his battalion of Cybions. He is a traitor to the empire. We need to keep him out until reinforcements arrive. I am protecting what's left of the UIC inspection team."

"Yes, sir." The Warrant Officer opened coms to the United Intergalactic Coalition Armada. Within seconds, they reached

Admiral Renolfo. Her image appeared on screen. "What is the meaning of this?"

Bobot stepped forward, placing a hand on Cegnis Kazar's shoulder. "Admiral, we were attacked by Emperor Hiron as part of a double-cross."

"What? They dare to attack our inspection team?"

"It was Emperor Hiron. Vice Executor Kazar thwarted the attack and has taken us into protective custody. There is civil unrest on this planet, and Hiron's general is returning from the countryside with a battalion of Cybions. Vice Executor Kazar can use the palace defenses to hold them off, but not indefinitely."

"Where is Hiron?"

"Dead."

"And Hubritia Liguri?"

"She was murdered in cold blood, Admiral."

"Where is Vice Executor Kazar?"

"He is mobilizing the palace defenses. This is his wife, Cegnis Kazar."

"We are shocked and ashamed that it has come to this," said Cegnis, bowing her head. "But my husband has assumed command. He was not a part of Emperor Hiron's treachery."

"It is true," said Kazar from his control room, patching into the transmission. "I was not a part of any of this."

Renolfo nodded. "Yes, your sympathy with United Intergalactic Coalition is well-known, Vice Executor Kazar. I am sending our top battle group to stabilize Feng. They will be there within the cycle."

"Thank you, Admiral," said both Kazar and Bobot.

Her image flickered off the screen.

"What happens now?" asked Cegnis.

"The UIC will initiate the Pax Galactus Initiative, as we discussed," said Bobot. "They will stabilize Feng and install a constitution. The Feng Empire will become a democracy, and you will be in the driver's seat."

"Good," said Vice Executor Kazar over the coms. "If we can keep General Utang out long enough."

* * *

Captain Trevor Reinhardt strode down a corridor on the Resilience as he made his way towards the battle bridge. As he rounded a corner, Commander Mariu Ashwani joined him, keeping pace.

"What's the situation?" asked Ashwani.

"The Feng have attacked the inspection team."

"Jesus, I didn't think they were *that* brazen."

"Emperor Hiron was killed, and the vice executor is holed up in the palace, supposedly protecting what's left of the team."

"So we're talking full-blown coup."

"Yes, but the palace is under siege by General Yoshi Utang."

"Do you think the palace will hold their own until we get there?'"

"Utang has a battalion of Cybions."

Ashwani knew what that meant. "I bet they never thought they had to defend against their own, and Cybions no less. Are we expecting any resistance from the Feng Armada?"

"Vice Executor Kazar said he's given strict orders for them not to engage when we arrive."

They arrived at the battle bridge. A sensor scanned Reinhardt's pupils, and an affirmative tone preceded the blast door opening. He stepped inside, followed by Ashwani. The room was alight with monitors and holographic displays of various points of data—sonar, radar, planned position indicators.

"Captain on deck!" Everyone in the room stood and saluted. Reinhardt returned the salute, and they all went back to their stations.

"Can we trust him?" asked Ashwani.

"I'm not," said Reinhardt. Then to a Warrant Officer, "Put me in contact with the operations room."

"Yes, sir."

Reinhardt and Ashwani entered the conference room just off the bridge. They took their places at the table, and Reinhardt pressed a button, and Admiral Renolfo appeared as a holograph. They saluted, she returned the salute, and they each took a seat.

"Captain Reinhardt, I assume you received the communique about the situation on Feng?"

"Yes, Admiral."

"We are sending a combined joint task force for pacification, and I would like you to be Task Force Commander."

Reinhardt looked at Ashwani, uncertain of how to react.

Renolfo frowned. "I know you must be wondering, 'Why you?'"

"The thought had crossed my mind."

"If I appointed a Humani Task Force Commander, the optics could be detrimental. The Feng have already been trying to spin our activities as unwanted aggression to create a coalition against the UIC."

Reinhardt flashed a joyless smile. "So if the pacification is led by a Human TFC, it won't be a Humani vs. Feng thing."

"Exactly. I will serve as Theater Commander. You will be reporting directly to me." Renolfo said it as if it was to offer some sort of consolation. Reinhardt knew it was more for the Humani behind the scenes watching nervously than for him.

"Who are the players in this joint task force?" asked Reinhardt.

Renolfo sent encrypted data, which was tabulated on screen in the conference room. "Homunculi, Human, and Vampiri. Minimal Humani, mostly pilots."

"What do we have to work with?" asked Ashwani.

"A division of strike marines and an armored division. Marines, mechs and tanks."

"You're welcome," quipped Reinhardt.

The joke was lost on Renolfo. "When you arrive and secure orbit around Feng, you will dispatch scouts for reconnaissance while collaborating with the Feng planetary defense in regards to orbital artillery. Your first objective on the ground will be to secure the Feng Imperial Palace. Once that has been achieved, you will dispatch marine assault carriers and landing ships and collaborate with Feng air and ground sections to secure the capital."

"Do we want to use Feng infantry outside the capital?" asked Reinhardt. "I don't think we should be using Feng to pacify Feng. Too unreliable. We won't know who's siding with who."

Renolfo nodded her agreement. "Once we secure the capital, you will create a military staging base on the geographical fringe."

"We'll lay down preparatory fire in multiple surrounding landing zones and send in the strike marines to fan out and sweep the manors. I'll detach fighter squadrons and flights as needed to address any hot spots of insurgency."

"I'll make sure we establish logistic supply chains to the staging base and ground units," added Ashwani. "And we'll need Feng assault vehicles. They're better designed for the harsh Feng climate than our assault vehicles."

"I am sending you data on Feng topography, climate, manor, and district structure as well as any other relevant information."

Ashwani consulted their data feed. "Got it."

"I also sent you the modified rules of engagement for this operation."

Reinhardt looked them over. "Kinda tight."

Renolfo nodded. "We must be cautious. The universe is watching."

Ashwani pointed at their screen. "Not so tight regarding the Cybions. Kill on sight."

"There is to be no hesitation with them, and only Cybions on the planet are with General Utang, who has been deemed an insurgent."

"Got it," said Reinhardt.

"I will contact you once we have entered the Feng system," said Renolfo.

They all stood, saluted, and Renolfo's hologram disapparated. Reinhardt and Ashwani left the conference room and took their places on the bridge.

Reinhardt turned to Ashwani. "Commander, prepare to take us to the nearest wormhole node."

Ashwani consulted one of the holographic charts. "Plot vector to the nearest wormhole node, destination: the Feng System."

"Vector plotted, Commander," answered the helmsman.

"Take us there, three-quarter conduction speed for Spacetime handshake."

"Nodal handshake in T-minus sixty micros," crackled the voice on the other end.

"A lot can happen in an Earth hour," said Reinhardt, frowning.

* * *

On planet Feng, General Yoshi Utang heard the sirens screeching from the Imperial Palace. He knew what it meant, but he couldn't believe it. The palace was under attack. He and his battalion of Cybions raced on their darkcycles to the palace to find the moats opened, ice deployed, and blast doors down.

They pulled to a stop just before the main entrance. He activated his com. "This is General Yoshi Utang. I am outside the front entrance. Acknowledge."

He waited as the Cybions perched on their cycles, frozen in time with the stillness only machines could achieve. When there was no answer, General Utang repeated his transmission. "This is General Yoshi Utang. I am outside the front entrance. Acknowledge."

Still, no answer.

He decided to ride around the palace on his cycle, the obedient Cybions in tow, to survey the situation. As he rounded the palace checking his scanners, the furious sky roiling above, he saw that there was no sign of any enemy units assailing the palace.

He raised communication again as he sped around the palace perimeter. "This is General Utang, what is your situation? Acknowledge!"

The lines were silent.

Utang drove past the hangar bays, which were also sealed. He saw the icy, inclined ramparts and the open moats. This only meant one thing—Invasion Protocol Alpha. He looked up at the sky and saw no ships entering the atmosphere. Something triggered the palace defenses, but he didn't know what.

He got back on his com, this time using Emperor Hiron's classified frequency. "Emperor Hiron, this is General Utang outside the palace walls. Please acknowledge."

Silence.

Frustrated at not knowing what exactly was happening and his inability to raise anyone inside the Imperial Palace, Utang pounded the console on his darkcycle.

*

"There is someone outside the palace wall," announced Lieutenant Haza in the control room.

"It is General Utang," said Vice Executor Kazar.

"What do you want me to do?"

"Nothing. We need to buy all the time we can. Let him plod around outside in the cold. He does not know what has happened. The longer it takes him to figure it out, the better for us."

"The UIC Armada is on its way," said Bobot.

"How long?" asked Kazar.

"They are less than a sexagen out from nodal handshake. Spacefold will take another twenty minutes."

"So, we are talking another couple of sexagens," said Kazar, his voice impatient.

"Blast Utang into oblivion with the rail guns," suggested Cegnis.

"Only if he figures out what is happening," insisted Kazar. "So far, he is driving around the palace attempting to raise anyone inside."

"He is not stupid, Monsu," pressed Cegnis.

"If he makes a move to assault the palace, I will fire. Until then, we need every minute."

*

Suddenly, General Utang had an idea. He instructed one of the Cybions to breach the palace. The Cybion's eyes gleamed with acknowledgement. It raised a mechanical arm and cycled through various projectiles, summoning a small grappling spike. He fired into the wall in front of them, but the ice was so hard and thick the spike merely bounced off, failing to find purchase.

It fired again at the blast door, hoping the metal was more pregnable, but the emergency blast door also repelled the grappling spike. The Cybion took a running start and leapt over the chasm, landing on the icy incline on the other side. It deployed elbow spikes and shin blades as it slid down the incline towards the yawning gap below. The sharp edges dug into the ice as the cyborg slid to the edge, stopping short of falling into the pit.

It selected the flamethrower from its arsenal and began to melt the ice on the incline. General Utang then sent the order for one hundred other Cybions to leap the moat. They were able to latch onto the now iceless incline with relative ease and began to shimmy their way over to the emergency blast door.

They deployed their metal cutters and began working on the door as a unit, targeting the spots were the hydraulics held the doors in place.

*

"Sir, the Cybions are attempting to breach the main entrance," said Lieutenant Haza.

"Activate perimeter guns," said Kazar. "Open fire."

*

There was the sound of mechanical doors opening over the frigid, howling wind. General Utang turned to see the perimeter guns deploying, targeting the Cybions. He ducked down behind his darkcycle as the guns fired, lighting up the Cybions cutting through the blast door. Their bodies shook as they were riddled with the impact of the bullets, and they fell backwards into the abyss, silently meeting their end by incineration, their remains engulfed by lava.

"I knew it!" shouted Utang to no one in particular.

He instructed the remaining Cybions to take out the guns. They leapt into action, dodging gunfire and deploying their blades, guns, and flamethrowers. They sliced and diced the perimeter guns as Utang hopped back on his darkcycle.

He tore off through the corridor that the Cybions created, and they followed on their cycles, some taking fire as they sped off away from the palace.

General Utang cursed himself for doubting Talbo Cyclesse. The Imperial Palace had been taken, and the status of Emperor Hiron was unknown. He knew those Barberoi inspectors were behind this, and he knew deep within his gullet that they had help from within Feng ranks. He cursed Monsu Kazar under his breath as he sped off back through the industrial sector and into the countryside.

He raced back toward Lord Xiang's manor with only four hundred or so Cybions. The palace defenses had cut his battalion down by half in minutes. He was not going to breach the palace under current conditions.

He sprinted through countryside alongside the Crystelline Forest with his two remaining companies of Cybions. Despite the situation at the palace, there were no other signs of skirmishes or battles.

Lord Xiang's manor was closest. As he passed through the gatehouse, Xiang's guard parted, recognizing the general and the Cybions and allowing them to pass. From a distance, he saw the house, having heard the sirens, was on high alert.

As he rode up, Xiang's inner guard blocked Utang's entry, standing fast in front of the large, closed iron doors. He stopped his darkcycle right in front, the Cybions flanking him.

"I must see Lord Xiang immediately," said General Utang.

"We have been given orders to admit no one," said the lieutenant, eying the Cybions nervously.

Utang strode up and practically stood nose-to-nose with the lieutenant. "Do you have any idea who I am?"

"Yes, sir. You are General Utang of the Imperial Army. I am only obeying my lord."

"Your loyalty is to the empire first, and your lord second," snarled Utang.

"The empire is under attack," stated the lieutenant.

"Which is why we need to see Lord Xiang," insisted Utang. "I am declaring martial law. The Imperial Palace is under siege."

The lieutenant pressed his finger to his helmet. He was receiving a transmission. "Lord Xiang will see you now."

Utang was outraged that he was only being granted an audience because Lord Xiang allowed it. However, time was of the essence. The manor guard opened the doors and stepped aside, and General Utang and his Cybions entered the manor proper.

Utang ordered his cyborgs to fan out across the property and remain on high alert. Treason was in the air on Planet Feng, and he didn't want to be taken off guard, especially since he was uncertain of where Xiang's allegiance lie.

Two Cybions accompanied Utang into the manor house where they were met by Lord Xiang in the antechamber.

"Come, let us speak privately in my den," said Lord Xiang.

Utang nodded, following Xiang up the stairs and to the left. Lord Xiang threw open the doors and gestured for Utang to enter. Utang stationed his two Cybions at the door and entered, followed by Xiang, who sealed the doors behind them.

"The palace is on high alert," said Lord Xiang. "Yet, there is no sign of any threat."

"The palace has been taken from within," said Utang, removing his helmet and placing it on an ornate table carved with the Xiang family crest. "The coalition inspection team is behind this."

"They would not *dare*," said Xiang in disbelief.

"I believe they had help."

"Who within the palace would commit such treason?" gasped Xiang, placing a hand over his mouth.

"I have reason to believe that Vice Executor Kazar is behind this."

"Impossible," said Xiang.

"He has been a UIC sympathizer since his rise to the office of vice executor."

"But what you speak of is treason. Emperor Hiron would not allow it."

"I have not heard from our emperor," said Utang, his expression grave. "I fear that something has happened to him."

"If that is true, then it is not only an act of treason, it is an act of war by the United Intergalactic Coalition."

"Exactly," said Utang, pacing the room. "They would not seize the palace without an exit strategy."

"The Coalition Armada," said Xiang. "They are going to invade."

Utang nodded. "I am afraid so. I need to alert the planetary defense, and we need to rally the manors and launch an assault to retake the palace."

Lord Xiang frowned. "But you just came from the palace, and forgive me for saying, but your battalion looks significantly lighter than when you were here before."

General Utang stopped pacing the room. "We attempted to breach the palace and were fired upon. That is how I know the palace has been taken. I need to send a transmission to the planetary defense from your control room. Now."

"But of course," said Lord Xiang. "Follow me."

Lord Xiang led General Utang to his personal control room. "I do not think that you can reach planetary defense from here."

"I am going to tap into the satellite using remote access of the palace's communications network." Utang shoved Xiang aside and began his hack into the palace system, using his classified authorization code. The screen flashed the words, 'Access Denied,' in red. "Frak it all! That scoundrel Kazar locked me out!"

Xiang narrowed his eyes, examining the lower left corner of the screen. "It appears that the Imperial Palace has jammed all communications on and off the planet. The communications grid cannot be accessed."

"We must mobilize the other manors. Our only hope is to retake the palace. Assemble your messengers. I will need an inventory of all of your warriors, from your enforcers to the manor house guard."

Lord Xiang looked dubious. "General Utang, the Imperial Palace is under siege, and we are unaware of the status of our Holy Emperor. You and your Cybion storm troopers have swarmed the countryside, inflicting Eugenesis on my manor and interrogating my fiefs. Now you expect me to sacrifice my men, leaving my manor vulnerable, so that you can wage war against what you think is the United Intergalactic Coalition staging a coup with our vice executor?"

Rage welled up inside General Utang. He crossed the room, menacing the insubordinate Lord Xiang. "Do you choose to engage in treason against the Feng Empire as well? Under the authority of martial law, I command you to do as I say without question."

"Forgive me, General, but I have no confirmation on the emperor's status, or that of the vice executor for that matter. I answer to them before you."

Utang growled at the recalcitrant lord. "I can have the Cybions rip your precious manor apart."

"I am afraid that you have already done so, General."

"Do you dare defy me?"

"I know what you have done to Lord Talbo Cyclesse. You murdered him, a true loyalist of the empire, in cold blood in his own manor house, along with his dear wife."

"That was a mistake," said Utang.

"I am loyal to the emperor and the vice executor," said Xiang. "You have offered no evidence that the palace has been commandeered by traitors or the United Intergalactic Coalition. You said so, yourself, you were fired upon by the palace defenses. How do I know *you* are not the traitor in this scenario?"

"You disobedient son-of-a-tuthgar!" Utang grabbed Xiang by the throat and squeezed. The impotent lord made no move to resist.

Utang released the man and paced across the room as Xiang clutched his throat and gasped for air.

General Utang wondered if he had so beaten down this lord and his manor that they were not only unable to help, but they also no longer had the will. He also wondered if the other manors would react the same way, especially after Hiron unleashed his Cybion monsters on the citizenry to quell all sedition.

He felt chest pains as he realized that the Feng Empire was crumbling before his very eyes, and he was powerless to do anything about it. As he bent over clutching his chest, the monitor in Xiang's control room displayed Vice Executor Kazar's face.

"Manors and houses of the Feng Empire, I, Vice Executor of the Feng Empire, am addressing you with grave news. As I am sure you have heard, I have activated palace defenses in a state of dire emergency as we have come under attack.

"In an attempt to derail the treaty between the Feng Empire and the United Intergalactic Coalition, our very own General Yoshi Utang of the Feng Imperial Army has attempted to stage a coup within the Imperial Palace, resulting in the murder of Emperor Hiron and an important United Intergalactic Coalition official.

"I have regained control of the palace and have assumed authority of the Feng Empire. General Yoshi Utang remains at large with a battalion of Cybions, but their numbers have been vastly reduced in the battle to regain control of the palace. He is a fugitive among you, and remains incredibly dangerous.

"I recommend that you secure your manors to the best of your ability and do not offer refuge to this traitor. If he attempts to make contact, notify the palace immediately. Any attempts of your enforcer's forces to take him into custody must be executed with extreme caution. Please be advised, as he is a traitor, it is not necessary to take him alive.

"I have, in collaboration with the United Intergalactic Coalition, requested assistance from the Coalition Armada in securing our palace and territories. They make spacefold shortly and will offer much needed support. In the meantime, take care of your manors and try to remain safe. Take all of the necessary precautions as we bring this assassin and traitor to justice.

"I will address you at a later time with our progress. The Feng Empire will live on and prosper in these dark times."

The image flickered off screen.

General Utang, his suspicions validated, was outraged. He turned to Lord Xiang, who now had a gun on him. Utang hadn't even seen him make a move for it. Everything was just spiraling out of control.

"Now wait a minute," pleaded Utang.

"I have heard all that I have needed to hear," said Lord Xiang. "Please, do not resist."

"Your guard will never make it past my Cybions into this room."

"Your Cybions will not make it into this room before I blast a hole in your skull, General."

"Kazar is lying," said Utang. "He is behind this."

"Once again, where is your proof?"

"Why would the vice executor bring the Coalition Armada here when we have our own floating in orbit around the planet?"

"It would leave the planet vulnerable," explained Lord Xiang.

The expression on Utang's face was desperate. "Do you not see? The United Intergalactic Coalition is going to use the Pax Galactus Initiative! They are going to topple the Feng government!"

"Perhaps it is time for new leadership."

"Lord Xiang, how do you think lords will fare in a coalition democracy?"

"Better than they fare under a despot who punishes his own people."

"Listen to me."

"You have no authority here, General."

Utang threw his hands up in resignation. "So, what happens now? If you shoot me, my Cybions will break into this room and eviscerate you where you stand."

"If they come into this room, I will shoot. I do not have to be a marksman at this range, General."

"Let me go. I will leave without harming anyone in your manor. I swear it."

Xiang wore a joyless grin. "Well, it is refreshing to have *you* in a position where you must beg for mercy. How does it feel?"

Utang was no longer angry. He just felt defeated, resigned to the reality unfolding before him. "I beg of you, Lord Xiang. Spare me. Let me go."

Lord Xiang weighed his options in his mind. This was a true standoff. He had to let the traitor go. "Go, but leave your helmet here. My snipers will track you until you leave the manor grounds. Turn to attack, and your head will be burst open like a hu li melon."

General Utang nodded. "Thank you. I regret any harm that I have done to your house."

Lord Xiang huffed at the remark. "Do not thank me, General. With the manors hunting you and the United Intergalactic Coalition arriving, your fate is inevitable." Then he opened his com. "Let the general go, but I want snipers keeping his exposed head in their sights until he has left the manor."

General Utang nodded again and left the room, leaving his helmet on the wooden table. Lord Xiang walked over to the helmet and ran his clawed fingers over the cold metal.

He was uncertain of his future and that of his manor in the time to come, but he knew for certain this was the last time he would see General Yoshi Utang alive.

CHAPTER 16

"Entering spacefold in T-minus twenty microns."

Captain Reinhardt and Commander Ashwani braced themselves as the neural network on the hull of the command carrier Resilience initiated a handshake with the Spacetime node. In seconds, the ship and its accompanying battle group leapt into a wormhole taking them to the Feng System.

As they exited the wormhole, the battle group lurched back into Spacetime just inside the Feng system in battle formation.

"Launch hunter-killers," commanded Reinhardt.

"Hunter-killers launched," confirmed Ashwani.

"On screen," said Reinhardt. "I want readings on the positions of every vessel in the planetary defense's outer screen."

"Aye, Captain," said Ashwani.

Within microns, the readouts detailed positions on the locations of all Feng Armada vessels outside of orbit.

"Open communication to the Feng outer screen."

"Com link opened, sir," answered a communications officer.

"This is Captain Trevor Reinhardt of the command carrier Resilience of the United Intergalactic Coalition Armada. We are about to enter Feng space to aid in the pacification of planet Feng in accordance with the Pax Galactus Initiative."

He paused, waiting for a response.

"Captain Reinhardt," said a voice on the other end of the com as translated by the Resilience's quantum translation processors, "this is Commander Fros of the Feng Armada Planetary Outer Defense Screen..."

"That's a mouthful," said Ashwani. Reinhardt shot her a look.

"...we have been expecting you."

"Permission to enter Feng space," said Reinhardt.

"Permission granted. You may pass through to the inner screen and then prepare to enter planetary orbit."

"Hunter-killers show that the Feng vessels are on high alert, but their weapons systems are in cooldown," said Lieutenant Poi.

"Always a good sign," said Ashwani.

Reinhardt nodded. "Proceed ahead, half conduction, weapons hot. We're on high alert."

"You heard the captain," echoed Ashwani. "Ahead, half conduction, weapons hot, high alert."

The United Intergalactic Coalition battle group entered the outer screen as the Feng vessels sat motionless, allowing them to pass.

"I can't believe it," said Ashwani. "They're actually standing down."

"We're not out of the woods yet, Commander."

"Sir, hunter-killers have now entered the Feng inner screen," said Lieutenant Poi.

More readings collected on the various displays on Feng Armada formation—assessment of High Valued Units, Class A through D Threat Assessment, calculations of Order of Engagement.

"Not much of an armada," said Ashwani, reading the data.

"The Feng Empire has been weakened considerably," said Reinhardt. "They're a shell of their former glory."

Ashwani smirked. "You sound almost disappointed, sir."

"It's a warrior-to-warrior thing," said Reinhardt.

"Would you prefer that they be at full complement to offer up a greater challenge?"

"What I prefer, Commander, is that we enter orbit and dispatch fighter squadrons and marines to stabilize the planet without incident."

"The Feng are hailing us, sir," said a communication's officer.

"Open channel," said Reinhardt.

"Captain Reinhardt," said Commander Fros, "the Feng inner screen has been commanded to stand down and allow you passage into Feng orbit."

"Hunter-killers confirm," said Lieutenant Poi. "The Feng inner screen is on high alert but weapons systems are cooled down."

"Thank you, Commander Fros," said Reinhardt.

"Admiral Razaal will greet you just outside of orbit," said Commander Fros. "From there, you will receive approach vectors for entering planetary orbit."

"Understood. Captain Reinhardt out." The communications officer terminated the com link.

All of the crew on the Resilience battle bridge were on edge as they passed Feng battleships, destroyers, and dreadnaughts. They were coming up on a massive, looming Feng command carrier. It was almost three times the size of the Resilience.

"Jesus Christ," gasped Ashwani.

Reinhardt wore a wry grin. "Never saw one up close and personal before, Commander?"

"No."

"Humbling, isn't it?"

* * *

Disgraced and a fugitive, General Yoshi Utang sped off towards Talbo Cyclesse's fallen manor house with the remnants of his battalion of Cybions. If the United Intergalactic Coalition was going to come waltzing in to topple the Feng way of life, he was in no position to stop them. However, he wasn't going to make it easy for them either. He knew that his surrender would result in his prosecution as a war criminal in both the Feng and Coalition courts, necessitating a death sentence.

As he sped past gleaming, metallic industrial spheres hovering over vast ice fields, the manufacturing sites of the Feng shipbuilding industry, he marveled at the stark beauty of his homeland. The raw, frigid landscape juxtaposed with the spectacle of technology. The industrial spheres, nature's perfect shape maximizing volume, the epitome of efficiency, floating like miniature planets over an unforgiving, untamed land. The combination was a reminder of the Feng people's fierce duality.

The Crystalline Forest flanked him once more, its barren, glimmering beauty his companion as he fled further into the countryside, away from the Imperial Palace. He encountered the confused remnants of Talbo's manor enforcers, the Cybions making quick work of them. They were no match for the clinical cyborgs.

They opened fire as the Cybions formed a protective barrier around Yoshi Utang on their darkcycles. They returned fire, deploying edged weapons, shooting and slashing their way through the barricade like a hot sword through snow, completing the utter devastation of the Cyclesse manor.

When he reached the open gates, he proceeded inside the manor property, racing up to the manor house. The snow was still littered with the bodies of Talbo's guard and house staff, lying in pools of black blood on the stark white frozen ground.

Utang dismounted and darted into the manor house, sending commands for the Cybions to establish a tight perimeter outside. The house was eerily vacant as he barged in, devoid of the sounds of house servants darting to and fro on their mundane tasks in serving their lord. The place had been abandoned.

He climbed the grand staircase and stalked down a long corridor, stopping outside a room. He waved a hand, opening the door, and he entered Talbo's sensory deprivation room where two Aether chambers sat, one for Talbo and one for Terret.

Utang activated Talbo's, firing up the matter transmutor. When he entered the desired settings, he stripped himself of the remainder of his armor down to his naked body. He entered the chamber, the door sealing him off from the outside world, as dark matter began to pour in. Within seconds, the darkness of the chamber became denser until it became the pitch of the void, and Utang was enveloped.

He closed his eyes, a futile act as his vision was irrelevant, and concentrated on the universe around him. He sensed the life forces of the planet, and he reached out with his being to the galaxies. He spanned systems until he sensed the faint presence of his brother, Mongo.

'Brother, it is Yoshi.'

There was a wordless answer in the void as the two brothers linked presences, merging memories, sharing experiences, and synergizing thought.

* * *

The command carrier Resilience drifted into the vast, looming shadow of the Feng command carrier surrounded by its battle group, and its battle group surrounded by Feng battleships, destroyers, and dreadnaughts. Although the United Intergalactic Coalition battle group was larger than the Feng's inner screen, the hulking Feng command carrier was an intimidating sight.

"Open com link with the Feng command carrier," instructed Reinhardt.

"Com link open," said the communications officer.

"This is Captain Reinhardt of the UIC command carrier Resilience, requesting permission to enter Feng orbit."

Reinhardt, the communications officer, and every member on the battle bridge and operations room waited expectantly for a reply. After a few micros, Reinhardt opened a channel and hailed the leviathan command carrier again. However, again, there was no response.

Ashwani frowned. "What's the hold-up?"

"I don't know," said Reinhardt. "Open channel."

The communication officer nodded.

"This is Captain Reinhardt of the United Intergalactic Coalition Armada requesting permission to enter Feng orbit. Please acknowledge."

Silence.

"Dammit," said Reinhardt. "Every micro we are delayed places the inspection team in greater jeopardy."

"You don't think they got cold feet, do you?" asked Ashwani.

"Captain," said Lieutenant Poi. "We're being targeted. The command carrier's weapons are heating up."

"So much for rolling out the red carpet," said Reinhardt. He nodded to his commander.

"Initiate Order of Engagement within the battlespace," ordered Ashwani. "Target Class A and B threats. Mobilize hunter-killers to engage the Feng command carrier."

"Sir, the Feng Armada is assuming battle formation," said Lieutenant Poi.

"Feng hunter-killer detected above the thermo-gradient," said a radarman.

"Localize," commanded Ashwani.

"Zig zag evasive maneuver," said Reinhardt to the helmsman. The move would interfere with the hunter-killer's target motion analysis and buy them some time.

"A second hunter-killer detected within our inner screen, sir."

"The command carrier is hailing us," said the communications officer.

"Open com," said Reinhardt.

The image of a Feng officer appeared on screen. "I am Admiral Razaal of the Feng Planetary Defense."

"I am Captain Reinhardt of the United Intergalactic Coalition Armada. Why have you targeted my battle group?"

"We ask that you maintain your positions until we give you clearance," said Admiral Razaal.

"Admiral Razaal, the longer we wait up here, the greater jeopardy our inspection team is in."

"Understood, Captain Reinhardt. Nevertheless, we order you to maintain your position until I grant you clearance to make an approach. Failure to do so will result in an armed response." His image flickered off the screen as the link terminated.

"What do we do, Captain?" asked Ashwani.

All eyes were on Reinhardt.

"We wait," he answered. "Dammit, we wait."

* * *

"There is a transmission coming from Admiral Razaal," said a communications officer to Vice Executor Kazar.

"Put him through."

"Vice Executor, the UIC Armada has arrived."

"Yes, let them through," said Kazar.

"Before I grant them passage, I must relay to you a transmission from Captain Mongo Utang."

"Captain Utang? Where is he?" asked Kazar.

"I do not know, sir, but he has advised me not to let the UIC Armada through."

"Admiral, you take your orders from me."

"Of course, sir. I was just wondering why Captain Utang would caution me about the UIC Armada. Given the unusual circumstances…"

"Unusual circumstances indeed. His brother is a traitor to the Feng Empire. General Yoshi Utang is responsible for the murder of our Holy Emperor and is currently a fugitive. Naturally, he wants to protect his brother.

"Send approach vectors to the UIC Armada immediately. Let them pass."

"Yes, sir. Consider it done." The link was severed.

"Trouble from within the ranks?" asked Bobot.

"Just a loose end that needs to be addressed," said Kazar.

"Does General Utang's brother pose a threat?"

"Not immediately," said Kazar. "However, he is working on a classified project that Hiron placed great faith in. Once we have secured the government, we will redirect our attention to the outstanding armada scattered throughout the galaxies and hunt him down."

"After you hunt down his brother, the general, first," chided Bobot.

"Yes, I am well aware of our current problems, Bobot."

"Once we have regained control of the planet, the United Intergalactic Coalition will hunt down any nuisance remainders from the old empire," assured Bobot.

Kazar didn't like the authority in Bobot's statement. The Feng were not used to taking directives from other races, particularly the Humani. However, the uneasy alliance was a necessary evil in his rise to being the first Prime Minister of Feng.

* * *

"What the hell is he waiting for?"

Captain Reinhardt, his command carrier targeted by two invisible Feng hunter-killers, had his battle group in formation, their weapons heating up. As they waited for clearance from Admiral Razaal to enter orbit around Feng, his crew in the battle bridge and operations room perched nervously over their controls with itchy trigger fingers.

"This is Admiral Razaal…" His picture appeared on screen. He looked as severe as before. "…I am forwarding approach vectors to your ship."

Reinhardt, who hadn't realized that he was holding his breath, released it. "Thank you, Admiral."

Razaal terminated the transmission.

"Not much of a conversationalist, that one," said Reinhardt.

"We have the vectors," confirmed Lieutenant Poi. They began to flash up on the displays.

"Execute," said Reinhardt.

The United Intergalactic Coalition battle group entered into orbit around the planet in battle formation, picking up speed.

"Raise communication with the Imperial Palace," said Reinhardt.

The communications officer established a com link. "Vice Executor Monsu Kazar is on the line whenever you are ready, sir."

"Put him through."

Kazar appeared on screen.

"I am Captain—"

"I know who you are. Welcome, Captain Reinhardt," interrupted Kazar. "I am Vice Executor Monsu Kazar of the Feng. We have been expecting you."

"Oh? I couldn't tell from the cold reception of your Admiral Razaal."

"A misunderstanding," said Kazar, smiling. "We are not accustomed to letting United Intergalactic Coalition battle groups into our planetary orbit."

"What is the situation on the planet?"

"We have secured the palace, and I have the Feng Air Command enforcing a protective zone around the capital. However, the traitorous General Yoshi Utang is still at large, roaming outside the capital with two companies of Cybions. The Air Command is too sparse to comb the countryside."

Reinhardt nodded. "After we secure the palace and a staging base, we will provide air support and help hunt him down. What about the various manors?"

"Most are sympathetic with our cause, following my orders. Riots have broken out in a few, the manor enforcers having been overwhelmed."

"Send me the coordinates of the unstable sectors, and I'll dispatch marines to win the peace on the ground."

"Very good, Captain. We are relieved that you are here."

"Well, let's not pop the corks on the champagne until we've won the peace."

"I am sorry?" Vice Executor Kazar was unfamiliar with the expression.

"It is premature to celebrate," explained Reinhardt.

"Yes, of course," said Kazar apologetically. "I am sending you the information you requested as we speak."

The communications officers on the Resilience began receiving the data, and Lieutenant Poi confirmed with a nod.

"We will be in touch," said Reinhardt, and he terminated the link. "Dispatch the scouts. I want confirmation that the capital is a safe zone, and I want our own coordinates of the unstable sectors," he said to Ashwani.

"Aye, Captain."

"And keep our battle group on high alert. I don't want the Feng Armada shooting us in the back while we're helping them."

*

Almost two sexagens passed as UIC scouts collected data on any and all Feng air and ground units. Reinhardt had established contact with the Feng air unit commander as well as the artillery liaison officer, who were both relaying data up to the Resilience.

Reinhardt was consulting with his communications officers and the operations room. He looked up at Ashwani. "Commander, do we have the support of the Feng orbital artillery?"

She looked up from her screen. "Aye, Captain. They're standing by."

"Dispatch Colonel Pappas to secure the palace. Detach a squadron and give him some air support."

"Aye, Captain."

It was important that they secured the palace and the inspection team within the first cycle. Once Reinhardt received confirmation from Pappas, he sent air support to three potential landing zones on the outskirts of the capital for preparatory fire. The landing party of marines inserted in one of the landing zones in thirty micro windows between rounds of preparatory fire.

Ashwani was conferring with a communications officer assigned to the landing party. "We have established contact with the ground commander. The armored division has mobilized."

Reinhardt nodded. "I want a secure channel with the commanding general as well as his deputy commanding generals for operations, support, and maneuvers."

"Aye, Captain."

"I want a full inventory of marines, mechs, and armor. Do we have permission to use Feng airfields?"

"Aye, Captain."

"Let's get our birds out there and ready. I want to launch air assault operations in no more than one cycle. We need to start sweeping the manors."

"We also have full use of Feng assault vehicles located within the capital," said Ashwani.

"Do our soldiers know how to operate them?"

"Vice Executor Kazar has relayed rapid digital tutorials to the ground commander for dissemination and training."

"Excellent, Commander."

Six cycles later, the UIC Marines fanned out from the capital, sweeping and securing manors with air support and orbital artillery support.

The pacification of Feng had begun.

* * *

One Phase (Three Cycles) Later

Commander Massa and the Razor's Edge launched from one of the Feng airbases within the capital.

"Receiving coordinates, we have a hot zone in Sector Seventeen," said Commander Massa.

Their Vortex fighters screeched across the sky, flying nap of the planet to minimize warning, noise, and detection.

The Feng landscape was vast, with large sections of unoccupied land, so the marines were transported from manor to manor via air transport.

"Break down into four flights and head to your designated sub-sectors," said Massa. "Flight A, you will provide air support to the troop transports landing in the Xiang and Cyclesse manors."

"That is us," said Nakai. "Taking the lead."

"Roger that," said Pequo.

"Roger," said Lieutenant Akron.

They took off to meet the incoming troop transports.

"I see them," said Pequo. "Calculating their velocity vectors."

"Roger," said Nakai. "I will go for the lead. You two will go for the lag."

The three-fighter flight intercepted the two transports. Nakai's vortex fell in front of the two transports, and Pequo's and Akron's fell behind, bringing up the rear.

"Scanning for insurgents," said Akron.

"Approaching Xiang Manor," said one of the transport pilots. "There is activity on the ground. It is a definite hot spot. Preparing to disengage escort."

As they passed over the rioting on the ground, they began to turn.

"No anti-aircraft on scanners," said Akron.

"Disengage escort on second pass," said Nakai.

"Roger," said the transport pilot.

When they passed over a second time, the troop transport broke from the escort and landed in the middle of the manor property, right by the manor house. The back door swung open, and marines began to pour out, fanning out across the area in formations.

"Proceed to the next hot spot," said Nakai.

"Roger," answered Pequo, Akron, and the remaining transport pilot.

Within minutes, they were coming up on the Cyclesse Manor. The Crystalline Forest below appeared to be made of glass from their vantage point.

"Scanning for insurgent activity," said Pequo. His eyes focused on data points in his helmet as they flew over the manor house. "I am picking up some serious readings. They are registering as faint lifeforms, but they are registering as hot on thermal scans. There is one normal lifeform reading."

"How many?" asked Nakai.

"About fifty or so."

"Those would be the Cybions. General Utang must be with them."

"We cannot land the transport until we take them out," said Nakai.

"Roger that," said Pequo and Akron.

"Light 'em up," said Nakai.

*

Yoshi Utang was enveloped in the Aether. 'Brother, you must carry on without the support of the armada. Feng has fallen.'

'Yoshi, I will save you.'

'No, you must forget about me and focus on the greater good. You must go back and save Emperor Hiron.'

'I intend to do both, Yoshi.'

'You will destabilize Spacetime. Save the emperor, restore the empire.'

'You misunderstand me. There is a way I can save you both and the empire in one deft stroke. When I do, none of this will matter because none of it will have happened.'

'I know what you intend to do, but I fear you are guided by your thirst for vengeance.'

'What I will do will both restore the empire and satisfy my bloodlust.'

'One deft move.'

'Yes.'

There was a loud explosion that yanked Yoshi out of the Aether, toppling the dark matter chamber. The door opened, and Yoshi's naked body spilled out onto Talbo's tile floor. He grabbed his communicator. The Cybions outside sent reports of three attacking Vortex fighters flooded his screen.

Utang slipped back into his uniform and battle armor as the house shook from nearby missile strikes. He dashed out into the hallway and down the stairs. He knew his death was imminent, but he was going to go down fighting and take as many of the Humani scum with him into the Aether.

He dashed outside into the frosty air as he saw his Cybions under siege. Equipped for land-based battle, they were no match for the Vortex fighters. Some returned fire, while others lay strewn about, lifeless and cold as the ground beneath them.

He took advantage of the chaos and hopped on his darkcycle, taking off towards the Crystalline Forest. As the Vortex fighters fired their guns, Cybions leapt in the path of the bullets, sacrificing themselves as they were programmed to do.

The Vortex fighters screamed overhead as they made pass after pass on the compound. Yoshi Utang worked the throttle, pushing the cycle to its limit as he careened over ice and snow. As he approached the tree line, he did not dare slow down. Narrowly avoiding gunfire and missile strikes, he crashed through low-lying branches and disappeared into the dense forest.

The impact threw him off his darkcycle and into a frozen tree trunk, his armor taking the brunt of the blow, knocking the wind out of him. He gasped and struggled to fill his lungs with air as bullets ripped through the glassy branches, sending shards of ice flying everywhere.

He rose to his feet and inspected the bike. It was wrapped around a tree trunk, shattered components littering the ground. Having to continue his trek on foot, he staggered through the woods, stomping through the snow, its depth making it a slow progression.

He searched his memory, struggling to remember the path his brother-in-law once showed him. The Vortex fighters made passes overhead, firing blindly down onto the sparkling canopy, the glassy branches obstructing line of sight and throwing off their sensors.

At last, he arrived at a spot in a clearing in front of a rather thick tree trunk where there sat a large mound of snow. Utang grabbed the edge of a white camouflage screen and pulled. As it slid off the structure beneath, it revealed Talbo's X15 Dragon fighter from his days in the Air Command. Mothballed decades ago, the X15 was a superior fighter, decommissioned because it was too expensive to manufacture.

He opened the cockpit, slid inside, and put on the flight helmet. He closed the cockpit and fired up the engines, checking all systems, sensors, and weapons. The X15 Dragon needed no runway to take off. Its jets pivoted, allowing it to hover.

Once the engines were fired up, he pivoted the jets and began to lift off the forest floor. He saw the Vortex fighters flying overhead, and his sensors indicated that he had been detected. He quickly rose to the top of the canopy, and as one of the Vortex fighters veered right at him, he pivoted the jets and took off on a collision course, narrowly avoiding the Humani craft.

CHAPTER 17

"We have a bogey," cried Akron, "and he is closing in on me fast!"

"I see him," said Nakai.

"Me, too," said Pequo. "Where did Utang get his hands on a fighter?"

"Alpha 3, turn to bring him back around," Nakai instructed Akron. "The transport landed safely. We are free to engage."

"Roger." Akron pulled a 10G min radius turn as Utang followed. "He is targeting me!" Akron began barrel rolling, but Utang was hot on his tail.

"Hold on, we are right behind you," said Nakai as she and Pequo turned to intersect Utang's flightpath.

Akron rolled and rolled, keeping Utang just out of his turn radius. "Hurry! He is right on me!"

For a brief moment, Utang's flightpath crossed Akron's, and he got tone. He fired on Akron, blowing him out of the sky in a ball of flame.

"He got Akron," said Pequo.

"I am going into pursuit," said Nakai. "Cover me."

Nakai fell into lag pursuit as Utang now began to displacement roll to throw her off. She turned and burned behind him, trying to cross flightpaths.

"This frak is a slippery one," she said as she tried to achieve a firing solution.

Utang went into a turn as Nakai spiraled upward and banked left, falling in behind him. However, she was coming too fast and ended up pulling a wingline overshoot, ending up in front of his X15 and within his weapons range.

"Alpha One, pull out!" Pequo cried, but it was too late. Too close for missiles, Utang switched to guns and proceeded to make Swiss cheese out of her afterburners. She ejected, and her Vortex fell into a slice turn, colliding with the icy ground. The wreckage was engulfed in flames as Nakai drifted in her shoot towards the ground.

Utang rolled and turned to engage her as she fell, but Pequo didn't allow him the opportunity. He fired his guns at Utang, causing Utang to disengage and roll into another flightpath, allowing Nakai to fall to the ground safely.

Now it was just Utang versus Pequo, fighter to fighter, and it was clear that Utang was in the superior craft. Pequo, however, was a superior pilot, evening the odds.

Staying above Utang and careful not to overshoot, Pequo attempted a high-side gun pass. His Vortex swooped low in a powered dive as he fired his guns at Utang's jets. He missed and climbed back to the higher altitude.

Utang pivoted his jets and went into a slice turn, causing Pequo to overshoot, but Pequo rolled out of the flightpath and banked right, climbing in a pitch turn. As they each swung around, Utang from below and Pequo from above, they passed each other, narrowly avoiding collision.

As Pequo switched to visually guided missiles, a reticle appeared inside his helmet over his left eye. As they pitched and rolled, a dance of two fighters, he craned his neck to try and obtain line of sight. When he had it for a fleeting moment, he fired a missile, but he quickly lost it as Utang refused to remain on a single flightpath.

The missile bobbed and weaved in hot pursuit, unable to obtain a fix. Utang released countermeasures, one of which detonated the missile. As the sky ballad continued, Utang managed to turn and roll, reversing positions, and fell into a lag pursuit. Given the speed of the X15, it was seconds before he'd overtake Pequo.

Pequo increased the angle of attack, gunning the jets, creating massive wingtip vortices. Utang, careening towards Pequo's Vortex fighter, narrowly avoided collision, but instead passed through Pequo's wake turbulence, two large horizontal tornadoes curving downward behind his wings.

Utang struggled as he overshot the Vortex fighter and his conduction engines failed. Pequo quickly swept down behind him, getting tone and lighting him up. Utang's X15 erupted into flames as it fell out of the sky, colliding with the Crystalline Forest below.

On the ground, Nakai, in her flight mech, expended the last of her ammunition as the remaining half company of Cybions battled the UIC Marines. She saw Utang's X15 Dragon shot out of the sky in her periphery, and within seconds, the lethal Cybions froze in place, immobile.

"Nice work, Alpha 2," said Nakai from her mech suit below.

"How is the situation on the ground?" asked Pequo, checking his scanners as he made a pass above.

"The remaining Cybions went dormant as soon as you cut off their orders from the general."

"Roger," said Pequo, smiling under his helmet. "I will notify command that the general has been neutralized."

The United Intergalactic Coalition forces quickly stabilized the rest of the Feng Empire. The majority of the manors readily surrendered, quick to assert their loyalty to the new governmental order. With General Yoshi Utang neutralized, the Feng Air Command was able to fan out their patrol patterns. The Feng planetary defense maintained their positions, compensating for the presence of the United Intergalactic Coalition battle group drifting in orbit.

* * *

Captain Reinhardt and Commander Ashwani stood in the conference room awaiting the arrival of Admiral Renolfo. After almost two phases, Operation Fire and Ice had been a success, and under the oversight of a Human no less. This was a momentous occasion, not just for the coalition, but for the Human race as well.

There was a tone, the door opened, and Admiral Renolfo entered. They traded salutes, but they remained standing.

"Welcome aboard the Resilience," offered Reinhardt.

"Thank you, Captain," replied Renolfo. "And may I commend you on a successful mission. Most impressive, for a Human."

Reinhardt wasn't sure if that last remark was a barb or genuine admiration. "Thank you, Admiral."

"I hope you understand that the fall of the Feng Empire is the most important historical event of recent eras."

"Fall, ma'am?"

Renolfo frowned at Reinhardt. "Emperor Hiron is dead, a victim of his own attempted coup gone wrong. We have secured the empire. We will be accepting Vice Executor Kazar's surrender momentarily."

Ashwani traded a concerned look with Reinhardt. It was Reinhardt's place to ask. "With all due respect, Admiral, do you think the vice executor sees this as a surrender?"

"I really do not care what he sees this as. What matters is that we will begin nation-building immediately afterwards." Renolfo was flashing gold in true Humani fashion, her arrogance radiating off of her in waves.

"Is he prepared to surrender?" pressed Reinhardt.

"He has Bobot Tegrit coaching him," said Renolfo, dismissive. "From what Bobot tells me, Kazar is quite ready to do anything to begin his new role as president. He is not recalcitrant like Hiron was."

"I understand," said Reinhardt. "When do we leave?"

"Immediately," replied Renolfo.

Reinhardt turned to Ashwani. "Commander, you have the ship. I want everyone to remain on high alert. I still don't trust these Feng."

"Aye, Captain." She traded salutes with Reinhardt and Renolfo as they left the conference room to head to their shuttle.

Reinhardt and Renolfo strode down the corridors of the command carrier together towards the shuttle bay of the Resilience.

"Is the Razor's Edge pilot who shot down General Utang available?" asked Renolfo.

"Yes, ma'am. He was summoned back to the ship as per your order. He's waiting for you in the shuttle bay."

"Excellent."

In the shuttle bay, they saw the young pilot standing by the shuttle, waiting in uniform sans his flight mech suit. As he saw Admiral Renolfo and Captain Reinhardt approaching, his body grew rigid and he stood at attention. When Reinhardt reached the shuttle, Lieutenant Pequo snapped a salute that both Renolfo and Reinhardt quickly returned.

"At ease, Lieutenant," said Renolfo.

Pequo widened his stance, clasping his hands behind his back.

"That was some show you put on out there," said Reinhardt.

"Thank you, Captain." His skin flushed yellow and purple. Was this nervousness? Embarrassment? Or was it humility? Reinhardt didn't believe that the Humani were capable of that particular emotion.

"You went head-to-head with an X15 Dragon and won. Not an easy feat, as those were superior to our Vortex fighters," added Renolfo.

"His craft was superior, but General Utang was an amateur pilot," said Pequo, flashing gold.

'Ah, there it is, that patent Humani pride,' thought Reinhardt. "Yes, well, nevertheless, congratulations. I will be personally recommending you for the Distinguished Service Lemniscate."

"Thank you, sir."

"The vice executor himself has personally requested your attendance at this historic summit. He wishes to express his gratitude in person."

"However I can be of service, sir."

Renolfo gestured for Reinhardt and Pequo to board the shuttle and followed behind them. As they took their seats, the shuttle pilot checked all systems and confirmed the readiness of their escort. After all was confirmed, they left the shuttle bay and were quickly intercepted by the Vortex escort.

Pequo looked out the window and recognized the fighters. It was Commander Massa, Lieutenant Nakai in a new fighter, and two others, Lieutenants Gretal and Huboi.

Pequo thought back on his conversation with Commander Massa with great pride. Massa congratulated him after a rushed debriefing. Pequo had been surprised to hear that Admiral Renolfo had requested that he join her and Captain Reinhardt on his trip to the planet to accept the vice executor's official surrender.

As they entered the atmosphere and dipped below the clouds, the frozen Feng landscape sprawled out beneath them. Pequo craned his long neck and took in the vast glassy ice fields speckled with metallic spheres of various sizes and modern structures. In the center of the capital was the massive Feng Imperial Palace, its jagged icy turrets piercing the angry sky.

A storm had rolled in, and snow had begun to fall. As it blanketed the landscape powdery white, it covered the bodies of the fallen—Cybions, Lord Cyclesse's manor staff and soldiers, insurgents, rioters—erasing any trace of what had transpired, lending the Feng world a fresh start.

Renolfo looked outside, and then she watched Pequo's reaction. "Astonishing, is it not?"

"Yes. I did not expect it to be so beautiful."

"It's like sugar," said Reinhardt.

Renolfo regarded him with a quizzical expression that was quickly replaced with indifference.

"A crystalline sweetener derived from the cane plant," said Pequo, acknowledging the reference.

Reinhardt smiled. He liked this Humani. He wasn't arrogant like the others. This one was a deep thinker, and he seemed eager to please his Human captain. Neither was a characteristically Humani trait.

"Look at it. The Feng world is a melding of forces of nature and Feng technology," said Reinhardt in genuine admiration. "The Feng, given their shortcomings, are a remarkable race. Their Rule of Nature is primitive, but clean, honest."

"Sir?"

"Yes, do explain, Captain," said Renolfo, flashing a light orange.

Reinhardt extended a demonstrative hand, palm facing up. "It represents an honor code. As a fellow warrior, I appreciate that."

As they watched out the window, they saw steam rise from the hot factory spheres.

"Do you think they are ready for democracy?"

Renolfo bristled at the sentiment behind the question. "Lieutenant, their readiness is immaterial."

Reinhardt smiled at the question. Pequo immediately flashed yellow, anxious that such a question was inappropriate at his paygrade.

"Commander Massa told me you were a bit of a philosopher," said Reinhardt. "The Feng vice executor has been a United Intergalactic Coalition sympathizer for some time now. He's laid the groundwork for this. It's my hope that he can prepare his people expeditiously."

"I have read that Feng culture has been prime for a change," said Pequo. "The devaluing of their currency, civil unrest, and the disappearance of a middle class and a reversion to a feudal system are prime conditions for change in governmental regime."

Reinhardt couldn't help but smile. "I am told that you're a student of alien cultures. You even take special interest in Human culture."

Pequo didn't like the term 'alien,' a Human xenophobic term.

Renolfo flashed a deeper nuance of orange. "Peace is won when other cultures and races take an interest in democracy and cooperation."

"I believe that peace can be won by understanding other cultures," offered Pequo.

Challenging the admiral. Reinhardt really liked this Humani pilot. "That's an interesting position taken by a warrior."

"Do not misunderstand me, Captain," said Pequo, flashing yellow and purple again. "I am not so naïve to think that diplomacy is the end-all, be-all. I am fully aware that military force is necessary."

"Of course," said Renolfo. "You are obviously well-read on the subject."

"I enjoy reading up on it, but I also feel that it is my responsibility as a warrior, ma'am."

Reinhardt grinned ironically. "Responsible warriors. I like that idea, Lieutenant. I also believe that the Feng vice executor would share your sentiment. Although the Feng are a warrior people, this vice executor appears to be more progressive."

As the shuttle descended into the palace landing bay, it was greeted by the company of UIC Marines. After landing the shuttle hatch opened, and Reinhardt's security detail stepped out, followed by Renolfo, Reinhardt, and Pequo.

"Welcome, Admiral Renolfo. Captain Reinhardt. I am Captain Greely."

"Thank you, Captain Greely," said Reinhardt, happy to see another human. In fact, the company of marines was entirely human. "This is Lieutenant Rolo Pequo of the Razor's Edge."

Pequo saluted the captain.

"So, you're the one who shot General Utang out of the sky."

"Yes, sir."

"Huzzah."

"The vice executor is expecting us?" interrupted Renolfo.

"Yes, ma'am."

"I have been given full authorization by the supreme chancellor to accept the terms of his surrender and begin nation-building."

"Very good, ma'am. He eagerly awaits your introduction. Follow me," said Greely.

"Of course."

They were escorted to the Feng Imperial conference room, where Monsu Kazar and Bobot Tegrit stood in waiting. Kazar eagerly greeted Renolfo, Reinhardt, and Pequo.

"Greetings! I am Vice Executor Monsu Kazar of the Feng people!" He extended his hand.

Renolfo paused, uncertain of how to respond to Kazar's forward gesture. Reinhardt extended his hand, but was taken off guard when the vice executor gripped his forearm. Reinhardt followed suit. When in Rome. "I am Captain Reinhardt, Task Force Commander. It is a pleasure to meet you, Vice Executor."

"The pleasure is mine," said Kazar, eying Renolfo nervously.

"I am Admiral Renolfo, and with us is Lieutenant Rolo Pequo of our elite Razor's Edge Squadron."

"Greetings, Admiral." He turned to Pequo. "Yes! You are the one who brought the traitorous General Utang to justice, and most impressively, I hear."

Pequo flashed yellow and purple again, the epidermal microexpression amusing Kazar, as he tittered with delight at the display.

"Yes, sir. I am."

"Wonderful! The Feng people owe you their thanks, as do I, Lieutenant." His gaze lingered uncomfortably on Pequo until Bobot cleared his throat with great exaggeration.

"I believe you know Bobot Tegrit of the United Intergalactic Coalition," said Kazar, maintaining his enthusiasm.

"It is a pleasure to meet you in person," said Reinhardt.

Bobot hastily shook his hand and then quickly turned his attention to Admiral Renolfo. "It is a great honor to meet the one who oversaw this historic operation. I owe you my gratitude for saving my life."

"And I owe you my gratitude for your efforts in the peace process and facilitating this operation with the vice executor from the palace," reciprocated Renolfo.

The two were glittering gold as they showered each other with compliments. It was all Reinhardt could do to stop himself from rolling his eyes. 'Jesus Christ,' he thought. 'These two Humani are giving me diabetes.'

Bobot then addressed the pilot. "Lieutenant Pequo. Nice to see that a Humani pilot brought General Utang down."

"I am happy to serve the United Intergalactic Coalition," said Pequo. His humility even astonished Bobot.

"How do you want to proceed with the surrender?" Kazar asked Renolfo.

"I assume that we can have all the relevant parties present."

"Of course, Admiral," said Kazar.

Renolfo nodded her approval. "Excellent. Supreme Chancellor Wignani will be present in holographic form."

Kazar clapped his hands together in excitement. "The supreme chancellor himself! This is a momentous occasion indeed."

"I would like to begin immediately," said Renolfo.

"Excellent. Please be seated." Kazar gestured for each of the others to take a seat around the conference table.

"It is imperative that this meeting be transmitted across all Feng multimedia," insisted Renolfo.

Reinhardt knew why Renolfo insisted on this. It wasn't enough for Kazar to surrender. His people, the Feng, had to witness it. It was crucial that they saw him in a vulnerable state, highlighting his fallibility as a leader. It was important that they witnessed his supplication before the United Intergalactic Coalition.

"Yes, we are fully capable for such a broadcast."

"That's some storm you have outside," said Reinhardt.

"It will not affect our transmission," assured Kazar. "I am ready when you are."

Renolfo placed her right hand out, palm up. "I have forwarded the com link to Supreme Chancellor Wignani. You may open the com when you are ready."

Vice Executor Kazar began transmission to all Feng multimedia and opened the com link. Supreme Chancellor Wignani materialized in his designated seat as a hologram.

"Greetings, Vice Executor Monsu Kazar," said Wignani. "I am Supreme Chancellor Lavel Wignani of the United Intergalactic Coalition."

"Greetings," said Kazar. "As you can see, Admiral Renolfo, Captain Reinhardt, Lieutenant Pequo, and Bobot Tegrit are in attendance."

Wignani frowned at Pequo. "It is highly irregular for a fighter pilot to attend such an occasion."

"He is here at my personal request," apologized the vice executor. "He is responsible for neutralizing the traitor and co-conspirator responsible for the attempted subterfuge that nearly derailed the peace process between the Feng and the United Intergalactic Coalition. I am in his debt."

Wignani nodded, although it was clear that he didn't approve. "Very well. This meeting has convened to accept the conditions of your surrender to the United Intergalactic Coalition. I have authorized Admiral Renolfo to be the executor of the proceedings and Captain Reinhardt to serve as witness."

Kazar reacted to the word 'surrender.' Bobot Tegrit had not mentioned a surrender, nor one to be offered so publically.

However, he knew he was in no position to refuse, and if he was to rise to power in the new Feng Republic, he'd have to cooperate. Still, the Feng in him bristled. "On behalf of the Feng Empire, I, Monsu Kazar, Vice Executor, surrender to the United Intergalactic Coalition as represented here by Admiral Renolfo of the United Intergalactic Coalition Armada."

Renolfo nodded officiously. "I, Admiral Renolfo of the United Intergalactic Coalition Armada, hereby accept your surrender, as witnessed by Captain Reinhardt of the UIC Armada."

Reinhardt nodded in acknowledgement.

"It is my recommendation that I stay on in service to the new government to assure a safe and productive transition to the new democratic government," continued Kazar.

Supreme Chancellor Wignani nodded in agreement. "Granted. You, Monsu Kazar, will serve as the President of the new Feng Republic until elections are held to secure the office."

"Thank you, Supreme Chancellor."

"And what of your cabinet?"

"It is with deep sadness that I report to you that, with the exception of one outstanding member, the Feng high council has been murdered in the incident resulting in the death of our Emperor Hiron."

Bobot Tegrit leaned forward in his seat. "With all due respect, Supreme Chancellor, I would like to interject."

"You may," said Wignani.

Bobot bowed slightly in deference and continued. "I have been present during this whole episode. Despite the attack on my team of inspectors, I have been treated fairly and well by Monsu Kazar. I have dined with the Feng and even participated in their religious service. These people, despite the treachery of a few zealots, show promise both technologically and culturally.

"I humbly request to stay on as an advisor to help Monsu Kazar as the new president selects his cabinet and executive officers in a cautious and judicious manner."

Wignani turned to Monsu Kazar. "Are you agreeable to this stipulation?"

"Yes, of course," agreed Kazar. "I have several lords of the manor who have served the Feng Empire with great devotion and efficiency. I believe their participation in the transition would be most welcome. They are prime candidates for high office in the new republic."

Supreme Chancellor Wignani nodded. "Under the new constitution provided by us, the new Feng republic will hold elections for public office, and these lords will be allowed to enter as candidates.

"However, they will be stripped of all lands and duties, retaining only their domiciles, and will function as feudal lords no longer. Their fiefs are hereby granted their freedom to pursue their own destinies in all matters, including employment and personal finances."

"And what of the Feng industries, until now operated under the auspices of the Feng government under the supervision of these prior feudal lords?" asked Kazar.

"The stakes in these industries will be made available for public purchase, each according to his ability to afford them. Ownership of facilities, capital, and operations will henceforth be democratized."

"The transition will be overseen by the United Intergalactic Coalition military," added Admiral Renolfo, "during which all outstanding military assets and personnel will be inventoried and reigned in across the galaxies for reassignment. A representative portion of the Feng military will be reassigned to various posts across the galaxies in support of United Intergalactic Coalition military efforts in peacekeeping and warfare."

Kazar suddenly looked uncomfortable. "Regarding the outstanding military…Captain Mongo Utang, brother of the traitorous General Yoshi Utang, is still at large, his location currently undetermined."

"With the help of reassigned Feng Armada vessels, we will pursue Captain Utang until he is either apprehended or neutralized," assured Admiral Renolfo.

"Captain Utang has been working on a project of a deeply classified nature," added Kazar. "Only Emperor Hiron and General Yoshi Utang were aware of its nature and status."

"You perceive this operation to be an immediate threat?" asked Wignani.

"I am not sure."

"Fear not," said Admiral Renolfo. "Wherever Captain Utang is, he is cut off and alone. Without resources and support from Feng command, any operation he is overseeing will be starved out and eventually abandoned."

"In the meantime, a team of constitutional attorneys will be dispatched to Feng to install the new constitution and get things going," said Supreme Chancellor Wignani. "In conclusion, we ask that you take a knee and pledge your support to the United Intergalactic Coalition."

This final demand startled Kazar. Although he wasn't a fierce warrior like Emperor Hiron or Yoshi Utang, the very notion of kneeling before any Barberoi was offensive to him as a Feng. In addition, as these proceedings were being broadcast across the Feng manors, such a gesture would have made him appear weak in the eyes of the Feng people.

All eyes were on him as they anticipated his pledge. Kazar knew why this was required. It was the reason why the coalition required the proceedings to be simulcast over all Feng multimedia. The Feng people needed to see their leader kneel. Only then would there be no question as to the Feng's obligation to the United Intergalactic Coalition.

Monsu Kazar stood, stepped away from his chair at the table, and took a knee in front of the hologram of the supreme chancellor. Unable to bring himself to make eye contact with Wignani, he instead averted his gaze to the intricate carvings of legendary Feng warriors on the table legs and couldn't help but feel disconcerted.

*

When the proceedings were over and the holographic representations of Wignani and Renolfo had vanished in the conference room, Monsu Kazar, obviously perturbed, approached Renolfo. "So, that is that."

"Yes," said Renolfo. "You did well, for yourself and the Feng people."

Kazar smiled and nodded, but his expression was dubious...regretful even. "Yes, well, if you do not mind, Admiral, I have many pressing matters to attend to."

"Of course," said Renolfo.

Bobot put an arm around the new president of the Feng Republic, his skin sparkling gold in an epidermal microexpression. "He need not worry. He is in good hands."

They walked off to attend to the matters of regime transfer.

"He took that well," said Reinhardt.

"Yes, of course he did," said Renolfo, his sarcasm lost on her.

*

Her duty performed, Admiral Renolfo had boarded a separate shuttle to return to her command carrier, escorted by a squadron of Vortex fighters. Reinhardt and Pequo boarded their shuttle transport, and it rejoined its escort of Vortex fighters as it took off for the Resilience.

"You've been very quiet," said Reinhardt to Pequo. "Penny for your thoughts."

Pequo smiled pensively, appreciating the Human colloquialism. "Permission to speak freely, sir."

"Of course."

"Even though the emperor has fallen, he is being replaced by the vice executor, who will now be the chief executive of the new government."

"There will be elections held. Monsu Kazar may not hold onto his title for much longer."

Pequo shook his head. "Let us be frank, sir. Running as a candidate in elections takes money. The only Feng with the means to finance such a run will be those who have been in power all along.

Monsu Kazar and the feudal lords will easily win these positions and retain much of their power, only under the guise of democracy."

Reinhardt smirked. "That's a rather cynical view for a fighter pilot. Perhaps the underclass will organize and oust the ruling class from their positions of power."

"With all due respect, Captain, that is highly unlikely. Especially without the provision of campaign finance limits. The socioeconomic strata will maintain its relative status quo."

"You believe that's by design, Lieutenant?"

"I believe that it is the most efficient way to transition with the least amount of disruption," said Pequo.

"So then it's the best way."

"Efficient doesn't mean just, sir."

Reinhardt nodded, grinning from ear to ear. Now he really liked this Humani. He reclined in his seat. "Well, Lieutenant, we are just blunt instruments. Philosophical and ethical considerations like these are well above our pay grade."

Pequo found his captain's folksiness and candor to be unusual but refreshing. "Remember, responsible warriors."

"That's right," said Reinhardt, closing his eyes. "Responsible warriors."

* * *

Captain Mongo Utang stood behind the Drekaari mining complex next to Chief RagnakTok, his cape billowing in the hot, dry wind. He squinted against the blazing sun as grains of sand in the wind assaulted his rough, battle hardened face.

RagnakTok issued an order, and the ground in front of them began to open up, the sand sinking into yawning chasms as vast caves opened up across the desert. Captain Feng's battle group descended from the sky and hovered above the openings, lowering into them slowly, by degree.

When they disappeared into the immense desert, settling beneath the surface, sand began to cover the openings, pumped in by the Drekaari. There was no place in the galaxy they would be able to run from the United Intergalactic Coalition. Instead, they had to hide in plain sight while they completed Operation: Catalyst.

A hot tear streamed down Captain Utang's face. His brother Yoshi was the second family member the United Intergalactic Coalition took from him. When he felt Yoshi's living presence fade and vanish from the Aether, something inside him had died.

His sole purpose in his pained existence was to bring both his brother and Emperor Hiron back. He would go back to the tipping point in Spacetime that stole the Feng Empire's destiny away from them. That key battle where the tide changed due to the folly of a ridiculous race.

He was going to return to the Feng invasion of Humani in the last Intergalactic War and tip the tables back.

PART IV

HEISENBERG AND UNCERTAINTY

"The Prophet is the source of Light and Truth, piercing the darkness of time and space, and all who defy Him shall perish."

Quote from a Harbingers of Light Propaganda Transmission

CHAPTER 18

Command Carrier Titan
Golgath System

Reassigned to a new command carrier after taking leave, Commander Massa stood in the briefing room, addressing his squadron. He clicked on the screen behind him, and a topographic map of the mining planet Golgath appeared. "A freighter carrying forty Humani Avatars has gone missing in the Drekaar sector. Contact was lost a megacycle ago.

"Command thought it might have been due to a re-ignited skirmish between the Iguani and the Drekaar, but there have been no readings indicating any military activity within the mining sector."

"What is the emergency?" asked Lieutenant Nakai. "Command does not think it will resurface?"

"Normally, our squadron would not be dispatched for one newly missing freighter," explained Massa. "However, an emancipated Avatar of great importance was aboard that freighter, one who is important to Humani shipbuilding operations. He was sent to oversee the development of a new mine, using experimental technology to extract kronite more efficiently. On top of that, a recon vessel has gone missing without a trace."

"Do you think it is the Feng?" asked Lieutenant Pequo.

"Once again, there has been no military activity detected in the Drekaar sector, including Feng activity." Commander Massa paused. "In fact, there's a reassigned Feng expeditionary strike group en route to provide support."

Lieutenant Mesoi chortled. "Yeah, right. They just want to make sure we do not declare martial law and seize the precious kronite mines in the name of the United Intergalactic Coalition."

Massa shook his head. "They are entering the UIC now, so that is not a likely scenario. Either way, when you run into them, I want you to be polite until our orders from Admiral Renolfo change. Am I clear?"

"Yes, sir," the squadron answered in unison.

"This is reconnaissance only," said Commander Massa. "Observe and report." The squadron's reassignment was as per armada policy. Having seen action in recent missions, they were reassigned for this recon mission to break things up. "Report to launch deck for immediate launch."

His squadron stood and saluted. Commander Massa returned the salute and briskly left the briefing room.

"You heard him, you animals," shouted Nakai, "to the launch deck!"

After suiting up in his combat mech, Commander Massa slid into his Vortex fighter sitting at the beginning of the rail. He attached his mech suit to the leads in the cockpit, automatically illuminating the combat and guidance systems.

"Commander Massa," said a voice in his helmet. It was the battle group commander.

"Yes, sir."

"Be advised, a Feng carrier has arrived and is entering orbit around Golgath."

"Yes, sir." Massa opened a channel to his squadron of sixteen. "I was just advised that the Feng carrier is entering orbit."

"Great," huffed Pequo. "Company."

"Cut the chatter," said Commander Massa, "and stay frosty. Just because we have to play nice does not mean we let our guard down."

"Yes, sir."

"Prepare for launch in ninety microns," said the battle group commander on an open channel to the fighters.

Commander Massa opened a pic of Missani and Catori on the display in his helmet. It was a ritual he practiced right before slingshot on the rail. It was a reminder of what he was fighting for, and if he should have an accident on the rail, it was the last thing he wanted to see before he left this existence.

"Slingshot in sixty microns," said the battle group commander.

Commander Massa felt the magnets of the rail grip the ventral fin of his vortex fighter. His guidance system plotted a vector across quintessence fields to orbit with Golgath, communicating with the other fighters so there was no overlap.

Lieutenant Nakai smiled as she felt the rail grip her Vortex fighter, her teeth rattling from the resonance. *Best ride in the park.* She lived for speed, and she never calculated the odds, which is why slingshot never scared her.

"Fifteen microns," announced the battle group commander.

The other pilots made final adjustments and braced themselves as they felt the grip of the magnets on their mech suits inside their cockpits. Commander Massa always found comfort in the grip, as if a large, invisible hand, the hand of the Engineer, held him fast and safe.

"Five microns."

Massa looked around at his squadron and then up at the landing lights on the ceiling through the translucent image of his family.

"Slingshot," said the battle group commander.

The lights on the ceiling of the launch deck streaked in a blur as Massa's Vortex glided along the rail until he hit open space. He turned off the pic of his family and drew his attention to the navigation as it conducted him through orbifold planes, his squadron appearing on his navigation on parallel vectors.

"Entering orbital speed in forty microns," said Massa.

"Check," said Nakai.

Massa saw the Feng carrier and its strike group off in the distance, drifting behind the Titan. The carrier was massive, looming like a leviathan predator over the Humani carrier.

"Orbital speed in thirty microns."

"Commander, the Feng carrier launched a squadron of Warmongers," said Nakai.

"Do not worry about them," reminded Massa. "They are just here so that the Feng Empire can save face. Remember, observe and report."

The squadron of Warmongers scattered, maintaining a loose formation.

"Their weapons are heating up," said Nakai, nervous.

"They are not targeting us," reassured Massa. "Just Feng bravado. Shields up. Orbital speed in ten microns." As his navigation plotted a vector through to the planet's atmosphere, he hoped he was right. He didn't think the Feng would break their truce with the United Intergalactic Coalition easily. Doing so would mean all-out war.

"Orbital speed in three microns. Two. One."

The stars against the black of space streaked as Commander Massa's Vortex leapt forward into orbital speed. His navigation lit up, tracking the waning dark energy of the fighters giving way to the gravity of Golgath, as he soared down towards the planet.

His fighter broke orbital speed and hit the planet's atmosphere with a bang that rattled his mech suit. He extended the brackets around his fighter until they formed wings suited for atmospheric flight. His squadron followed suit.

"The Warmongers have not entered orbit," said Pequo. "They are not following us."

"I noticed," said Commander Massa. "Like I said, they are backup. Plotting a course to the Drekaar mining sector."

"Roger that," confirmed Pequo.

"Activate all surveillance equipment," instructed Massa. "We are going to sweep the mines."

"I am not expecting much," said Nakai.

"Approaching surveillance altitude," said Massa. He took point as his squadron fell into formation, scanners creating a topographical display in the cockpit, simultaneously spitting out readouts for thermal, magnetic, and microwave energy signatures, the quantum computer monitoring and decoding all transmissions.

The squadron flew over the perimeter of the Drekaar mining base. "They know we are here," said Massa. "They are scanning us."

"No sign of Iguani activity so far," said Pequo.

"Normal readings for Drekaar mining operations," said Nakai. "Nothing out of the ordinary."

"Wait a minute," said Massa. "I am picking up a small craft…it is another Vortex…that is impossible." He checked his scanners again. How was it possible for another Vortex to be flying over the mining complex? Massa's readout began to glitch.

"It is not a Vortex," said Nakai. "The energy signature does not match."

"Sure looks like a Vortex," said Pequo.

Massa opened up a hailing frequency, pinging the craft. "Small craft, please identify yourself."

He waited, but there was no response.

He opened it up again, pinging the craft. "Small craft, this is Commander Massa of the Galactic Armada, identify yourself immediately."

They were coming up on the small craft. It was facing them head-on.

"It is in attack stance," said Nakai.

"Small craft, be advised that if you do not break attack stance and identify yourself, we will engage," said Massa.

"Its weapons are heating up," said Pequo.

The rogue Vortex began firing on the Drekaar mining complex.

"It is firing! It is attacking the complex!" shouted Nakai.

"Engage!" commanded Massa.

As the rogue Vortex passed between them, they banked around and fell into lag pursuit. The rogue Vortex dropped below the hard deck and screamed across the sky right over the mining colony.

"He is no longer firing on the complex. He is bugging out," said Nakai.

Massa had a quick decision to make. As it was, they were above the rogue Vortex fighter, but to fire upon it would risk accidentally hitting the Drekaar mining base and adding insult to injury. "Drop below the hard deck and pursue."

"But that is breaking the Rules of Engagement," replied Nakai.

"We cannot risk this Vortex damaging the mining complex and causing an intergalactic incident."

"Too late," crackled Pequo over the com. "The Feng Warmongers are entering orbit in attack formation."

"The Feng strike group is engaging ours," added Nakai.

The rogue Vortex abruptly went into a near vertical climb, narrowly missing Massa's and Nakai's fighters.

"Holy smokes!" cried Nakai.

"What is he doing?" asked Pequo.

"He is going to attack the Feng Warmongers," said Massa.

The formation banked and entered a near vertical climb in pursuit of the rogue Vortex. It had some distance on them, but they were closing in fast. So were the Feng Warmongers from the other direction.

The rogue Vortex began to fire up at the descending Warmongers.

"I have tone," said Massa.

"Me, too," said Nakai.

Both opened fire at the rogue Vortex, but it rolled as gunfire whizzed around it, bolts of light darting past it.

The Warmongers entered the atmosphere with a loud bang. Their kronite cores fully charged from the dark energy fields of space, the Feng fighters extended liquid metal wings and switched to rockets.

They immediately opened fire on the rogue Vortex, which declined any evasive maneuvers. It took a couple of simultaneous direct hits and vanished.

Massa's squadron scattered, and the Warmongers began to open fire on the Razor's Edge.

"We are taking fire!" shouted Lieutenant Tolso, whose fighter was hit in the dark energy reactor and exploded.

"Tolso is hit!" said Pequo.

One by one, the Vortex fighters of the Razor's Edge were picked apart. The Feng weren't taking prisoners.

"What the frak is going on?" cried Pequo in panic. "Why are they firing?"

Massa, Nakai, Pequo, and Hazoi—the last of their squadron—were now flying back over the Drekaar mining complex.

"Drop below the hard deck," said Massa. "They will not risk hitting the complex." He said nothing of the Feng following the Rules of Engagement, as such a notion was preposterous.

They dropped below the hard deck and skimmed the top of the complex. The Feng Warmongers followed them, opening fire. Pequo was struck down first, his ship crashing into a squat structure as he bailed out in his battle mech, the Feng blasting holes in his chute.

Massa was hit next, and he pulled the ripcord, and Nakai and Hazoi followed as Warmongers screamed over them, punching holes in their parachutes with spears of light.

* * *

Captain Trevor Reinhardt was sitting in his office with an open com link to Admiral Renolfo.

"Good evening, Admiral."

"Captain Reinhardt, we have a bit of a situation. A week ago, Navigo reported that a team of Avatar technicians on Golgath has not reported in for a megacycle."

"Golgath." He punched up several displays elaborating data on the mining planet—climate, topography, population. "A mining planet inhabited by the Drekaar and Iguani tribes. A desert planet. We're not exactly in the vicinity, and we've just seen action on Feng not that long ago."

Renolfo's expression was grave. "I dispatched two hunter-killers in orbit around the planet. They have recorded unusual data, fluctuations in gravitational waves and dark energy around the planet, ripples in Spacetime, one which nearly took out one of our cloaked vessels."

"Ripples, huh? Wasn't the Navigo team there to start teaching the Drekaar the rudiments of dark matter conduction?"

"That is correct, Captain. It was the beginning of an initiative to introduce space travel to the Drekaar."

"Interesting choice in race," remarked Reinhardt.

"I think that you know that establishing a foothold on Golgath is in the best interest of the UIC."

Reinhart stroked his chin thoughtfully. "Kronite."

"I dispatched a reconnaissance vessel to investigate further. It dropped off the radar."

"It was shot down?"

"I then sent the Titan expeditionary strike group to investigate. For some reason, one of our pilots in the Razor's Edge Squadron opened fire on the mining complex. Feng Warmongers engaged the squadron, and the Feng strike group engaged and disabled the Titan."

Reinhardt sat forward in his chair. "What the hell? What was the Feng strike group's reason for engaging?"

"That is just it," said Admiral Renolfo. "The Feng command carrier is not responding to our attempts to hail it."

"And now you want to send my battle group in."

"I need you to ascertain what happened on Golgath, why one of our pilots opened fire on the Drekaar mining complex, and why the Feng have attacked our ships. You will de-escalate the situation and head up an official investigation into what transpired there."

Reinhardt frowned. "Has there been any action on the ground between the Drekaar and Iguani?

"Our intelligence indicates that all has been quiet. I will forward you all the data we have. If there is something strange going on there, I want you to find out what it is."

"Yes, ma'am."

The transmission terminated. Reinhardt sat in his chair, deep in thought. Then he pressed his com. "Commander Ashwani."

"Aye, Captain."

"I'm reporting to Neuroscience, and then I'm heading to the bridge. Set coordinates to the Golgath system. I want to enter spacefold within the sexagen. I'll brief you when I get there."

"Aye, Captain."

*

Captain Reinhardt opened his eyes, and his vision was whitewashed from the bright lights. He squinted until his eyes adjusted.

"Captain Reinhardt," said a voice from somewhere within the light, "your retinal gateway chips on your optic nerves have been switched over to fact-finding mode."

"Yes."

"Do you acknowledge that from this point forward you are to serve in mind and body as a Fact-Finder for the United Intergalactic Coalition regarding the matter of the Razor's Edge Squadron's involvement on the attack on Golgath?"

"Yes, I do."

"You acknowledge that your memories from this point forward will be transmitted to UIC Command in real time and serve as an official record of your investigation, to which the United Intergalactic Coalition will have complete access to."

That was a joke. All in service of the UIC were property of the UIC, mind and body. By enlisting, one gave up any right to privacy. Memories were harvested from dead soldiers and analyzed like a black box.

"Yes."

Reinhardt felt clamps release from his head, and he was able to stand upright. He rubbed his temples tenderly.

Warrant Officer Neil Serling, a Humani, stepped forward. "You are to begin, effective immediately. The four surviving members of the Razor's Edge are pinned down inside the Drekaar mining facility. Admiral Renolfo wants them back alive for questioning."

"I understand."

"Captain, you may be their only chance at clearing their names and getting us out of this whole mess. Even if you are only Human, sir." Serling smirked as he said that last part. Funny, how there wasn't an epidermal microexpression for humor. Serling was another Humani that Reinhardt liked, part of a very small list.

Reinhardt raised a sardonic eyebrow. "They'll have to get over that little fact. What about the Drekaar?"

"They are crying foul, accusing the UIC of exercising the Pax Galactus Initiative to take over their mining operations. It appears a Feng faction is threatening war with the UIC."

Reinhardt chuckled bitterly. "Yeah, right. So much for a smooth transition into the fold."

"The admiral will debrief you once you are on the bridge as to the latest developments."

"Thank you, Serling."

Serling smiled. "Good luck, sir."

As he made his way to the bridge, Reinhardt cleared his mind, focusing only on the mission at hand. Every officer above lieutenant commander was fully trained in the mental discipline of forensic mnemonics, in the event that they would one day be called upon for a fact-finding mission.

When he reached the bridge, Commander Ashwani stood straight and saluted. "Captain on the bridge," she announced, and all stood and saluted Reinhardt.

When he saw her, certain emotions and bodily responses began to make their way to the forefront of his consciousness. Reinhardt forced them out of his awareness, focusing on the other crew on the bridge, so these feelings and sensations wouldn't be recorded by his chip.

"At ease," said Reinhardt.

Ashwani frowned at the aversion of his gaze. "Captain, Lieutenant Commander Chen is uploading the recent data on the situation, as well as maps of Golgath and the surrounding sector."

"So we have missing Navigo engineers, a rogue pilot, and a disabled strike group," Reinhardt asked more than said.

Ashwani nodded. "I've read the files you sent ahead."

Chen looked up. "Captain, Admiral Renolfo requires your presence in the briefing room."

Reinhardt nodded. "Tell her we'll be there."

Ashwani followed Reinhardt through a pair of red doors into a modestly sized conference room. Reinhardt stood at the head, Ashwani to his right. Admiral Renolfo's holograph appeared at the opposite end. Reinhardt and Ashwani both saluted her.

Renolfo saluted back. "Captain, Commander," she said in acknowledgement.

They all took a seat.

"Captain Reinhardt," Renolfo began, "we have quite the mess. Feng Warmongers neutralized all but four pilots of the Razor's Edge. Commander Massa, Lieutenant Nakai, Lieutenant Pequo, and Lieutenant Hazoi were shot down and retreated into the mining base. They are currently pinned down inside. Three of their mech suits are online, but the Feng have surrounded Golgath and are jamming any communications on or off."

"Are they going to allow us to take our pilots into custody?" asked Reinhardt.

Renolfo frowned. "The Feng vessel issued a text statement claiming the UIC instigated the conflict to assume control of the mining colony."

"Under the Pax Galactus Initiative," said Reinhardt.

"Yes," answered Renolfo. "They are threatening to destroy the Titan and all on board if we do not back off Golgath."

"And what about our pilots?"

"That is still unclear. You will be escorting the Golgath diplomat, Captain, who will attempt to convince them that we are taking the survivors into custody and will be launching a full investigation into what transpired."

"Martin Rayban?"

"That is correct."

Reinhardt sighed. "Why do I think they won't be receptive?"

"That is why we're sending a Human diplomat. As a species, you are more or less neutral. If we sent in a Humani response team, the Feng would accuse the Humani of covering for their own. "

That wasn't exactly true. The tension between Humans and Humani was well-known. "I'm there in case negotiations break down," said Reinhardt.

"That is correct, Captain. In the meantime, the Feng are declaring that they will take the pilots into custody and conduct their own investigation. If they have their way, our pilots will stand trial in the Feng judicial system on one of their colonies."

"Our pilots won't stand a chance."

Renolfo nodded. "That is right. Not only that, the Feng will have an opportunity to spin the incident in their favor, making the UIC look like imperialists. They are suggesting retracting their surrender to the UIC, even throwing around words like rebellion and war."

Reinhardt looked at Ashwani, who shook her head. "That's what doesn't make sense," she said. "They wouldn't stand a chance against the UIC, especially now. This is just a small faction, an offshoot. We now have the Feng planet."

Renolfo gestured and a map of the Charted Territories materialized in the air. "The worlds in blue are members of the United Intergalactic Coalition. Those in red are autonomous. Those in yellow are autonomous but at-risk worlds fraught with internal strife and civil wars, politically unstable planets."

"Planets that can be turned against the UIC," Reinhardt added.

Renolfo swiped her hand, removing the map. "Intelligence gathered indicates that this Feng faction has been reaching out to these worlds, spreading propaganda about the imperialism of the UIC. They are looking to form a coalition."

"I'm sure these worlds won't want to side with a small, outnumbered bunch of old empire Feng hold-outs," said Reinhardt.

"It is not that simple," said Renolfo. "The alleged attack on the Drekaar base by one of ours could be construed as an act of imperialist aggression. There are even worlds within the UIC who would not be comfortable with such a move. We cannot afford to lose the support of our current member worlds. There are too many at-risk worlds, and our resources are already spread too thinly."

Reinhardt was reminded of his Ancient Roman history. The scuttlebutt around the Charted Sectors has been that the United Intergalactic Coalition has grown too large and has become too unwieldy.

"Due to already strained resources, we have been forced to grant member worlds a little more autonomy than we are comfortable with," said Renolfo, as if she had read his thoughts. "Some of the outsider worlds are interpreting that as weakness."

"But I don't understand," said Ashwani. "Why threaten war when they're on the balls of their feet? They haven't formed any significant coalitions yet. At best, this is a small group of insurgents clinging to the old empire."

"They hope to use this incident on Golgath to spur a coalition," said Renolfo. "They will argue that time is of the essence, and that the United Intergalactic Coalition will need to be stopped in its tracks sooner, rather than later, while it is overextended and weak."

Reinhardt stroked his chin thoughtfully, his brow furrowed. "That's why we need to retrieve our wayward pilots on Golgath."

Renolfo nodded. "Exactly. If we do not, it could set off a chain reaction that will undo everything the United Intergalactic Coalition has achieved in bringing peace to the Charted Territories. This mission cannot fail."

"I understand," said Reinhardt.

"Good luck, Captain," said Admiral Renolfo, standing.

Reinhardt and Ashwani stood and saluted the admiral, who saluted back. The transmission terminated and her holographic image disappeared.

"We have our work cut out for us," said Ashwani.

"You ain't kidding," said Reinhardt.

They stepped out of the briefing room and back onto the bridge.

"Mr. Rayban is aboard, sir," said Chen.

Reinhardt nodded. "Excellent. I'm going to greet him in my quarters."

"I'll send a security detail to escort him right away, sir," said Chen.

"Commander," said Reinhardt, "how long until space fold?"

"Ten minutes," said Ashwani.

"Rayban got aboard just in time," said Reinhardt. "Nothing like cutting it close to the wire."

*

Martin Rayban was waiting outside Reinhardt's quarters with two security officers when Reinhardt arrived. When he saw Reinhardt, his face lit up.

"Thank you, gentlemen," said Reinhardt, dismissing the security detail.

"Captain Reinhardt," said Rayban, extending his hand. "It's a pleasure to meet you."

Reinhardt shook his hand. "Glad to have you aboard." He swiped his hand, and the portal to his chamber opened. "After you, Mr. Rayban."

Rayban nodded in courtesy and entered the captain's quarters. He looked around and saw a modest living space with a small bed off by the window. There were paintings from various cultures from various worlds on the walls, some pottery, a desk over in the far corner with computer equipment, and a modest seating area with comfortable furniture. Captain Reinhardt had made the most of his Spartan accommodations.

"Please," gestured Reinhardt to one of the plush chairs, "have a seat."

"Thank you," said Rayban, planting himself in the comfortable chair.

Reinhardt detested entertaining politicians. They were outside the chain of command, and their exchanges were often replete with meaningless but pleasant small talk, and glad-handing platitudes. 'Kissing hands and shaking babies,' as Reinhardt would frequently say.

"Can I offer you something to drink?"

"You wouldn't happen to have any Humani Sangoi, would you?"

"As a matter of fact, I do." Reinhardt walked over to a modest bar and fixed the diplomat his drink. "Would you like ice with that?"

"Yes, please." Rayban was looking around the room, taking it all in.

Reinhardt knew he was sizing him up, getting a sense of who he was talking to. He handed Rayban a glass filled with a turquoise elixir.

"Thank you, Captain."

Reinhardt sat on the chair across from him, but he didn't sit comfortably like Rayban did. Not when there was business to attend to. "Mr. Rayban, if you don't mind, time is short, and I'd like to get to the brass tacks."

Rayban took a sip of his Humani beverage. "Of course, Captain."

"It would appear we have our work cut out for us."

"I know how the Drekaar operate," said Rayban, a little too confidently for Reinhardt's taste. "There was some kind of misunderstanding, and they're overreacting."

"With all due respect," said Reinhardt, "it's not the Drekaar I'm worried about."

"The Feng?" said Rayban. "They're just concerned that we're trying to take over the Drekaar mining operation. Once they see a diplomat's been dispatched to resolve the issue, they'll back off."

"I'm not so sure," said Reinhardt. "They're orbiting the planet and are jamming communications. They've already disabled one of our strike groups. The Titan group is drifting just outside of orbit around Golgath at the Feng's mercy."

"I appreciate your concern, Captain, but I assure you that this is one giant misunderstanding. Perhaps the Vortex fighters that fired on the mining complex malfunctioned, or the pilots were provoked in some way."

"Intelligence has indicated that the Iguani have been quiet in recent days," said Reinhardt. "As far as anyone knew, there were normal mining operations when our squadron did a fly by over the complex."

"However, there is a matter of the missing Humani Avatars," said Rayban. "They failed to report back for thirty-seven cycles. No distress call. No communique out of the mining complex."

"It cannot even be confirmed if they even made it to the complex at all," said Reinhardt. "What are you thinking?"

Rayban took another sip. "Mmm. This is very good."

Reinhardt nodded. "I'm glad you're enjoying it."

"I'm thinking that the Iguani intercepted the Avatar transport, maybe shooting it down, before it even reached the mining complex, and now the Drekaar are afraid they're going to be blamed for it."

"But the intelligence, as I said, indicated that there hasn't been Iguani activity in the region," said Reinhardt.

Rayban shrugged his shoulders. "Maybe the intelligence is inaccurate. It wouldn't be the first time."

"My concern is the Feng presence in the area and their rapid response. They were Johnny on the Spot."

Rayban waved a hand. "That's just a small group of insurgents."

"I don't know," said Reinhardt. "Something doesn't add up."

Rayban sat forward, raising his glass in a toast to himself, grinning like a used conveyance salesman. "That's why I'm here, Captain."

Reinhardt resisted the urge to roll his eyes.

CHAPTER 19

Drekaar Mining Complex
Golgath

Lieutenant Alita Nakai awoke in her mech suit, her head throbbing from the concussion of falling through a Drekaar dome in the mining complex. She heard gunfire throughout the complex and saw Warmongers streaking overhead.

"Alpha Two, are you all right?" asked Massa on his com.

"Yes," she replied, standing. She checked her systems. Tracking sensors and combat systems were intact. "What is the situation?"

"Alpha Three and I are one structure over from you. We are taking some fire from the Drekaar, but we are holding them off."

"I see you," said Nakai, calling up a map of the mining compound on her internal helmet display. "Alpha Six is in the same dome as me. I am going to regroup with him, and then I am on my way. What is our exit strategy?"

"The Titan is under attack and the Feng are surrounding the planet. Extraction is not an option."

"What do we do?" asked Nakai, fighting back panic and remembering her training.

"When in a hole, we dig in deeper," replied Massa.

Nakai knew what this meant. They weren't leaving the planet, at last not at the moment. Priority one was survival. Plain and simple.

She began to dart down the inside of the long structure she was in, alongside a track guiding carts of kronite coming up from the mines below. It glowed from the heat and radiation from underneath the crust, but her mech suit protected her.

She saw dark shadows moving from the far side of the structure and the tell-tale silhouettes of the curved tails ending in poisonous barbs. The Drekaar opened fire on her, but they were long bursts of automatic fire. The Drekaar were nothing if not undisciplined.

"Self-destruct in T-minus two micros," she said to the quantum computer onboard her crashed Vortex via her suit.

She magnetized her right mech hand and collected their bullets in a field as she dashed towards the exit, pistons pumping and hydraulics working. As the Drekaar advanced, her ship exploded, taking them out and the structure around it.

She was glad she didn't have to expend any ammunition. She had to choose her shots carefully. Her firearm was lightweight and only had two alternating revolving chambers. Just enough to get a pilot out of a scrape until reinforcements arrived.

The Drekaar, immune to heat and radiation, wore no protective suits, so when they ran right into the explosion, they were obliterated. However, soon more Drekaar arrived. She saw their shadows in the dust and falling rubble.

There were too many for her to engage alone. In high enough numbers, they would overpower her, even in her mech suit. Her only alternatives were to get Hazoi and find the others.

She frantically searched for Hazoi, but his mech suit wasn't appearing on her scanners. Perhaps his suit or her tracking system was damaged in the crash landing. She picked up two Drekaar moving quickly in her direction.

She wheeled around in time to catch the barb of a tail in her hand inches before it struck her helmet. She crushed it, ripped it off, and stabbed the Drekaar with it as it clawed at her suit.

As it collapsed to the ground, the other Drekaar tackled her. They grappled on the floor, rolling around, as the Drekaar attempted to strike her with its barb. As they rolled around, the barb kept missing her helmet, striking the ground instead.

The Drekaar managed to grab her wrists in its claws and pin her down. It retracted its tail for another strike when Hazoi grabbed it in his mech hand. He yanked the Drekaar off of Nakai. She lifted off the ground as the Drekaar assailant was yanked backwards, still retaining its grip on her.

Nakai regained her footing as she was jerked around in a bizarre tug of war, and she jammed her gun under the Drekaar's chin. She pulled the trigger, blowing its brains out the top of its head, and it released her. Hazoi dropped its lifeless tail.

"Thanks," said Nakai.

"No problem," said Hazoi.

His mech suit lurched forward and he bent over, revealing the barb of another Drekaar planted in the back of his neck. The Drekaar's eyes burned as it glared at her over Hazoi's mech.

"Frakking scudna!" Nakai pointed her gun at it, but it pulled Hazoi in front of it, using him as a Humani shield.

Nakai ran a scan on Hazoi's fading vitals as the venom pumped into his body, strangling the life out of it.

"Leave," grunted Hazoi. "I have this."

Nakai nodded. She turned and ran as Hazoi set the self-destruct on his suit. The Drekaar was unable to remove the barb lodged in Hazoi's flight mech, and he perished in the blast.

Nakai found double metal doors and charged them, smashing through and pulling them off their hinges. She darted across a small stretch of open area, looking up as Warmongers darted around the sky, scanning the complex. A couple began pelting the squat structure Massa and Pequo were pinned down in…the one she was running into.

She smashed through another set of double doors as the room was filled with a large blast. Massa and Pequo must've detonated their Vortexes. The shockwaves nearly pushed her back out the doorway. In the cloud of dry Golgath dust, her tracking system immediately highlighted the Drekaar in the vast room. She, Massa, and Pequo fired at them, flanking them inside the structure.

"Took you long enough," said Pequo over the coms.

"Divide and conquer," Nakai said.

The Drekaar in the structure were quickly overwhelmed. Creamy white blood splattered the stone walls as the three surviving members of the Razor's Edge blasted the scorpion-like insurgents.

One dashed at Massa's mech with such speed that it nearly knocked him off his mechanical feet when it collided with his suit. He caught it by the arms and grappled with it. Extending the hydraulics in his arms, he held it at length as its tail whipped around, thrusting its barb at the compartment where his body was housed, glancing off as he twisted and turned.

The structure shook and pieces of ceiling rained down as he struggled with the Drekaar. It looked up at the ceiling in a moment of confusion, and Massa sought to capitalize on the opportunity.

He tried to release its arms and kick it away, but its claws latched onto his arms. The blow dropped it to its knees, but it held on tight. In that moment, Massa knew that he wouldn't be able to fend off every tail strike, so he pulled it to its feet and pulled it close, embracing it.

Its eyes burned with rage. Massa redirected all power to his arms, and he began to tighten his embrace on his enemy. As his embrace tightened, he felt the shell of its exoskeleton push back.

The Drekaar wriggled in his grip and lurched backward. Because all Massa's power was rerouted to the torque multipliers in his arms, his legs offered little resistance, and he was dragged across the dry dirt as it struggled to break free.

Its tail strikes ceased as Massa began to feel its organic exoskeleton crack under the pressure of his mechanical bear hug. Finally, its eyes went dim as he crushed it like a mogo nut shell, spilling its creamy blood all over his suit and onto the dirt, and it went limp in his mechanical arms.

He quickly restored power to the rest of his suit as he saw another two Drekaar rushing toward him. Nakai and Pequo laid down suppressive fire, giving him enough time to recover. When they all slaughtered the last of the attacking Drekaar, they regrouped in the center of the room, scanners probing around for any other bogies.

"Are you all right?"

"I am fine," said Nakai. "What about you two?"

"Where is Hazoi?" asked Massa.

"He died saving me."

"We have to get out of here," said Massa.

The ground shook as they heard heavy thuds outside the structure. Nakai knew what that meant.

"Feng troop transports," said Massa. "Our only chance is to recede into the mine. Are all suits intact?"

"Yes, sir," replied Pequo, as Nakai ran rapid diagnostics on her suit. "Yes, sir," she replied.

The suits would have to be to withstand the radiation.

"We move," said Massa.

All three dashed towards the mouth of the mine as the structure fell apart around them. Massa's sensors picked up the brigade of Feng advancing on the structure. He caught a glimpse of Golgath daylight through the opening in the roof as he entered the mine, as all three pilots ran along the track, shoving aside carts of glowing kronite.

As they turned blind corners, their sonar sensors scanned the shaft, bouncing off the walls. They shoved their way past unarmed Drekaar miners, who offered little in the way of resistance. They weren't soldiers, but they jumped on their coms, no doubt reporting the pilots' advancement.

Nakai had an idea. As she darted past a Drekaar miner, its tail coiled in fear, she grabbed its com out of its hand and gave it a good shove, its tail strike glancing off of her armor. She immediately synched it with her suit's universal translator.

"Good thinking," said Massa over his com, his mech suit lumbering down the shaft. "What are they saying?"

Nakai listened to the feed inside her suit. "That is odd."

"What is odd?" asked Massa.

"They are frantic over our retreat into the mine shaft."

"Why? They will have us pinned down," said Pequo.

"It is a bottle neck," said Massa. "No matter how large their numbers, they can only advance a couple at a time in column formation."

"We will pick them off as they come," said Nakai.

"Exactly," said Massa.

"I have bogies coming up around the bend," said Pequo.

"More miners," said Massa.

The shaft erupted with flashes of light as the three pilot mechs took fire from the supposedly unarmed miners.

* * *

The Resilience battle group exited a wormhole into the Golgath system.

"Lieutenant Commander Chen, please summon our diplomat to the bridge," ordered Reinhardt.

"Aye, sir."

"Dispatch hunter-killers, establish the outer screen. I want immediate eyes on the Feng strike group."

Within minutes, Martin Rayban was on the bridge, dressed to the nines, looking polished and wearing his best shit-eating grin.

Reinhardt frowned. "Mr. Rayban, I was just about to raise the Feng carrier orbiting Golgath. I thought you should be present."

"Yes, of course," said Rayban, puffing out his chest. He looked around the bridge for a place to sit.

Reinhardt nodded to Ashwani, who gave up her seat. "Right here is fine, Mr. Rayban."

"Ah, thank you, Commander Ashwani." He took a seat, doing his best Captain Kirk impression.

This time, Reinhardt actually rolled his eyes. "Connelly, open a channel to the Feng command carrier."

"Yes, sir."

Within seconds, an image from the Feng carrier appeared on screen. There stood a large man with broad shoulders, his hair in a long, black ponytail. He wore plated, horned armor and a dour expression. "This is Captain Mongo Utang of the Feng Dynasty, commanding officer on the command carrier Superion."

Reinhardt's face went white. This was one of the outstanding Feng armada captains they had been searching the known galaxies for. He quickly cleared his throat. "This is Captain Reinhardt of the UIC command carrier Resilience. It is an honor to be speaking with the distinguished Captain Utang."

"Why do you approach the planet Golgath in attack formation?"

So much for small talk.

Rayban looked as if he wanted to speak, but Reinhardt held out a hand, signaling for him to wait. "We would like to negotiate for the release of the UIC command carrier Titan and its strike group, and we wish to take our wayward squadron into custody in light of the recent events on Golgath."

Captain Utang smiled at this, but it wasn't a friendly smile. It was a toothy display of menace. "Ha! *Recent events.* The United Intergalactic Coalition has had its sights on the Drekaar mines for quite some time now, and it has been itching to use the Pax Galactus Initiative to declare martial law."

Reinhardt shook his head. "That's not the case, Captain Utang. We want to get to the bottom of what happened just as badly as you do. We have no designs on Golgath."

"You just want to protect your own," sneered Utang.

"We have been searching for you, Captain. I don't know if you've heard, but the Feng Empire is now joining the United Intergalactic Coalition. We're technically on the same side."

"Hardly, Captain Reinhardt. I do not recognize the Feng alliance with the United Intergalactic Coalition, nor your supposed authority in this matter."

Rayban sat forward in his seat, opening his mouth to speak yet again, but yet again Reinhardt's hand went out to silence him. Utang hadn't taken any notice of the diplomat. Instead, his gaze focused on Reinhardt like a laser.

"You have orders from Vice Executor Kazar to stand down and report to Feng Command for reassignment."

"Ha! Kazar is responsible for the murder of our Holy Emperor, and as I understand it, your precious Razor's Edge is responsible for the murder of my brother, Yoshi."

"Your brother stood accused of treason and conspiracy to violate the UIC peace accord," insisted Reinhardt. "He then fired on our pilots. They simply defended themselves."

"I hope the pilot who shot down my brother was not killed in my attack," growled Captain Utang. "I cannot wait to torture them one by one to see which one did it."

"None of those pilots are subject to your brand of justice, Captain," said Reinhardt.

"Not only have they murdered my brother, a loyalist of the empire, it now appears that they have attacked the Drekaar."

"I find it hard to believe that they initiated an unprovoked attack on the mining complex," said Reinhardt.

"There is a legion of Cybions converging on the mining complex," said Utang. "If your pilots survive capture, they will face interrogation and justice in Feng courts on one of our colonies."

Rayban looked as if he was going to burst. He was dying to interject, but Reinhardt shot him a look that demanded that he wait. Rayban's face turned red with frustration and embarrassment at being told to remain silent, he being an important diplomat and all.

"I'm afraid I cannot allow that," said Reinhardt.

"You speak as if you have a choice," said Utang. "Besides, if the shoe was on the other foot and the UIC took custody of Feng spies, the UIC would not honor extradition."

"Captain Utang, I am well aware of your exploits in battle," said Reinhardt. "Your accomplishments in battle border on legend. However, do not delude yourself that you are any match for the United Intergalactic Coalition Armada. You must tread carefully, Captain."

Utang's sneer turned into a snarl. "It is you who must tread carefully, Captain Reinhardt. Word of the UIC's attempt on Golgath is spreading over independent planets. Coalitions against the UIC are already forming, aligning themselves with the Feng Empire. Any act of aggression on your part will only hasten these efforts, to the detriment of the already overextended Coalition."

"At least let's agree on setting the Titan strike group free. They did not order the attack on the Drekaar mining facility, and they've only fired upon you in self-defense."

Utang shook his head in defiance. "The Feng do not take direction from Barberoi, let alone Humans. Titan and its strike group will remain in our custody until you have vacated the system."

"Captain Utang, we will not vacate the system. We will not fire upon you unless we are fired upon. In the meantime, I ask that you reconsider our offer. We want to avoid confrontation, but you must be reasonable."

Before Utang could reply, Reinhardt signaled Connelly to end transmission.

"That was intense," said Ashwani. "He's not backing down."

This time, Rayban was unable to contain himself. "How *dare* you silence me during the negotiations, the very reason why I am on board this vessel!"

"The negotiations haven't even begun," said Reinhardt. "That was just foreplay."

"You have very likely jeopardized our mission," said Rayban in rebuke.

"Do you know who that is?" asked Reinhardt.

Ashwani nodded. "He's a famous Feng Captain in their fleet."

"That's Utang the Ice Dragon," said Reinhardt, "son of a famous general from the last Intergalactic War, and brother to the general of the Feng Empire's military, the other Ice Dragon. You know, the one Lieutenant Pequo shot down."

"Nice pedigree," said Ashwani.

"He's one ruthless son-of-a-bitch. Any of the worlds who have slipped from the UIC's grasp were because of him," said Reinhardt.

"And here you are getting into a pissing contest with this man when he currently holds the upper hand," said Rayban.

"I was setting the tone for future interactions," said Reinhardt. "He is a warrior who follows the Rule of Nature. He needs to know that we're to be taken seriously. If we opened immediately with negotiations, he would've interpreted it as a sign of weakness."

"But we *are* in a position of weakness," said Rayban.

"How do we deal with him?" asked Ashwani, ignoring Rayban's remark. "He doesn't seem open to negotiation."

"The question is," said Reinhardt, "why is he here? Why now?"

"I don't follow, sir," said Ashwani.

"He just happened to be in the neighborhood of Golgath? Why would he break our treaty and risk all-out war over this?"

Ashwani understood. "Why is he so interested in our pilots?"

"Right," said Reinhardt. "And what does he know about what happened down there?"

"Do you think the Feng had something to do with the attack on the mining complex?"

"The Razor's Edge is our top fighter squadron. They've served under me numerous times before. Commander Massa is a stand-up guy, even for a Humani, with a distinguished service record. Something had to have provoked them to open fire on the Drekaar mining complex."

* * *

Pequo was the first to sense the armed Drekaar miners as they rounded the corner. He held up his mechanical hand, magnetizing it as they opened fire, but a few rounds got through, one clipping his leg, taking out the hydraulics.

He dropped to one knee as he collected Drekaar rounds in his magnetic field. He aimed his gun, but having expended most of his ammunition in the outer structure, his chambers were almost immediately emptied.

Nakai rotated out her empty chambers and swapped in her remaining full chambers from her mech's right thigh compartment, her sensors isolating the Drekaar brain stems. She fired in controlled shots, painting the walls with creamy Drekaar blood.

Massa was empty, so he stood in front of Pequo, both mechanical hands magnetized, collecting incoming rounds. Within minutes, the shaft was still and the armed Drekaar miners lay dead.

"Why were those miners armed?" asked Pequo.

"Because they were not miners," said Massa. "They were protecting something."

"I am picking up a legion of Cybions entering the mining structure," said Nakai.

"We go deeper into the mine," said Massa. "Maybe there is a way out, a shaft leading to the outside."

"And right into Iguani territory," added Nakai.

"Would you rather face a legion of Cybions?" asked Massa.

Nakai was silent. She got his point. The Iguani were the lesser of the evils.

"My suit's ambulation is disabled," said Pequo, trying to stand.

Massa grabbed one of Pequo's mechanical arms and swung it over his shoulders. He pulled the damaged mech up, and Pequo was able to stand on one leg.

"What about the radiation?" asked Nakai.

Pequo's suit was compromised.

"No time to attempt repairs," said Massa. Then to Pequo, "Your choice—radiation sickness or death by Cybions?" The question was rhetorical.

"Let us go," said Pequo. "We do not have much time."

"Alpha Two, you take point," said Massa. "Alpha Three, watch our six."

They ambled their way deeper into the shaft, bouncing sonar down the tunnels at each fork, taking radiation readings, assessing. They made educated guesses as to which tunnels to take, trying to avoid going deeper under the surface. The deeper they went, the more radiation there would be and the further away from an exit shaft to the surface.

"That is strange," said Pequo, looking at his in-helmet display. "There is no increase in radiation."

"We are trying to stay towards the surface," explained Nakai, "so we do not fry your sorry ass."

"No, he's right," said Massa. "This is unusual for an active mine."

"Unless, this mine is not active," said Pequo.

"The Cybions have entered the shaft," said Nakai. "It will not be long before they are on us."

"Leave me here," said Pequo. "I am slowing us down."

"No way," said Massa. "We will all share the same fate."

Deep down, Pequo was relieved to hear that. Although he didn't want to jeopardize his comrades, the prospect of death by Cybion dismemberment terrified him.

They stumbled upon a large cavern holding a small ship. There were Avatars surrounding it, working on the outside, making repairs and operating diagnostic scanners.

"What the frak is that?" asked Nakai.

"It is what the Drekaar were protecting," said Massa.

"Well, we found the missing Avatars," said Pequo.

The Avatars went about their work, as they were bred to do, taking no notice of the three mechs. That is, all except for one Avatar. He was dressed in fancier clothing, and he was looking right at Massa, Pequo, and Nakai.

"What are you doing here?"

"Heck of a way to greet your rescue party," quipped Pequo.

"The Cybions are moving quickly through the tunnels. They will be all over us in minutes," said Nakai.

"You should not be here," said the Avatar.

"Let me slip out of my suit," said Pequo. "We can use it to blow the shaft and buy us some time."

"Good thinking," said Massa.

"On it," said Nakai. She threw Pequo's arm around her shoulders and they staggered over to the mouth of the tunnel. Pequo activated the self-destruct and slipped out of his suit.

"We have to leave, now," Massa told the Avatar.

"That is not possible."

Massa wasn't taking no for an answer. "Do you know how to operate this ship?"

"Yes, but—"

"We are leaving," interrupted Massa. "Everyone on board the ship," he announced. The Avatars stopped what they were doing and gazed blankly at him.

Pequo ran alongside Nakai's mech until they reached Massa and the Avatar by the ship.

"Fire in the hole," said Nakai.

Massa and the Avatar turned to look, and they saw the glowing red eyes of the Cybions in the darkness. Pequo's mech exploded, caving in the opening to the shaft, sealing it.

"That should buy us a few micros," said Pequo.

Massa pointed towards the craft. "Pequo, escort this Avatar onto the ship."

"Yes, sir." Pequo grabbed the Avatar under the arm, turned him, and they boarded the ship. Massa and Nakai followed in their mechs.

"What about the other Avatars?" asked Pequo.

"Frak 'em," said Massa. "They will not fit, and we are out of time."

Nakai was scanning the interior of the ship, sizing up the controls. "This is Feng construction. What is it doing in a Drekaar mine shaft?"

"We can theorize later," said Massa. "Avatar, take us out of here."

"My name is Plato," said the Avatar.

They heard blasting and the grinding of metal on the other side of the caved-in shaft.

"Plato, if you do not take us out of here, we are going to be ripped to shreds by a legion of Cybions," said Massa. "So, you understand my urgency."

"I think I can fly this," said Nakai.

"No," said Plato.

"She can fly anything," said Pequo. "It is a gift."

"I mean, I will pilot," said Plato. He stepped in front of her mech and activated the controls.

"Interesting, how you know how to operate a Feng interface," said Massa.

"Do you want to hurl accusations or escape?" asked Plato.

The pile of rock at the mouth of the shaft began to shift and move.

"Take us out of here, Plato," ordered Massa.

The ship fired up and began to rise off the ground.

"Uh, I do not mean to be a buzzkill, but I do not think we are fitting through that shaft," said Pequo, pointing to the only other shaft, one too small to accommodate the ship.

"Where do you want to go?" said Plato.

"Anywhere but here," said Nakai.

"Pequo is right," said Massa. "How are we getting out of here?"

"Where do you want to go?" asked Plato.

The rubble shifted behind them as the Cybions were almost through. The Avatars on the outside of the ship watched passively, waiting for cruel and imminent death.

Massa held up his empty firearm to Plato's head in a bluff. "Move it!"

Plato reached over and hit a button. There was a strange whirring sound that came from somewhere inside the strange ship. Outside, the cavern began to bend and stretch.

"What the frak is going on?" asked Nakai, her sensors inside her mech going wild.

"If I were you, I would hold on," said Plato.

He touched another button, and Pequo felt like his soul was being ripped out of his body. There were glitches on Massa's scanners as they registered everything and nothing simultaneously. Nakai felt a wave of dread and panic as she momentarily became disoriented.

The Cybions broke through and swarmed the cavern, painting the walls and floor with the blood of the Avatars in a flash of claw and blade.

Inside the ship, everyone braced for whatever was going to happen next. The Cybions toggled to firearms and opened up on the ship, but the bullets passed right through them.

"What is going on?" said Pequo.

Before anyone could answer, the cavern disappeared, and in an instant, they were outside the mining complex, surrounded by Feng Warmongers.

"Holy shreg!" said Pequo.

"What did you do?" Massa asked Plato, shoving his empty gun in the Avatar's face.

"I got us out of the mine," said Plato, "like you specified."

"The Warmongers have spotted us," said Nakai. "Their weapons are heating up."

"They will not fire on us," said Plato.

"I do not want to stick around to find out," said Massa. "Get us out of here!"

"I am afraid I cannot do that."

"What is this guy's deal?" asked Pequo.

Their ship became surrounded by Warmongers, who hovered around them, weapons targeting the strange ship.

"I saw what Plato did," said Nakai. "I think I can get us out of here."

"I am afraid you do not grasp how to pilot this ship," said Plato.

Pequo grabbed him and shoved him out of her way. "Lead, follow, or get out of the way."

"Do you think you can fly this thing?" asked Massa.

The ship's com crackled. "This is Commander Walong of the Feng. Surrender the ship immediately, or we will blow you out of the sky."

"I can do it," said Nakai. "It looks like Feng technology. How hard can it be?"

"You could not possibly understand how this ship works," insisted Plato. "You are going to get us all killed."

Massa pointed his gun in Plato's face, silencing him. "Well, we are dead either way. Do it, Nakai."

She nodded and stepped in front of the controls. She was about to punch the button, when Plato yelled, "No! I will do it!"

Nakai looked at Massa, who looked at Plato. "Then do it already!"

Plato stepped in front of the controls and started punching in coordinates in time and space, which resulted in whirring sounds coming from the dark matter conductor.

"Surrender the ship immediately," ordered Commander Walong over the com. "This is your final warning."

"I do not think so," said Massa.

"They are not firing," said Pequo in astonishment.

"Hold on to your asses," said Nakai.

Plato punched a button, and the desert and Warmonger ships around them began to bend and stretch.

Pequo grabbed his gut as his stomach lurched. Massa looked on as the ship's scanners were all over the map, yielding impossible readings on location, time, and kinesthetic. In a flash, the Warmonger ships and the Drekaar mining complex were gone.

CHAPTER 20

"Captain," said Lieutenant Chen, "there's a strange ship that appeared on the outside of the mining complex. It's emanating distortions in dark energy. The Feng are surrounding it."

"Identify."

"Negative. It cannot be identified using known records of catalogued vessels…Wait a minute…it's gone."

"What do you mean it's gone?"

"It's gone, sir, as in no longer there."

"Where did it go?"

"I don't know, sir."

Proximity alarms erupted on the bridge of the Resilience.

"Captain, the Feng strike team is engaging!"

"Battle stations, everyone!"

"Captain, there is another Feng battle group exiting a wormhole in this system!"

"What? One of ours?"

"Negative, sir. They're targeting us."

"Jesus Christ! Evasive maneuvers! We need to get into a better position!"

Sandwiched between two rogue Feng strike groups, the second larger than Reinhardt's battle group, he now had to defend two fronts.

"The Feng have breached our outer screen on both sides," said Ashwani. "Our destroyers are engaging."

They watched on screen as their ships fought and were quickly disabled and destroyed by the more numerous Feng forces.

"Launch Vortex squadrons!"

"Launching Vortex squadrons," echoed Ashwani.

The Feng command carriers launched their Warmongers, and within minutes, the cloud of Vortex fighters swarmed the cloud of Warmongers, whirling and rolling in zero gravity dogfighting.

The Vortex fighters were clearly outnumbered, and as each was neutralized, the data was compiled and displayed in the operations room and on the bridge, the casualty list growing exponentially.

Within a sexagen, the Feng forces had located and neutralized the UIC hunter-killers and destroyers.

"Send a request to command for reinforcements!" cried Reinhardt.

"The Feng are blocking our transmissions." responded Lieutenant Chen. "The Feng have breached our inner screens. They're now targeting our HVU's!"

"Goddammit, get me UIC Command!"

"Negative, sir. They're jamming us!"

It was all spiraling out of control so quickly. The battleships fought valiantly against the Feng dreadnaughts and battleships, taking a few with them in a blaze of glory, but there were too many, and they were now targeting the Resilience.

The Resilience shook as it took fire.

"Feng hunter-killers are targeting the Resilience!"

"The dreadnaughts are targeting us!"

Reinhardt gripped his captain's chair to steady himself and clamped a hand on Ashwani's shoulder. "This was how the Titan strike group was overwhelmed! Captain Utang has been a busy boy, rounding up other rogue groups. But he's not declaring war."

"I don't understand, sir."

"It sure seems like it," cried Rayban.

"No," insisted Reinhardt. "He's protecting something on the planet."

The rogue Feng forces were not enough to fight the entire United Intergalactic Coalition Armada. However, they were enough to overwhelm Captain Reinhardt. The UIC being stretched thin, he was all the United Intergalactic Coalition had to offer at the moment.

Reinhardt knew the attack was suicide. Once word got back to UIC Command that there was a Feng faction that took down the Resilience battle group, they would throw everything they had at them to eradicate the Feng insurgents. He knew that they were protecting something important.

The Feng began to engage Reinhardt's strike group.

"Defensive maneuvers," said Reinhardt. "Engage!"

"There's too many of them," said Ashwani.

They watched on screen as their few battleships and two destroyers traded fire with Utang's six battleships and two massive dreadnaughts.

"Captain, two of the Feng battleships took critical damage to their chemical reactors and life support."

"Sir, we've lost two battleships. The third and the destroyer are engaging the damaged destroyers."

"Negative," said Reinhardt. "Have them engage the other battleships."

"Sir, that's suicide."

Reinhardt swallowed hard. "We are going to lose them anyway. Maybe we can distribute some of the damage. Have them target the weapons systems. If we can de-fang them, it'll buy us some time."

"Aye, Captain."

Reinhardt's remaining battleship and destroyer managed to take out the weapons system of a third Feng battleship before being taken out.

"Sir, we've lost them."

"Dammit," said Reinhardt, running his hand through his hair in exasperation. This was no simulation. The men in those lost ships were dead.

"The Feng are advancing!"

Reinhardt gripped his chair as his carrier shook from taking on fire. This time blast doors deployed, sealing off sections from hull breaches and nanite webs sealed off gaping holes in the hull, but at the expense of the all-or-nothing armor.

"They're targeting our weapons!"

"Losing weapons tracking systems, sir!"

"They're targeting life support!"

Ashwani grabbed his arm. "Captain, you have to get to the battle bridge!"

"I'm not leaving!"

"It's deeper within the ship! It makes tactical sense! You can continue the fight from there!"

Reinhardt knew she was right.

"Poi, Chen, come with me. I want the armor reconfigured to protect engineering and life support!"

Lieutenants Poi, Chen, and Commander Ashwani all entered the express lift together. The doors quickly sealed behind them, and the lift sank so rapidly that Reinhardt felt his stomach hit the roof of his mouth. It raced down to deck thirty.

When the lift doors opened, they entered the battle bridge, and the displays from scanners on and off the ship, ship vitals and diagnostics, weapons systems, engineering were all piping in from the operations room.

Reinhardt stood behind his Captain's chair. "How far from the next wormhole node?"

"Point eleven AU, Captain!"

"We're not going to fight our way out of this. Our only option is retreat. Get us there, full conductance, and get me Captain Utang!"

Within seconds, Captain Utang appeared on the monitor. "Called to say goodbye, Captain?"

"This move of yours is suicide! You are protecting something on Golgath. What is it?"

"Suicide, Captain Reinhardt? Do you think me that desperate?"

"The UIC Armada will smite you from the universe."

Utang laughed, amused by the threat. "My dear Captain, in the end, none of this will have mattered."

"That's rather nihilistic, even for a Feng."

Utang consulted his monitors and displays. "I see you are making a run for the nearest wormhole. You will never make it."

Reinhardt ran a finger across his throat, and the communications officer terminated the com link with Utang.

"Status."

"He's right, Captain," said the helmsman. "At this rate, we'll never make it."

"Change bearing," said Reinhardt. "Enter planetary orbit."

"Sir?"

"We'll pick up speed and slingshot around the planet to the wormhole."

Ashwani shook her head. "They'll follow us. It won't do any good."

Reinhardt curled his right hand into a fist, his eyes narrowed in determination. "They'll have to regroup above us before pursuing. We'll build some distance between us. Their ships are all bigger and heavier. We'll outrun them."

"That's not true, Captain," said Lieutenant Poi. "The greater the mass, the faster the orbit. They'll catch us."

"Jesus, Poi, why let facts get in the way of a good plan?"

"We can decrease our orbit, letting the increased gravity of Golgath speed us along. The Feng will follow suit, but they'll be a step behind us. It'll be close."

Reinhardt nodded.

"Do it," said Ashwani to the helmsman.

The command carrier Resilience began to dip towards the planet as the two Feng strike groups coalesced above and began to follow them down in pursuit.

"Now we only have one front to worry about, one battlespace to defend," said Reinhardt.

"Preparing to enter orbit, sir."

"We're taking fire on the upper decks."

"We have hull breaches on decks one and four."

"Evacuate crew to decks twenty through thirty and seal the outer modules," said Reinhardt.

"Aye, Captain."

Alarms sounded around the ship with an announcement of the evacuation. Reinhardt didn't need all of the operations of the massive vessel. At the moment, he just needed them to haul ass.

"Entering orbit!"

"The Feng Warmongers and dreadnaughts have also entered orbit!"

Reinhardt wasn't worried about the Warmongers. They were fast, but they were smaller, and their damage would be minimal...or so he hoped. Indications of distance to Golgath and the specific orbital energy piped in from the operations room.

"We're going to pick up speed at the periapsis," said the helmsman.

"The Feng dreadnaughts and the command carrier are gaining velocity and closing in." The dreadnaughts were somewhat smaller in size to the Resilience and lighter, but the Superion was massive and gaining quickly using Golgath's gravity.

"Sir, Captain Utang is hailing us."

"On screen," said Reinhardt.

Utang appeared on screen looking as amused as ever. "Taking the long way around, Captain Reinhardt?"

"I'm giving you a run for your money."

"The Superion is faster in Golgath's gravity. We will overtake you, but thank you for making it interesting."

Reinhardt stood, defiant against his antagonist. "Everything is being recorded as a matter of official record and is being transmitted to UIC Command. Once the galaxy sees that you have attacked us unprovoked, other worlds will think twice about any alliance. You're finished, Utang."

A holographic display appeared in front of Reinhardt that Utang was unable to see indicating that the Resilience was closing in on the wormhole.

"You Humans, always so focused on the now, when the past is so much richer, particularly for the Feng. Soon your imminent death will not have happened, but unfortunately, that will not spare you the agony you are about to experience."

The Superion opened fire on the Resilience with its rail cannons and guns, shredding sections of the hull over engineering, sheering off the nanite armor.

"Terminate com link," ordered Reinhardt, and Utang flickered off the screen.

"Captain, we've lost all power to the conductors!"

The Resilience began to drift in orbit on its own momentum as the Feng dreadnaughts closed in for the kill.

"The hull's neural net sustained too much damage," said Poi. "Even if we made it to the wormhole, we won't be able to execute a handshake."

"Transmissions are still jammed, sir."

Reinhardt shook his fist. "Frak it all! He's making sure I cannot transmit my witness data back to Command. How is he jamming us?"

"He's manipulating gravitational and magnetic waves."

"Life support?"

"Seventy-two percent, sir."

The Feng continued to fire at the Resilience.

"Sir, they're targeting stabilizers!"

The crew on the battle bridge stumbled as the command carrier was losing maintenance of its orientation. Lights flickered and monitors glitched.

"Reconfigure shields to protect life support systems!"

"Sir, he's hailing us again."

"Dammit, we're sitting ducks!"

Ashwani was looking over readings from Poi's and Chen's displays. "It would appear so, sir."

"Life support is at sixty-nine percent but stable."

"The dreadnaughts' rail cannons are heating up, sir."

Reinhardt was defeated. There was nothing he could do. It had all happened so quickly. His Hail Mary had failed, and he took full responsibility for the fate of his crew, but that offered no consolation.

"Open a com link to Captain Utang."

Utang reappeared on screen. "Yes, Captain?"

"As Captain of the Resilience, I offer my surrender." Ashwani was pained as she heard her captain utter those words, but she knew he had no other alternative.

The crew on the battle bridge observed in silence, their minds racing, contemplating the horrors of being taken prisoner by this insurgent madman.

"How kind of you, Captain. I suppose I could let you wait as the wake of Spacetime erases us from existence, as a courtesy, warrior-to-warrior."

"What are you talking about?" asked Reinhardt. "You're talking as if you've invented time travel."

Utang smiled. "Funny you should say that, Captain Reinhardt. In ten micros, one of my officers piloting a very special vessel is going to go back to a very important tipping point in our history, altering the future—our present."

* * *

Lieutenant Votan was on Golgath in a separate shaft of the Drekaar mining complex inside the other Spacetime travelling ship with only a pilot. There was no need for any further accompaniment. His only mission's objective was to warn Admiral Fengus Utang, Captain Mongo Utang's father, of the impending wormhole generated by the filthy Humans during the invasion of Humana.

"Ready when you are, Lieutenant," said the pilot.

"Initiate," said Votan.

The pilot executed the Spacetime coordinates for the Invasion of Humana in the last Intergalactic War, and the ship began to vibrate and hum. The cave outside began to distort, and Votan felt a queasy feeling as the cave vanished. Outside the window of the ship was the vast, cold void of space filled with Feng Armada ships in battle formation, the majority of the ships in front of Votan's little ship.

Captain Mongo Utang was an avid student of the war and this particular battle. He had tirelessly consulted the Aether and historical records to obtain the precise coordinates for Votan's arrival to avoid inadvertently placing him on the Humani side or in the outer screen of the Feng Armada during engagement.

"Lieutenant, the command carrier Dominance is targeting us," said the pilot.

"Good," said Votan. "Hail the Dominance."

"Hailing, sir."

"This is the command carrier Dominance of the Feng Empire," said a voice on the other end. "Identify yourself."

"I am Lieutenant Votan on a hunter-killer of the Feng Empire returning from a reconnaissance mission."

"We do not recognize your vessel," said the voice on the other end. "Security clearance code."

Votan used the one that Captain Utang gave him, one that was used in this time period. "I need to speak with the admiral immediately," added Votan. "It is emergent."

There was a pause followed by an acknowledgement. "Lieutenant, enter hangar bay twelve."

"Acknowledged," answered Votan.

He admired the massive size of the Dominance as they approached, a marvel of a ship, even by modern standards. Within minutes, they were landing in the hangar bay.

As they exited the ship, they were greeted by a small security detail. "I am Master-at-Arms Rang. We have been unable to identify you, Lieutenant."

Votan bowed slightly. "That is because I am part of an experimental program, shadow operations." Votan provided the Master-at-Arms with another security clearance code, one that would link up with the quantum computer aboard Votan's ship containing Votan's mocked up file as a Feng shadow operative.

Rang ran it through his digi-tab and found the file. He saluted the lieutenant. "Apologies, sir. In these times, we cannot be too careful."

Votan saluted back. "Understandable. I need to speak with the admiral immediately."

"Follow me." Rang led Votan to a briefing room and left him there. After twenty minutes, Captain Plaxo Klingu appeared.

Votan stood and saluted.

Captain Klingu returned the salute. "At ease. What do you want, Lieutenant?"

"With all due respect, sir, I specifically asked for Admiral Utang," said Votan, disappointed.

"The admiral is very busy, as am I."

"The Humans are going to be arriving in a wormhole in," he consulted his Spacetime recorder, "one sexagen."

"We are not worried about Humans," said Captain Klingu. "They are a bungling race of animals."

"They are going to open up a wormhole in the middle of our battle group, precisely on top of this command carrier."

Captain Klingu looked incredulous. "That would be suicide. Even the Humans would not be so daft."

Votan knew that if he said it will be an accident, Klingu would ask him how he would know something like that in advance. Then Votan would have to explain the ship and Spacetime travel, Klingu would want to inspect the ship, and the sexagen would be expended.

"The United Intergalactic Coalition sees no other use for the Humans."

"I would need to verify your intelligence," said Captain Klingu.

"Of course," said Votan. He remotely accessed his ship's quantum computer on his own digi-tab and produced the fabricated surveillance data corroborating his story.

Captain Klingu read it carefully. When he was finished, he clapped a heavy hand on Votan's shoulder. "You have done well. I will forward this to the admiral immediately."

"Thank you, sir."

"In the meantime, we could use you to help oversee our salvage operations."

"Yes, sir."

"Excellent. Report to the deck department immediately."

*

Within the sexagen, the Feng invasion battle group adjusted their coordinates, avoiding the oncoming wormhole. In anticipation, they focused a few squadrons and a battleship on the coordinates, and they picked off the Human ships as they emerged, sending them to oblivion.

The Feng then refocused on the invasion, overwhelming the Humani planetary defense forces. Lieutenant Votan helped coordinate the salvage groups addressing the disabled and destroyed Humani ships.

The planet was taken in a little over forty sexagens. The Feng established their own planetary screen to defend their occupation from any Coalition reinforcements. The salvaging operations nearly complete, Lieutenant Votan was summoned to the admiral's office.

He stood in front of the door sensor, and there was an affirmative tone.

"Enter," said the admiral inside.

The door opened, and Votan entered. He stood rigid and saluted.

"At ease," said the admiral, after returning the salute "Have a seat."

Lieutenant Votan took in Admiral Fengus Utang, a legend in the Feng Armada (now even more so) and father of his commanding officer. The man was massive, but intelligent. His demeanor was curt and officious, which only made him more intimidating.

"Your intelligence has single-handedly allowed us to avoid disaster," said Admiral Utang.

"I was happy to assist, sir."

"Without your assistance, we would have taken on serious casualties." He paused. "Your vessel is not a hunter-killer."

"That is correct."

"So you lied to Captain Klingu. If your actions had not saved our invasion force, I would have you court-marshalled and executed."

Votan swallowed hard. The man was insulted.

"Why did you lie about your ship?"

"Because the truth was not expedient at the moment," replied Votan. "The ship is a Spacetime travelling vessel sent from the future."

"If I did not have my ship's engineers investigate every inch of your little ship, I would tear out your throat where you sit for insulting my intelligence. However, they have confirmed a new technology that appeared to manipulate gravitational waves and Spacetime."

"That is correct, sir."

"Assuming your report is accurate, who sent you?"

This was the moment of truth.

"Your son, Captain Mongo Utang."

The imposing admiral was silent. Votan took the opportunity to produce digital pics of Mongo and the corresponding genetic profile. Admiral Utang scrutinized it carefully.

"I will have this analyzed and confirmed by our biotechnicians."

"Of course, sir. Captain Mongo Utang wishes that he could have been here to see you again, but he had to fight to defend my passage to this time from the United Intergalactic Coalition."

"My son," said Admiral Utang, his demeanor softening. "He is but a young boy at home with my wife and his brother." He was actually smiling slightly. "He became a fierce warrior, my son?"

Votan nodded, beaming with pride. "They call him the Ice Dragon, sir."

The admiral's smile grew into a grin. "A name reserved for a true warrior."

"He was destined to bring balance back to the universe," said Votan. "To bring back the glory of the old Feng Empire."

"You mean this empire."

"Correct, sir."

"So, before this intervention, the Feng lost the Intergalactic War?"

"The losses you would have sustained, your death, was a tipping point in the United Intergalactic Coalition's favor," explained Votan. "The Feng would have lost the war and continued to exist as a shell of its former self. The emperor, Hiron, would have been assassinated."

The admiral listened to this with great attention. "The empire owes you and my son great thanks. When you return, you will tell him so."

"That is just it," said Votan. "I cannot return. That vector in the event cone has been erased."

"My son is gone?"

"That version of him. The version that suffered with redemption on his mind and vengeance in his heart. He agonized over the events leading to your death and the weakening of our Holy Empire. That warrior suffers no more."

"Then you have helped bring my son peace. For that, I thank you." The admiral appraised Votan for a moment. "How is it that you are still here? Why has this version of you not been erased?"

"It was a gift from your son. The technology allows us to manipulate not just time, but space, merging alternate possibilities with our own, solving certain time paradoxes. On some plane of existence lies the possibility that my future self continues to exist. He has merged that reality with this one, isolating the event vector of my existence from the effects of my intervention here."

"I have no idea what any of that means, but our scientists, with your help, will begin to unravel it all. In the meantime, you will be promoted and will have your choice of assignments."

"Thank you, sir. I have one request."

"Name it."

"Back on my home planet of Wassu, I am an infant. I wish to go visit myself."

"A strange request, but these are strange times. Granted."

"Thank you, sir."

"Dismissed."

* * *

Captain Reinhardt shook his head, unable to wrap his brain around the notion that the Feng had apparently developed time travel. "But how? I don't understand."

Captain Mongo Utang sat back in his chair and waved a clawed hand. "The Aether holds the answers to many mysteries, Captain Reinhardt. Our entire means of space travel has always been predicated on the physical definition of time."

"Expansion of the universe," said Lieutenant Poi.

Utang nodded. "We have merely found a way to access the undiscovered dimensions of the multiverse."

Reinhardt was suddenly reminded of Pequo's remark about responsible warriors. "Such technology is dangerous. If used irresponsibly, the consequences could be catastrophic."

"Irresponsible? As determined by you, Captain Reinhardt? The United Intergalactic Coalition? You are no longer in a position to pontificate what is responsible."

"That ship that appeared on Golgath's surface outside the mining complex, it disappeared off our scanners," said Reinhardt.

"Another Spacetime travel craft hijacked by the remainder of your fighter squadron," explained Utang. "However, they have no idea what they have and have no knowledge of when we are sending the other," assured Utang. "They are lost in Spacetime."

"If they knew how to escape your forces, they must know how to operate it. They can set things right," insisted Reinhardt. "They can screw up your plans."

"They have already tried," said Utang. "They were the unidentified Vortex fighter that attacked the mining complex. They were attempting to destroy the craft. They did not count on interference from themselves in our present Spacetime."

Reinhardt's hopes were immediately dashed. He fell into his captain's chair and rubbed his temples with his fingertips. "I don't understand. Why make two?"

"To correct for any mistakes made. As your pilots have demonstrated with their craft, Spacetime manipulation is an inexact science. Also, each craft is fitted to serve a particular function."

"Since we're going to be history anyway, why don't you explain the functions?"

Utang nodded in agreement. "Since none of this matters…"

"Of course," agreed Reinhardt.

"You are familiar with the attempted invasion of Humana in the last Intergalactic War, Captain…"

Reinhardt rolled his eyes. "Yes, I am."

"Then you recall that in a monumental blunder, your race inadvertently exited a wormhole right in the center of the Feng invasion force, wiping out the lead command carrier and our greatest tactician."

"Yes, your father," said Reinhardt. "As colossal a blunder as it was, it turned the tide."

Utang nodded. "One ship will warn the Feng command carrier of the coordinates of the Human wormhole exit. They will have time to evade the massive collision."

"And the other ship?"

"The other ship, the ones your pilots have stolen, is loaded with explosives. Disguised as a Vortex fighter, it will dock in the Humani lead planetary defense command carrier and detonate."

"Quite the one-two punch," said Reinhardt.

"With the changes in events, this scenario will no longer exist," explained Utang. "You and I will live in another scenario shaped by our changes, but our current versions of ourselves will be wiped from existence, its memory briefly registered in the Aether as a transient afterimage."

A lightbulb went off in Reinhardt's mind. That explained the Razor's Edge pilots' phantom memories. The memories that vanished upon reassessment.

"Captain, there's a surge in dark energy," said Lieutenant Poi.

"Where?" asked Ashwani.

Poi squinted, perplexed. "Everywhere."

Utang grinned, resigned to his fate. "That is the harbinger of nonexistence. Make peace with your maker as this iteration of yourself evaporates into the Aether and is enveloped by oblivion."

Reinhardt shook his head at Ashwani. "Man, does this guy ever shut—?"

In an instant, gravitational waves distorted and both the Feng and Resilience battle groups vanished in orbit over Golgath. Multiple Feng strike groups appeared in their stead and battalions of Feng soldiers and Cybions covered the planet's surface, their numbers more vast than they had been in recent days, the recent days of an obsolete time trajectory that no longer existed.

The Feng now occupied Golgath and its kronite mines, and there wasn't a single United Intergalactic Coalition patrol in sight.

* * *

"Where are we?" demanded Commander Massa as he looked out at the barren desert landscape.

"The more appropriate question is *when* are we?" said Plato.

"You are real mouthy for an Avatar," snapped Nakai.

"Easy does it," admonished Pequo. "He saved our lives."

"We are still on planet Golgath," explained Plato, "an eon in the past."

"What? What are you talking about?" asked Massa.

"He is lying to save his own skin," chimed in Nakai.

"What do you mean 'an eon in the past?'" asked Pequo, raising a hand to silence the others.

"I mean an eon ago."

"You mean we are in a time-travelling ship?" asked Pequo.

Nakai snorted at the notion. "Yeah, right. The Feng developed time travel technology."

"Actually, to be more precise, Spacetime travel," said Plato.

Commander Massa squeezed past Plato and studied the controls and readouts. "By the Engineer, I think he is telling the truth."

Plato shrugged his shoulders. "Why would I lie?"

Nakai sneered at the Avatar. "I think the bigger question is: what were you doing helping the Feng?"

"I had no choice. They threatened me with a slow and painful death."

"Do you think a test tube Humani's life is worth more than those of the natural Humani world?" Nakai's question was more of an accusation than an actual question.

"Well, now they are minus one Spacetime travelling ship," retorted Plato.

"You mean there are more?" asked Massa.

"Just one, located in another cave within the mines."

"What are the Feng doing with time-travelling ships?"

"They did not exactly explain it to me."

Nakai threw her hands up in the air. "Of course not."

Plato shrugged. "A Captain Utang only explained that it would restore the glory of the old Feng Empire. Something about setting things right."

"Captain Utang," Pequo and Nakai said in unison.

"He has been unaccounted for since Feng toppled," said Massa.

"It would appear that you have found him," said Plato.

"Did he say anything else?" asked Massa.

"No."

"He must want to go back and prevent the death of Emperor Hiron," speculated Massa.

"That is possible," said Plato. "However, Drekaar Chieftain RagnakTok told me that Captain Utang was obsessed with the Invasion of Humana during the last Intergalactic War. He would rave on and on about it."

"The Drekaar chief told you this?" asked Massa, dubious.

"Prior to my discovery of Captain Utang's presence on the planet, I had the opportunity to dine and even hunt with the Drekaar chieftain and his tribe."

Nakai laughed out loud. "Wait a minute, you mean to tell me that you hunted? With the Drekaar?"

"I even helped bring down a massive Gargantuok."

"A Gargantu-what?"

Their conversation was interrupted by movement around the ship. The sand began to shift around it, moving into a swirl and picking up momentum. A massive vortex spun the ship around as it began to drop below the desert surface.

"Get us out of here," said Massa.

"I cannot travel in Spacetime at this moment," explained Plato. "The Spacetime continuum is unstable from our journey and needs to regenerate."

"Then how about you fly us out of here?"

Plato activated the kronite core and fired up the jets. However, as he began to lift off, the ship had already sunk a hundred pracics below the surface, and sand was filling the opening above.

"We are going to be sealed in!" shouted Nakai.

When the last bit of daylight had been cut off, along with their only apparent exit, Plato let off on the throttle, landing the ship.

"What are you doing?" cried Nakai.

"It would appear that I have no other option."

"He is right," said Massa. "We have to search for another way."

Plato nodded and opened the hatch. Pequo and Nakai exited the ship. Massa gestured for Plato to exit. "There is no way I am leaving you unattended on this ship."

"Very well," said Plato. Accommodating Commander Massa, he exited the craft and joined the others, Massa bringing up the rear with his hand on his gun.

"We are in a big, subterranean cavern," said Pequo, the sand muffling his voice and stifling any echo.

"Check it out," said Nakai.

They were surrounded by a series of caves. Burning coals began to appear in the dark tunnels, oddly grouped in pairs. Dozens of crablike creatures measuring ten pracics tall scurried into the cavern, their eyes on stalks, snapping their claws and whipping barbed tails at the Humani outsiders.

Massa, Nakai, and Pequo drew their arms. Their weapons were empty of rounds, but they hoped to bluff their way out of whatever confrontation might ensue.

Plato cocked his head sideways, sizing up these familiar creatures. They resembled the Drekaar, but were more crablike than scorpion.

The crabs hoisted themselves up on their hind legs and began to dance around the Humani, snapping their claws in bravado. It was a rather ostentatious display, more posturing than actual threat.

"What the frak are they doing?" asked Nakai, pointing her empty weapon at several crabs as they scurried around.

Plato stepped forward, cleared his throat, and did his best impersonation of a greeting in Drekaari.

The crabs settled down and fell back on all legs, their eyes burning as they listened to this strange off-worlder utter something similar to their native tongue. One crab, slightly larger than the others and bearing odd bead-like decorations, scuttled forward and began to grunt and click.

Massa banged his helmet. "Damned translator chip is malfunctioning. I cannot make out what he is saying."

Plato uttered the same greeting to the adorned king crab, and again the creature clicked and croaked in return.

"I do not believe it," said Massa.

Pequo stepped closer to Plato. "It understands you?"

"I think so."

"Can you understand it?"

"No. My universal translator is useless without network support, but if I am guessing correctly, it would not matter."

The creature issued the same sequence of sounds and then another sounding like hissing water.

"What do you mean?" asked Massa.

"I believe that these are the ancient Dreguani?"

"The what?"

"Before the Drekaar and the Iguani were at war with each other, they were one people."

"How do you know this?"

"Chief RagnakTok told me."

"By the Engineer, you learned a lot about the Drekaar in your short time on the planet," remarked Pequo, impressed.

"I find them quite fascinating as a race. They are not quite as primitive as some would have you believe."

"Well, that is all well and good," said Massa, "but can we figure out if they want to be friend or foe?"

"I can try," said Plato. He stepped forward closer to the king crab.

"Easy," said Nakai, sighting the crab with her empty weapon.

Plato ignored her warning and began to issue a primitive greeting as best as he could articulate with Humani vocal chords. He recalled words that RagnakTok had used as compliments when addressing him, particularly after the hunt when he emerged from the Gargantuok—brave, strong, surprising, impressive.

He was familiar with individual Drekaari words, but he was not facile in their syntax, so his conversation must have sounded like it was coming from a toddler.

The crabs' eyes glowed, and there was chittering all around. Plato recognized this reaction. It was the same that the Drekaar had to him. They were surprised and interested.

"How do you know how to speak Drekaari?" asked Massa.

"He did spend a month or so with them," said Pequo.

Plato shrugged his shoulders. "Captain Utang had my universal translator jammed so I would not hear his conversations, so I learned Drekaari the old fashioned way—immersion."

"Impressive for an Avatar," remarked Massa.

"Impressive for anyone," corrected Pequo, to Plato's surprise and delight.

"Wait a minute," said Plato. "If the Feng were going to use this craft to travel Spacetime and mimic other ships, would it not make sense to equip it with some kind of translator independent of the network?"

"This ship can mimic other ships?" asked Massa. "Now you have got to be shanking me."

Plato waved a dismissive hand. "Yes, it uses nanite technology to apply a magnetic charge to a liquid metal allowing it to change shape."

Nakai shook her head as if trying to clear her ears. "Can you say that again, like in Humani?"

Plato held up a finger to the large king crab and darted back onto the ship, leaving the three pilots alone with their new hosts. The other crabs began to chitter, their eyes glowing. Was it fear, outrage, or some other emotion?

"First, he starts a conversation with them, and then he leaves them hanging," said Nakai. "Not very polite."

"What if these things attack?" asked Pequo.

"We have no ammunition," said Massa. "We fight hand-to-hand, Nakai and I using the enhanced strength of our mech suits." He eyed the crabs shifting around in the sand, whipping their barbed tails behind them. He saw venom dripping from the tips.

Plato emerged from the ship with his finger to his temple. His return sparked a louder chittering response from the indigenous creatures. However, the alien utterances were crudely translated in all of their universal translator chips.

"Why come you back? Where go you?" said the king crab.

"Are you guys getting this?" asked Massa.

Pequo turned to Plato, who stood there grinning with self-satisfaction, and gave a thumbs up. "He activated the translator program."

"Why do they sound stupid?" asked Nakai.

"The translation is a rough one," explained Plato. "There are no records of Dreguani speech to operate off of. The program recognizes elements of Drekaari and Iguani, but not enough for a perfect translation."

"Where come you? What you?" asked the king crab.

"Great, so we now understand them," said Massa. "But do they understand us?"

"They are not equipped with universal translator chips," said Plato.

"Well, we have to find a way to communicate," said Pequo.

Plato stepped forward again and bowed his head. Then he tried to remember some other words he heard RagnakTok say. He used the words 'from' and 'desert.' He likely sounded as crude to them as they sounded to him.

There was more chittering, an acknowledgement of some kind, but no eyes burned.

"Friend or monster?" asked the king crab.

Plato indicated that they meant no harm by using a term of endearment that RagnakTok reserved for him, not knowing if it was sincere or sarcastic. He hoped for the former.

"Me name YoulokTuk. Me the big."

"His name is YoulokTuk," repeated Plato.

"We heard him," said Massa. "What does he mean by *the big*?"

"I think he means he is their leader," offered Pequo.

"I think you are right, Lieutenant," agreed Plato.

"What did you tell him about us?" asked Massa.

"I told him that we are friends from the desert."

"Do you think it wise to lie to them?"

The king crab watched Massa and Plato's exchange with great interest but no comprehension.

"Technically, I am not lying, Commander. We appeared in the middle of the desert, so we are indeed from the desert."

Massa shot Plato an impatient look. "Tell them we need to leave this cavern."

"I am afraid I do not know how," said Plato.

"Eat you," said the king crab.

"What did he just say?" asked Nakai, tensing the hydraulics on her arms.

"Eat you," king crab repeated.

"I think he is getting hungry," said Massa, tensing the arms and legs of his mech suit, preparing to fight.

"Wait," said Plato, holding out a hand, but it was unclear if he was speaking to the pilots or the crabs.

Suddenly, the crabs rushed the four stranded Humani and seized them. The pilots fought in their mech suits, but the crabs immobilized their arms and legs with their massive claws, holding them fast and carrying them off into one of the dark tunnels.

CHAPTER 21

"What the frak are they doing?" cried Nakai as she struggled against the grip of the claws holding her hands and feet. The grips were strong, but they stopped short of crushing the metal mech suits like aluminum cans. Pequo did not have his mech suit to protect him, but the claws gripping his ankles applied only enough pressure to hold him as they dragged him through the tunnel.

"I do not think they want to hurt us," said Plato.

They all struggled as they were jostled about, carried and dragged through the darkness, a feeling almost as unsettling as being carried off by a bunch of giant crabs.

When they reached yet another, larger cavern, the crabs released the Humani and parted, revealing a long table. Massa quickly pushed himself to his feet, as did the other pilots, each inspecting any damage done to their suits. Surprisingly, there was none.

Plato remained on the ground, eyeing the table. He recognized the table. The Drekaar feasted on such a table back at their camp.

"Eat you…please," said the king crab named YoulokTuk.

"Is he asking our permission to eat us?" asked Nakai.

"No," said Plato. "I think he is inviting us for a meal."

"Well, that is great," said Pequo, brushing himself off. "I am starved."

The crabs skittered around them and ushered them to sit around the table. The four Humani did as they were guided to do, careful not to insult their large hosts.

"We really do not have time for this," said Massa. "We have to get back to our ship."

"I do not think a little meal will hurt matters," insisted Pequo.

"Men," huffed Nakai. "Always thinking of their stomachs."

"If the Avatar is correct," pressed Massa, "the Feng are plotting to disrupt history and win Intergalactic War 4.0."

The crabs skittered to their seats around the table as one crab began to dispense a beverage in crude goblets.

"We have all the time in the world," said Plato.

"How do you figure that?" asked Massa, scanning the contents of his crude stone goblet as they were poured.

"Whatever the Feng are doing will not happen for just shy of an eon."

Nakai scanned the beverage in her goblet. The readings indicated that it was non-toxic. She pulled off her helmet, revealing her face. The crabs chittered in reaction, eyes glowing like the coals in a fire. "I *am* thirsty." She reached for her goblet.

"I would not drink—" warned Plato, but Nakai already had the elixir in her mouth. Her eyes nearly bulged out of her head, and she spit the liquid out, spraying the table. She coughed as she struggled to find her voice. "What the frak is that?"

"It is one of their customary beverages," said Plato. "Very pungent, barely edible. I will request some water." He uttered the word for water. The servant crab appeared to understand as he snatched Nakai's goblet up in his claw and remove it.

"Plato, do you think these creatures are armed?" asked Massa, looking around. "I do not see any evidence of weapons."

"At this point in their history, the Drekaar and Iguani are not at war, so the only weapons they likely have are for hunting."

The servant crab returned with fresh goblets of water for the four Humani, placing the new goblets next to the old ones. Nakai shoved the first goblet away from her in favor of the one filled with water. She replaced her helmet, scanned it, and removed her helmet. "This looks like water. Warm water."

Nakai clasped the goblet carefully with her mech hand and brought it to her lips. She let the water flow into her mouth. Although it was warm, hard water, it still offered some relief.

At last, Massa removed his helmet and placed it on the floor next to where he sat on the dirt floor. He reached out and took a drink from his goblet as well.

There was a clanging sound, and the crabs around the table stirred with excitement.

"What now?" complained Nakai.

The servant crab returned from a small, darkened tunnel with a large platter holding a large, coiled-up snake. He slammed the platter down on the table, and the other grabs grabbed the dead serpent and began to stretch its carcass out across the length of the table.

"Ugh," said Nakai, recoiling. "Disgusting."

Plato smiled impishly. "Just wait for it."

"Wait for what?" she asked, mortified.

The crabs began to slice the large serpent open with the sharp serrations on their claws, opening the carcass. Out spilled numerous smaller, infant serpents, writhing and undulating all over the table.

"Son of a bastog!" howled Nakai.

The crabs all reached across the table in a frenzy, snatching up the slithering delicacy.

YoulokTuk clicked loudly, silencing the other crabs. "Give friends."

The crabs passed down a few of the little serpents down the table to the four Humani. Pequo held his down with his hand as it tried to snap at him. Nakai recoiled from hers, pushing it back across the table. Massa allowed his to slither off the table and into the shadows to live another day. The crabs dove in, consuming the young serpents in earnest.

Plato snatched his up just under its head and slammed its head on the edge of the table four times. When it was still, he pulled its head off rather easily, its young body being soft, and he took a hearty bite.

Massa, Nakai, and Pequo looked on in total disbelief.

"What?" asked Plato with a mouth full of baby serpent. "When in Rome..."

"When in Rome, what?" asked Massa.

"What is a Rome?" asked Nakai.

Pequo, a student of Human culture like Plato, understood the expression. He crushed the skull of his baby serpent in his bare hand. He ripped its head clear off, raised the carcass to his face, and sniffed it.

"Rolo Pequo, you do not dare," scolded Nakai.

Pequo smirked and sunk his teeth into the body, tearing away soft, succulent flesh. As Nakai and Massa looked on in revulsion, Pequo chewed it, rolling the tender meat over his tongue. He swallowed it down and grinned. "It is not so bad. Actually, it is quite good."

Nakai buried her face in her hands, and Massa shook his head.

After the serpent course was finished, YoulokTuk belched loudly and addressed his guests. "Full you."

Plato responded in the affirmative, making a big demonstration of rubbing his distended belly. YoulokTuk clicked in apparent approval. His eyes rested on Pequo for a moment, who in turn rubbed his belly. YoulokTuk, clicking loudly, was pleased by the gesture.

Then his eyes focused on Nakai and Massa. "No like you."

"I am not so crazy about you either, buddy," said Nakai.

"No, he is observing that you did not like the meal," corrected Plato.

"Yeah, well, you can tell him I am on a diet," said Nakai. "A girl has to watch her figure."

Massa leaned forward. "You need to tell him that we need to get back to our ship."

"I do not want to insult his hospitality."

"Tell him."

Plato turned to YoulokTuk and used two words he heard often during his captivity in the Drekaar mining facility. "Back to work," and he added "me." Then, for good measure, he added "important."

YoulokTuk listened intently, expressionless. After a moment of consideration, he clicked in response, "Show light."

Plato whispered those words to himself, pondering their meaning. 'Show light.'

"What does he mean?" asked Nakai.

"It does not matter," insisted Massa. "Tell him we need to get back to our ship, and he needs to show us a way out."

YoulokTuk watched the exchange and then clicked enthusiastically, as if he understood. "Show light."

"Perhaps that is what he intends to do," offered Plato.

Massa frowned, weighing his options. "Very well. We will see what he has to show us. I just hope it is a way out of here."

"I do not understand your sense of urgency, Commander," said Plato.

"If you were armada, you would, Avatar."

YoulokTuk rose from his place at the head of the table, as did he other crabs. "Follow you."

"Yes," said Plato in Drekaari, bowing his head slightly. "Follow we," he said in Drekaari.

The Massa and Nakai grabbed their helmets and placed them back on. The crabs scurried out the cave, and the four Humani followed down one of the dark tunnels.

"These cave networks must be extensive," said Plato. "A wonderful adaption to the extreme desert heat."

"Yes, wonderful." Nakai's sarcasm masked an underlying anxiety. She did not understand these primitive creatures, yet she was being led around in the dark by them.

"Only an Avatar would be so enamored by these things," mocked Massa.

Pequo shook his head in the dark. Unlike his comrades, he found them fascinating. If these creatures were indeed the ancestors of the

Drekaar and the Iguani, then they were gaining great insight into Golgathi culture.

As they rounded a turn, there was a bright light at the end of the tunnel.

"What is that?" asked Nakai.

"I do not know," said Massa, checking the topography and geodetic readouts in his helmet, "but it cannot be sunlight. We are still subterranean."

"I am detecting rising radiation levels," said Nakai, consulting her own readouts.

For a moment, Plato looked as if he was swooning. Pequo reached out and grabbed his arm, steadying him. "Are you all right?"

"Yes," nodded Plato.

"Maybe you two should stay behind," said Massa. "You have no suits for protection."

Plato shook his head adamantly. "No. I want to see this."

"But the radiation…"

YoulokTuk stopped and turned, noticing the pilots had stopped in the tunnel. His eyes flashed in the darkness and he chittered. "Show light. Light good."

"We can go," said Massa to Plato. "Pequo, you stay behind."

YoulokTuk, sensing Plato's hesitation, crawled over to the Avatar and clicked his claws. "Light change you. Help."

"Oh, for the Engineer's sake," said Massa. "I will carry the Avatar."

"He does not look so well," warned Pequo, looking pale himself.

"Lieutenant, if we do not follow them, we do not get back to this ship and out of this cave."

"It is okay," said Plato. "Take my arm. I can walk with your help."

Massa gripped his arm firmly. YoulokTuk chittered and turned to skitter back in the direction of the illumination. Massa, Nakai, and Plato followed, Plato supported by Massa. Pequo remained behind, backing away from the lighted cave.

As they made their way down the tunnel, the light grew brighter, whitewashing their vision. Massa and Nakai relied on their scanners and helmet readouts.

At last, YoulokTuk led them into a vast chamber bathed in the ethereal light. As their scanners adjusted, the pilots saw that they were in some kind of subterranean quarry. The rock walls bore chunks of a glowing element, the source of the bright light.

"I cannot identify this element," said Nakai, reading her scanners.

"It is emitting a powerful radiation," said Massa. "These creatures' hard protein exoskeletons must protect them."

Plato was now fully leaning on Massa, clutching the hydraulics of his mechanized arm for support.

"Ask him why he is showing us this," said Massa to Plato.

"He does not look so good," said Nakai. "He is weak."

"Ask him," pressed Massa.

"It is okay," said Plato. "Prop me up."

Massa grabbed Plato under his arms and lifted, supporting his body weight, which had now become too burdensome for the Avatar.

"Why show?" asked Plato in Drekaari, his voice hoarse.

YoulokTuk scrambled over to him, eyes glowing. "Light power."

"Ask him how do we get our ship above ground," said Massa. "Tell him we need to leave."

"We go now," said Plato in Drekaari. "Help with leave."

"Show light. Light power," said YoulokTuk.

Plato's eyes began to close.

"He is losing consciousness," said Nakai. "We need to get him out of here. Now."

"Light good," said the king crab.

"All right. Everyone out, back the way we came," ordered Massa. He hefted the Avatar into his arms and led Nakai back out of the cavern. The crabs remained behind, basking in the strange light.

Massa consulted the maps in his helmet display, retracing their steps until they reached the cave with the long table. Pequo was there waiting for them.

Nakai swept her arm across the table, clearing the surface of stone goblets, and Massa laid the Avatar down.

"He is unconscious," said Nakai.

"We need him to operate the Spacetime controls," said Massa, pacing back and forth. "We are wasting time."

Nakai scanned Plato's vitals. "He is in no condition to do anything right now."

"Will he recover?" asked Massa.

"He took a heavy dose of radiation," said Nakai. "With rest, he may regain consciousness."

"We just need him to enter the coordinates to the Invasion of Humana," said Massa.

Pequo stepped in front of Massa, stopping him from pacing. "He did his best to try and help us, sir. Maybe you should cut him some slack."

Massa removed his helmet. "Excuse me, Lieutenant?"

"If it was not for him, those things might have torn us to pieces at the first encounter."

Nakai stepped next to them. "Boys, this is not the time."

"Because of this wild gonari chase, we have wasted valuable time," said Massa.

"You heard Plato," said Pequo. "The ship needs to recharge and the Spacetime continuum needs to stabilize before we make another jump. If we have to wait, what difference does it make if we wait down here or up on the surface?"

"He is right, Commander," said Nakai.

Massa pointed a finger into Pequo's chest. "This Avatar better wake up and be able to punch in the coordinates."

Pequo pulled himself away and turned his back on his commander before he said or did something he'd regret. "Do not forget that you are the one who insisted he join you in the cave without protection."

Nakai noticed that Pequo looked flushed. "You do not look so good yourself."

Pequo kept his back to the others. "I will be okay. I just need rest. We all need rest."

The crabs skittered back into the cave, their exoskeletons exhibiting a faint glow. YoulokTuk scampered over to the table where Plato lay and looked him over, running his claws over his body. "Rest him. Better beyond now."

Commander Massa walked over to the king crab. "What was that light?"

YoulokTuk listened but didn't comprehend.

Massa repeated, "What was that light? Why did you take us there?"

However, without the benefit of a universal translator chip, YoulokTuk only heard nonsensical guttural sounds.

"Rest him. Better beyond now."

"Engineer be damned!" Massa turned away from the creature, frustrated.

YoulokTuk clicked orders to the other crabs, and two approached the table. They gingerly took Plato up in their claws and carried him off to the corner of the room where they laid him down gently.

"Rest you," said YoulokTuk. "Better beyond now. All."

"He wants us to rest, too," explained Pequo. "Sounds like a good idea to me."

Nakai stood next to Massa, leaning in. "We have to wait anyway, for the ship to recharge and for the Avatar to wake up."

"Okay," said Massa, resigned to the reality of the situation. "But we take shifts keeping watch. I do not exactly trust our hosts."

"They do not seem to mean any harm," said Pequo.

"They led us into a highly radioactive cavern," said Massa.

"They had no way of knowing how it would affect us, sir."

"You have first watch," Massa told Nakai.

The three pilots settled down in the corner of the cave around Plato's unconscious body. One of the crabs brought over goblets of water, one for each of them. The pilots drank the warm, sulfurous liquid. Pequo raised Plato's head and poured some water into his mouth.

The crabs had retired to another cave, leaving them alone. The pilots were unsure if their hosts were sleeping, but they were left undisturbed to tend to their fallen navigator.

After Massa and Pequo had fallen asleep, weary from the day's events, Nakai's eyelids felt like lead inside her helmet. She began to blink. Her scanners reached out across the cave, but they registered no movement.

She looked down at Plato, who lay inert, and then at her comrades. Her vision began to blur from exhaustion as she checked the time. Her brain felt foggy. In these caves, without the cues from the sun, it was difficult to determine if it was day or night. She struggled to keep her eyes open until the end of her watch, pondering whether or not they would ever return to their own time.

*

YoulokTuk crept into the cave where the pilots slept, careful not to make a sound and rouse them from their slumber. He skittered over to where they lay and noticed that the three pilots were asleep, but the other one who spoke Dreguani was not with them.

He carefully left the cave, traversed a few tunnels, and returned to the cave where the strangers' ship was, where he knew he'd find the Avatar.

The hatch was open, and Plato was hard at work on the ship's quantum computer. YoulokTuk crept up the hatch door and waited, clicking quietly.

Plato turned around, surprised but unafraid. "Oh, it is you."

"Feel you?"

Oddly, he felt good. Great, actually. "Good much," was all he could manage in Drekaari.

YoulokTuk understood, clicking in delight. "Light good. Better beyond before."

"What light be?" asked Plato.

"Light good."

Plato smiled, shaking his head. He searched his memory for applicable words from his interactions with RagnakTok. "Light electric? Light rock? Light what be?"

YoulokTuk chittered loudly, his eyes burning. "Light God."

Plato didn't quite know how to respond to that one. 'Light God.' Did the Dreguani think the element was God or a deity? He remembered his conversation with RagnakTok and the Drekaar historian. Some did believe that, some did not. It was the basis of their great cultural schism.

"Light feel good?" Plato asked.

"Light…better you. Strong."

Plato didn't need the translator to comprehend that last word. It was a word lavished upon him by RagnakTok after the hunt.

"Strong me. New."

YoulokTuk clucked in excitement. "Yes, yes. Show you. Follow."

The king crab suddenly turned and scrambled off into one of the dark tunnels. Plato quickly followed after, careful not to lose the creature. The king crab was all hot and bothered to show him something.

He caught up to YoulokTuk in the tunnel, and the Dreguani stopped just outside the opening to another cavern. He waited for Plato and then entered.

As Plato followed him in, he saw a large cavern where the crab-like creatures slept all on top of one another in a large, messy heap. However, YoulokTuk was directing his attention to the opposite corner of the room.

There, in the corner, sat a crab on what appeared to be hundreds of eggs. It was awake, and when it saw YoulokTuk, it clicked softly at him. When its eyes pivoted to Plato, they burned.

YoulokTuk clicked softly back to her, which appeared to soothe her, as her eyes dimmed and her clicking ceased. YoulokTuk gestured for Plato to come closer, and Plato approached tentatively. He knew enough about various species of fauna than to frighten a mother protecting her young.

"Look. Wonder," said YoulokTuk.

One by one, the eggs began to hatch. Little barbed tails poked through the shell, whipping around, removing pieces. Underneath the shell were miniature scorpion-like babies. As they hatched, they climbed up onto their mother's body.

When they all had hatched and ascended to their mother's back, they all began to chitter in unison. It reminded Plato of music. He smiled as YoulokTuk bounced up and down on his legs in anticipation.

In unison the babies stung their mother with their barbs, whipping their tails violently. She hissed and cried in response, the sound like escaping steam. Plato recoiled as they pierced her brittle exoskeleton, revealing soft flesh underneath. The babies began to feed on their mother, her eyes blazing, but her body powerless from the venom.

Plato made as if to turn away, but YoulokTuk grabbed him firmly by the arm with one of his claws. It appeared he wanted Plato to see this.

Within minutes, the mother crab's eyes went dim and then vacant, and the babies continued to dine on her as Plato watched, horrified. YoulokTuk released his arm.

"Why see me?" managed Plato, grimacing. He didn't know the Drekaari word for horror.

YoulokTuk, however, read his body language and interpreted it correctly as revulsion. "Not…(there was an incomprehensible word)…not kill…"

"Kill her they," insisted Plato, failing to see any other interpretation for the act.

"No…love."

Love? Plato thought he misunderstood the Dreguani. However, the word was understood through the translator, not his memory of past conversations with the Drekaar. Was the translation incorrect?

As he forced himself to look as the babies fed on their mother's carcass, the significance revealed itself to Plato as an epiphany. Of, course. Love. The mother gave her life so that her young may feed and live on. It was the ultimate sacrifice.

YoulokTuk saw Plato watching, his expression changing. In fact, he was exhibiting an epidermal microexpression—a caramel, cider color. It was the color of warm feelings and comfort.

The king crab clicked softly to Plato in the same way he did to the mother crab.

*

The three pilots awoke in their cave, their heads swimming. Commander Massa sat up, placing his mechanized hand on his helmet. "My head is killing me."

Nakai sat up, letting out a heavy sigh. She squinted her eyes as her helmet displays came into focus. "I feel like I consumed too much Humani Ale."

Pequo looked around the cave. "Where is Plato?"

Massa pounded his fist on the ground. "Engineer be damned, what happened to the watch?"

Nakai scanned one of the empty stone goblets next to her turned over on its side it the dirt. She analyzed the residue. "There was more than water in those goblets."

"Those crabs drugged us," said Massa, finishing her thought.

They each stood, Nakai grabbing onto Massa for support. Pequo didn't feel drugged at all. In fact, fully recovered from his brief exposure to the radiation, he felt refreshed.

"The ship," said Massa.

"No, I think I might know where he is," said Pequo. "The cavern with the strange element."

"Nakai, check the cavern. Pequo and I will check on the ship."

They split up, Nakai darting down the dark tunnel towards the cavern of light according to her mech's mnemonic mapping. When she reached the cavern with light pouring out of its mouth, her scanners registered increased radiation. She entered.

Through the bright light, she saw YoulokTuk and several of the crabs standing around Plato, who lay prone on the ground. She walked over, shoving their way through the crabs. Plato's eyes were open, but barely.

"What the frak are you doing?" shouted Nakai to YoulokTuk. "You are killing him."

YoulokTuk watched her attentively, but he didn't understand.

"I need to take him out of here," said Nakai. Once again, the crabs listened but didn't comprehend.

Nakai squatted down and snatched Plato's limp body up in her mech's arms. The crabs reacted to this. Their eyes burned, and they grabbed Nakai's arms in their massive claws, holding them fast but otherwise inflicting no damage.

"Let me go!" cried Nakai as she attempted to wrestle out of their grip.

Massa barged into the cave, waving around his empty weapon, shoving it in YoulokTuk's face. YoulokTuk recoiled, and the other crabs retreated to surround him protectively.

Massa stepped in front of Nakai. "Get out of here. I will cover you."

Nakai backed out of the cave and down the darkened tunnel. Massa backed out of the cave, the crabs following closely, eyes fiery, but maintaining their distance from Massa's weapon.

"Get to the ship," shouted Massa.

They retreated down the tunnels to where their ship waited. When they found it, Pequo was waiting. Nakai, carrying Plato, climbed the open hatch.

"What happened?" asked Pequo.

"Get in the ship," directed Massa. "We are getting out of here." As Pequo boarded the ship with Nakai and Plato, Massa covered them just outside with his useless weapon.

"It looks like someone has been in here," said Nakai.

"I was," rasped Plato, his eyes open.

Pequo looked down at him. "Last night? What were you doing?"

"I programmed two vectors into the quantum computer. One to take you to the Invasion of Humani, and one to get you home from there to the Spacetime we originated from."

"Why did they take you in that cavern again?"

"They are here, and they look pissed!" said Massa from outside the ship. "Fire it up already!"

"They will not harm you," said Plato, his voice hoarse. "Take me to them."

"Plato wants to talk to them," said Pequo to Massa.

"Tell him to start the ship. It should be recharged," said Massa.

"No," said Plato. "Let me talk to them. Please."

Pequo snatched up Plato in his arms and tried to exit the ship when Nakai grabbed his arm. "What do you think you are doing?"

"Trust me," said Pequo.

She hesitated and released his arm. Pequo left the ship and stood next to Massa, who was waving his empty firearm around frantically. The crabs encroached gradually, clicking and hissing, recoiling when the firearm was pointed directly at them.

He did a double take when he saw Pequo with Plato in his arms. "What are you doing here? I told you to start the ship!"

When they saw Plato, the Dreguani quieted down and watched him with blazing eyes. "No take he you," demanded YoulokTuk.

Nakai slinked out of the ship and took her place next to Pequo, her scanners peeled.

Plato raised a weak hand, and they quieted down. He uttered some words in Drekaari, which appeared to de-escalate the situation. There was clicking amongst the crabs, drowning out YoulokTuk's half-translated speech so that none of the pilots were able to follow the conversation.

After some back and forth, the crabs began to retreat back into one of the dark tunnels. YoulokTuk approached Plato, raised a claw, and clicked softly before joining the others, leaving the four Humani alone.

Massa lowered his weapon. "What did you tell them?"

Plato struggled to raise his head. Pequo propped his head up with his arm as if holding an infant. "I told them that you were leaving."

"Why did they back off?"

"Because I told them I would remain here with them."

Massa shook his head. "Negative. We need you to pilot the ship."

"He already set two vectors. One to the Invasion of Humani, and one to get us back home," said Pequo.

Massa shook his head. "What if something goes wrong and we need you?"

Plato struggled to speak. "Even at my best, I am in no position to help you with your mission against the Feng. I am not a soldier."

"What if we cannot execute the second vector?"

"If you survive your mission, you will be able to execute the vector. I made it...Human proof." He chuckled at his own joke, causing him to cough.

Massa didn't like this outcome. He didn't like it one bit, but he had to play the hand he was dealt. "Very well. We leave now."

"We cannot just leave him here," said Pequo.

"The Avatar served his purpose," said Massa.

"Just like Pequo," said Nakai, "getting attached to subspecies."

"He is a Humani, just like us," demanded Pequo.

"He wants to remain behind," explained Massa. Then to Plato, "Right?"

"Yes."

Massa considered the matter closed for discussion. "I want you on the ship in two micros. Say your goodbyes." He turned and boarded the ship. Nakai stood there for a moment, looking at Pequo through her helmet. Pequo wasn't able to see her expression. Then she, too, boarded.

Pequo was alone with Plato. He squatted, knelt on both knees, and placed Plato down gingerly. He stared at him in pity.

"It is okay," said Plato. "I want to remain here. There is no place for me back on Humana."

"That is not true. You are a valuable asset to Navigo. That is why my brother sent you to Golgath."

Plato smiled, but it was a sad smile. "Your brother sent me because I am expendable. It is okay. These Dreguani do not think of me as an indentured servant. They see me as something more."

"I never saw you that way," said Pequo.

Plato smiled again. "I know. You are different. I wish there were more like you on Humana."

Pequo placed a hand on Plato's shoulder. "I just want you to know that we could not have done this without you. You are a hero."

"Thank you. Now go. Save Humana and the universe."

Pequo nodded and stood up, but Plato grabbed his arm. "One more thing."

"Yes."

"I isolated your time vectors using the fourth dimension so that no matter what happens, the past you change will not erase you three as you are now."

"Do you think that wise?"

"It is a gift and a precaution."

Pequo did not know what he meant, but he was out of time. He stood up, giving Plato one last look. Then he turned and boarded the ship. As he took his place next to Nakai, Massa initiated the first Spacetime vector. As the ship began to whir and hum, it transformed around them into a Humani Vortex fighter.

As the ship vibrated with incremental intensity, they saw the Dreguani emerge from the tunnel and surround Plato. They carefully picked him up with their claws and carried him off back into the tunnel.

Pequo saw Plato's hand raise in goodbye when the cave around them stretched and vanished in an instant.

CHAPTER 22

The three Humani pilots emerged just outside of Humana orbit exactly according to their preset coordinates. As soon as their vision cleared, they looked outside.

Nakai was the first to break the stunned silence. "So, where is everybody?'

There was no one around them, let alone a raging battle. Massa checked the coordinates. "The coordinates are correct. This should be the Invasion of Humana in Intergalactic War 4.0."

"Are you sure we are not early?" asked Nakai. Massa shot her a look. "Just asking."

Pequo looked down at the communicator. "We are being hailed by Planetary Defense. They are pinging our ship and targeting us."

Massa opened the channel.

"This is the Humani Planetary Defense. Identify yourself. Acknowledge."

"This is Commander Massa of the Razor's Edge Squadron. Permission to approach."

There was a brief hesitation. "We cannot identify a Razor's Edge Squadron. What battle group are you assigned to?"

Pequo grabbed Massa's arm. "There is no Razor's Edge Squadron in this time. Do you know of a squadron and battle group in this time?"

Massa paused, thinking. Then he reopened the channel. "We are a part of the Valiant battle group."

There was another pause as the claim was verified. "The Valiant is not patrolling in this system. Stand by for armed escort."

"Acknowledged," said Massa. He closed the channel. "They do not trust us. I do not understand. The Valiant was present during the Invasion of Humana."

"The only way that there can be no invasion here is if something changed before this point in Spacetime," said Pequo.

"Do you think we were wrong, and the Feng ventured back before the Invasion of Humana and altered the past relative to this point?" asked Nakai.

"It is possible," said Massa. "We will debrief on Humana and get our bearings."

"How will we explain…us in this ship?" asked Pequo.

"One thing at a time, Lieutenant." But, Massa knew he was right. In this time, they were all children. In fact, Nakai probably wasn't even born yet. They would have to explain their presence and this ship.

The armed escort, a squadron of Vortex Fighters, intercepted them. Nakai leaned over the sensor panel. "They are targeting us."

The navigation displayed a vector to the planet's surface relayed from the Humani Air Command control room. "Follow us to the planet, and do not break your flightpath," ordered the squadron leader.

"Roger that," said Nakai, slipping behind the controls.

Together, they entered orbit and then the atmosphere. Wings extended and the ship's kronite core fueling the jets, they descended to a landing field outside the Lukoi Base.

"We are picking up unusual energy readings from your ship," said the squadron leader.

Nakai checked the kronite core indicators. "He is right."

Massa leaned over. "What do you mean?"

"I mean that our kronite core has no kronite."

"That is impossible."

"There is a mystery element in the core…wait a minute…" She ran core diagnostics. "I do not believe this."

"What? What is it, Lieutenant?"

"It is the mystery element in that cavern on Golgath."

"The one with the bright light?" asked Pequo.

"Yup. And it is making the conductor overheat. If we do not land soon, the core will melt the conductor and our jets."

"Punch it," said Massa.

Nakai increased the throttle. Their visors glitched, and the airbase that appeared far below them was in an instant right beneath them.

"Son of a bastog!" cried Nakai as she pulled back on the throttle, raising the ship just before impact with the landing strip.

"What are you doing?" shouted the squadron leader. "I told you not to break flightpath. All patterns are full!"

Nakai narrowly avoided colliding with an ascending Vortex, rolling away and into the path of a destroyer. She missed hull contact within nano-tics.

"Return to base or we will be forced to engage!"

She landed the ship quickly, crushing the landing gear and scraping the bottom of the ship until it skidded to a halt. The squadron flew by overhead as ground security rushed out to the wreckage.

"What did you do?" asked Massa.

Nakai released the controls and stared at her hands as if they had acted outside her voluntary control. "I do not know."

MP's stormed the tarmac hefting assault rifles. They surrounded the ship, taking aim. "Step out of the vessel with your hands in the air!"

Nakai raised a sardonic eyebrow. "Welcome home."

*

After spending some time in the brig, then some time having their genetic profiles harvested and confirmed, followed by hours in Neuroscience for mnemonic retrieval, and then exhaustive interviews from a team of Intelligence Specialists, the remaining pilots of the Razor's Edge sat, waiting in a debriefing room, this time without restraints.

"What in the Engineer's Name is going on?" asked Nakai. "We are being treated like the enemy."

"We arrived outside of planetary orbit in an unfamiliar vessel asking to speak to the admiral," explained Massa. "They are trying to verify that we are who we say we are."

"They must be wrestling with the memories retrieved," said Pequo. "It will be fun explaining that."

"That is evidence of our account," said Massa, "as outlandish as it may seem to them."

There was a tone at the door, and it opened. An officer entered, followed by another of lesser rank. The pilots stood and saluted, recognizing the shoulder insignia of a vice admiral.

"Be seated," instructed the vice admiral after returning the salute. They all sat down. "I am Vice Admiral Ducato in charge of Intelligence at Space Warfare Command. This is Chief Petty Officer Hukui. I apologize for your treatment, but you must understand the position we are in."

"Understood," said Massa, speaking for the squadron.

"We have quite the preponderance of evidence based on your reports as well as digital memories harvested, and quite frankly, our Intelligence Specialists do not know what to make of any of it."

"Let me guess," said Massa, "upon second mnemonic retrieval, those memories were missing."

"That is correct," said Hukui, perplexed that Massa would know that.

Vice Admiral Ducato nodded. "The ones involving your experience in ancient Golgath and at the Drekaar mining complex, anyway."

"The same thing happened on the Resilience after a mission when we encountered Feng forces on Aquilassi," said Massa. "It baffled Captain Reinhardt as well."

"Our technicians have pored over your unique vessel," said Ducato. "There is tech on there that we have never seen before. Additionally, as you made your approach to our landing strip, your ship made a jump to light speed, a feat that we have only seen in one race, the Astrals."

"Light speed, sir?" asked Massa. He was unfamiliar with the Astrals as well.

"That is right, Commander," said Hukui. "For a very brief moment, your ship jumped to light speed. That is Astral technology, and we are wondering where Humani pilots could have obtained it."

"Who are the Astrals?"

Vice Admiral Ducato fielded this one. "The Astrals are a race hailing from Golgath. Not much is known about them, but they are a theocracy with space travel capabilities. They call themselves 'the Harbingers of Light' and adhere to a little understood religion they call Platonics."

Massa, Pequo, and Nakai all looked at each other in astonishment.

"You mentioned 'Platonics.' What is that?" asked Massa.

"The Astrals claim to bring balance and enlightenment to other worlds and races, what they refer to as the Truth," said Ducato. "They have referenced a prophet named Plato as one who introduced them to the Truth, bringing their people out of the Darkness, what they consider to have been a state of ignorance."

Nakai put her face in her hands. Pequo said to Massa, "I told you we should have taken him with us."

Ducato became impatient. "What is it? You all look as if you have seen a ghost."

"We just heard about one," said Nakai.

"We left an Avatar on Golgath before we arrived in the here-and-now," explained Massa.

"His name was Plato," added Pequo.

"I do not understand," said Ducato. "What does this have to do with anything?"

"If you recall in our report, we encountered an unfamiliar element on ancient Golgath during our time with the Dreguani," said Massa. "This Avatar sustained severe radiation poisoning."

"The one who was too ill to make the trip," said Ducato. "Do you think that this is the same Plato that the Astrals venerate?"

Massa nodded. "Lieutenant Pequo believes he installed some of that element in our Kronite core. Perhaps that explained our brief jump to light speed."

Ducato nodded. "That is a possibility. Conventional wisdom throughout the galaxies has been that travel at the speed of light or faster was physically impossible. That is, until the Astrals started showing up.

"They are a race of terrorists that seek to convert other races to their Platonics. They have been a thorn in the side of the United Intergalactic Coalition as well as the Feng Empire, showing up faster than our defenses can react and striking battle groups as well as Terran establishments on our member worlds. They have not as yet attacked any soft targets, but that is because we think that would undermine their conversion efforts."

"You mentioned the Feng," said Massa. "They are not at war with the United Intergalactic Coalition?"

Ducato shook his head. "I reviewed your account of the Intergalactic War 4.0. There has been no such war. Not yet, anyway.

"In fact, the presence of the Astrals has prevented a full-scale war between the Feng Empire and the United Intergalactic Coalition. Currently, there exists a truce, an uneasy understanding between the UIC and the Feng."

"So why not just form a coalition against these Astrals and take Golgath?" asked Massa.

"Two reasons. The Astrals are an autonomous race. There is no civil strife on Golgath or any of their satellite worlds, which places them outside of the Pax Galactus Initiative."

"Satellite worlds? You mean they have an empire?" asked Massa in disbelief.

"That brings us to reason number two," continued Ducato. "They are members of the Kronite Collective, a series of worlds that have banded together as a guild to regulate the kronite market. If they withhold their kronite, our space travel and military operations will be quickly crippled, leaving us vulnerable to the Feng.

"Until now, the Feng have been unwilling to test the Collective's resolve. An attack on Golgath would bring dire consequences for their operations as well, leaving them vulnerable to us. That, coupled with the Astrals' technology, would render a military action costly and difficult. Although we outnumber the Astrals, a few of their ships can easily wipe out a battle group."

"It sounds like a stalemate," said Massa.

Ducato nodded and leaned forward in his seat. "Until now. It appears that, for the first time, we have access to the classified Astral technology. Your ship, to put a fine point on it."

"What if we went back and took the Avatar Plato back with us, preventing the development of this race?" offered Massa.

"That is one possibility," said Ducato. "However, your ship has sustained severe damage. Lucky for us, the explosive payload did not detonate."

"Can it be fixed?" asked Massa.

"We would have to learn your ship's technology first," explained Ducato. "There is, however, another problem. The Astrals are an autonomous race. Going back in Spacetime to intervene would be an execution of the Pax Galactus Initiative against an autonomous race."

"You have to be shrugging me," said Nakai. "These Astrals have attacked the UIC and the Feng. Is that not an act of war?"

Ducato frowned. "There are some in the Intergalactic Assembly that would agree with you, Lieutenant. And then there are those who would see such an intervention as worse than nation-building. Preventing the evolution of an autonomous race is a far more serious measure, one that would have to be discussed at length and defined within the framework of the Grenadot Convention."

"You have got to be kidding me," snapped Nakai. Massa shot her a reproachful look.

Vice Admiral Ducato pointed a long finger into the air in front of him. "Which brings us to another possibility—rapid study of the technology on your ship and reverse engineer it for our vessels."

"Our technicians have hypothesized that the utilization of this unidentified element can cause a ship to skip through Spacetime, giving it the appearance of light speed or faster," added Hukui.

Ducato nodded. "I have been instructed by the Chief of Humani Armada Operations, who has been instructed by the Assistant Secretary of the Humani Armada, to investigate both options. Figuring out the technology will open up both options for us."

Pequo shook his head.

Ducato looked annoyed. "Something on your mind, Lieutenant?"

"Plato assured me that he plotted the vector back to our Spacetime, our present, from here and now," said Pequo. "However, I am not so sure we can do that or go back in time to the precise moment we left him behind on Golgath anyway."

"Why is that, Lieutenant?" asked Ducato.

"Plato manipulated the sequence of event cones, using the fourth axis to merge realities. He said he did it as a gift and as a precaution."

"That is an odd way to phrase it," said Ducato.

"That *is* a problem," said Hukui, nodding. "The number of event cones going that far back is massive. Pinpointing the exact one is like finding a needle in a grass stack. Going back to your present, our future, would be impossible as the trajectory of history has shifted."

"We can just retrace our steps using the ship's quantum computer," offered Massa.

Hukui shook his head. "That would be possible if we were just going back on a temporal axis. This Plato has, in effect, created a new reality. This Spacetime vector no longer traces back to that point in Spacetime. Not without manipulation of that fourth axis, which only he and the Feng from your time knew how to do."

"So, this is a different reality than our own?" asked Pequo, keeping pace.

His head beginning to spin as he struggled to wrap his brain around the discussion, Ducato deferred to Hukui, who answered the question. "If what you say about this technology is correct, your reality has been altered, while we will not know the difference. This has always been our reality as we have known it. In the meantime, all Spacetime parameters have shifted, like waves on an ocean. Nothing is as it was, and nothing will be as it should be as you know it."

"Does this mean that we will be erased?" asked Nakai, her head hurting from trying to grasp their predicament.

Pequo shook his head. "It would have happened already. Plato assured me that the merging of realities with one that guaranteed our existence on the fourth axis would prevent that. His gift, I suppose."

"How is that possible?" asked Massa.

"This gets into advanced quantum theory," said Hukui. "Theoretically, event cones are not oriented linearly. Like molecules, they spin, making it difficult to locate any point in Spacetime with any accuracy. We call it the Temporal-Spatial Cloud Model."

"Well, apparently the Feng have figured it out," said Nakai.

"The Feng of your Spacetime," reminded Ducato.

Alarms erupted throughout the airbase.

"What in the Engineer's Name is that?" asked Ducato. His communicator lit up. He answered. "What is it?"

"Sir, three Astral Photons have entered the atmosphere."

"By the Engineer! They are attacking!"

"They have come for the ship," said Chief Petty Officer Hukui.

"How did they find it so fast?" exclaimed Ducato.

"Where is it?" asked Massa.

"In a supermax laboratory seven levels under the surface," said Hukui.

A captain barged into the room. "Sir, we have to get you down below to safety," she said, addressing Ducato.

"We want to help," said Massa.

"Negative," said Ducato. "You possess valuable information that we cannot afford to lose. You are joining me down below."

Within seconds, there were explosions outside the building. The ground shook as the three strange ships whisked through the airbase, pounding the buildings and grounded aircraft with what appeared to be energy displacement weapons. Each metallic gold Astral ship looked like two crescents arranged perpendicularly so that four points jutted out in front.

As the captain led Ducato and the others down a long corridor, the lights flickered from the impact of the bombing outside. Pequo looked over his shoulder as he turned a corner, following the others, and he could've sworn he saw something flicker in and out of the hallway.

He dismissed it as a trick of the flickering lights when electric discharges lit up the corridor as if it were one big Tesla coil. Something flickered just outside of his periphery, and then right next to him, and then the hallway vanished.

Nakai looked over her shoulder. "Where is Pequo?"

Massa stopped to look, but Ducato and Hukui continued ahead with the captain, stopping for nothing or no one. Massa scanned the flickering corridor. "Lieutenant, we have to go."

She shook her head defiantly. "Not without Pequo."

Massa grabbed her arm. "He is gone. We have to go with Ducato."

Nakai, reluctant to move on without Pequo, looked one more time. 'Where the frak *was* he?' The building shook more violently. She clenched her jaw and nodded her agreement. This was one time she couldn't help Pequo.

Massa pulled her along until they caught up with the captain, Ducato, and Hukui waiting in a secure elevator.

"Hurry up," shouted Ducato, hanging part of the way out. "We have to get below ground."

Massa and Nakai dashed into the elevator, nearly crashing into the rear wall. Ducato and company parted to make room. As the doors closed, sealing shut in front of them, the sounds of the Astral assault became muffled. However, the ground still trembled as the secure elevator descended down to lower levels, magnetic doors sealing above them as they went.

"Where is Lieutenant Pequo?" asked Ducato.

Massa shook his head, Nakai averted her gaze, and that was all the answer Ducato required at the moment.

When the doors opened on the seventh level, the group was escorted into a secure bunker equipped with surveillance equipment and monitors manned by cryptological technicians.

Massa looked on in awe, having heard of such facilities but never having seen one firsthand. On the monitors, he saw the Astral Photon fighters glitching across the sky, seeming to appear and disappear as they pulverized the base.

Their movement, barely visible to the Humani eye, reminded Nakai of the glitching that little Frax used to do when playing video games with his brother, lagging so that Luoi couldn't track him. It was a dirty move, but it evened the odds, compensating for Frax's younger reflexes.

However, what she was now watching on the surface was not a video game. It was reality, the new reality that she, Massa, and Pequo had inadvertently set into motion when they left the Avatar on ancient Golgath.

"We have to do something," said Massa, clenching his fists.

Chief Petty Officer Hukui opened a cabinet stocked with assault rifles and began to disseminate them to the vice admiral, the captain, and the pilots. Ducato accepted his. "No matter what, we protect your ship."

Massa nodded, accepting his weapon, as did Nakai. A security shade opened, revealing the laboratory where the Spacetime travel vessel sat, swarmed with technicians and engineers, even as the airbase was under siege.

Nakai was overcome with guilt as she pondered the ramifications, and the guilt gave way to queasiness as she realized that they were now engaged in a different reality in a Spacetime where-when the Humani were unequipped to send them home.

As she considered the possibility that she would never see her family again, Massa came to the same realization on his own, thinking of his wife and son. In this Spacetime, neither had even been born yet. He, like Nakai, flashed yellow as he realized that he was now cut-off from everything that he had known and held dear.

They looked on as pilots scrambled to their Vortex fighters, being picked off by the lightning fast Photons, their ships being reduced to flames and torn, twisted metal.

The Astral Photons emerged and vanished in the plumes of black smoke as the Lukoi Base burned. Then, as fast as the fighters appeared, they retreated, disappearing in streaks of light into orbit and beyond, completely untouched by Humana's outer screen and planetary defense.

The ground had ceased to shake, and the alarms had eventually gone quiet. On the surface, the airbase was left in utter ruin.

Ducato hefted his rifle and handed it back to Hukui. "They will return, now that they know we possess this technology. It is imperative that we unlock it and exploit it." Then to the communications officer, "Get me the chief of armada operations."

"He and the assistant secretary are hailing us, sir."

"On screen."

The screen split, displaying both across a heavily encrypted channel on the monitor in the bunker.

"What in the Engineer's name is going on?" demanded Opoti Requoti, Assistant Secretary of the Humani Armada.

"We have been attacked by three Astral Photon fighters, sir," said Vice Admiral Ducato. "They are aware that we have come into possession of their technology. It is my belief that they will return. We need to move this ship to a secure, undisclosed location. Immediately."

"Who else knows about this?" asked Admiral Fassa Takai, Chief of Armada Operations.

"Only we do, sir."

"Are these the pilots referenced in your report?" asked Requoti.

"That is correct, sir."

"In your report, you said there were three."

"We lost one in the attack."

"I see. Have them accompany the ship."

"I have already selected a suitable location and have transmitted the coordinates through an encrypted channel," said Admiral Takai.

The communications officer nodded to Vice Admiral Ducato, confirming it.

"Received," said Ducato. "Thank you, sir. We will move within the hour."

The channel closed, the screen flickering off.

"Commander Massa, Lieutenant Nakai, follow me," instructed Ducato.

"What happens now, sir?" asked Massa, following with Nakai.

"The secretary will consult with the supreme chancellor regarding how much we should share with the Feng. We want to establish a coalition, but we do not want them to know that we possess Astral technology."

"How will we move without the Astrals tracking us? They could be watching without us even knowing."

"That is a chance we will have to take," said Ducato. "Remaining here is no longer an option. They will be back in greater numbers, and our forces have taken on heavy casualties. You will be escorted by two battle groups to the new coordinates."

"How do we know they will not hit us at the new coordinates?" asked Massa.

"The coordinates are in the Uncharted Sectors. Neither the Astrals nor the Kronite Collective have established footholds there."

"I had no idea the UIC had either," said Massa. He wondered if it was because such information was classified or this was all part of this new reality.

As they rejoined their broken ship and awaited their heavily armed escort, Nakai secretly prayed to the Engineer for Pequo.

* * *

Lieutenant Pequo blinked, and he was no longer in the corridor. There was a brief but intense feeling of malaise that overtook him, and his gut wrenched. His surroundings were unfamiliar. He stood inside a small room configured like an airlock, but there was only one set of doors leading into whatever vessel this was. There was no second set of doors leading to space.

To his right stood a small mech covered in the same lightening and discharges as the corridor. The suit glowed as the lightening coursed up and down, until it finally came to rest. When the suit cooled down, Pequo saw that it was merely an exoskeleton over a hulking bipedal, Humanoid body.

Pequo turned to address it. "Where am I?"

The figure did not answer him. It kept staring forward, as if expecting someone or something to come through the doors.

"Who are you?"

Again, no response, although Pequo had an idea who he was dealing with. This figure was, no doubt, from one of the Astral ships. Underneath the mechanical exoskeleton was, no doubt, an Astral.

The doors whooshed open, and two tall figures emerged, silhouetted in a bright light emanating behind them. "Come with us," they said in unison.

Pequo was astounded by the clarity of their speech. There must've been a quantum computer on board with the ability to interact with his universal translator chip. Pequo stepped forward and followed the two figures into the bright light.

It warmed him as he passed into it, bathing him in a strange kind of energy. He vaguely recognized it. It was much like the illumination from the cave on ancient Golgath.

He followed them down a curving corridor, the one inside the mech suit parting ways behind him. Pequo's gait was unsteady as his vision flickered, disorienting him. He reached out and placed his hand on the cool metal wall, steadying himself. He looked down at his legs and saw that his body, too, was flickering in synch with the ship.

As he looked ahead at his escorts, he saw that they were Humanoid, but covered in a hard exterior shell, much like the Drekaar or the Dreguani. He half-expected to see claws, but their arms ended in hands with digits, the first and fifth opposable. On their hips, in holsters, were unusual-looking guns.

They led him to another room, gesturing for him to enter with a sweep of their hands. The doors opened, and Pequo stepped inside. However, the two escorts did not follow, and the doors closed behind Pequo.

He turned and examined the doors sealing him inside this chamber, looking for a control panel. There was none. Pequo waved a hand in front of the doors, but they remained sealed. Captive, he began to examine the small room while he waited for what was to happen next.

CHAPTER 23

Pequo looked around the small chamber. It was an odd room. There was no desk, no bed, no toileting facilities of any kind, no computer equipment, only decorations and an odd menagerie of bric-a-brac, some he recognized as Humani or Human, others completely unfamiliar. On a small shelf sat a stone goblet, like those he saw on Golgath. Next to it was a dried, shriveled claw that once belonged to a living creature. On the walls hung various digital representations of art, some quite realistic, others very abstract.

The air in the room tingled with electricity, and Pequo turned to find a bright figure standing behind him. It was Plato. He was smiling.

"Hello, Lieutenant Pequo."

"Plato? How is this possible?"

"We have much to discuss, my old friend."

"Old friend. We have just met."

"From your perspective. From mine, an entire eon has passed since our introduction."

"Where are we?"

"We are on one of my vessels orbiting Humana."

"How can you maintain orbit? You will be shot down."

Plato shook his head, his smile serene. "Planetary Defense cannot detect us."

Pequo steadied himself. "We are glitching. That is the cause of the strange sensation I am feeling?"

"Yes. The malaise that you feel will soon pass as you become accustomed to it."

Pequo tracked Plato as he crossed the small room, stopping in front of a digital duplicate of an Earthen painting. He gazed at it meaningfully, lost in a private moment.

Pequo had questions. "This glitching technology…I assume it is all based on that glowing element on Golgath?"

Plato looked away from the School of Athens. "Yes."

"And that mech suit, or exoskeleton of the one who grabbed me…"

"Also powered by light matter," answered Plato.

"Plato, what have you done?"

"I calculated the exact coordinates in Spacetime that you and your squadron were going to emerge, and I figured I would meet you here."

Pequo frowned. "That is not what I am referring to."

"You mean the Dreguani."

"Yes."

"Pequo, I chose you instead of your comrades to visit my ship because you have always shown me kindness and understanding."

"But I do not understand, Plato."

Plato gave Pequo a warm, patient smile. "While you are generous in nature, you do not understand what it is like to be a member of the underclass and treated as such. To be ridiculed and be prevented from living up to your potential. To have your fate sealed before you were even created."

Pequo made a sweeping gesture with his hand. "I do not see what any of that has to do with all of this."

Plato nodded, acknowledging Pequo's confusion. "The Humani have swayed the United Intergalactic Coalition for nearly a quarter of an eon. They exert undue influence, meddling in the development of other worlds and species, always claiming to know what is best for them, when in reality they are assuring their dominance. Rigging the game, so-to-speak."

Pequo crossed the small room and stood in front of Plato, meeting his ethereal gaze. "So, you saw fit to bring a primitive race into the future, proving them wrong, vindicating yourself."

Plato looked back at the painting, his eyes focusing on the depiction of Plato pointing upwards and then Aristotle gesturing downwards in response. "I often wondered what a so-called 'primitive race' could do if they were afforded a Renaissance and an Industrial Revolution, rather than being held back." He looked at Pequo. "I was sent to Golgath to hold the Drekaar back."

"I thought you were sent to bring them into space travel."

Plato shook his head, laughing as if Pequo was being naïve. "I was sent to teach them the rudiments of dark energy conduction, all so Navigo could gain a foothold on the mining complex."

"You believe Navigo was using you."

"That is right, Lieutenant Pequo. When I was held captive by the Feng, who also intended to use the Drekaar, Navigo and Humana turned their backs on my crew and me."

"That is not true," insisted Pequo. "We were sent to find you."

"You were sent to protect Humana's interests in the Drekaar mining facilities. Nothing more."

"There is nothing wrong with self-interest. Navigo and Humana were providing valuable knowledge to the Drekaar. Nothing is free in the universe. You know that."

"Indeed, Lieutenant. We all pay a price."

"I do not understand," said Pequo. "Why the sudden cynicism?"

Plato's smile became pensive. "Once again, for me, it has been an eon, plenty of time for resentment to fester. It is time for Humana to pay its price, the price it has been deferring for quite some time."

"So, you have spent that time playing god with a primitive species, shaping them in your own image. How is it that you have even lived this long?"

"The light matter, the glowing element in the cave…the Dreguani knew of its healing powers. You, too, had some brief exposure."

"It made me sick."

"Yes, but how did you feel afterwards?"

Pequo reflected on this. "Wonderful. Renewed."

"As a result, your physiology was altered. You will live a bit longer than a typical Humani, and you will have fewer illnesses."

Pequo's eyes widened. "How much have you been exposed?"

Plato's serene smile returned. "It has been an eon."

"That is how you have survived this long?"

"That, and as it ends up, skipping through Spacetime retards the aging process. Between both, it has arrested altogether."

"So, you are an immortal." The amazement in Pequo's voice was gone and replaced with fear.

"The Dreguani revere me as one of the many manifestations of their light matter deity."

"So, you are their god."

"No, more like a prophet. Delivering them technological and cultural advances has solidified that status in their minds. It has been a busy eon. I built them schools, trained teachers, taught them writing, reading, mathematics. Then I progressed to art, elementary physics and chemistry, engineering."

"By the Engineer," gasped Pequo.

"No, by me. Imagine progress obtained unfettered by natural constraints, evolution. There was no serendipitous discovery, no happy accidents. Their development has been entirely directed."

"By you."

"Yes, by me."

"They appear different. Their anatomy…"

Plato smiled. "Also a result of facilitated descent with modification. In order to operate utensils, computers, and machinery, they had to develop digits in place of claws."

Pequo shook his head. "Yes, but this would imply that those with claws would not survive to reproduce."

"I got the idea from my brief interaction with the Feng on Golgath when I was held captive. They exercise what they call Eugenesis."

"You murdered those who did not fit your mold?" Pequo's question was more of an accusation.

"I merely controlled the selection pressures in their evolution. The Dreguani do not perceive it to be murder."

"I fail to see how it is not."

"Lieutenant, you have never seen a Dreguani birth. When the eggs hatch, hundreds of babies crawl all over the mother…and then they eat her alive."

"That is terrible."

"The Dreguani view it as love, the ultimate sacrifice. They have no qualms about dispensing with the old and the weak to make way for the new."

"Plato, what you have done is unnatural. Species do not progress through artificial manipulation."

Plato chuckled, but it was a bitter sound. "That is ironic coming from a Humani, a race that created the likes of me in a laboratory so that they may take to the stars. You even worship a deity called the Engineer."

"You are not a deity, Plato."

"I know that. I am a prophet."

"If anything, you are a teacher."

"A prophet teaches, shares wisdom, portends the future."

"Using the Feng's Spacetime travel technology," said Pequo. "Does that make them prophets, too?"

"In this Spacetime, they no longer possess this technology," said Plato.

"You saw to that, personally. Erased that pathway in Spacetime, merging it with an alternate trajectory to preserve your version of it."

"That is right."

Pequo shook his head in disapproval. "Plato, progress has to be earned incrementally through discovery and labor. No species, no race is entitled to it. Entitlement breeds arrogance, and arrogance breeds reckless, even dangerous behavior."

"Lieutenant, light matter has unlocked some of the many mysteries of existence. I have been at it only an eon and have only scratched the surface. There are other worlds to discover in the far reaches of the universe, other species with which to make contact. There are other realities in which the natural order is different, even reversed.

"Witnessing it all provides one with a perspective beyond normal experience, beyond that of the wisest sages and magisters across the galaxies."

Pequo leveled his gaze at Plato. "The Humani seem to view you as terrorists. With that kind of knowledge comes a great responsibility. Yet, you squander all of your astronomical perspectives on cowardly attacks on your own people, and on the Feng."

"The Humani are no longer my people," snapped Plato, momentarily losing his calm. "They threw me away as if I was garbage. The Dreguani took me in, made me feel like I was a part of something bigger than myself."

"The way you speak, it does not sound like you believe in anything bigger than yourself, Plato. Do you still even revere the Engineer?"

"Lieutenant, He is your creator, not mine."

"Well, then, the Humani are your creators!"

"I cannot revere them because I have surpassed my creators in every way. I possess knowledge and technology beyond their wildest comprehension, and I intend to use it for the greater good. Their perspective is selfish and limited. I see that now."

"So, what is it you are after? Revenge? Domination?"

Plato placed both hands out in front of him, palms up as if he were a Humani scale. "Balance."

"Or your version of balance as you see fit."

"Lieutenant Pequo, if things keep progressing as they are, the UIC and the Feng are going to rip the universe apart. The Feng threatened the very fabric of existence, the Aether, as we know it with what little they knew of this technology. They all need to relinquish some of their power for the greater good, for all of our sakes."

"Why are you telling me all of this? Do you expect me to help you?"

"I do not seek the destruction of the Humani, or the Feng for that matter, but they will need to step off of their pedestals if balance is to be achieved."

Pequo was now growing angry. "Do you expect me to be your liaison to the Humani? I will not do it."

"This is a great deal of information for you to process all at once," said Plato. "I do not expect you to receive it all in the spirit that I intend. In time, I hope to share this knowledge with you, so that you may be enlightened as I have been."

"You have come for the ship," said Pequo. "You want it back. You do not want the Humani to have your precious technology."

Plato laughed again. "Now who is the cynic? They can have it for the moment. I am an eon ahead of them. It will take them at least as long to even begin to comprehend what they have."

"Then why did you attack their airbase?"

"Because I want them to take it and flee."

Pequo looked perplexed. "I do not understand."

"The UIC has been maintaining a hidden base in the Uncharted Sector, the location of which has eluded me. When they run with the stolen technology, I will be able to track the light energy signature, even through spacefold."

Pequo was pacing back and forth, with his finger held up to his pursed lips as he pondered the situation. He knew that, once attacked, absconding with the Spacetime travelling ship was exactly what the Humani would do.

"Release me," he demanded. "Release me at once, or kill me. I will have no part of this."

Plato regarded him with a derisive sympathy. "Your role in this is out of your hands, I am afraid."

Pequo exploded, lunging at the would-be prophet, reaching out to clutch him by his throat. However, Pequo passed through him as if he was an apparition, and collided with the wall, knocking the digital painting of the School of Athens askew.

The apparition of Plato had vanished, and Pequo was alone once again. He ran to the doors and pounded on them, shouting demands to be released, but there was no response. Instead, he stood inside that room, a prisoner, waiting for his fate, which was in the hands of the apparent leader of the Astrals.

*

Separated and vulnerable, the remaining pilots of the Razor's Edge considered their situation. They had come seeking one war and had stumbled into another, one inadvertently of their making.

While trying to prevent the rise of one empire, they affected the rise of another. Home, as they knew it, no longer existed, and they now had to cope with the current reality, their new normal.

An Avatar they regarded as less than Humani had become a prophet, a traveler of Spacetime and alternate realities, his influence leading to the evolution of a new race.

Everything as they knew it was turned on its head, and somewhere across the galaxy, on a small, primitive blue planet, Trevor Reinhardt was just being born.

THE END

CHECK OUT OTHER GREAT SCIENCE FICTION BOOKS

IN PERPETUITY
by Jake Bible

For two thousand years, Earth and her many colonies across the galaxy have fought against the Estelian menace. Having faced overwhelming losses, the CSC has instituted the largest military draft ever, conscripting millions into the battle against the aliens. Major Bartram North has been tasked with the unenviable task of coordinating the military education of hundreds of thousands of recruits and turning them into troops ready to fight and die for the cause.

As Major North struggles to maintain a training pace that the CSC insists upon, he realizes something isn't right on the Perpetuity. But before he can investigate, the station dissolves into madness brought on by the physical booster known as pharma. Unfortunately for Major North, that is not the only nightmare he faces- an armada of Estelian warships is on the edge of the solar system and headed right for Earth!

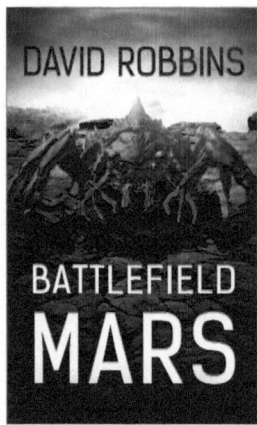

BATTLEFIELD MARS
by David Robbins

Several centuries into the future, Earth has established three colonies on Mars. No indigenous life has been discovered, and humankind looks forward to making the Red Planet their own.

Then 'something' emerges out of a long-extinct volcano and doesn't like what the humans are doing.

Captain Archard Rahn, United Nations Interplanetary Corps, tries to stem the rising tide of slaughter. But the Martians are more than they seem, and it isn't long before Mars erupts in all-out war.

CHECK OUT OTHER GREAT SCIENCE FICTION BOOKS

MAUSOLEUM 2069
by **Rick Jones**

Political dignitaries including the President of the Federation gather for a ceremony onboard Mausoleum 2069. But when a cloud of interstellar dust passes through the galaxy and eclipses Earth, the tenants within the walls of Mausoleum 2069 are reborn and the undead begin to rise. As the struggle between life and death onboard the mausoleum develops, Eriq Wyman, a one-time member of a Special ops team called the Force Elite, is given the task to lead the President to the safety of Earth. But is Earth like Mausoleum 2069? A landscape of the living dead? Has the war of the Apocalypse finally begun? With so many questions there is only one certainty: in space there is nowhere to run and nowhere to hide.

RED CARBON
by **D.J. Goodman**

Diamonds have been discovered on Mars.

After years of neglect to space programs around the world, a ruthless corporation has made it to the Red Planet first, establishing their own mining operation with its own rules and laws, its own class system, and little oversight from Earth. Conditions are harsh, but its people have learned how to make the Martian colony home.

But something has gone catastrophically wrong on Earth. As the colony leaders try to cover it up, hacker Leah Hartnup is getting suspicious. Her boundless curiosity will lead her to a horrifying truth: they are cut off, possibly forever. There are no more supplies coming. There will be no more support. There is no more mission to accomplish. All that's left is one goal: survival.

CHECK OUT OTHER GREAT SCIENCE FICTION BOOKS

SALVAGE MERC ONE
by Jake Bible

Joseph Laribeau was born to be a Marine in the Galactic Fleet. He was born to fight the alien enemies known as the Skrang Alliance and travel the galaxy doing his duty as a Marine Sergeant. But when the War ended and Joe found himself medically discharged, the best job ever was over and he never thought he'd find his way again.

Then a beautiful alien walked into his life and offered him a chance at something even greater than the Fleet, a chance to serve with the Salvage Merc Corp.

Now known as Salvage Merc One Eighty-Four, Joe Laribeau is given the ultimate assignment by the SMC bosses. To his surprise it is neither a military nor a corporate salvage. Rather, Joe has to risk his life for one of his own. He has to find and bring back the legend that started the Corp.

SERENGETI
by J.B. Rockwell

It was supposed to be an easy job: find the Dark Star Revolution Starships, destroy them, and go home. But a booby-trapped vessel decimates the Meridian Alliance fleet, leaving Serengeti—a Valkyrie class warship with a sentient AI brain—on her own; wrecked and abandoned in an empty expanse of space. On the edge of total failure, Serengeti thinks only of her crew. She herds the survivors into a lifeboat, intending to sling them into space. But the escape pod sticks in her belly, locking the cryogenically frozen crew inside.

Then a scavenger ship arrives to pick Serengeti's bones clean. Her engines dead, her guns long silenced, Serengeti and her last two robots must find a way to fight the scavengers off and save the crew trapped inside her.

SEVEREDPRESS

f facebook.com/severedpress
🐦 twitter.com/severedpress

CHECK OUT OTHER GREAT SCIENCE FICTION BOOKS

FURNACE
by Joseph Williams

On a routine escort mission to a human colony, Lieutenant Michael Chalmers is pulled out of hyper-sleep a month early. The RSA Rockne Hummel is well off course and—as the ship's navigator—it's up to him to figure out why. It's supposed to be a simple fix, but when he attempts to identify their position in the known universe, nothing registers on his scans. The vessel has catapulted beyond the reach of starlight by at least a hundred trillion light-years. Then a planetary-mass object materializes behind them. It's burning brightly even without a star to heat it. Hundreds of damaged ships are locked in its orbit. The crew discovers there are no life-signs aboard any of them. As system failures sweep through the Hummel, neither Chalmers nor the pilot can prevent the vessel from crashing into the surface near a mysterious ancient city. And that's where the real nightmare begins.

LUNA
by Rick Chesler

On the threshold of opening the moon to tourist excursions, a private space firm owned by a visionary billionaire takes a team of non-astronauts to the lunar surface. To address concerns that the moon's barren rock may not hold long-term allure for an uber-wealthy clientele, the company's charismatic owner reveals to the group the ultimate discovery: life on the moon.

But what is initially a triumphant and world-changing moment soon gives way to unrelenting terror as the team experiences firsthand that despite their technological prowess, the moon still holds many secrets.